Just Friends

BOOKS BY JO LOVETT

JO LOVETT

Just Friends

bookouture

Published by Bookouture in 2022

An imprint of Storyfire Ltd.
Carmelite House
50 Victoria Embankment
London EC4Y 0DZ

www.bookouture.com

ISBN: 978-1-80019-798-5
eBook ISBN: 978-1-80019-797-8

To Sophia

ONE

LILY

Lily took a long sip of her wine, beamed at her friends and gestured at the white-sand beach immediately on the other side of the low wall next to their restaurant table, and the gorgeous glistening sea beyond.

'Look at that yacht,' she said. 'The one called *The Butterfly*. Next to the really big one. It's got a slide from the deck straight into the sea.'

'That's so cool,' her friend Aaliyah said. 'I did a home visit recently to a family who had a slide instead of stairs. I couldn't decide whether it was weird or fabulous.'

'I love visiting amazing and unusual houses.' Lily took another sip of wine. 'If I hadn't been a midwife, I'd have liked to have been an estate agent.'

'*Or* a rich business person who could afford a yacht like that.' Their friend Meg pointed at one of the other very swish white boats bobbing around and said something about it, but Lily didn't hear what she was saying because she was too busy choking on her wine.

Aaliyah, who was sitting on the same side of their four-person table as Lily, started whacking her hard on the back.

'Heimlich?' Meg pushed her chair back and stood up. Since she'd left nursing to become a Pilates instructor, she was always keen to put her medical skills to good use.

'No,' Lily spluttered, holding her hand up. 'I'm fine.' She was fine in the sense that she wasn't going to choke to death right now. She was *not* fine in the sense that she was pretty sure that her ex, Matt, was one of the large group of men who'd just walked into the restaurant.

Matt was her best friend Tess's cousin. Tess was getting married on the island on Friday. Lily hadn't asked Tess about him, but she'd been expecting that Matt would be coming to the wedding, and she'd – more or less – psyched herself up for that. She had not psyched herself up for seeing him now. At least she was wearing a nice 'I'm on holiday with my girlfriends for the first time in years *partayyyy*' dress and had gone fancyish on her make-up this evening. Although not fancy *enough*. If she'd known there was any chance of seeing him, she'd have gone full-on glam.

It had to be him. He had his back to her, plus she didn't want to be too obvious with her staring, so she didn't have a *great* view of him, but it would be a very big coincidence for another wide-shouldered man with dark, wavy hair and perma-stubble to have pitched up on this small island in a group of English-speaking men, who mainly looked to be in their thirties, four days before his cousin Tess's wedding to her thirty-something fiancé, Tom. Who Lily had just clocked in the middle of the group.

Lily had thought that, like Tess, Tom would be spending a few days before the wedding holidaying on the island with just his best friends. This looked more like a full-blown stag.

The man who she thought was Matt did a quarter-turn to greet someone and now she could see his profile properly.

And yes, it was him. Of course it was. It was eight years since they were last together but everything she could see of him was instantly achingly familiar. The shape of his nose, chin and cheekbone, his long eyelashes, the way he tipped his head back slightly when he laughed. She couldn't see his eyes from here but she knew that they were a deep brown, and held kindness, and often laughter, that drew you in. They'd drawn her in, anyway. And clearly his ex-wife.

He turned very slightly in her direction and for a moment she thought he'd seen her, but he turned away again and, no, he seemed totally unaware of her.

'Lily?' Someone was speaking to her but she couldn't process what they were saying. There was a loud whooshing in her ears and she was finding it really difficult to remember how to work any part of her body.

'Lily?' It was Meg who was speaking. She was saying her name.

With difficulty, Lily consciously moved her gaze away from Matt and towards the table in front of her. She was shaking. She lifted one of her hands and held it above the table flat in front of her. Yep, literally shaking. At this rate she was going to need to get her inhaler out and take some extra puffs for the first time in a while.

She picked up her glass and gulped some more of her wine and started coughing again.

'Are you okay?' Meg asked.

'Totally fine,' Lily spluttered.

She really wasn't.

She should probably have paid more attention to the minutiae of Tess's wedding preps over the past few months. She was fairly sure that Tess would have mentioned Tom's pre-wedding plans.

It had been difficult, though, juggling work, her best friend morphing into a bridezilla and the challenge of living in London while helping to organise a wedding on a Greek island. Not just any wedding, either, but an elaborate one. And not just any island, but a tiny one, Antiparos, that could only be reached by boat from the neighbouring island of Paros, which you could only reach either by plane or boat from mainland Greece. So she hadn't *totally* listened to every *single* conversation about things she wasn't involved in – like the groom's holiday and stag plans.

She adjusted her sunglasses against the low July evening sun and sneaked another look at the men as they sat down on the opposite side of the taverna's beach-side terrace.

Matt was wearing a pale-blue shirt, open at the neck, and he looked even more gorgeous than she remembered. It was a struggle to look away from him. Because of her dark glasses, no one would be able to tell, as long as she kept her head turned towards her friends and just swivelled her eyes towards him, but it wasn't doing her pride any good that she couldn't help watching him while he apparently hadn't noticed her at all. Or he'd noticed her but hadn't even twitched.

She really didn't want to sound too interested. She wasn't going to ask.

She absolutely wasn't going to ask.

She had to ask.

She waited until Meg and Aaliyah were distracted by a discussion about whether or not to get another bottle of red or start in on the cocktails, and leaned in so that only Tess would hear. 'Soooo, there are just the four of us, but Tom has at least fifteen friends here?' Seventeen actually. She'd just counted them all twice. 'And tonight we're all at the same restaurant?'

'Yup.' Tess took a big slurp of wine. 'I know what you're going to say. Tom and I shouldn't see each other before the wedding. But it's fine. It's still three and a half days away. It's only the night before that you shouldn't see each other. And it's a small island and they're a big group so they didn't have a lot of restaurant options this evening. And they're over there and we're here, so technically we aren't in exactly the same place.'

That had not been what Lily wanted to say. What she wanted to say was *But Matt's here. Why is he here? Why didn't you tell me he'd be here? And what's he doing here? Since when is he one of Tom's best friends?* To be fair, seventeen friends wasn't a *tiny* inner friendship circle. But still. Matt was Tom's fiancée's cousin. Not his friend. So why had Tom invited him on his pre-wedding holiday? She'd thought Matt would just do a one-nighter for the wedding, and probably spend the rest of his time out here on Paros, at his aunt's house. And why did he look so bloody good? How come the several grey hairs and extra pounds it looked like he'd gained over the past eight years suited him so well? Lily was pretty sure the last eight years hadn't treated her so kindly on the looks front.

'Very true.' She kept her head pointed in Tess's direction while continuing to swivel her eyes under cover of her sunglasses in Matt's direction. Hooray for the still-bright sun. And finally he'd just glanced again in her direction. He'd definitely noticed her. Definitely. He'd looked over towards her for just a couple of seconds too long and then shifted his position slightly so that he was facing almost entirely away from her.

Okay, well, fine. *Fine.* Really. Fine. She was thirty-three years old and *way* beyond being pathetic about seeing an ex, even *the* ex. Also, she was good at acting. She was going to act now. She absolutely was going to be fine. She wasn't going to pass out from her now-galloping heart. She wasn't going to give in to temptation and wipe her suddenly clammy hands on her dress. She wasn't going to choke again. She was going to ignore him and enjoy this beautiful evening in a great local restaurant next to a stunning beach with her three best friends. 'I just, yep, no, nothing.'

'I think we should try a couple of cocktails.' Aaliyah pointed halfway down the drinks menu. 'This honeydew ouzo one looks amazing.' This week was the first time she'd ever left her three kids for even a single night, and she was so keen to let her hair down she'd be looking like Rapunzel soon.

'You think Tom and I shouldn't see each other at *all* this week, don't you?' said Tess, like Aaliyah hadn't spoken. Finally there was an upside to Tess's extreme all-things-wedding-related obsession. Normally she was far too eagle-eyed where her friends were concerned, but right now – unless it impacted on the wedding in some way – she'd never notice that Lily didn't give a flying anything about whether or not Tess and Tom saw each other but *did* care hugely about whether she and Matt were going to have to speak.

'No.' Lily shook her head, still with half an eye on Matt, who was chatting and laughing with a few of the other men now, definitely not looking at her any more. *How* could he look so bloody carefree? Was he not affected by having seen her? He'd totally registered that she was here. 'I think it's fine. I mean, as you say, we're in different parts of the terrace. And the tradition's only about the night before. And it's only a tradition. It doesn't matter. But if you're worried, we could move to a different restaurant when we've finished these drinks. Since we haven't ordered yet.' Lily didn't need to feel selfish about suggesting that; Tess would probably genuinely feel less anxious if they did move.

'Yes, maybe we *should* move. We don't want anything to ruin your wedding.' Meg was big on superstition. She'd thrown salt over her shoulder at dinner the night before and ruined the stuffed aubergines of a woman at the next table.

Tess's face crumpled a little and Lily immediately felt terrible. She shouldn't have suggested that they move. She should just grow up and deal with Matt being here. She'd known that she'd see him at the wedding. This was just a few days early.

Thank God for her dark glasses.

'No,' she said, 'I don't know why I said that. It's *totally* fine us all being here. *Obviously*. Let's order some of those ouzo cocktails. Look, it says the ouzo's produced on the island. We have to try it.'

'Actually, yes, I think you're right,' Meg said. 'Arguably we're really quite separate, and it's nearly four days until the wedding. I'm sure it's only the night before and the morning of the actual day that count. It would be a big hassle to move.'

Tess looked over at Tom and said, 'It does feel a bit weird being in the same restaurant but not speaking to each other, actually. And we're supposed to be having separate holidays. Why don't we go and find somewhere else?'

'Are you *sure* you want to?' Lily asked. 'Not because you're worried about seeing him because it's *totally* fine you seeing each other, I'm sure.'

'Thank you, lovely Lily. Yes, I am sure. Shall we explain to the waiter and book a table here for tomorrow evening instead? So that we don't look rude, and also I love the look of the menu.' Tess looked at the three of them expectantly.

'Good plan,' Lily said, while Aaliyah clapped the drinks menu closed quite forcefully and Meg sighed a little bit too loudly. 'So I'll explain then.'

'Thanks.' Tess stood up and began to gather her things up while Aaliyah rolled her eyes and Lily tried really hard to ignore her. Tess *was* at the higher maintenance end of the bride-to-be range but a *lot* of people got a bit tense before their weddings and it was totally understandable.

Forty-five minutes later, they were all seated in a very nice little restaurant – the third one they'd schlepped inside since leaving the original one because Tess hadn't thought the ambiences of the others were quite right (Aaliyah had told Lily and Meg quite loudly that the only bad ambience was Tess's sodding fussiness) and without the sea views (Aaliyah had said *Oh my God* when Tess had raised that issue, and Lily had pointed out to Tess that live music and a table in a gorgeous little white-painted courtyard surrounded by bright flowers made up for the sea and they were going to see the sea again tomorrow, all day, and Tess had eventually seen sense) – and they had a cocktail each and they were all happy again.

Lily snuck a quick look at her watch. Yep, they'd been here for long enough. It wouldn't look suspicious if she mentioned Tom and his friends, as long as she edged the conversation round to them in a natural way. She *really* wanted to know what Matt was doing here. Well, apart from the obvious, going to the wedding on Friday and apparently attending Tom's stag holiday first. For her sanity, she needed to know what the men's plans were this week and whether she was likely to bump into Matt at all and have to talk to him.

And whether he'd met anyone else since his divorce.

'And that is why,' Meg said after a *very* long monologue, which Lily hadn't totally listened to because she'd been thinking about Matt, 'my ideal man is a farmer.' Bingo. The ideal opening to work the conversation round.

Lily swallowed her olive and said, 'Maybe one of Tom's friends is a farmer. He seems to have quite a lot of friends with him.'

'Oh God. Do you think I should have asked more people to come early?' Tess said. 'Or he should have asked fewer? Do you think we should have had the same number?' Dammit. Lily just wanted to know about Matt, not get sucked into more has-the-wedding-been-planned-perfectly chat.

'No. It doesn't bloody matter how many people you have with you on your pre-wedding holiday. Most people don't have pre-wedding holidays at all.' Aaliyah waved at the nearest waiter and pointed at their glasses. 'Same again all round. Thank you *so* much.'

'You had your lovely massive hen night, didn't you?' Meg said. They'd had to organise a spa day and afternoon tea for

Tess in London, which had cost everyone a fortune. It had been even more expensive for Lily, because Tess had wanted a vegan afternoon tea but had worried that vegan cake often tasted vinegary, and since she hadn't wanted to put on any weight prewedding had asked the others to sample several for her. Meg lived in Edinburgh now and could only make it down to London for a couple of the tastings, and Aaliyah had told Lily that no way was she eating cake every Saturday for six weeks when she'd worked *so* hard to get rid of her third-baby weight, so in the end Lily had done a series of vegan afternoon teas with different friends, which had been very nice but hadn't done her bank balance or waistline many favours.

'It *was* a lovely hen night,' Lily said.

'Yes, it was.' Tess nodded. 'Thank you all so much. Wonderful best friends and bridesmaids.' She held out her arms and they all leaned in for a hug. 'Are we sure, though, that it doesn't seem weird that Tom's brought so many more friends?'

'Yes. Because he didn't have a stag when you had your hen.' Lily *really* wanted to ask about Matt but they needed to get off this topic or, going by last night, when Tess had suddenly started obsessing very vocally and at length about the wedding flowers, Aaliyah might snap and yell at her. And Meg, who was as keen to find a man as Lily was to remain single, might start looking wistful again, because she was sure she was *never* going to get married. And, actually, Lily *was* happy to remain single and it really didn't matter to her why Matt was here and if she *did* have to speak to him that would be fine, she'd deal with it like the mature adult she was, so there was no need for her to ask anything about him. 'Shall we order our food? This spicy squid starter looks amazing.'

Half an hour later, the restaurant owner took another look at the gigantic meze platter that he'd placed in the middle of their table and had just talked them through at – very charming – length, and said, 'Okay, then. Enjoy!'

'It looks *amazing*,' Meg said. 'Could I ask your name? I'm Meg.' She looked at the others. 'And my friends are Tess, Lily and Aaliyah.'

'My name's Pythagoras.' The smile he shared around the table was as charming as his meze chat.

'I *love* that name.' Meg beamed at him. 'Wasn't there a famous ancient Greek called Pythagoras?'

'Yes.' He beamed back at her. 'My father was a mathematics professor and he named me after him.'

'That's so cool,' Meg breathed. 'And so interesting.'

Pythagoras, still smiling, opened his mouth and started speaking but was interrupted by a big crash from the interior, from the direction of the kitchen. 'Oops. I'd better go and check what just happened. *Bon appétit*.'

'I'm in love,' Meg said.

'With?' Aaliyah speared some squid with a cocktail stick.

'With Pythagoras, obviously.' Meg indicated with her eyes in the direction of the kitchen. 'Genuinely. He's my One. I've finally met him. Love at first sight.'

'Honestly,' said Aaliyah, spearing more squid. 'About half an hour ago your ideal man was a farmer. And there's no such thing as love at first sight. This squid's *good*.'

'It was pretty much love at first sight for me and Tom,' Tess said.

'What?' said Aaliyah. 'You worked together for three years before you went on your first date. And you both went out with other people in that time.'

'But we loved each other the whole time,' Tess said.

Aaliyah coughed some words that sounded a bit like, 'Rewriting history.' The four of them had always got on very well but Aaliyah had lost a tiny bit of her tolerance recently due to her third child, who'd just turned one, being a demon at night (Aaliyah's words) and apparently never having slept more than two hours in a row for the entire first year of her life. And, to be fair to Aaliyah, if there was ever a time when anyone might lose tolerance with Tess, it was now.

'So when did you know that Patrick was the one for you?' Lily asked Aaliyah before Tess could argue. Or, worse, get upset. There'd been a lot of tears from Tess recently.

'Quite quickly, if I'm honest, but not the first time I met him. I mean, I *liked* him, and obviously he *was* The One, but it clearly wasn't love at first sight because how can you love someone you don't know?'

'I think you just *feel* something,' said Meg. 'Right inside you. Like you might not know all the *facts* about them yet, but you still know. That's how I feel about Pythagoras.' Lily totally knew what Meg meant. That had been how she'd felt when she'd met Matt. It had been during a charity overnight walking marathon that Tess had organised, and she'd just *known*. The moment they'd met it was like she knew him, inside and out, and she'd known that they were right for each other. Forever. And they had been. Until they weren't.

'You've said that before,' Aaliyah said.

'I'm not saying there's only *one* The One.' Meg's eyes started to glisten. Oh, God. She was about to do her The One That Got Away spiel. Almost certainly with reference to her three-week relationship circa 2014 with Terence-from-Walsall (perfect husband material according to Meg, despite early indications like, in no particular order, his hate-love knuckle tattoos, his drinking habit and the way he spoke to her). 'But there are very few Ones. I don't want Pythagoras to be another One That Got Away. I want to settle down. I want to have kids.'

'If you and Pythagoras had babies, they'd be *gorgeous*,' Tess said. 'Tom and I are planning to try to start a family quite soon. Maybe a honeymoon baby.'

'That's so exciting, Tess.' Meg's eyes were filling quite fast now. 'I'm so pleased for you.'

'Meg, hun.' Aaliyah pushed the platter towards her. 'Have

some of this divine squid. It *will* happen for you one day. Definitely. And if it doesn't, other doors will open.'

'I don't want that door to close for me.' Meg did a big, honking sniff. Amazing that she could look beautiful no matter what facial expressions she did or sounds she made.

'I'm sure it won't close,' said Lily, signalling *Shhh* at Aaliyah with her eyes and passing a tissue to Meg under the table. 'It'll happen. But maybe when you're least expecting it. Maybe The Ones That Get Away aren't really *The* Ones.' She heard men's voices at the restaurant door, tensed and looked over. No, it wasn't Matt. And obviously it wasn't; the men weren't going to switch restaurants mid-way through the evening, were they, because they had no reason to.

God, she was going to be a nervous wreck within hours at this rate. Nearly five days to go until she'd be off the island. It was a small island. That was a lot of potential for bumping into him.

Meg wiped her eyes with the tissue. 'Sorry,' she said. 'Just full of emotion. I *know* Pythagoras is the one. I *know* that if we don't get married and grow old together I'll always regret it and I'll know for the rest of my life that he's my *The* One That Got Away.'

'Well, unless you meet someone else and settle down very happily with them,' Aaliyah said, munching. 'Which is actually very likely to happen. Maybe someone who lives a bit closer to Edinburgh.'

Meg shook her head. 'No,' she said. 'It's him. I'm going to ask him for his number before we leave this evening.'

Aaliyah rolled her eyes.

Tess said, 'Tom would have been my One That Got Away if we hadn't got engaged, and I'd have been sad forever.'

Aaliyah rolled her eyes more and Meg gave a miserable little whimper.

Lily thought *Matt's clearly my One That Got Away* and was

immediately furious with herself. He wasn't. When the chips were down, *her* chips, she'd realised that they weren't right for each other. Serious romance probably wasn't right for her full stop, and she was happy with that. She liked her life.

And given all of that, she should be completely relaxed about the fact that she and Matt were on the island together. He was just someone she'd once known.

Knowing, though, that she'd been going to see him, she'd really wanted to blow him away again, just once. Out of pride. And hurt. Because, with all his declarations of undying love and undying misery post their split, why the *hell* had he married someone else *less than one year* afterwards?

She'd trusted him, she'd trusted what he'd told her; but it couldn't have been true.

Which was absolutely completely fine, because they really hadn't been right for each other, and splitting up with him had definitely been the right decision.

'Lily, are you okay?' Aaliyah had a forkful of stuffed vine leaf halfway to her mouth. 'You're frowning.'

'Yeah, fine. Just thinking about a difficult client,' she said. A very plausible answer. She met a *lot* of awkward clients in the new business she'd set up, photo curation, and they were always good for a story or two, obviously on a strictly anonymous basis.

'I'm going to go and ask him now.' Meg pushed her chair back and stood up. 'When you have very strong feelings, you have to act on them, improve your life.'

Lily had very strong feelings right now and she was *not* going to act on them. No way would it improve her life if she went back to the hotel, made herself look as good as she could possibly manage, and then hunted Matt down and yelled, 'Okay, fair enough, it was my decision for us to split up, but why did you marry *her* so soon afterwards?' She wasn't going to do any of that. She was going to be dignified.

'Got it.' Meg was almost dancing back to the table, waving a piece of paper. 'I think he feels the same way.'

'Hun, I hope this doesn't end in tears.' Aaliyah pushed her plate away. 'I'm done. Don't want to blow my diet.'

'It won't end in tears,' Meg said. 'I just *know*.'

Yeah. In Lily's experience that meant nothing.

————

The next morning, Lily slid her hand towards her beach bag and pulled her phone out, very slowly. She waited a few seconds, to check no one had noticed, and then tilted it towards her and tapped the screen gently. Keeping her head in the same position, face up to the sun, and holding an 'I'm *loving* this' little smile, she moved her eyes so that she could see the screen.

What? No way. How could it be only eleven fifteen?

She checked again. Still eleven fifteen. So they'd only been here for forty-five minutes. Realistically, they weren't going to be heading off for lunch for at least another hour. She was going to *fry*.

And die of boredom. Why weren't any of the other three talking or reading? How could they just lie there, doing absolutely nothing?

She looked to her right at the beautiful fine, white sand and the gorgeous turquoise sea. And then to her left at the beautiful fine, white sand and more gorgeous turquoise sea, and some very nice palm trees and some shrubs with fiercely pink flowers. Idyllic.

Heavenly.

God, she was bored.

And so, so hot.

She was pretty sure that she'd been good at sunbathing ten, fifteen years ago. When she thought about ways in which she'd aged, it wasn't a surprise that she got the hangovers from hell nowadays, or that she was a full dress size bigger than she'd been then. Or even that despite her hair being blonde – she'd always thought that only dark-haired people would have to go down the dye route in their thirties – her roots were hideously grey unless she coloured her hair every three weeks. But she really would not have expected to have lost the ability to sunbathe properly.

She looked over at a couple of boats bobbing on the horizon, and then around at all the sand again.

Right.

She needed to do something, for her sanity, otherwise she wasn't even going to make it to lunchtime of Day One of three pretty solid days of sunbathing – right now she was really looking forward to their hair and nail appointments, just for the variety – without losing it slightly.

She rolled to her right – another ability she'd lost since her early twenties was a sit-up without something *very* heavy on her feet, although she was a lot more flexible recently after some Pilates lessons from Meg – and pushed herself up.

'I might just pop up to the shops,' she said. 'I think I forgot to pack any aftersun.' She totally hadn't. She'd packed two tubes, just in case.

'I might come with you actually. I forgot aftersun too.' Aaliyah sat up fast and scattered sand with her feet. 'Whoops, sorry.'

Lily slipped a beach dress on over her head and looked down at Meg and Tess. 'You want anything?'

'I'm good, thanks,' said Meg, which wasn't a surprise. Since they'd met in the first term of their nursing degree at Leeds uni, Lily was pretty sure that Meg hadn't once forgotten anything. And she was probably busy doing some Pilates-type meditation while she lay there.

Tess just gave a very small snore.

'Did you actually forget your aftersun?' Aaliyah asked as

they walked up the wooden slatted path from the beach to the road.

'Nope. You?'

'No. Bored out of my mind.'

'Same,' said Lily, pleased. 'I'm loving being here, I really am; it's just quite hard to be in the middle of mega amounts of work one minute and then just doing nothing the next. I think I could relax better if I had something to *do*. I keep thinking about all the photo files I have to go through and feeling like I'm really wasting my time not getting on with those, but I can't see my screen well enough with all this – lovely, obviously – sunshine.'

'Same. Twenty-four hours ago, I'd got up at the crack of dawn after about five broken hours' sleep, got three children dressed and breakfasted and out the door, done the school run, unloaded and re-loaded the dishwasher, put a load of laundry on, answered about ten emails from school and another ten from work even though I'm on holiday, made a tagine for them all to eat yesterday evening and dashed to the airport. This morning, I've got up after my first good night's sleep for years, had a leisurely breakfast with no children in sight, and sunbathed. I mean, obviously I'm *loving* being here, but it's just a bit weird.'

'You missing the kids a lot?'

'Yep. But, you know, this is great.'

'Yeah.' Lily nodded. It *was* great. Absolutely. 'Come on.' She put her arm through Aaliyah's. 'Let's shop slowly and then maybe go back just in time for lunch.'

Ten minutes later, they were under the awning of a shop, looking at sarongs. Lily held a purple one up against herself.

'What do you think?'

Aaliyah turned round and nodded. 'That's gorgeous, and a great colour for you. It'll be perfect with your lime-green bikini.'

Lily turned the sarong over to check the price tag and nodded. 'Yep, I'm going to get it. What about you? You said you might get some new sunglasses?' Aaliyah had told them yesterday that hers were chipped from where her toddler had got hold of them and chucked them against a wall.

'Is there any point, though? They'll just get broken again. And when you have young kids, no one really notices what *you* look like.' Pre-kids – in fact even after she'd had her older two – Aaliyah would never in a million years have worn chipped sunglasses. She'd always gone down the full-on glamour route. It didn't seem like she'd just got more chilled because she had different priorities now, it seemed more like she'd given up a little bit. Probably because she was so tired all the time.

'Why don't you just try a few pairs on?' Lily suggested, moving over to a locked glass case of designer sunglasses. 'Why don't I ask someone to come and open this cabinet?'

Five minutes later, a little of the old Aaliyah had reappeared. She had a pair of Prada shades on and was posing.

'You look amazing,' Lily told her. Aaliyah's perfect features meant she'd look good in all sunglasses ever.

Aaliyah adjusted the sunglasses down and did an exaggerated pout and Lily laughed. She reached to take another pair out of the cabinet and then froze, with her hand out. Was that Matt she could see out of the corner of her eye?

No, probably not. She'd lost count of how many fake Matt-sightings she'd had on the way back to the hotel yesterday evening and on the way to the beach this morning and while they were *on* the beach.

The man was coming closer.

Oh. It *was* him.

He was so close now that the bright sunlight behind Aaliyah was partially blocked for a moment. Very apt.

He was getting even closer.

It felt like she was going to have to speak to him at some point, but – despite a somewhat sleepless night running through imaginary conversations in her head – she wasn't prepared for that yet.

So it seemed like her best option right now was to hide.

She looked round. There was a tall display of scarves behind her and just to the right, which was definitely big enough to camouflage her.

Oh, God, he was turning towards them.

She whipped the purple sarong up so that it covered her face and jumped behind the scarf display.

'Lily?' she heard Aaliyah say. And then, 'Hi, Matt. You probably don't remember me. I'm Tess and Lily's friend, Aaliyah.'

Marvellous.

TWO

MATT

Matt was struggling not to laugh, which was ridiculous, because this was not funny.

Well, the fact that Lily had draped a large purple thing over her head and leapt behind some scarves to avoid him was funny.

But the fact that now they were clearly going to have to speak to each other was not so funny.

He'd really thought that Tom had told him that Tess had had a big hen weekend in London a few weeks ago, so he'd assumed that her friends wouldn't be here for longer than a day or so before the wedding and that he wouldn't have to see Lily until later in the week.

When they'd split up and she'd refused to speak to him again, he hadn't understood where she was coming from. Right now, he did understand. Last night, when he'd seen her in the restaurant, he'd felt like his head and heart might explode just at the sight of her, let alone at the prospect of holding an actual conversation with her. It was just too much. He needed to be prepared, and he wasn't prepared yet. He should have worked out something to say when they next met while he was lying awake last night thinking about her.

'Matt?' Aaliyah repeated.

'Hi, Aaliyah,' he said. 'Of course I remember you.' He'd spent a lot of time with Tess, Aaliyah and the fourth of their group, Meg, during the fifteen months that he and Lily had been together. He'd barely seen Aaliyah and Meg since, though. Aaliyah put her arms out and they shared a quick hug. 'It's been a while. What have you been up to?'

'Having babies, basically,' Aaliyah said. 'I have three kids now. And I work part-time as a GP practice nurse. How've you been?'

'Wow. That sounds busy. Congratulations. Yeah, I'm good, thanks.' He smiled at her, and tried hard – and failed – not to glance over to Lily, still under the purple thing. He didn't do social media and he'd always avoided talking to Tess about Lily since their split, because he just hadn't wanted to know. Now he *did* want to know. Did *she* have a partner and three kids?

And was she happy? He hoped so.

Aaliyah's eyes were moving backwards and forwards between him and Lily behind the scarf display.

'Hi, Lily,' he said reluctantly. God, his voice sounded odd.

Lily didn't move for a moment, and then she lowered the purple thing slowly and looked out round the display and gave a little shake of her head with her eyebrows raised, like she was trying to act surprised.

And despite the renewed sense of unfinished business festering inside him – apparently he really hadn't parked his feelings about her at all – and the purple fabric still draped across Lily's cheek and shoulder, all he could think was how beautiful her heart-shaped face was and how he wished she was smiling right now because he'd always loved her smile.

She had her hair done differently. It was naturally wavy and she never used to straighten it – it would be down or up on top of her head, but always with lots of curls – but today, and last night too – she'd done something to make it straight and had it up in a thick, highish ponytail.

'Oh, hello, Matt. I didn't see you there. I was just looking at these lovely scarves. How *are* you?' She flung her arms out in a parody of a surprised gesture and knocked the scarf display with her right arm. 'Ouch,' she said, as the whole display careened away from her and crashed – surprisingly quietly – at an angle onto a display of bags, piles of brightly coloured scarves cascading to the floor.

'Are you okay?' Matt asked, stepping forward and pulling the display back to vertical. It looked like her arm had hit the edge of one of the shelves with quite serious force.

'Yes, thank you.' She flexed her arm a little without looking at it. Lily's automatic response to everything had always been that she was fine. The time she broke her wrist skiing when they were together, she'd refused to admit it was even hurting, until he'd caught her cradling the wrist with her other hand with tears in her eyes. So she might be okay, or she might be really hurt. 'I can't believe I just did that.'

She looped the purple thing over her shoulder, bent down and began to gather up scarves. It looked like her wrist was okay, actually.

Matt stared down at her. If he was honest, he just wanted to leave the shop immediately, to not have to talk to Lily, but obviously he had to help her clear up. He bent down too.

Damn. He was too close to her; he could smell her scent, the same one that she'd always used, hints of almond and vanilla he remembered her telling him one time, when they'd been standing in her bathroom together. God, that had been an intimate moment. Which he shouldn't be thinking about now.

He edged backwards and looked hard at the scarves on the floor, to give his heart rate a chance to settle.

'Why don't I take that?' Aaliyah reached over Matt's head for the purple thing on Lily's shoulder. 'There isn't space for me to squeeze in down there too.' She looked behind her to where the shop worker was busy with another customer. 'He genuinely doesn't seem to have noticed. Why don't I go and chat to him about sunglasses to distract him while you tidy?'

'Good plan, thank you,' Lily said, smoothing, folding, piling and replacing scarves really quickly.

'You've got a serious talent for stacking shelves with scarves.' Matt was going as fast as he could, at about a quarter of her rate.

'I know and I never realised.' Lily didn't pause her lightning scarf-work to speak. 'Such an important life skill. I'm not quite so talented at crouching like this, though. My thighs are killing me.' She placed a pile of red scarves neatly on a shelf and shifted from her squat to a cross-legged sitting position before moving on to a heap of blue scarves.

She was wearing a dress over a bikini, and every time he glanced at her it was a struggle not to register that the dress was slightly see-through. It felt really inappropriate to be noticing so much. He shook his head slightly and reached out to start on the green scarves, at exactly the same moment that Lily did. Their hands brushed and he almost leapt backwards from his crouch, in serious danger of knocking another display unit over.

God, this was annoying. She should not be having any kind of effect on him.

'What's the purple thing you were holding?' he asked, for something to say while he moved himself into a sitting position a little bit further away from Lily.

'A sarong. For tying round my waist. On the beach. I have a lime-green bikini it'll go nicely with. You know, purple and green go well together. I mean, not every purple and green. But most of them. Definitely deep purple and lime green. Actually, most purples and greens. Well, not dark green. Unless the purple was like a lilac, or a very light vibrant one.' She stopped babbling, looked at him briefly and pressed her lips together.

Matt couldn't help smiling. Pretty satisfying, if he was

honest, that she was clearly feeling as jumpy around him as he was around her.

He picked up the finished pile of folded green scarves and placed them on a shelf.

'No.' Lily shook her head.

'No?'

'You can't put them there. They look horrible next to those yellow ones.'

'Do they?'

'*Yes*. Seriously. Look at them.' She gestured.

'But they must have been next to each other before. Look where they fell.'

Lily shook her head. 'No. They really don't look good. Put the green ones there.' She pointed at a higher shelf. 'So that the pink ones are between the green and the yellow.'

'So we've knocked their display down and now we're rearranging how they display their scarves because we know better than they do about colour combos?'

'Yeah, when you put it like that, I actually did them a favour knocking the display over.' She shot him a grin and, oh *God*, he loved that smile. 'I should knock more down.'

He smiled back at her – he couldn't help it – and then they worked on the scarves in silence; and a couple of minutes later, they'd finished.

Matt stood up, stretching his muscles as he did. 'I'm getting old. Genuinely feeling the effects of sitting bent down like that.' He reached a hand out to help Lily, just as she pushed herself up in one fluid movement from cross-legged to standing. He blinked. 'Wow.' That was new, wasn't it? Wouldn't he have known if she could do moves like that?

Lily laughed. 'Yep, not just a skilled scarf arranger. Meg's a Pilates teacher now and she's had us doing all sorts of new stuff.'

Matt felt a flash of, what was that? Misery? That she'd had a whole eight years without him, living her life, doing things like learning to stand up in an absurdly supple way? Ridiculous. He'd lived his life too. They'd split up. Not his choice at the time but it was what it was and that's what happened when relationships finished. You moved on.

'Impressive,' he said.

After too long a pause, Lily said, 'So, thank you for helping with the scarves. Can't believe I was such a klutz. And I can't believe the shop assistant hasn't noticed yet.'

Matt looked over. 'Aaliyah's doing an amazing job distracting him.' She was talking very animatedly and waving different pairs of sunglasses around.

'I'd better own up, now that things don't look quite so scarf-apocalyptic.'

They both moved towards the counter.

'Oh hello.' Aaliyah put down the sunglasses she'd been trying on and said to the man behind the counter, 'Thank you so much for all your help, Jason. I'm going to think about it and come back later. Your sarong's here, Lily. I'll meet you back at the beach. I need to pop to the pharmacy. Thank you again, Jason.'

And off she went – really quickly – definitely, no question, purposely leaving Matt and Lily together in the shop. Did she think they had stuff to discuss? They really didn't. They might have done eight years ago – well, from his perspective they *had* left important discussions undiscussed then – but it was all way in the past now. Matt caught Lily's eye and she gave a half smile and then shifted her eyes from him to Jason.

Lily began to explain to Jason what had happened with the scarves while Matt wondered how quickly he'd be able to escape.

'To tell you the truth, I saw you putting them away and I let you carry on because I was enjoying talking to your friend.' Jason was leaning on the counter, grinning at Lily.

She laughed. 'Cheeky. But totally fair enough. So what do

you think of our arrangement?' She did a ta-dah gesture with her hands.

'You are right. It looks very nice now. You want to change all my other displays?' Jason twinkled at Lily and she laughed some more, and Matt suddenly *really* wanted to leave. He just didn't want to be here, watching Lily being Lily.

He cleared his throat. 'I'd better get going.'

'Do you need anything before you go?' Jason asked.

'No, I'm good, thanks. Well, maybe just some flip-flops.' Kind of rude to come into a shop, participate in the partial destruction of the displays and then not buy anything.

He chose a pair of black flip-flops while Lily paid for her sarong.

'Black. You don't like colour?' the man said.

'I'm good with black,' Matt said.

Lily nodded and he said, 'What?'

'Nothing.'

Matt shook his head. 'When you know what suits you, why wouldn't you stick with it?'

'Absolutely.' Lily sniggered. She'd always teased him about how conservatively he dressed, and he'd teased her back about her obsession with colour.

He nudged her arm with his elbow and said, 'Shut up,' and then wished he hadn't. Far too intimate a gesture.

They sank into another silence while they both finished paying, and then walked out of the shop together, still in silence, and paused just outside the door, in the shade under the shop's awning.

'So, great to see you,' Matt said. Whichever way she went now, he was going the other way.

'Yes, lovely to see you. Bye, then. Probably see you at the wedding.' She switched a big fake smile on, which jolted him right to his core – not the fact that it was fake, but the fact that he *knew* it was fake. It was the one she'd used when they'd been at work dinners at his firm when she hadn't been enjoying the conversation. When she looked like that in the past, he'd catch her eye and smile a secret smile at her, and her expression would lighten and he'd know that that real smile was just for him.

And right now he was the one making her smile her pretend smile.

'Bye. See you there.' Matt hesitated for a moment and then leaned forward and pecked her cheek. No, not good. Too much of a sensory overload, plus he'd just had a wave of extreme desolation at behaving like a distant acquaintance with someone he'd spent over a year hoping he'd spend the rest of his life with.

Lily half-raised the hand that wasn't holding the sarong before beginning to walk in the direction of the beach.

Matt watched her go for a second and then ducked under the shop awning and began a slightly self-conscious amble in the opposite direction.

He stopped in front of a little art gallery and looked in through the window to kill a few moments.

Meeting Lily shouldn't feel awkward, or a big deal, or anything. It was eight years now since they'd split up and he'd been married and divorced in that time. Anything between them was way in the past. But, Lily. She'd broken his heart even more than his actual divorce had, if he was honest.

Well, their first meeting was done now. And there was no point wishing that he hadn't agreed to join Tom on this stag holiday. He'd met Tom at a barbecue with Tess several years ago and had hit it off immediately, and then he and Tom had become close friends in their own right. He couldn't have said no to the wedding invitation given how close he was to Tess and Tom, plus his parents couldn't make it because they'd already had a big trip organised to Australia to visit Matt's older brother and his family, and someone should be representing their side of the family; and equally he couldn't have said no when Tom had invited him to his stag do.

Anyway, he and Lily might see each other at a distance over the next couple of days, and obviously a little at the wedding, but not to talk to – no reason for any substantive chat – and then they'd both be on their way and that would be that.

'Can I interest you in any of my artwork?' An orange-suited man had emerged from the gallery. Damn. Clearly Matt had been standing staring into space for too long.

'Maybe later,' he said. 'It all looks great but I'm a little busy at the moment.'

He turned round, scanned the street to check that Lily had disappeared into the distance, and began the walk back to the beach.

He hoped he wasn't going to spend the next three days permanently on edge.

There was something about unfinished business, though. Hurtful unfinished business. He still wanted to know why they'd split up.

He and the rest of the stags were finishing a long, relaxed lunch when a woman's loud voice boomed, 'Hello, my darlings,' and Matt was enveloped from behind in a perfume-laden hug.

'Hello, Auntie Carole,' he said.

'Hi, Carole,' said Tom.

'Don't worry about me. I'm not here to cramp your style.' Five-foot-two Carole pinched six-foot-two Tom's cheek like he was about six years old and roared with laughter. 'Sorry, Tom. Your face is a picture. I know you don't want to see your aunt-in-law on your stag party, but I thought I'd pop over and see Matty and have a quick chat about the work we want to do. There are some houses on the island I want you to have a look at, and I don't want to tell you about it during the wedding.'

Matt was an architect and his aunt Carole, the sister of both Matt and Tess's mums, had lived on Paros for decades and had decided recently that she wanted to spend some of the proceeds of the sale of her lingerie business on building some holiday cottages on her land, and she'd asked Matt to draw up the plans for her while he was over.

'I'm impressed that you found us,' Matt said.

'I have my sources.' Carole tapped her nose. 'And a big group of lively young men on a small island isn't hard to track down. Anyway, can I borrow you for a couple of hours to go through some things with you and show you on a map where the houses are that I'd like you to take a look at?'

'Of course.' Matt smiled at her. Carole and her husband, Norman, were childless and their nieces and nephew had spent many summer holidays here in Greece with them, and Matt adored her.

'Car's out there.' She indicated with her head towards a bright-pink jeep in the street.

Fifteen minutes later, the two of them were sitting outside a hidden-gem-style café in a village in the interior of the island and Carole was spreading papers out all over the table.

'I've brought you iced tea and some of my homemade honey cookies,' Calista, the café owner, told them, inserting plates and glasses between the papers.

'Thank you so much. These look delicious.' Matt smiled at Calista and offered the plate to Carole.

'Thank you, my darling. I'm only going to have one.' She took the biggest one, from the far side of the plate. 'I'm watching my figure.'

Matt took a cookie too, as Carole said, 'Now. I've done some preliminary plans of my own.' She picked up a wodge of papers

and waved them in his face. He blinked. *Some* was an understatement.

'Looks like you've been quite busy,' he said.

'If you're going to do something, do it properly. Anyway,
these should show you what I want. Three separate cottages of
different sizes, pool and barbecue area each. Now, they need a
USP. So I'm thinking *either* they're mini copies of the house
that a certain Hollywood star has on this island *or* they're copies
of the underground house that someone built on this island that
got shortlisted for shedloads of awards.'

'Okay. *Or* I could come up with something original, based
on a style that you like but appropriate to the specific location?'

Carole raised her eyebrows and scrunched her nose up. 'Do
you think you can actually do that? Being honest?'

'I mean, yes? I'm an architect? It's my job? That's why
you're paying me to do this?'

'I'm sorry, my love. I forget sometimes that you're a fully
fledged adult now with a proper career. How old are you now?'

Matt laughed. 'I'm thirty-six. Very much a fully fledged
adult. Okay. Why don't we go through your plans and what
kind of exterior design you like and take it from there? And
obviously I'm more than happy to go and check out famous
houses if we can see them from the road.'

'You can't see them from the road per *se*,' Carole said, 'but
luckily I have friends who live in nearby houses and you can get
a good look from their gardens. And luckily they're both happy
for you to go round on Saturday and have a nosey before you
come over to us after the wedding. Are you sure you can only
stay for one night?'

'Sadly, yes, but I'd love to come out to visit again soon. It's
been too long.'

. . .

An hour and a half later, after they'd finished going through Carole's – very ambitious – plans and drunk a lot of tea and eaten a lot of Calista's cookies, Carole looked at her watch.

'I need to get back,' she said. 'Got to cook Norm's dinner. Let's do a quick drive round the island and I'll point out a couple of houses, and then I'll drop you back with your party and get myself back on the ferry.'

'So how are you?' she asked a few minutes later as they rattled along a dusty back road in the pink jeep. 'This is the first time I've seen you since your divorce. You know, the only time I ever met Gemma was at your wedding. You never came here with her. The only girlfriend you ever brought was that lovely girl, a long time ago. What was her name? Blonde hair and a big smile?'

'Lily.' They'd only been together a couple of months when he'd asked her if she'd like to come to Greece. It had felt natural because he'd already begun to assume that they'd spend the rest of their lives together. Stupid.

'I liked her. But she's not the one you married. How've you been since the divorce?'

'Yeah, I'm fine, thank you.'

'Really?'

'Yes, really.' Matt pointed at the road ahead as Carole took her eyes off it to look at him. He'd better give her some more details or she'd drive them into the bushes. 'The most difficult thing now is custody of the dog. We have joint custody and we've both really struggled with it. Makes you realise what a nightmare it would be if you had kids and split up.' It also, when he said it out loud, made him realise that he probably shouldn't have married Gemma in the first place, if only a couple of years after their divorce he was more upset about losing the dog than her. And if he reflected any more about things, the fact that he couldn't stop thinking about having seen Lily again indicated that he probably hadn't been ready to marry someone else so soon after he and Lily split up. He'd thought he was in love with Gemma at the time, but in retrospect it had probably been classic rebound.

'So what happened?'

'She met someone else.' He wasn't going to go into any of the sordid facts with Carole about having found Gemma in their own bed doing stuff he hadn't thought she'd ever done or would ever want to do. He wasn't going to go into those facts with anyone, actually.

'I'm sorry, sweetie. Good job you're taking a break now.' Carole threw the jeep round a corner and Matt grabbed the door handle as the whole car rocked for a second. 'Have we not been in a car together before? How is that possible? Norm must have been driving last time you came. I wouldn't have had you pegged as a nervous passenger.'

'I'm not a nervous passenger,' Matt told her. 'Just a rational one.' You definitely wouldn't choose Carole to drive you along a winding mountain road, for example.

As they bounced back down towards the beach where all the others were, Matt caught a flash of purple as some women rounded a corner in the road. Had that been Lily? Actually wearing the strange purple thing that she'd had over her head? Could well have been. There was every chance they'd bump into each other several times on this tiny island. They hadn't seen each other a single time in London since they split up but the population of London had to be several thousand times that of Antiparos.

'Matt? Matty?'

Matt looked back round at Carole.

'You didn't hear a word that I said, did you?' She smiled at him good-naturedly. 'Million miles away?'

'Oops, yes, sorry,' he said. Carole had always known when they were lying when they were kids, and he was pretty sure things wouldn't be any different now.

'I was asking if you'd seen Tess yet.'

'No, not yet. Bumped into two of her bridesmaids in a shop this morning but that's the closest I've come to her.' Odd to talk about Lily as Tess's bridesmaid rather than as herself, the funny, gorgeous, vibrant, heartbreaking individual – who he clearly hadn't known as well as he'd thought he had – that she was.

Turned out he still really wanted to know what had actually gone wrong between them. Maybe he should just ask her if he got the opportunity. This unfinished business thing was not healthy.

'Matty. You're paying no attention whatsoever to me.'

'Sorry?' he said. He pushed thoughts of Lily away and grinned at Carole.

'I could never resist that smile.' She took her right hand off the steering wheel to reach up to ruffle his hair and they lurched to the left and Matt let out a yelp. 'Stop it. You're far too nervous a passenger. Come on, let's get you back. I hope you're going to be concentrating harder on your architect plans than on my conversation.'

Matt re-joined the rest of the stags on the beach late afternoon for a raucous volleyball tournament.

Midway through a game, he caught a swing of a blonde ponytail as a couple of women strolled past them along the water's edge. Was that Lily? He turned to look, irritated beyond belief as he did so by the fact that he knew that he shouldn't but he couldn't help it. And that his heart rate had quickened a little.

No, not her.

Oof. The ball had just hit him hard on the back of his shoulder.

'Mate,' Carlton, one of Tom's friends, yelled, 'what were you *doing*? The game's this way, not in the bloody sea.' Yup.

. . .

Lily and the others weren't in the same bar or restaurant that Matt's group went to that evening and, by the next morning, Matt was only keeping an eye out for her maybe fifty per cent of the time – a big improvement.

Piling ham and cheese onto his plate at breakfast time, he remembered hotel breakfasts with her. She'd had a very strong belief that eating meat for breakfast was just plain *wrong*, like an aberration – her stomach just couldn't deal with that kind of food first thing – much how he felt about the way she sometimes used to like an evening in pyjamas with a bowl of cereal and chocolate for her dinner. She was the only person he'd ever met who'd never had a full English breakfast even once. He wondered if she'd be having what had been her usual – croissant followed by Greek yoghurt and fruit – or if she'd moved on in her breakfast tastes.

They were all going to be playing golf mid-morning. Matt decided to go and find a quiet corner in a café and spend an hour working on plans for Carole's cottages before he met the others.

Drinking a delicious – and incredibly strong – coffee while he worked, he thought for a moment that he heard Lily's laugh from somewhere and looked up. Nope, no sign of her in the street outside. There were women's voices coming from somewhere nearby, and while he couldn't make out individual words, he was pretty sure that they were speaking English. So what, though? There were bound to be other English tourists here in July. And even if it *was* Lily, it didn't matter, did it?

This was actually becoming ridiculous. He'd thought about her all the time after they split up, and that had not been a good time in his life. He really didn't want to revisit even a fraction of that pain.

He needed either to put her completely out of his mind and

just acknowledge her as someone from his past who he'd loved a lot but from whom he'd moved on, or just actually ask her what had happened between them at the end so that he no longer had that question mark in his mind.

Right now, though, he was going to stop thinking about her and enjoy his day with a great group of men on a holiday paradise island.

Time to get another coffee and then wander back in time for the golf.

Half an hour later, he thanked the café owner again, walked out onto the street and turned left.

'Matt,' called a voice from behind him. It sounded exactly like Lily.

He turned round, slowly.

It was her. Looking very odd.

Oh God. He was going to laugh. He really, really shouldn't.

He clamped his lips together and Lily glared at him.

THREE

LILY

Lily continued to give Matt the evil eye while he visibly battled to keep a straight face.

'Hi,' he said eventually.

Seriously, the things you had to do as chief bridesmaid when your best friend got married.

They'd just finished getting their hair done as a practice run for the real thing.

It was just the two of them, Lily and Tess, because Aaliyah wasn't letting anyone near her hair – she was amazing at doing it herself and didn't trust anyone else to touch it – and Meg's hair was bob-length and she'd only had it cut a couple of weeks ago, so she'd refused to have anything done to it hairdressing-wise and was just having flowers in it. Wise, *wise* decisions on both their parts as it turned out.

When Lily and Tess had set out for the hairdresser's, Aaliyah had said she was going to FaceTime her kids and then read by herself in the hotel garden, and Meg had vaguely said she was going for a walk, which Lily suspected was going to involve Pythagoras, the handsome restaurant owner from the other night, who they'd just *happened* to bump into on the beach yesterday, after which Meg had wandered off with him and not returned until early evening.

The entire fifteen-minute walk from the hotel, Tess had raved about how amazing the hairdresser – who'd been recommended by a friend of a friend of her own hairdresser in London – was going to be, so Lily had genuinely not been worried at all, and when her stylist, Angela, had said that she'd had full instructions from Tess about what sort of style to go for, and would Lily like to leave it to her, she'd said yes, because Tess had excellent taste.

Big, *big* mistake.

She'd almost screamed out loud when she'd seen herself in the mirror when Angela had finished, and had then spent a couple of minutes having to fight tears.

She now had a *fringe*, and *short sides*, for the first time in her entire life. She also had poodle-style curls in the rest of her hair and a ridiculous bow in them, and looked like total shit, but that was a secondary consideration because she could remove the bow and wash out the hairspray and poodle curls. She couldn't un-cut her fringe and the sides, though. Angela had got her scissors out and said she might neaten up some of the ends. That had sounded okay, because it had not sounded like she was going to cut *inches* off. *Why* hadn't Lily paid more attention? *Why* had she just meekly said okay when Angela had turned her chair away from the mirror and said she worked better like that?

'I didn't think you were going to cut that much off,' she'd said in an unsteady voice when Angela had turned her round to show off her stunning creation in the mirror.

'It was just a little,' Angela had said. 'It's beautiful, isn't it?'

It was not beautiful. It was a complete eyesore. It was the worst hairstyle Lily had ever seen and she'd had a colleague for a long time who'd been a fan of the pull-wispy-lengths-of-hair-over-balding-patch school of wishful I'm-not-really-going-bald thinking.

She'd really, really wanted to have the tantrum from hell.

'Isn't it?' Angela had repeated.

Lily couldn't have a tantrum. Tess was getting married in two days' time and Lily was the never-freaking-out, supportive one. Of *course* she wasn't going to have a tantrum.

'Yep,' she'd managed.

And *then*, while Lily had been busy screaming internally about her fringe and looking in the mirrors all around them and comparing Tess's *gorgeous* hairstyle with her own hideous one, Tess had spied Matt walking past the salon door and had told Lily that she had to go and check with him that Tom was nowhere in the vicinity because Tess was sure that it would be terrible luck if Tom saw her with her wedding hairstyle before the moment when she began the walk down the aisle.

'But I can't go like this,' Lily had said, gesturing at her own hair in horror. She couldn't speak to *any* human being looking like this, but especially *Matt*, and even more so after the scarf display incident yesterday. He'd think she'd turned into some kind of disaster magnet.

But Tess had hissed, 'Lily, you *have* to or the whole wedding could be ruined. My whole *marriage* could be ruined. My whole *life* could be ruined.'

'But I look *ridiculous*,' Lily had said. Whispered, actually, so that Angela wouldn't overhear and be upset.

'My *marriage*,' Tess had wailed.

Right.

Lily had felt so stressed from her bad hair and having to talk to Matt that she'd had to get her inhaler out and take some puffs before she'd left the hairdresser's.

And now here she was, standing in the middle of the pavement, in front of Matt, who – like he had yesterday – was looking his usual handsome self, even better than he had done when they were younger, and with his hair obviously looking totally normal, and clearly torn between laughter and pity.

Which wasn't surprising, because Lily looked like an eighties footballer, or an ageing rocker. Rod Stewart with a perm. A blonde Brian May.

It was really annoying. It was like fate was pranking her.

Before this week, she'd planned so well how she was going to be looking her best when she saw Matt, and yesterday she'd looked like an idiot with the scarves and today she was standing in front of him with the worst haircut she'd ever had in her entire life. Thirty-three years to get a shit cut, and all had always been well, and now, *now*, was the time she'd done it. Marvellous. Splendid.

Matt's lips twitched again.

'Don't laugh,' she said.

'I'm sorry. I'm really sorry.' Matt pressed his lips together and looked at the ground and back at her. 'I haven't seen you like this before.'

'Tess and I have just had our practice hair styling for the wedding.'

'Oh. How's hers looking?'

'Hers looks genuinely fantastic.'

'Well, that's good.'

'Yep.'

Yesterday, it had really unsettled Lily how when they were so close to each other on the floor with the scarves she'd felt like every nerve in her body was attuned to him and today it was unsettling her how gorgeous he looked. They'd split up, it was a long time ago, and they were nothing to each other now. She shouldn't be reacting to him.

And his thick, wavy hair looked as good as usual and hers looked so bad she could almost have laughed herself if she hadn't wanted to cry.

'Ask about Tom,' Tess hissed from behind the hairdresser's door.

Lily took a deep breath and managed not to snap at Tess – *sometimes* things were a bigger deal than some tiny pre-wedding detail, and both seeing your love-of-your-life-ex two days running and having *shit hair* for the next few months felt like huge deals. Instead she said, 'Tess would like me to ask if Tom's nearby because she doesn't want to see him with her perfect wedding hair until the actual wedding.'

Matt leaned in and lowered his voice. 'And her hair is really, genuinely perfect?'

'Yes. Genuinely. We didn't have the same stylist.'

Matt nodded and pressed his lips hard together again like he was trying not to laugh again.

Lily shook her head. She didn't want to have to talk to *anyone* right now, let alone Matt, or Tess, actually; she just wanted to go back to the hotel and wash her hair and try to work out how to live with the fringe and the short sides. 'So is Tom nearby?'

'Sorry. No. We're about to head over to the golf course for a game. I think he's probably already on his way over there. Other side of the island. I think Tess's safe to come out.'

'Yay.' Tess burst out of the hairdresser's and threw herself at Matt. 'My favourite cousin. It's so nice to see you. Thank you for coming out for the wedding. *I'm getting married on Friday.*'

'It's great to see you too,' said Matt, returning her enthusiastic hug and smiling. 'Wouldn't have missed the wedding for the world. And your hair does look lovely.'

'Thank you.' Tess patted the loose curls the hairdresser had created from nowhere – her hair was naturally poker straight – and preened. Then she said, 'OMG, don't tell Tom about it, will you?'

'Dammit, I've already surreptitiously taken a photo and sent it to him,' Matt said.

'Oh my God,' Tess screeched. 'Why would you do such a thing?'

'I think it was a weak joke,' Lily said.

'Was it?' Tess asked.

Matt nodded. 'Obviously.'

'Why would you make a joke like that?' Tess said.

'Um?' Matt swivelled his eyes a little.

'These wedding preparations are serious business,' Lily told him. If he hadn't worked that out already, he'd realise soon. Tess had an excellent sense of humour and would laugh about anything normally, but not so much when she was only two days away from her wedding. Or even two months away from it, actually.

'The wedding's going to be perfect,' Tess said. 'Lily's been an amazing help.' She turned to face Lily and gasped. 'Oh. My. God. Lily. Oh. My. God. Your hair.' So *that* was why she hadn't freaked about it earlier. She just hadn't noticed. Even when Lily had said that she looked ridiculous. To be fair, Tess's own style was stunning and she was the bride. She'd had lots of mirror-gazing to do. 'It's literally the worst hairstyle I've ever seen. Anywhere. Ever. You look like you've had a poodle perm cut into a mullet.'

'Yes, I know that,' Lily said.

'Oh my *God*. You've got a massive *fringe*. And weird *sides*. They've ruined your hair. How are you going to look okay with a fringe and short bits like that?'

'Yup.' Lily was pretty sure that she wasn't going to cry – in front of anyone else, anyway – but she couldn't smile right now. What was actually *wrong* with Angela? A couple of years ago during lockdown when the hairdressers were all closed, Lily and Manjeeta, one of her colleagues, had one day suddenly had enough of their over-long hair and had each cut about three inches off the bottom of each other's hair so that they'd both gone back to just below shoulder-length, and both their haircuts had been *fine*. She'd have been *way* better off with Manjeeta – a midwife, not a hairdresser – now, rather than Angela.

'Oh my God. We need to do something. Otherwise you'll ruin all my photos.' Tess stopped talking and stared at some large, bright-flower-filled pots outside a bakery on the opposite side of the street, while Lily tried really hard to focus on the fact that her hair grew very fast. Maybe she could ask Aaliyah for some hair styling tips while she was growing it out.

'Are you okay?' Matt said to her. Oh God. Pity from Matt. Now she could feel hot tears forming behind her eyelids.

'Yes, thank you.' Lily opened her eyes wide and then blinked hard. It would be mortifying to cry in front of him. Especially since the tears weren't just about her hair, but also because being here on the island with him, having actual conversations, was just... overwhelming, that was the word. 'It'll be fine. Just one of those things.'

'It *is* just one of those things,' he said. 'You always used to say that your hair grows really fast, and you look lovely no matter what. The first thing anyone ever notices about you is your smile.'

Lily's tears were definitely going to spill out now. Simultaneous pity and niceness from Matt. And a memory: one of the first things he'd told her was that she had a lovely smile. And then he'd said he hoped she didn't think he was chatting her up. And then he'd said that actually he kind of was. And she'd laughed and told him she liked his smile too.

She sniffed.

Sunglasses. She should have thought of them before. She opened her bag and pulled them out and stuck them on. That was much better.

'Thank you,' she said.

Tess turned to face them both and said, 'I've been trying to work out whether we can keep you out of the photos, Lily, but

we can't. It would seem weird. We're going to have to get you a
new hairstyle.'

'I could just do my own hair?' said Lily, trying really hard,
and failing, not to feel fairly pissed off with Tess. Yes, wedding
photos were important but, also, this was Lily's *hair*, that she
had to *live* with. She'd had long hair – all one length, no stupid
fringe and side bits – *forever* and she'd *liked* it like that. And
very few people would be happy standing in front of their ex
looking like a dog's dinner. And, also, keep a best friend out of
wedding photos because of her hair? Really?

'Nope.' Tess shook her head again. 'You need to have it done
by a professional.'

'Um, that hasn't worked well so far, and Aaliyah's doing her
own?' Lily really wished she was as good at doing her own hair
and as scary-forthright as Aaliyah was at the moment.

So scary that, when Lily had got back to the beach
yesterday and Aaliyah had asked her if she'd had a good clear-
ing-the-air conversation with Matt after she'd left the shop, she
hadn't said anything about the fact that, *what*, Aaliyah had left
them alone on purpose? She'd just gritted her teeth, told
Aaliyah that it had been nice to see him and changed the
subject.

When they were younger, Aaliyah never used to be the way
she was now. And Tess didn't either, pre insane wedding preps.
And Meg hadn't been as desperate when they were younger.
Really, apart from right now when she was so flustered about
seeing Matt again and pissed off about her hair, Lily seemed to
be navigating her thirties more easily than her best friends were.
There was clearly something to be said for having decided that
you were probably better off long-term single.

'Aaliyah's really good at styling her own hair and also she
terrifies me at the moment and she wanted to do it,' Tess said.
'*Oh.* I've just had a brainwave.'

'She could do mine?'

'Exactly.' Yessss.

Tess reached up and hugged Matt. 'See you later. We have to go and find Aaliyah now.'

'Bye then,' Lily said, not moving within hugging distance. She didn't think she could cope with actually touching him right now. When their hands had brushed yesterday over the scarves, and when he'd kissed her cheek outside the shop, it had been excruciating.

'Good luck,' Matt said, not moving in her direction either. 'I honestly think you'll be happy with your hair again once you've washed it yourself, Lily. It's just a bit different. Doesn't mean it can't look good.'

'I mean, really?' Lily said.

'Did that sound patronising?'

'Patronising and really fake.'

'Sorry? But not fake. Hair grows. Maybe you'll have to have it in a, um, much shorter style for a bit, but with a different hairdresser it's bound to be fine, isn't it?'

'Would you like to shave your head right now? For example?'

'No. But I don't have to.'

'You're really annoying,' Lily said over her shoulder to him as Tess took her arm and started to march her off in the direction of the hotel. Annoying was better than devastatingly attractive, at least.

Twenty minutes later, they were in Lily's room with the others, and Aaliyah had Lily sitting on the stool at her dressing table and was inspecting her from all angles.

'Okay,' she pronounced eventually. 'I don't think it's as bad as you think it is at first sight because I don't think she's actually cut that much off the sides. She's done most of the side mullet bit with hairspray. Lily, you need to get in the shower and wash everything out of your hair and while she's doing that you need to go and buy some hairdressing scissors, Tess.'

'Me?' said Tess.

'Er, yes?' Aaliyah raised one eyebrow.

'But I'm the bride.'

'Tess, hun,' said Aaliyah in a voice of steel. 'I love you, you know I do, we all do, but I'm not joking, you've turned into a complete bride-fucking-zilla. Lily has a *bad* hairstyle right now and we need to sort it, and *not* just because of your sodding photos but because we care about her and I'm pretty sure that she's really upset about it but not saying so. You need to stop thinking only of yourself and start caring about other people again.'

You could have heard a pin drop.

Lily sat in frozen silence, trying surreptitiously to get a look at Tess in the dressing table mirror without moving her head. She could see Meg out of the corner of her eye, also frozen.

'Go,' said Aaliyah, not at all frozen.

'Okay,' said Tess, in a slightly wobbly voice. 'Sorry about your hair, Lily.'

When the door had closed behind Lily, they all looked at each other.

'Are you okay, Lily?' Aaliyah asked.

'Feeling a lot better now that you're going to be in charge of my hair,' Lily said.

'Pretty punchy there, Aaliyah,' Meg said. 'Are *you* okay?'

'She's just been pissing me off,' Aaliyah said. 'She's *so* self-centred being more worried about her photos than how you feel with the haircut from hell. She wants to try looking after three monster kids on close to no sleep for a whole year and *then* she'd know what stress was like.'

Lily and Meg both nodded and Lily tried not to think about the *haircut from hell* comment.

Aaliyah did a massive sniff and said, 'I *really* miss the kids but also I *really* need a break from them.'

'Hey, come here.' Lily stood up and put her arms round her. 'That's why it's perfect that you're here for a few days. You clearly *do* need a break and there's nothing wrong with that and you'll be delighted to see them when you get home.'

'Yeah, you're right. Thank you.' Aaliyah squeezed her arm. 'Now get in the shower.'

Tess was back with the scissors by the time Lily was out of the shower and sitting at her bedside table with Aaliyah standing behind her wielding a comb and lots of hair clips.

'Tess, go and take a rest,' Aaliyah instructed, 'and Meg, stay here so that you can tell me how's it looking.'

'I kind of arranged to meet someone for lunch,' Meg said as Tess left the room.

'Pythagoras can wait,' Aaliyah said. 'Stay here. Lily, I'm going to have to take some of the length off the back to balance things but I think I can make you look good. Actually, you know what, I think I might work better with no one watching. Go and see Pythagoras, Meg.'

'Your wish is my command.' Meg practically skipped out of the door.

'Right.' Aaliyah clipped some of Lily's hair up and took hold of the bottom right-hand part. 'We're going to go layered. You're beautiful. You're going to look fab when I've finished.'

Oh, God. It didn't feel good that this was Lily's only haircut option.

'Wow,' she breathed two and a quarter hours later, studying herself in the mirror. She actually looked okay. 'You're a genius. A very slow haircutter, but definitely a genius one.'

'Why, thank you.' Aaliyah bowed. 'If I'm honest, that was a little bit nerve-wracking. I've never cut anyone's hair before. That's why I took my time.'

'What, ever?'

'Never. But needs must.'

'Wow.' Lily turned her head to each side. She'd liked her hair the way it was but, given the situation, this was good. She had layers and bounce and Aaliyah had done something which meant that she only had a wispy fringe and the rest of it was part of the layers. It genuinely looked nice. Great, even. 'You're very clever.'

'I am, actually, as it turns out.'

They both laughed and then Aaliyah said, 'So, I've been thinking, about all of us. I can see that parenting three kids and not sleeping and juggling that with work has turned me into a bit of a witch and I can't do anything about that and right now I don't want to because I'm *over* being polite for the sake of it and I'm tired and basically everyone who annoys me can piss off.' Lily nodded. Fair enough. And, also, now didn't feel like the time to contradict Aaliyah.

'Tess's lovely normally but *oh my God* she's annoying me this week,' Aaliyah continued, banging the back of Lily's hairbrush on the bed for emphasis. 'Meg's lovely but getting a little bit too desperate to settle down. And you're just lovely. Like, always lovely. Always there for everyone else. I mean, just now. Your hair looked *terrible*. You're beautiful but even you couldn't carry that off brilliantly. And Tess was being ridiculously self-centred. And you didn't lose it with her.'

'To be fair to Tess,' said Lily, delighted that Aaliyah agreed about her bad haircut and Tess but really not wanting to say so, 'I of all people do know that photos are incredibly important to people, and wedding photos and new baby ones are basically the most important of all.' It was a couple of years now since Lily had started her business helping other people to curate (or just cull, basically) their photos. It had been surprisingly successful – even more people than she'd expected felt overwhelmed by how many photos they had and wanted to get the numbers down to a manageable level so that they could easily look at them and enjoy them but couldn't bring themselves to delete a single one of their children playing in the garden or their holiday to Ibiza or their fortieth birthday party. So now she was only working three days a week in her job as a midwife and concentrating the rest of the time on the business.

'Photos *are* important,' Aaliyah said, 'but she was still being ridiculously self-centred, because *hair's* important too. And you just smiled and carried on.'

'Yeah.' That was true. That was what Lily did.

'I know you don't like going into details when you're upset about anything.'

'Mmm.' Lily did not want to have this conversation.

'Basically, I just wanted to say that you never really told us exactly what happened with Matt beyond that you were really upset and could we all please get very drunk with you, and I know it was a really long time ago but I've always worried that you didn't completely get over him. I mean, you haven't really had a serious relationship since then. I don't think you've been out with anyone for more than about three months since him. I hope that isn't because you're in some awful still-hung-up-on-Matt place a lot of years down the line. How many years is it now?'

'Eight,' said Lily, 'but, no, honestly, I'm not, I'm fine.'

'You knew immediately how long ago it was though.'

'I'm anal like that.' She wasn't. But she still knew they'd gone out for one year, two months, three weeks and one day.

'Hmm. Well, just to say I hope you're okay. And you know if you ever want to talk we're all here. Well, Meg and I are. I think Tess will be in a month or two once she's over her wedding.'

'Thank you for caring.' Lily wasn't about to discuss her feelings, or any weaknesses, in any greater depth. Even with her best friends, it still often felt like it would flip her straight back into how she'd been as a child – always the ill one, always the one who needed everyone else's support – and she just couldn't go there. She'd binned that person when she'd left school and gone to uni, and she wasn't revisiting her. That person had had a really bad time at school, always the odd one out, often not able to take part in things, never invited to parties. Adult Lily, who rarely admitted to much beyond superficial problems, like a bad haircut or an annoying neighbour, was a much happier, way more popular person.

She'd told Aaliyah, Tess and Meg about all of that, during a nightmare time at uni when she'd had an asthma attack during her exams, and they'd been amazing, and they were gorgeously willing to support her however much she did or didn't want to share with them. It felt like they were the only people in the world who got that about her. 'I do really appreciate it. Thank you. Especially for letting me *not* talk when I just can't. Obviously in an ideal world, Matt wouldn't be here, but he is, and, honestly, it's fine.' Oh God. *Oh God.* What if he had a new partner and she was coming out for the wedding and Lily had to see him with her? Why hadn't that occurred to her before? No. Stop thinking about it. 'And thank you so much for being an amazing hair stylist. New career for you if you ever get fed up with your job.'

'Come here.' Aaliyah leaned forward and hugged her. 'I'm so sorry that you have to see Matt and I totally get that you don't want to talk about it. Let's go and find Meg. And we should probably look for bloody Tess too.'

They found Tess on a lounger next to the hotel pool, inching round to exactly follow the direction of the sun while slathering on more Factor 50. She'd been telling them all week that she needed to look sun-kissed on top of her fake tan but clearly in no way burnt. There'd been ructions at one point the afternoon they arrived when she'd fallen asleep in the sun and woken up to discover a branch was casting a line of shade across the middle of her back and arms.

'Oh, wow, you look amazing,' Tess said. 'My wedding photos are saved.'

'And?' said Aaliyah, like Tess was a naughty toddler who needed to be taught some manners.

'And thank you so much, Aaliyah, for saving Lily's hair and I'm so pleased for you, Lily, that your hair looks so gorgeous now, and I never doubted that it would all be fine,' said Tess. 'And I'm getting married on Friday and I'm *so relieved* that you're going to look gorgeous in my *very important* photos.'

'Come on,' said Lily, before Aaliyah could *yell* at Tess. 'Let's go and look for Meg.'

'There they are,' said Aaliyah about fifteen minutes later.

'Wasn't that quite quick for golf?' said Lily, watching Matt and the others in the distance strolling and chatting.

'Maybe they only did nine holes.' Tess grabbed Aaliyah's large straw hat and stuck it on her own head. 'I need to hide my hair in case Tom looks in our direction. Does he look sunburnt to you?'

Lily squinted at them all. Tom looked fine. Matt looked gorgeous. She could see his hair ruffling in the slight breeze. And now he was laughing at something someone had said, and gesticulating. Tess had asked something about Tom. 'I don't think so,' she said.

'You have such serious Tom-radar,' Aaliyah said. 'I can't believe you saw them from here. Meg, who we came to find, is right there about twenty feet away, with Pythagoras. Aww.

Look at them. They're like something out of an ad for a tropical beach holiday. Or maybe for washing powder. Or a dating app.'

She was right. They were both dressed in flowing white things – Meg a dress and Pythagoras a linen shirt – and were wandering barefoot along the beach, the water lapping at their ankles, holding hands and gazing into each other's eyes.

'You're right, I do,' Tess said. 'It's like I can always sense where he is. And that's just one of the reasons I'm marrying him.'

Right now it felt like Lily could always sense where Matt was, and she certainly *wasn't* marrying him.

'Hey.' Meg was standing in front of them, still holding Pythagoras's hand, beaming at them. 'Lily, your hair looks out of this world. Did you do this, Aaliyah?'

'Yes, I did.' Aaliyah took hold of Lily's shoulders and moved her round in a little circle. 'Doesn't she look amazing?'

'She really does. Wow,' said Meg.

'Great haircut, Lily,' said Pythagoras.

'What about mine?' asked Tess, lifting the hat.

'Self-centred bride-bloody-zilla,' Aaliyah muttered, not totally under her breath, while Pythagoras did his obvious duty and told Tess that of course her haircut was beautiful and she was going to be a stunning bride.

And Lily stood there furious with herself for really wanting Matt to look over towards them and see her with her rescued hairstyle.

FOUR

MATT

'Metaxa shots all round.' Donny, Tom's best man, and his friend Carlton put trays of glasses down on their tables.

'It's four p.m.?' said Matt, thinking of the couple of hours of work he'd been hoping to squeeze in between now and dinner.

'Yeah, you're right, we should have started earlier.' Donny put two in front of each man and an extra one in front of Tom. 'Tonight is Tom's actual stag night. Gives him all of tomorrow to recover before the wedding.'

'I don't think I need an actual massive stag night,' Tom said. 'Just a chilled holiday with my mates.'

'Don't be stupid.' Donny gave him an extra shot glass. 'Dereliction of my duty if I didn't give you a big night tonight. But don't worry, we're going to take it slowly. On account of the heat.'

'Oh God,' Tom said.

'That's right.' Carlton slapped him on the back.

'Okay.' Donny banged a spoon on the table. 'On the count of one, everyone downs their first. On the count of two, everyone downs their second. And on the count of three, Tom downs his third. And then we'll get the beers in.'

'Oh God,' Tom said again.

'Drink this,' Donny ordered everyone a few hours later when they'd moved into a private room at the back of a restaurant for dinner. Probably a few hours, anyway. It was hard to tell how much time had passed.

Matt was very pleased that they were about to eat. Soak up some of the alcohol. He was getting too old for this.

'Are these spiked?' he asked, trying to focus on the cup of black coffee that had just been placed in front of him.

'Nope. Straight up pure double espressos. Because you're all lightweights and the evening's young and you need to re-focus.'

'Oh God,' croaked Tom.

'Everyone needs to eat bread too,' said Carlton as their waiter distributed huge baskets of pittas and baguettes with dips and bowls of olives. 'And drink water after your coffee.'

The coffee, bread and water did help. By the time Donny and Carlton were checking their watches and nudging each other and looking over to the door, Matt's head was clear enough for him to know that they were blatantly waiting for something to happen and that Tom was about to be further stitched up in some way.

Donny and Carlton's nudging and smirking really took off as a woman dressed in a short, belted raincoat, bare legs and very high heels shimmied into the room.

They pointed at Tom and she walked up to him and sat herself on his lap.

'Woah, no thank you,' said Tom. 'Don't want to be rude but I'm nearly a husband. Can't have other women sitting on me.' He blinked several times like he was trying to focus and then said, 'Why are you wearing a coat? It's hot here.'

'You think I'm overdressed?' she purred. She slid off his lap and began to undo her belt as Donny pressed the play button on his phone for some dun-dun-*dun* music.

Tom put his head on the table and closed his eyes as she did her routine.

'I don't feel good about this now,' Donny told Matt and a few of the others. 'You know you feel you have to have a stripper on a stag, but this is just demeaning everyone.' He turned the music off and held his hand up. 'I'm sorry,' he told the woman. 'You've been fantastic. Thank you.' He pulled notes out of his wallet and handed them to her. 'A tip. Thank you again.'

'You want me to go?' she said.

'Yes, but not because you weren't *brilliant*,' Carlton said, standing up and beginning to walk with her to the door.

Tom lifted his head up and said, 'I'm glad she's gone. I don't want to mess things up with Tess.'

'Tess would understand,' Donny said. Apparently Donny didn't know Tess that well. 'This is your stag. It's tradition.'

'She would not understand,' Tom said. 'And it's not like she's going to be with a male stripper right now, is it? I don't want to upset her. I *love* her.' He banged his fingers vertically down onto the top of the table, hard, very hard, as he spoke. 'Ow. That hurt.' He studied his right hand for a moment, turning it all round. 'Very sore,' he said.

'Have another beer,' Donny said. 'That'll stop any pain.'

'I don't think I should have had a stag night like this,' said Tom as he sipped his beer. He'd clearly reached the morose stage of drunkenness. Matt had already reached the hangover stage, courtesy of all the coffee, water and bread. There was no way he was starting to drink again now. Apparently he was too old to want to go drunk, sober and drunk again in one day. He really hoped that having the headache from hell now meant that he wouldn't still be hungover in the morning. 'It doesn't feel right,' Tom said. 'Doing this on the same little island as Tess. She's amazing.' He slurped some more beer. Looked like he hadn't reached the sober-and-hungover-before-bed stage, probably something to do with the fact that his best friends had made sure that he drank more than everyone else. Good job he was a big man.

'She is great,' Matt agreed.

'I bet she was amazing when she was a kid as well,' Tom said.

Matt thought about how annoying she'd been. Three years younger than him, always following him and their other older cousins around, tantrumming when things didn't go her way. If he was honest, she'd only come into her own when she'd hit her mid-teens. And since then she'd been a lot of fun. And, when it came down to it, he loved her to bits and always had done. He was lucky to have such a great family.

'Yeah, she was great,' he said.

'You're the only person here who's known Tess all her life,' Tom said. 'I'm so lucky to have met her. I really, really, really love her.' He stabbed at the table again with his fingers and gave a surprisingly high-pitched scream for someone so large. 'My fingers hurt. One of them hurts more but I don't know which one.'

Matt peered at Tom's hand. 'Maybe the one that's sticking out weirdly.'

'Have some more beer,' Donny said. 'You won't feel anything then.'

'Tess would have been upset about the stripper. I'm glad she didn't finish the job. Tess would have been really upset. I don't ever want to get divorced,' Tom said. 'You're divorced, Matt. I don't want to be divorced. Because I love Tess. I love her so much. I'm sorry you're divorced. Are you sad you're divorced?'

'I'm fine,' Matt said. He genuinely almost was. Apart from the dog custody situation. And the fact that he missed Lily sometimes.

He missed Lily a lot. *So* much. And it was hurting all over again now he'd seen her on the island.

Lily. Wrong name. Wrong *person*.

He wasn't divorced from Lily. He was divorced from Gemma.

It was eight years since he and Lily had split up. It was insane that bumping into her briefly had got her so stuck in his mind again. This was not good.

It was because he still had questions about the end of their relationship. He should ask her.

'Roast chickens for everyone,' the waiter announced.

'I think that's a good thing,' Matt said.

'Yeah, I agree.' Donny gestured around the room. 'I don't think there's a lot of appetite for the massive night I had planned. I nearly booked private ferries to take us over to Paros for some serious clubbing but Carlton talked me out of it.'

'Didn't fancy losing Tom overboard or something,' Carlton said. 'Tess would have gone ballistic.'

'Yeah, she would. Yeah, that's the upside of a nice tame stag night. No injuries.'

———

Matt was filling his plate with bread and pastries to address his remaining hangover at breakfast the next morning, when Donny tapped him on the shoulder.

'Morning,' Matt said.

Donny looked over both his own shoulders like he was playing a spy in a low-budget James Bond farce and then spoke quietly out of the corner of his mouth. 'I think we need a hospital.'

'What? Why? Who for?'

'Tom. Think he's broken his finger.'

Matt sifted through his memories from the night before. Oh yes. He'd definitely hurt it. Broken, though?

'Properly broken?' he asked. 'Or maybe just bruised?'

'It really doesn't look good. Sticking out at an odd angle. Tom doesn't want Tess to find out and worry so he doesn't want to tell her but he thinks your aunt might be the best bet for help with advice about where to go. We tried asking at the hotel reception but we had a language barrier. Google wasn't that much help either. He doesn't have her number so he was hoping you could call her.'

'Yep, no problem. I'll call her now.'

'What an idiot,' Carole said after Matt had got a promise out of her that she wouldn't mention anything to Tess and then described the situation. 'I think there's a medical centre on Antiparos. Give me five minutes and I'll call you back with details.' After a good thirty years living on Paros, Carole spoke very good Greek and knew everyone. Norm knew everyone too but by his own admission he wasn't a linguist and his Greek didn't stretch much further than being able to ask for beers or a cup of coffee.

Mid-morning, Tom had been dispatched to the medical centre – by himself, saying he was already embarrassed enough without needing to drag a friend along with him – and Matt was feeling a lot less fragile after his large breakfast, a post-breakfast siesta under a tree with a newspaper and then a swim. All the others seemed to have gone for similarly quiet mornings, not a surprise given last night.

This afternoon, the majority of the other guests, including Tess's parents, would be arriving, and the stag would be coming to a natural end.

Matt was walking back to his room from the beach when he got a message from Tess.

Should have thought of this before. Now planning a family
dinner this evening – Carole's friend's house – will send address
separately later – 8 p.m. for drinks first – see you there. P.S. I'M
GETTING MARRIED TOMORROW

Family dinner. Just family, or would Tess ask her brides-maids to go too?

He put his key into his door and turned.

He'd decided last night that he was going to ask Lily what had happened at the end of their relationship, and today, sober, he was still planning to ask her that question. Now that he'd seen her a couple of times, and chatted, it felt like it wouldn't be too out-of-the-blue to ask her.

Other than having that conversation, though, it would probably be best not to spend too much time with her over the next couple of days. Clearly they were done, eight-years-in-the-past done, and he didn't need to see her, find her attractive, remember all the reasons that he'd fallen in love with her almost at first sight. He just needed to ask his question and move on.

As he put all his things down on a side table on his way into the bathroom for a post-swim shower before doing some work, his phone rang. Tom.

'How're you doing? How's your finger?' Matt asked.

'Broken and now in quite a serious splint. I have a favour to ask. Kind of a tricky one. Basically, I think Tess is feeling pretty superstitious about seeing me or even speaking to me today and obviously I totally get that and I don't want to upset her. But also she's worked incredibly hard to make everything perfect and I'm not sure she'll view me having my finger in a splint as perfect. So I'd like to warn her beforehand but I don't want to do it by text. Which I'm not even sure about anyway because she might think texting's a no go for the day before your wedding.'

'So you'd like me to warn her for you?'

'I'd be incredibly grateful. And if you could maybe do it in person rather than by phone? Just in case she freaks?'

'Not a problem,' Matt said. Tom was going to have to hope that Tess was less upset by his finger than she'd been by Lily's hair. She definitely wasn't going to be able to avoid having her husband in the photos. Maybe she could avoid having her husband's *finger* in photos though. An image of Lily standing in front of him yesterday with her truly terrible hairstyle and her beautiful smile came into his mind. He wondered if she'd got her hair sorted now. Anyway, Tom. 'Send me a photo of your finger so I know what I'm preparing Tess for?'

The photo came through almost immediately, and, *wow*, that was a serious splint and bandage job. The middle finger of Tom's right hand was so heavily swathed that his other fingers were splayed right out to the sides. It would definitely be visible in photos unless that hand was completely hidden.

'That's a lot of splinting,' Matt said, back on the call after gawping at the photo.

'They said it was a really nasty break. They actually wanted me to go to Paros or possibly even the mainland for an operation. I said no way could I leave the island in case I didn't make it back tonight for some reason. So they went down the incredibly big splint-and-bandages route and gave me a lot of painkillers. Which I'm not supposed to mix with alcohol. And I might have to have an operation anyway, next week.'

Wow. Matt went silent for a moment, his mind boggling at how Tess was likely to take the news that her honeymoon was going to be interrupted by her husband having to go and have surgery. Badly, if the way she'd reacted to Lily's hair was anything to go by.

'Matt?'

'Sorry. Just thinking. Yep, no problem. I'll give Tess a heads up.'

He phoned her straight after he'd finished his breakfast.

'Tess, hi. Could we meet up and have a quick chat at some point today?'

'Um, I'm actually quite busy? Because I'm getting married tomorrow? So I'll see you at dinner?'

Wow. Bridezilla was an understatement. You had to feel sorry for her bridesmaids and anyone else she was going to be taking her stress out on today. And Tom, whenever she found out about his finger. It *was* her wedding, though. One of the top ten most stressful life experiences. He was pretty sure Gemma had been stressed before their wedding too. Most people probably were.

He couldn't really imagine Lily behaving like this before her wedding, though.

He wouldn't be around if and when Lily got married.

Anyway, Tess...

'Yes, of course,' he said. 'I just had something to tell you. Kind of wedding related.'

'Oh my God, what? *What*? What do you know that I don't? Is it one of the guests? Is it Tom? Has something happened to Tom? Is it bad? What is it? What's happened? *What's happened?*'

'No, no, nothing bad, just something very small. Really, it's fine. Just a small thing.'

'Are you sure?'

'Really sure.'

'But why would you phone me if it was a small thing?'

'I mean, it's still worth mentioning, but it's small.'

'So why is it worth mentioning? What's *happened*?'

'It's *really* small, actually. Not *hugely* worth mentioning. But could we just meet up quickly just for a chat?'

'Let's chat at dinner. I'm really busy today. I have to get my nails done *right now*. I'll see you later when it will be *only nineteen hours to my wedding*.'

'Okay. Great. See you later. Enjoy your manicure.'

Right. Well, Matt had made an effort. There wasn't a lot else he could do now, other than text her to tell her. Maybe he'd do that.

But he liked Tom. And Tess was his cousin and great – apart from when she was getting married, it seemed. He'd promised Tom he wouldn't tell her by text. And there was a fair chance she'd lose it if the first she knew of the reality of the broken finger was during the actual wedding ceremony. When Tom fumbled the ring, for example, because he couldn't use his right middle finger. Or much of his right hand at all, actually, going by the photo. How *was* he going to get the ring onto Tess's finger, actually? Matt stood and looked at his own fingers and experimented. Yeah, there was a strong chance you'd drop the ring with your middle finger strapped up like that. Tess would not be happy about that. A lot of brides wouldn't.

Some would laugh. Some might cry.

Yeah, someone was going to have to tell Tess today.

So Matt would just do it during the dinner this evening.

But, no. If she got really upset maybe she wouldn't sleep well tonight. She'd be a lot better off finding out now so that she could talk it through with her friends and they could reassure her that it was *fine*.

Tricky to know what to do though.

Well, there was one thing he could do. He could obviously call Lily, if she hadn't changed her mobile number. He knew that he still had it in his contacts. He should probably have deleted it a long time ago.

He didn't really want to speak to her about fingers. If he was honest, he'd been finding it a bit odd talking to her about ordinary, everyday things. Unsettling. They weren't going to end up in each other's lives again, as friends, so he'd prefer just to ask her once and for all why she'd split up with him and then move on. No other chat. Or maybe just not ask her at all. He still wasn't sure. But definitely no more chat.

He was going to feel like a real arse if he let Tom and Tess down, though.

Assuming it was her – she could have changed her number – Lily didn't answer the first time. Or the second or third times. Maybe he should message her.

Except, what to say? He needed to let her know that it was about Tess and Tom so that she wouldn't think it was something personal. But she'd be with Tess today; what if Tess then somehow saw his message? How would he phrase it?

Probably best to try to have a quick chat in person. Tom would know the name of the hotel the women were staying in.

Twenty minutes later, he was in the foyer of their hotel asking if he could call up to Lily's room.

She picked up on the second ring. 'Hello?'

'Hi, Lily. It's Matt. Do you have a moment? I need to speak to you about Tess. I wondered if you'd be able to pop down to the foyer for a chat.'

'Um.' There was a bit of a silence and then she said, 'Okay. I have a few minutes but not too long because we have a nail appointment this morning. I'll see you in a second.'

She came round the bend in the stairs above him a couple of minutes later. She looked stunning. She was wearing denim shorts and an orangey loose vest top and her hair was incredibly different from how it had been yesterday.

'Wow.' He gestured at her hair. 'You look...'

'Better?' She laughed.

'Lovely is the word I was looking for. I mean, it's great.' It was *so* different. *So* much better. Was it even *real*? Was it a *wig*?

'Aaliyah did it. It was her first hairdressing attempt, which I didn't realise until afterwards, but luckily it turned out okay. Couldn't really have been worse.'

'It's amazing.' It really was.

'Are you saying my hair looked bad yesterday?' Lily had her eyes narrowed. He was pretty sure she was joking, but...

'No?'

'Ha.' Lily laughed. 'You looked panic-stricken there. I know it looked terrible yesterday.'

'Not terrible, just different. And it looks fantastic today.'

'Well, thank you. So you said you needed to talk to me about Tess? Is everything alright?'

'Could we go somewhere where we won't be overheard? Just while I explain?'

'Goodness, sounds quite a big deal. Um.' Lily looked around, her curls bouncing as she turned her head. 'Maybe the beach?'

'It's nothing to worry about,' Matt told her as they left the hotel. 'Basically, I have something to tell Tess on behalf of Tom, before the wedding, and she needs the full details so that she doesn't freak, but she doesn't want to speak to me because she's busy, so I wondered if you'd be able to tell her. And the reason that I thought us being out of earshot now would be best is that it might not sound great if she were to overhear a snippet.'

'Oh my goodness.' Lily stopped under a palm tree next to the beach and turned to face him. 'You're freaking *me* out and I'm not the bride. What's happened?'

'It's fine but Tom's broken the middle finger on his right hand.'

'What? How? This morning?'

'Yesterday, actually, but he's only just been to the medical centre.'

'Oh my goodness. Is he alright?'

'Yep, he's fine. I mean, I think as finger breaks go it's actually quite a bad one and quite painful, but it isn't going to stop him getting married, although he might have to have an operation next week. But the wedding can go ahead, no problem. It'll just be a story for their grandchildren.'

'Woah. That story's going to include Tess going *ballistic*. An operation in the middle of their honeymoon? What if he can't get his dressing wet so he can't swim or shower? They're going to a five-star hotel with an amazing pool and a private beach that they've saved up for for years. She's going to be *really* upset. Poor Tess. Well, at least it won't ruin the wedding itself.'

Matt had always loved how loyal a friend Lily was. It might be a good idea if she didn't exclaim so loudly now, though. Ruin was a strong word but it did seem that Tess was aiming for perfection wedding-wise, and they didn't need her to hear this. What if she came out of the hotel? Or had her bedroom window open? He made a shushing motion.

'Oh my God, it *is* going to ruin the wedding itself, isn't it?' Lily said, ignoring the shushing. 'Can he *use* the finger? Like for cutting the cake and things like that? And exchanging rings?'

'I mean, he has nine other fingers and thumbs.'

'What, so he *can't* use it? Oh my goodness. Tess is going to be *indescribably* upset. Wow. Nightmare. *Nightmare*. Well, at least it won't ruin the photos. At least he doesn't have a bad hairstyle.'

'Shhh,' Matt said again. 'The dressing's big.'

'What? How big's big? Oh my God,' Lily practically screamed. 'Visible-in-photos big?'

'Yup. And she can't really ban the groom from the wedding photos, and it might be quite hard to keep his hand out of all the photos.'

'Wow.' Lily went silent for a few moments and Matt tried really hard not to think about how gorgeous she looked today. Every day. Even yesterday when she'd had terrible hair. 'Poor Tom. Poor Tess. She's worked so hard for everything to be perfect. *Such* bad timing.'

'Could be worse. At least it isn't his ring finger.'

'Oh, okay.' Lily rolled her eyes. 'I'll tell Tess that and she'll be fine about it.'

'Yeah, you're right. Chances are she will not be fine about it. Sorry you have to be the messenger. I have a photo of the finger that I can send to you, which you can show her if she wants to see it.'

'Good idea. Shit, I've just seen the time. I'd better go now. I don't want to be late for the nail appointment.'

Matt nodded. 'Yeah, probably better not upset Tess any more than she's going to be. I'll send the photo to you in a minute.'

Lily was already hurrying back towards the hotel. She shot a smile at him over her shoulder, that got him somewhere deep inside – not right, surely – and said, 'Bye.'

Within thirty seconds of sending the photo he got an *OMG that's HUGE* text from Lily, followed by a string of astonished, sad, horrified, shocked, hand and finger emojis, which made him smile, even though he probably shouldn't. Lily had always loved an emoji.

———

Matt was finishing a post-massive-hangover suitably restrained lunch with Tom – who was not a natural at managing an out-of-action finger and was using his cutlery quite awkwardly – and a few of the other men, when he found that he had a missed call from Lily and a message saying that Tess would like to meet up with him *now* in the café next to the hairdresser's.

He looked at the coffee refill he'd just poured himself and sighed. He was going to have to go, clearly.

He chugged a couple of mouthfuls, stood up and told the others that he'd catch them later.

Lily, Aaliyah and Meg were all with Tess when he got there. Tess looked like she was spitting nails and the other three looked respectively concerned, irritable and resigned.

'Morning,' he said to all of them. 'Congratulations on your hairdressing skills, Aaliyah.'

'Thank you,' Aaliyah preened. 'I'm a genius with the scissors as it turns out.'

'Yep, an amazing transformation,' Matt said.

'Aaliyah's a miracle worker,' Lily said. 'I'm *so* grateful.'

'I'm actually tempted to let her loose on my hair.' Meg patted her own intimidatingly sleek hairdo.

'*Great*,' said Tess, really loudly, 'that Lily's hair looks good for the photos, but *what about Tom*? How's his finger? What happened exactly? Whose fault was it?'

'Nobody's fault,' Matt said, alarmed. 'Just one of those things. We'd probably all had a little bit too much to drink and he just over-gesticulated and hit his hand over-forcefully on the table. Just really bad luck.'

'Can he use his hand properly? Is it going to affect anything?' Tess's eyes were over-bright and opened far too widely under raised eyebrows. It was a good interrogation technique; Matt was feeling guilty even though he *knew* that none of this was remotely his fault and that Tess was his normally-very-fond, younger cousin.

'No, it'll be fine,' he said.

'I'd rather find out *now* than in the middle of the ceremony if he can't use his hand properly,' Tess said, her voice shrill.

'Come here,' Lily said, folding Tess into a hug. 'It's one finger. He probably won't be able to use his hand exactly as normal but he'll totally be able to use it. Of course he will. People break fingers all the time and they carry on with their everyday lives.'

'They don't normally break them straight before their weddings,' Tess said.

'Tess—' Aaliyah was looking at her watch '—it's going to be fine. We've still got quite a lot to do today. We should get going and stop worrying about the finger. Tom's about to be your husband and he adores you and you adore him and the wedding's going to be perfect and you'll just laugh about his finger in years to come. It'll just make the memories even more special.' That was maybe a stretch.

'Memories,' said Tess on a wail and burst into tears. Yep, definitely a stretch. 'Everything's going to be a disaster. And that's what we'll remember.'

'Tess—' Aaliyah sounded like she was talking to a stroppy four-year-old '—*stop crying*. You'll give yourself a headache.'

Tess just carried on weeping, her head on Lily's shoulder.

'And you'll get red eyes,' Lily said. 'Think of the photos.'

Which was genius, because like magic Tess did an enormous sniff and stopped crying.

'Matt probably doesn't have too much to add?' Lily said. 'Like, I think we know all there is to know. So we could let him get on with his day now?'

'I just want to know how Tom is in *person*, though,' Tess said. 'Can he use his hand normally?'

'Very close to normal,' Matt lied.

'We should really get going,' Lily told him. 'Tess is having a final dress fitting with a seamstress we found in the village. Why don't you suggest to Tom that he practise anything he might need to do tomorrow, like putting the ring on and cutting the cake, and then we'll know that there's literally nothing to worry about?'

'That's a really good idea,' Tess said. Again, genius from Lily. 'Okay, thanks, Matt. We'll see you this evening.'

We. Okay. As suspected. Lily would be at the dinner. Was it bad that he was kind of looking forward to seeing her there?

FIVE

LILY

'I think we should go back to the hotel now and get changed for dinner,' Tess said towards evening. 'This is the last time I'm going to go for a walk on the beach as a single woman.'

'*Last time as a single woman* again,' said Aaliyah, not that much under her breath, and rolling her eyes. 'Yes, it's definitely time to go back.' To be fair to Aaliyah, Tess had pointed out it was the last time she was doing this as a single woman about pretty much everything they'd done today since she'd stopped her two-hour histrionics over Tom's finger. And to be fair to Tess, it was huge getting married and it *was* her last day as a single woman and Aaliyah was being quite intolerant.

'I might just take a little walk by myself before I get ready,' said Meg.

'Say hi to Pythagoras,' said Aaliyah.

'Don't be late for dinner,' said Tess. 'And don't distract him from the catering.'

Lily didn't say anything because she was busy watching a beach yoga class and remembering how much Matt had made her laugh the one time they'd done yoga together. It hadn't been a success yoga-wise but they'd had a great time.

Her thoughts were interrupted by the arrival of Pythagoras.

'I thought I would come and meet you here, Meg. Good afternoon, everyone. Aaliyah, I have photocopies of those recipes you asked for. Obviously I'll have to kill you if you share them any more widely.' He grinned at her. 'They're family secrets.'

'Oh my God, thank you so much.' Aaliyah folded the papers he'd handed her and tucked them inside the front cover of the Sally Rooney she'd been carting around everywhere and not actually reading. 'This is dinner sorted when my parents next come over. My mum might finally admit I can cook. And not to worry, I'll guard the recipe details with my *life*.'

'Anyone like to join us for our walk?' Pythagoras asked the others.

'I can't. I've got like a *billion* things to do before tomorrow.' Tess really didn't have anything left to do other than panic. Belt and braces didn't even begin to cover the wedding preps so far. 'And, also, I really don't want to be rude *but* I can't help asking how long it's going to take to get the food ready for this evening?'

Pythagoras laughed. 'Don't worry, it's all under control. I have a couple of people already up at the villa and Meg and I will join them soon.' Carole had strong-armed a friend into hosting a garden dinner for them all this evening, and Meg had – with no difficulty, she said – persuaded Pythagoras into catering it.

'Thank you so much for the walk offer but I might just grab a little snooze.' Lily was not going to sleep; she was going to spend the maximum time available getting ready for this evening so that finally she looked okay in front of Matt. For pride's sake.

'I'm also going to have a little rest,' Aaliyah said. 'And drool over these recipes obviously. And then maybe join you in the kitchen for a few minutes to see you in action. Have *fun*.' She did an enormous pantomime wink as Meg and Pythagoras wandered off towards the beach.

'Honestly.' Lily nudged her. 'He's nice, isn't he? So much nicer than all her other boyfriends.'

'Yep.' Aaliyah nodded. 'Genuinely lovely. And the first one who's ever bothered speaking to us at *all*.'

'Such a pity that he lives here, and Meg in Edinburgh.'

'Come *on*.' Tess put an arm through each of theirs and started to march them towards the hotel. 'It's only two hours until dinner.'

———

Two and a quarter hours later, Lily and Tess arrived at Carole's friend's house. Meg and Aaliyah had gone ahead of them, to help Pythagoras in the kitchen. The house was in a beautifully peaceful hamlet on a hill overlooking the sea, and was gorgeous: traditionally styled, with white walls and blue shutters.

They were led straight into the back garden, which was *amazing*. Lily had an impression of a long, cactus-lined terrace, and beyond that lots of vegetation with a stunning sea view as a backdrop.

Tess was immediately swept away by her mother, while Lily took a glass of something sparkly from a table on the terrace before wandering a little further into the garden, kind of looking forward to seeing Matt.

She was pretty pleased with how she was looking this evening, if she said so herself. She wasn't hiding behind a scarf display or suffering from terrible hair or talking about broken fingers. Aaliyah had done a good job on her hair again, she'd spent a long time applying a generous amount of barely there, sun-kissed make-up, and she was wearing her favourite summer dress – a mint-green, Charleston-style one that always made her feel good. Obviously she'd split up with Matt and it had been his prerogative who he dated afterwards, and obviously this was *so* shallow, but she *really* wanted to make him wonder this evening why he'd married someone else less than a year after their split. Pride.

Lily was still drinking in the sight of lush grass framed by tall trees and beautifully vibrant flowers and, on the far side of the garden, a spectacular water feature, when she almost walked smack into Matt, who was standing talking to an older man, who Lily recognised as his uncle Norm, Carole's husband.

'It's Lily, isn't it?' Norm said. 'You holidayed with us a few years ago.'

'Yes, it is.' She put her hand into the one he was holding out to her. 'How lovely to see you again, Norm.'

'It's lovely to see you too. I remember very much enjoying your company. Now—' Norm had kept hold of her hand and now tucked it into his arm and with his other arm began to usher Matt further into the garden with them '—come with me, both of you, over here. You've both got your heads screwed on well. I'd like your opinion on something.'

'Sounds interesting,' said Matt as Norm escorted them across the lawn.

'I know you don't mean that,' said Norm. 'You think I'm just going to show you a nice flower or bush. However, look at this.' He led them round the back of the water feature and positioned them both looking towards the back of it.

Lily gasped, 'Goodness,' while Matt choked on his wine.

'Exactly.' Norm nodded. 'Never seen anything so phallic in my life. What are your thoughts? Must have been done on purpose, mustn't it?'

'Wow.' Lily hauled her jaw off the ground and said, 'Yes. It must have been.'

'You're the architect.' Norm nudged Matt. 'Ever had anyone ask you to design a giant penis and balls for their garden?'

'No.' Matt shook his head. 'They've done a good job. It's amazing how you only see it from this angle.'

'Once you've seen it, though, you can't un-see it,' Lily said. 'I *love* the weirdness of it.' She went round the other side to take a closer look and then went back. 'Knowing what you know now, go and take a look from the other side. It's actually *obscene*.'

Matt and Norm went round the front together and then reappeared, both snorting with laughter.

'I wonder who had this designed,' Lily said. Surely it couldn't have been Penelope, the owner of the villa, who was wearing a prim, floral-patterned dress and low heels, and giving off a very strait-laced vibe.

'Precisely.' Norm beamed at them both. 'That's what makes it even more special. Penelope had it installed about five years ago. Either she asked for the design or the designer played a little trick on her.'

'Wow,' Lily said.

'How did you see this in the first place? Did they *show* you?' asked Matt. 'No offence, Norm, but who sneaks behind a water feature in the back corner of someone else's garden?'

'Someone who wants a quick ciggie or a quiet beer out of view of his wife and her friends,' said Norm, like Matt was stupid.

A woman's voice hollered, 'Norm, Norm, where are you? I need you.'

'Exactly,' Norm said. 'As if by magic. That's Carole. I'd better go. Life not worth living if I don't do what I'm told.' He didn't totally look like he was joking. 'I'll look forward to speaking to you again later, Lily. Excuse me.' He disappeared back round the water-spouting phallus as Carole started shouting for him again.

And Lily was left with Matt, behind a naughty water

feature in his aunt's friend's garden on a small Greek island. Weird. She smiled at him and he smiled back.

'I like Norm a lot,' he said. 'He's a splendid uncle.'

Lily nodded. 'Me too. You tempted to check the water feature design out in detail and suggest incorporating it in future client plans?'

'Well, yes, obviously. Since I'm here. Although really that would be more the remit of a landscape gardener you'd think,' Matt said. 'Oh my God.'

'What?'

'Carole's asked me to design some holiday rental houses on her land, and she wanted me to check out some features of several houses on Antiparos. I'm pretty sure that one of them was this house.'

'Wow. So you might be designing naughty garden features for your own aunt and uncle soon.' Lily sniggered.

'I bloody hope not.'

'You wouldn't want to do a direct copy. You'd have to be original. Maybe some boob fountains or something.'

'Yeah, I don't even want to begin to think what the "or something" might be. I'd *really* like to hope Carole – let's face it, Norm isn't going to get a look in on the planning – doesn't have any plans like this. Although...' They looked at each other. 'That time...' Matt said.

'Yeah.' Lily winced. Even nine years on, you didn't want to be reminded of when your then-boyfriend's aunt had tried to get the two of you to model very risqué underwear for the latest catalogue for her global lingerie business. She'd just branched out into men's trunks at the time and had thought some moonlit beach shots of them up close and personal wearing almost nothing would be perfect.

'Remember when she told us, like she was going to clinch our agreement to do it, that she'd have full-body pictures of us on the back of London buses and we'd be famous,' Matt said.

'Yeah. And when she told me that I was perfect because people liked to see *real* women.' Lily had tried to take it as a compliment but hadn't *totally* succeeded. 'Remember those bras she showed us. Your face was *hilarious*. Yeah, when you think about it, you're *totally* going to be designing something naughty.'

'Yep, I am.'

When they were together, Matt would now have said something outrageous and she'd have giggled and then they'd have grabbed a quick snog right here while no one could see them. And probably more.

She was looking at him and he was looking back at her with an unreadable expression in his eyes. After a few seconds, Lily couldn't take the tension she could feel building between them any more, and shifted her gaze back to the water feature. Neither of them said anything. She stared at the water feature for too long and then looked back at him and then away again.

'So we should probably get back to the others,' Matt said, after, really, ages.

'Yes, we should,' Lily said. Why hadn't she suggested that? Why hadn't she thought of it? Why had her basic social skills deserted her? 'So you're still working as an architect?' she asked as they made their way back towards the rest of the party. She knew he was. He'd set up a firm with a couple of partners three or four years ago and seemed to be doing very well. She'd googled him from time to time over the years, *obviously*, and the last time had been a few weeks ago when it had occurred to her that she'd probably see him at Tess's wedding. And then obviously she'd done a cheeky extra google two nights ago because who wouldn't when they'd just seen him again.

'Yep. I'm lucky enough to have been able to set up a business with a couple of colleagues and we're all loving it.'

'That's so cool. What you always wanted to do.'

'Yeah, really lucky. I feel blessed if I'm honest. And what

about you?' They both took some fried octopus on cocktail sticks from a waiter holding a large platter. 'Still working as a midwife?'

'Yes, three days a week, and then the rest of the time I'm also lucky in having been able to start my own business.'

'Midwifery-related or something else?'

Before Lily could answer, Carole popped up in front of them, waving an open bottle of champagne. 'What were you two doing all the way over there? Let me top your drinks up.'

'Norm was showing us the water feature. He really likes it,' Matt said.

'I bet he does, the saucy bugger,' Carole said. 'I saw you all coming out from behind.'

Lily and Matt both laughed out loud as Carole continued, 'Let me introduce you to everyone else.' Disturbingly, Lily wasn't sure whether she was disappointed or happy to have her one-on-one conversation with Matt ended. Clearly she should be happy. But she'd kind of been enjoying being with him.

'Come on.' Carole inserted herself between them and put her arms through theirs.

An hour later, Lily and Aaliyah were chatting to Tess's parents – and Lily was, honestly, concentrating very well on the conversation, and, honestly, not distracted at all by the hum of Matt's low voice as he chatted to some of his cousins a few metres away – when Meg, followed by a smiling Pythagoras, came out of the house, looking very un-Meg-like in an apron.

Meg clapped her hands. 'If everyone could take their seats at the tables now, that would be fab. Tess has done a seating plan but basically it's Tess's generation on the tables in the middle, kids over there, and adults over here.' Lily hadn't noticed before, but several round, white-cloth-covered tables had been set up near to a long rectangular, drinks-and-crockery-laden table on the continuation of the terrace to the side of the house.

'Adults?' Tess's mother said. 'Are none of you adults?'

'I'm definitely an adult,' Aaliyah said. Meg had apparently shooed her out of the kitchen so that she could sit down and enjoy the meal given how busy she normally was. 'I didn't spend my whole life cooking, cleaning and nagging children and a husband when I was a kid.'

'Things will improve,' Tess's mother told her. 'It's hard when the kids are little.'

'Yes they will,' Aaliyah said. 'I'm making some changes when I get home.' She downed the rest of her champagne and smiled at them all.

'Good for you.' Tess's mother downed her own champagne and coughed. 'If I'd been born a generation later, I'd have done things differently too.'

'You would?' Tess's father was staring at her as though she'd just announced she was changing her name to Shirley Valentine and staying on in Greece by herself.

'Yes, I would.' Tess's mum took his hand. 'Dinner. Come on.'

'So what changes are you going to make?' Lily asked as she and Aaliyah made their way over to the tables to find their seats.

'Kick the husband out and have the kids adopted.'

'Er?' Lily said. The way Aaliyah had been recently, anything was possible.

'*Joking.* Obviously.' She turned round and looked at Lily. 'Oh, okay, that's how pissed off I've seemed. I *was* joking. I love them all. But I'm going to up my hours at the surgery and use the money to pay for a cleaner and a bit of childcare and I'm pretty sure I'll be a *much* nicer wife and mother then. I might also suggest to Patrick that we start going on some date nights even though when school mums use that expression I just want to slap them. I want to start enjoying the kids and my marriage again instead of drowning in chores and sleep deprivation.'

'That sounds like the perfect plan.' Lily hugged her. 'I'm so pleased for you.'

'Me too. These few days away have been amazing for me.' Aaliyah pulled backwards to fix Lily with the look Lily was pretty sure she used for her kids when they were being naughty. 'Maybe this holiday will have an effect on you too. You need to start making a fuss about yourself. And take help from other people. You don't always have to be the one who supports everyone else.'

'Okay,' said Lily, not because she meant it but because she wanted Aaliyah to stop looking at her like that.

'Good. Right. Let's find where we're sitting.'

They were on the same table as each other, with Meg too, although it looked like she was going to be spending most of the evening in the kitchen, 'helping' Pythagoras. Lily wasn't convinced Meg would actually know how to switch her own oven on at home, let alone help anyone produce restaurant-standard catering in a strange kitchen, but Pythagoras seemed very happy to have her company.

The rest of the people on the table seemed to be cousins of Tess's. Including Matt.

Lily gave an involuntary start when she saw his name at the place *next to hers* – not sure whether she was pleased or nervous and basically full of dread at the thought of sitting next to him for an entire meal – and then caught Aaliyah watching her and nodding.

'What?' she said. The know-it-all nodding was really annoying.

'You've done such a good job of pretending that nothing ever hurts you that people actually believe it,' Aaliyah said, indicating with her head towards Matt, who was walking towards them. 'Even in bridezilla-mode, Tess wouldn't have had you sitting next to Matt if she'd thought you minded. She genuinely thinks you're over him.'

'Shh,' Lily hissed. What if he *heard*? Or if *anyone* heard? 'And I'm *fine*. Thank you.' Of course she was fine. Totally over him. It had been eight years. It was just a bit awkward, that was all. Anyone in her position would find it awkward.

Aaliyah smiled at her, mouthed, 'Love you,' and sat herself down at her place on the other side of the table. Well, at least Aaliyah was looking a lot happier now.

Lily sat down too.

Another cousin of Tess and Matt's, Marie, and her husband, Ricky, were sitting on Lily's other side. It was going to be tempting to turn her back on Matt and just talk to them. But she didn't want to look like she was purposely ignoring Matt, especially with Aaliyah sitting right opposite and *definitely* glancing over from time to time to check. Also, she actually did want to know what he'd been up to, check that he was happy. Ideally not with another woman, though. And where had that thought come from? She'd really loved him and she absolutely *did* want him to be happy and he was someone who *should* be in a relationship, so she should absolutely want that for him. God, it had hurt, though, when Tess had told her about Gemma.

Okay, so she was going to chat to him, in a very casual, nothing-to-see-here manner, find out what he'd been up to, be charming and make him think that he should *not* have moved on from her so easily, no, not really, *yes*, really, and then talk to other people and *move back on with her life*.

She turned to speak to him and... he was deep in conversation with the person on his other side, his older sister.

Right. Fine. Good, actually.

Marie and Ricky were lovely and – only straining over her shoulder to hear snippets of Matt's conversation about half the time – she was happily mid-chat with them about Ricky's bizarre (in Marie's eyes) obsession with matching the colour of his socks to his mood, when Meg put a big, steaming casserole dish down in the centre of their table, and told everyone to dig in.

'I helped make this,' she said, 'and it's amazing.' She looked at Lily and Aaliyah, who both had their eyebrows raised. Meg was *not* a good cook. 'Okay, I stirred it,' she said, 'when Pythagoras was busy. And I tasted it just now.'

Lily looked up and saw Matt smiling at them all, and had a sudden flashback to when they used to go out with each other's friends. They'd all got on so well.

And that was all a very long time ago.

He was smiling at just her now and suddenly it felt like it was only the two of them here. There was definite babble going on around them, but she didn't have the brain space to make out any of the words; she was too busy staring, gazing, into Matt's eyes. Almost drowning in them. And now memories were jostling in her head, times when they'd sat together over dinners gazing at each other like this, the two of them a little unit, the rest of the world a distant backdrop.

She shook her head. She didn't need to do this, revisit the past. She looked around her. Everyone else had served themselves. She reached out for the ladle propped up against the side of the casserole dish and said, 'Pass your plate and I'll serve,' to Matt.

'Sure. Thank you. What is it? I missed what Meg said.'

Lily tried really hard not to look smug that Matt had also clearly not been concentrating on anyone except her just then. If she was going to be pathetic, she'd rather not be pathetic alone.

'I didn't hear either,' she said. 'I'm sure it'll be delicious though. We ate at Pythagoras's restaurant the other evening and the food was amazing.'

'Remember that time at that wedding in France,' Matt said

as Lily heaped spoonfuls of rice and then a gorgeously fragrant stew of some kind onto his plate. 'The innards.'

'Oh my God, yes. So disgusting.' She'd said yes please to a large plate of unidentified food and had nearly gagged on the first mouthful and had had to eat the whole lot under the eagle eye of the bride's grandmother. 'And remember you with the pig's ear.' They'd gone to a traditional New Year's dinner cooked by a Mongolian colleague of Lily's and all the food had been wonderful except for the very hairy and chewy pig's ear that Matt had struggled visibly with for minutes.

'Yeah.' Matt took a mouthful from his plate. 'This is the exact opposite fortunately. Genuinely melt in the mouth.'

'Mmm.' Lily tasted her own first mouthful. 'Yep. Gorgeous.'

Sitting next to Matt for dinner was way better than she'd have predicted. Maybe it was the amazing surroundings. She could *totally* see why Carole and Norm had decided to move out here. And Penelope.

Matt was looking at her with a definite smirk on his face.

'What?' she said. 'Why are you looking at me like that? Do I have sauce on my cheek or something?'

Matt shook his head. 'You're thinking how you'd like to move here, aren't you?'

'Oh my *goodness*. How do you *know* that?'

He laughed out loud. 'Every time. When you're in a great holiday location, you start to wonder whether you should move there.'

'Only slightly,' Lily said, narrowing her eyes at him. 'I'm a lot more mature now. I know that holidays are not real life, and all my friends and family are in the UK and I'm in no way planning to move.'

'What's the average house price on Antiparos?' Matt filled both their water glasses as he spoke, not looking at her, concentrating on his pouring.

'It's *way* higher than you'd think. Way higher than a lot of Paros.'

'Been round all the estate agents already?' Matt was grinning broadly.

'I might have popped into a couple.'

He was still smiling at her, and then his expression grew more serious.

'Lily, what exactly happened—' He was interrupted by two of the children, both girls, coming over from the kids' table.

'Mummy,' the bigger one, Lauren, said, 'Mimi can't breathe properly again.'

'Where's her inhaler? *Where's her inhaler?*' Ricky practically roared. '*Where is it?*'

'It's okay,' Marie said, pulling a bag out from under her chair. 'Everything's going to be fine.'

'Quick, do her puffs,' Ricky said.

'Let me just check her breathing first,' Marie said. She took a blue inhaler, a spacer and a phone out of the bag and spent fifteen seconds timing the rise and fall of Mimi's chest. 'Why don't we go and sit quietly over there, darling?' She hoisted her daughter up into her arms and began to shake the inhaler as she walked.

Lily looked away from Marie and Mimi, at the table. She couldn't get involved. She couldn't bear it. It brought back too many bad childhood memories.

She glanced at Ricky. He was twisting his napkin over and over in his hands. Lauren was standing next to him looking tearful.

Lily really didn't want to get involved.

Ricky was going to break his fingers in the napkin if he carried on like that.

'Daddy, I'm scared about Mimi,' Lauren said.

'Yeah.' Ricky pushed his chair out and strode over to Marie and Mimi.

Lily stood up and put her arm round Lauren. 'Why don't you come and show Matt that YouTube video I heard you talking about earlier? The one with the puppies doing Harry Potter impressions? I'll be back in a second.'

In the corner of the garden, Marie was sitting cuddling Mimi and periodically counting her breathing while Ricky paced around them.

Lily squatted down in front of Mimi.

'Hey, Mimi,' she said. 'How are you doing?'

'Okay.'

Lily looked at the portable oxygen saturation monitor that Marie had placed on Mimi's finger – her levels were good – and at Mimi's throat. 'She doesn't have a tug at her throat. That's good. Is she recessing?'

Marie checked her daughter's chest. 'I don't think so.' She drew a big, juddering breath herself. 'This is... hard.'

'I know.' Lily squeezed Marie's hand. 'What are her triggers?'

'We thought it was only viral-induced but I don't think she has a virus at the moment. She gets admitted to hospital a lot so we thought long and hard about coming on holiday to a small island like this, but then we thought it would be okay because it's the summer and she's normally only ill in the winter months. Are you a doctor?'

'No. I'm a midwife but I have personal experience of asthma. I totally understand your worries about being on the island but I'm sure there are medical options. Carole knows everyone. She'll absolutely be able to get you to Paros and to a hospital if necessary. But hopefully it won't be necessary, given that her sats are good and she isn't recessing and doesn't have a tug. It looks like the puffs are working, doesn't it?'

'I hope so.' Marie was looking almost grey with anxiety. 'I think we'll be too scared ever to leave London again.'

Lily looked at her. She never talked about her health with

anyone except medical professionals and very occasionally her three best friends. But it would be awful for another family to get as stressed as hers had, and maybe damage relationships as a result.

'I used to have very severe asthma as a child,' she said. 'Viral induced but also what we think must have been some allergies that we never quite worked out. And stress sometimes. I was admitted to hospital a lot. Many dozens of times. Literally at least once a month in the winter months when I was little. Sometimes every fortnight. And then as I got older I got much better, and my asthma's much milder now, and very well managed. I take a steroid inhaler religiously morning and night, but since I'm an adult that's no problem and I never forget because I do it straight before I clean my teeth, and I carry a blue inhaler with me but I don't have to use it that much. I have a completely normal life.'

'Oh wow. Thank you so much,' Marie said. 'That's really helpful.' She paused, glanced at Ricky, and then said, 'Could I ask how your parents coped with your asthma?' Ricky looked up and then down at his feet. Yep, clearly finding it very hard.

Lily really wasn't keen to go into too many details but it felt like she had no choice if it might help Marie and Ricky.

'Not brilliantly, if I'm honest,' she said. 'My parents both really struggled with it and they were both working full-time, so my granny ended up looking after me a lot – she retired early, in fact, so that she had the time to be with me – so I had a great relationship with her and more of a distant one with my parents. And my mother was so stressed about my health that she stopped me doing a lot of stuff. If I were giving advice, I think what I'd want to tell you would be that you maybe have to try hard just to view it as an annoying problem that you deal with when it happens, but don't let it ruin Mimi's childhood or your family life. Maybe don't try to stop her from doing things and don't let it define any of you. Which is obviously easier said than done.'

Ricky looked up from the ground and nodded. 'Wise words. Probably an easy trap to fall into. Thank you.'

'Yes, thank you so much.' Marie had several more questions for Lily about how her asthma had developed over the years, and her triggers.

'There are a lot of people with mild and moderate asthma,' Marie said eventually, 'but actually not that many with severe asthma. It really is reassuring and useful to hear your experience.'

'I'm so pleased to have helped,' said Lily. It had actually felt fine talking about it. Maybe she should find a way of using her experience to try to help other people in their position.

'I think we can go and find Lauren again now,' Marie said. 'Mimi's looking a lot better.'

As they sat down, Marie said again, 'Thank you so much, Lily. Hearing about your experiences has helped so much. Especially the fact that your asthma's so well managed now, having been so severe when you were young.'

'Honestly, I'm just pleased to have helped a little.'

Lily felt the hairs on the back of her neck rise. She turned and found Matt staring at her.

SIX

MATT

Lily looked at him and pushed her chair back. 'Excuse me for a moment,' she said, smiling at Marie and Ricky but not meeting Matt's eye.

'Is Mimi okay?' Matt asked Marie.

'I think she's going to be fine, thank you.' Marie kissed the top of Mimi's head and smiled at Matt.

'So great that Lily was able to help you.' God, he despised himself. He was totally prolonging this conversation so that he could ask about what he'd just heard. Lily had asthma? How could he not have known?

'I know.' Marie nodded. She had a lot to say about Lily's childhood and later experiences.

'Yeah, must be very comforting. I'm sure that Mimi will be okay as she gets older,' Matt said as Marie wound up, surprised to hear his voice holding steady against the wave of heat that had washed over him. What was it? Confusion? Hurt? Disappointment? Anger too, if he was honest. A mind-blowing combination of them all. He was almost shaking.

This wasn't him. He never felt like this. But.

Lily had been admitted to hospital on numerous occasions? She'd had severe asthma? Her parents had been beside themselves about it?

Matt had never been admitted to hospital himself, so, okay, he couldn't say for certain, but he was pretty sure that if he had been it would have been a big deal. Something he'd have told people about. Especially if it had involved life-threatening asthma and had happened very frequently. Why hadn't she ever mentioned any of this?

He caught a movement and looked up. Lily was walking back to the table.

She sat back down and said, 'So pudding's going to be as delicious as the main course. Some sugary little doughnuts with a sauce.'

Matt stared at her. She was maybe eighteen inches away from him. Her face was so familiar. The curve of her cheek. The way her nose wrinkled when she did a big smile. The way she always quirked one of her eyebrows when she was saying something sarcastic. Without having seen her for the past eight years he could still have described her extremely accurately; so many things about her were etched in his memory.

And yet... how well had he actually known her?

He'd honestly thought the answer to that question was *really well, in every way*.

He knew lots of small things about her, like she'd always hated peas and she'd been a huge S Club 7 fan when she was about eleven and she'd failed her Art GCSE.

But he hadn't known that she'd regularly been seriously ill as a child. If she'd spent that much time in hospital it had to have had a big effect on her. And she'd told Marie just now that she still had asthma, although thankfully now well-managed. And he hadn't even known that. Wasn't that something you'd tell your boyfriend about just for your own safety? They'd been on holiday together, on days out to the countryside together, miles from any hospital. Why hadn't she told him then?

He was pretty sure – no, certain – that he'd told her about everything big in his life. A lot of the small things too, everything that had ever occurred to him really. He'd hidden nothing from her.

What else had she not told him about herself?

God. Maybe she'd been seeing someone else, and that's why she'd broken it off with him. And that was an idea he'd literally never entertained before, even when he'd found Gemma in bed with Victor. She couldn't have been. Lily just wouldn't do that. He *knew* she wouldn't.

Because he *knew* her. Except... did he really?

He knew that he was glaring at her. She was looking straight back at him, her face immobile.

Marie and Ricky were both busy talking to their daughters now. Ricky stood up with Mimi in his arms and Marie stood up and took Lauren's hand, and the four of them began to walk away from the table.

'So I never knew that you had asthma,' Matt said, not caring whether the others were out of earshot.

'I mean, we weren't together for that long,' Lily said, her face expressionless. 'There was probably a lot of stuff we didn't tell each other.'

'We were together for fifteen months. We talked a *lot*. I know that of course there was stuff we didn't tell each other. But not big stuff. I thought.'

She shrugged. *Shrugged*. Like it didn't matter. 'I mean... It's something I don't like talking about. So I don't if I don't have to. I mentioned it just now because I feel like Marie and Ricky are understandably in a bad place about Mimi's asthma and I thought I should help.'

'Could I ask why you don't like talking about it?'

'Just... bad memories. You know.' Still no expression.

He waited. He was *sure* that wasn't everything. He waited some more and she said nothing.

'Marie said that your granny retired early to look after you so that your parents could carry on working when you were ill and that she was the one always in hospital with you and looking after you on a daily basis. But I remember you telling me she retired early from her teaching job because she wanted to set up her cake business. That's like you *chose* not to tell me about the asthma. And, thinking about it, I'm presuming that you must have literally *hidden* your inhalers from me.'

She shrugged again. 'Yeah. I kind of did choose not to tell you about it. I don't like talking about it, as I said.'

Right.

'Lily, why did we split up?' He'd been about to ask the question when Lauren and Mimi had come over to their parents. 'Was it because I'd been away working so much? Had you met someone else?'

She flinched, physically flinched, and then said after a pause, 'No. *No*. There was no one else. Not spending enough time together was part of it, I think. And also it was, I suppose, for exactly this reason.'

'This reason?'

'That you sort of push me to talk about things I really don't want to talk about. Meaning I'm not right for you. End of, really.'

'End of? Couldn't we have talked about this?'

She shook her head. 'I mean, no? Kind of my point.'

'But... we did talk. Could we not have talked... more? We told each other we loved each other. I meant it. I feel now like I hardly knew you.'

'Sorry, what?' Lily was frowning now. 'You said you loved me. You told me you'd never love anyone else the way you loved me. But you met someone soon afterwards and married her only a year after we split up. So did *I* actually know *you*? And, right now, who *are* you? We were together for fifteen months and I never once saw you like this.'

'Well, *firstly*, you left me and so I was clearly free to marry whoever the hell else I wanted whenever the hell I wanted, and *secondly*, you knew me a long time ago.' The angry words were just tumbling out of him. She was right: it was like he'd become a different person. 'Clearly I've grown up since then. And *thirdly*, I've never seen *you* like this before either.'

'Clearly you had the right to marry whoever you liked. I apologise for implying that you didn't.' Lily's voice was flat. 'And clearly everyone grows up.'

Matt shook his head, still watching her. It felt like this conversation – argument – was going nowhere. Had he learned anything now that he'd finally got to ask her the 'Why did we split up' question? Yeah, maybe he had. All of a sudden, his anger kind of disappeared, evaporated, and he just felt... deflated.

'From my side, I suppose I have to apologise for having asked you to talk about things you don't want to talk about. Your prerogative not to.' It sounded like maybe he'd pushed her away without even realising.

God, he'd obviously been too insensitive. Intrusive. That had probably been the problem. But also, it was just odd that she hadn't mentioned the asthma.

They'd moved closer to each other while they'd been arguing, hissing at each other, and were now only a few inches apart, looking into each other's eyes, neither of them smiling. Matt wasn't sure whether he wanted to shout and shout and shout, or drag her towards him and kiss the hell out of her. And, God, that was an inappropriate thought at this moment.

Lily's colour was heightened and her eyes were glistening and he'd never seen her like this before and the argument was his fault. The last remnants of his anger were replaced by a weary misery. He stretched his hand out and touched hers. She didn't move for a moment and then briefly returned the pressure of his hand on hers. She opened her mouth to speak and...

'Look at you two lovebirds.' Carole had appeared behind them and had bent down and had an arm round each of their shoulders. He wondered if she could feel the tension that he was pretty sure was making his frame almost entirely rigid.

Lily pulled her hand away and looked down at the table.

'Ha,' Matt said to Carole. 'Not lovebirds. Just old friends catching up.' God, life was hard work sometimes.

'Are you single, Lily?' Carole asked.

'Yep.' Lily nodded and gave Carole a small smile, not meeting Matt's eye at all. 'Very much so. And very happily so.'

'We'll see about that,' Carole said. 'I'm sure we can find you a young man.' She looked at Matt and winked.

Matt made another huge effort and said, 'Ha,' again, while Lily did another small smile.

'Anyway—' Could Carole genuinely be oblivious to the tension crackling around them? '—I just came to let you know that I think Norm and I are going to turn in now. We're staying here with Penelope tonight, so that we're on hand to help with anything from first thing tomorrow morning. Maybe you two should get an early night too.' She winked at them both again. Neither Matt nor Lily even twitched.

Matt really wanted to leave too. And tomorrow he'd keep his distance from Lily at the wedding and then he wouldn't see her again and he'd feel a lot better very soon.

If Tess and Tom had kids and had them christened, he'd have to remember to make an excuse not to go to the christening, in case Lily was there.

'Have a good one,' he told Carole. He pushed his chair backwards and stood up. 'I'm going to say good night too and make my way back to my hotel now. Good night, Carole.' He submitted to a big hug from her and then looked at Lily, who gave him a lips-tight-together smile.

'Night, my love,' Carole said.

'Good night,' Lily said.

Matt did a tight-lipped smile of his own, turned his back on Lily and walked across the garden to wish Tess a very good night's sleep before her wedding.

SEVEN

LILY

Then – eight years before

Lily sat down on the bed, sniffed and wiped the back of her hand across her eyes before pulling the letter out of the envelope. Oh, God, the pain of it. Just over a month ago they'd thought her granny's cancer was under control, and then, bam, they'd discovered that it wasn't, and two weeks ago she'd died. It was so hard to get her head around.

She couldn't believe that this was the last time she'd ever get a new letter in her granny's distinctive handwriting. She'd had a lot of letters from her over the years, because her granny believed in keeping in close touch and she did not believe in doing so by email or any other form of modern technology.

My darling Lily,

You'll be reading this the day after my funeral, unless someone messes up (and, frankly, lawyers do mess up, a lot, so who knows).

Or unless you're too sad to start reading it. Don't be sad, my darling. Well, do be a little sad, because it would be odd if you weren't. And I think grief is healthy. But don't be so sad that you can't function normally. You have so much to live for.

Anyway. I'm going to keep this short.

First things first. I love you and it's been an amazing privilege to be your grandmother. You know my thoughts on your parents both working all hours so that they couldn't look after you themselves. I think they should have arranged things so that they could have spent more time with you. HOWEVER, I'm so, so grateful that I had the opportunity to look after you instead of them, because I've adored every single minute of it. I could never have imagined in my wildest dreams that I'd be gifted such a wonderful granddaughter.

I'm so sorry to be leaving you now, my dearest, but it could be worse. We've done a good job keeping the cancer at bay for so long. Over twelve years now! And remember that initially they said I'd only have a year left. So we've stolen eleven years from the grim reaper. That's a long time. I love to prove a doctor wrong (not that there's anything wrong with healthcare professionals, my darling – I'm so proud that you're a midwife and it's a wonderful profession – it isn't because they're doctors that your parents are over-focused on their careers – I think they'd have been like that whatever they'd done).

Secondly, advice: well, I don't have much. You're fabulously funny, lovely, kind, caring and sensible. I would say, though, that you can only get away with those dungaree shorts because you're young and you have a gorgeous figure and amazing skin. I wouldn't necessarily recommend wearing them forever. And also it wouldn't HURT to have a couple of cooking lessons. Although there's no reason for a modern woman to be able to cook, thank God. But mainly, continue to follow your instincts. They're very sound.

Matt's wonderful. If you stay together long-term, I'm sure he'll make you an excellent life partner. If you don't, he will have been a lovely experience.

What you can achieve: anything. That tiny baby on a breathing machine, that toddler in and out of hospital with such severe asthma, that little girl who couldn't play outside in the winter because of the effect of the cold air on her airways – to grow up into the healthy, vigorous, fabulous young woman that you are – that's testament to what you can do, my darling.

You are fabulous. Never forget that.

And that's it for advice.

Thirdly: my ashes. I'd like YOU to be in charge of scattering them. And I'd like them to be scattered at Beachy Head. We had so many wonderful times there together. At a time of your choosing, though. I don't want to push you into having to go there soon if it's inconvenient. I'm very happy to spend a few weeks, or months, or years in an urn. Maybe on your mantelpiece. Maybe I'll haunt you.

I'm sorry. That was probably in very poor taste. It made me laugh when I wrote it, though. I'm not sure whether or not I'd like to become a ghost but I really don't believe in them so I don't think it's going to happen.

I need to finish now. I have so many things to say to you – I could just keep on writing and writing. But at the same time, you don't need any more advice from me, and you already know how infinitely proud of you I am and how infinitely much I love you.

Goodbye, my darling. I love you more than words can say.

You're perfect.

All my love,

Your granny

P.S. Remember, this grief WILL pass in its own way. You'll become accustomed to life without me. Remember your grandfather used to say, apropos of almost anything: 'Worse things happen at sea'. It sounded silly, but he was right. He was a good man. I've missed him so much over the past fifteen years and yet I'm so grateful that I've lived so much longer than he did, because I've enjoyed the richness of life, even without him. I've enjoyed YOU. And you in your turn will be able to continue to enjoy life without me (and also ideally without those dungarees).

Lily gave an enormous, shuddering sob. The *pain* and the *magnitude* of her loss. *How* was she going to be happy without her granny in her life? If anyone was funny and loving and kind and caring and sensible, it had been her grandmother. Lily *needed* her.

She heard a strange wailing sound, and realised that it was coming from somewhere deep inside her. She rolled over and buried her face in her pillow and just *sobbed*. Life was going to be a much bleaker place without her granny in it.

When her sobbing had subsided to sniffles, she sat up and re-read the letter. This time, she smiled a couple of times through her tears. The lawyers actually *had* messed up, because she was reading this the day before the funeral, not the day after. And she *liked* those dungaree shorts. Oh, God. She missed her granny *so much*. It was hard to believe that they'd never go shopping for clothes together again, squabble over the TV remote, play late-night cards, gossip together.

She was still sitting on the bed when the doorbell rang. The doorbell. She looked over her left shoulder at the clock.

Shit. She'd been sitting here for ages. It was Tess, Aaliyah and Meg. They'd insisted that they should come over to keep her company the night before the funeral because Matt was working away yet again and couldn't get back until tomorrow, just in time to meet her at the crematorium.

The bell rang again.

Shit. She really didn't want them to see her like this. She knew how much they cared about her and that they were already worried about her, and right now she didn't feel up to talking about things, even with them. She'd talk when things were a little less raw so she wouldn't get so emotional and feel like she'd flipped back into being the weak, fragile one.

She quickly but very carefully folded the letter and replaced it in its envelope, and tucked it under her pillow for the time being, before going to the front door.

The mirror in the hall told her on her way past that she looked absolutely atrocious. Puffy eyes with mascara rings underneath – big mistake to have been wearing make-up today – and a red nose and patchy cheeks.

She opened the flat's front door and said, 'Go through to the kitchen, back in a second, just got to go to the loo,' and whisked herself along the hall and into the bathroom.

She slapped cold water on her face, dried it and spent a couple of minutes wiping up the mascara and applying a lot more make-up, and then looked at herself critically in the mirror. Yep, all good; she genuinely didn't look now as though she'd just been crying.

When she got to the kitchen she discovered that it only contained Tess and Aaliyah. Tess was unscrewing a bottle of red while Aaliyah pulled glasses out of a cupboard.

'Where's Meg gone?' Lily asked.

'Er, she isn't here?' Aaliyah put the glasses on the table in the middle of the room and sat down. She and Tess were both staring at Lily like she'd gone mad.

'I was *really* desperate for the loo,' Lily said, to explain her inability to count to three this evening. Nothing to do with being overcome by grief.

'She can't make it,' Tess said, moving over to the table with the wine. 'She asked me to let you know that she's *really* sorry and she'll see you at the funeral and afterwards, obviously, but it's just that Rupert's going away for a month tomorrow and she thinks he's The One and she *had* to see him.'

'He clearly isn't The One,' Aaliyah said. 'The Actual One, if she ever meets him, will be someone who doesn't take her away from her friends. Every time. Literally. The first time she meets someone who she really likes *and* who's willing to hang out with us, we'll know that he's actually going to be good for her. Also, Rupert is not a good name.'

'I don't think we should be name-ist,' Lily said automatically.

'I mean, fine, whatever,' Aaliyah said. 'Oh, okay, you're right. Her Actual One might be called Rupert and obviously a lot of Ruperts must be nice, but I just don't like the name. Can't help it.'

'Fair enough,' Lily said. 'I think.'

'And this Rupert really is awful,' Tess said. 'I mean, she told him that it was the night before your granny's funeral, and he told her that if she wanted to see him again she'd put him above seeing the friends she already sees all the time.'

'Total arse.' Aaliyah nodded. 'I give it a month tops before she finds out that he's been sleeping with someone else and she's devastated and we have to pick up the pieces. Anyway, enough about Meg's love life. How are you doing, Lily? Are you coping?'

No, Lily was not coping. She felt like even smiling was too big an effort right now, let alone being her usual self.

'Come here.' Tess moved round the table and drew her into a hug. Oh, God. Lily *could* just let herself weep and weep on Tess's shoulder, and Tess and Aaliyah would both be there for her, she knew that, and maybe it would help, except then she'd have lost who she was, or rather who she'd become. And if she let herself crumple now, how would she gather herself together again? Other people didn't comfort her, or look after her, the way she was now. *She* looked after *them*. The only person who'd ever properly looked after her had been her granny. Oh, *God*.

Lily allowed herself a couple of moments to cry, *really* cry, against Tess, and then she did a gigantic sniff, a snort if she was honest, to stop herself. She started coughing and spluttering and Aaliyah whacked her on the back.

'Are you okay?' the other two asked her in unison.

'I'm fine. Literally just choked on my own snot,' Lily said, coughing, laughing and crying a bit all at once. 'That'll teach me to cry.' She shook her head, did another sniff, although more cautiously this time, to avoid any more snot-choking, shook her head again, and said, 'Where's my wine?'

Aaliyah pushed her glass towards her and said, 'I hope tomorrow isn't going to be too much of a nightmare.'

'How are you feeling about the funeral?' Tess asked.

Lily sniffed. 'Sad, obviously, but, you know, it is what it is and, as she said herself, we had her for eleven years longer than the doctors feared, so if you look at it like that, we've been lucky. Anyway, enough sad stuff. Much better not to talk about it. How's the new job?'

Tess looked at her for a long moment and then gave her another squishy hug. 'Always here to talk when you're ready.'

'Yes, always here,' Aaliyah said. 'But I'm guessing now's not the time?'

Lily shook her head and then nodded, and Aaliyah said, 'Love you, hun.'

Lily mouthed, 'Thank you.' If she'd tried to make an actual sound she'd have cried again.

'So your job, Tess?' Aaliyah said.

'The new job's good. My boss is shag-me-now gorgeous *and*

single, there are free Mars bars in the canteen on Fridays, and the nearest pub does all-night happy hour for nurses on Wednesdays.'

Lily laughed and found her voice to say, 'Thank you for being such lovely and understanding friends. And oh my *God* what an amazing-sounding job.'

———

Twenty hours later, she was standing with her parents welcoming people to the post-funeral drinks they'd organised in a local church hall.

Matt was approaching them from the kitchen at the far end of the hall. He'd made it back from Prague, where he'd been working on and off for the last couple of months, just in time for the start of the funeral service.

'The caterers have everything under control,' he said. He slipped an arm round Lily's waist and took up position next to her. Lily leaned into his gorgeous, solid warmth for a second.

'I'm so pleased that you're here to support Lily,' her mother said solemnly. 'She's going to need all the support she can get.' It was true. Everyone needed support at a time like this. But Lily was pretty sure that she was strong enough not to need any more support than your average bereaved person and her mother's tone of voice *really* grated. It was exactly the same one that she'd used in the past when she was referring in hushed tones to how *delicate* Lily was and how *worried* about her they were; and it had felt like no one ever saw Lily as an actual person; she was always just the ill girl.

Being fair to her mother, Lily *was* grief stricken. Her grandmother had effectively brought her up and they'd been very close and Lily really couldn't imagine the world without her in it. But she didn't want to be defined by her grief like she used to be defined by her health, or have people talk about her in hushed tones.

Matt was looking down at her with a mixture of pity and sympathy on his face. It was so lovely of him to care so much, but so much more than she could deal with right now. 'Would you mind just going to check that my friends are okay?' she asked him. Tess, Aaliyah and Meg were inside the hall. They'd be totally fine but she could really do without Matt being here with her parents at this moment. She should probably have introduced him to them before, well, of course she should, but she hadn't wanted him to witness the way her mother was with her, which was ironic because she was being even worse than usual today.

'Of course,' he said. He gave her shoulder a squeeze, which was nice, it really was, and obviously everyone *was* going to feel sympathetic towards her, but he was *so* sympathetic, and all the sympathy and *understanding* were dragging her down into feeling like she always had when she was ill, like people were treating her as though she was very unusual. She wasn't. She was just a regular person going through some of life's regular – albeit at this moment particularly shitty – shit.

'Lily, dear.' Doreen, one of Lily's granny's best friends, took Lily's hands and clasped them to her. 'We're all going to miss Letitia so much. Please, please look on me as another grand-mother now. I'd love you to come over and reminisce with me. And we do need to laugh as well as cry, because there are so many happy and comical memories.'

'I'd love to.' Lily loved the bony strength in Doreen's hands and the glint in her eye. And the fact that she was treating Lily like a perfectly normally healthy person still. Like her best friends did. She really didn't want to let go of Doreen.

'And would you come to line dancing with me soon?' Doreen's eyes were looking shiny now, like they were full of unshed tears. 'For old time's sake?' A group of them had been

line dancing together for the first time for Lily's granny's seven-
tieth, and then Doreen, Lily's granny and another couple of
their friends had carried on going.

'I'd love to,' Lily said again, meaning it. 'Except you're going
to put me to shame because you have five years of training
under your belt. Plus if I remember rightly you were a complete
natural.'

'I actually am a very good line dancer if I say so myself.'
Doreen did something nifty with her feet for a few steps, like
she wouldn't be out of place in *Riverdance*, all while still
holding Lily's hands.

'Doreen, I'm going to give you my number and I want to
come with you to your next session,' Lily said. 'Unless it's going
to be too advanced for me.'

'You're on.' Doreen let go of her hands and whipped a very
smart-looking phone out of her Anya Hindmarch handbag.

Lily's mother leaned in and said, 'This is so kind of you,
Maureen. Looking after Lily when she's so distraught.'

'It's Doreen,' Lily said, trying to keep her voice edge-free.
How could her mother not know her own mother's best friend's
name? Easily, actually; she almost certainly didn't know Lily's
best friends' names either. She'd know her own colleagues'
names very well, though.

'Lily was very close to her grandmother,' Lily's mother
continued as though Lily hadn't spoken. 'It's going to be a
struggle for her to cope with her loss.' And again, her tone had
flipped straight back into the one she used to use when she was
talking about Lily and her health. *Poor Lily. My ill daughter.*
Lily was feeling almost transported back in time, like she was
little again. Everyone would be looking at her, sympathising
with her mother about the stress of her frequent life-threatening
breathing episodes, while Lily was just the ill girl. The one
person who'd never treated her like that as a child was her
grandmother.

She missed her *so much*. Losing her was like having a limb torn off, like she was going to have to learn to balance all over again. But she was *not* going to be *poor bereaved Lily*.

'I know they were very close,' Doreen said, with a bit of a snap, 'because Letitia and I were very close, too. I know *all about* your family. And it is indeed a huge loss for Lily but she will be *fine* because she's a fighter.' She planted a kiss on Lily's cheek and Lily inhaled the scent of what she was sure was some very expensive perfume, wanting to cheer. 'Lily, I'm going to be in touch very soon about the line dancing. The next one's a week on Wednesday. Are you free then?'

'I'm not sure Lily will be up to anything as frivolous as that so soon after the loss of her grandmother,' her mother said in that *voice*.

For God's *sake*. Lily wanted to scream.

'It's your decision of course, Lily,' said Doreen in a voice even steelier than her chignonned grey hair, 'but I would point out that, while Letitia would of course have been offended if none of us missed her or mourned her, she would not have wanted you to mope.'

'You're right,' said Lily. 'And, yes, I am free a week on Wednesday and the line dancing's a date.' And she was immediately feeling a little better. This was clearly the way forward.

'That must have been hard,' Matt said on the Tube on the way back to his flat afterwards. 'How are you feeling?'

It had been very hard and Lily was feeling rubbish, like she permanently had tears ready to spill, exhausted but not in a physical way, and like the world was a more miserable place now. And also really pissed off that her mother had managed to turn this into a Poor-Lily-let's-treat-her-with-kid-gloves situation. Her granny wouldn't have wanted that for her; as she'd said in her letter, she wanted Lily to be happy and lead a busy, fulfilled life.

Lily couldn't go down the receiving-sympathy route right now. Yes, she should talk to Matt about how she was feeling, but what if he just treated her the way her mum had today, the way everyone used to? What if he started to see her differently from how he saw her now? And also, she'd barely seen him recently, he'd been away so much for work. You couldn't just start confiding in someone without building up to it.

'It was hard, like all funerals,' she said, 'but I'm okay. I'm going to have coffee soon with Doreen and go line dancing with her.'

She caught a glimpse of something in his eyes – hurt? Disappointment? – before he said, 'That's brave. That woman has serious energy.'

'Yeah, I'm going to have to get into training first. It's a week on Wednesday so I have time to fit a couple of runs in to try to get my stamina up. Which reminds me' – she rummaged in her bag for her phone to show him the review of a film she wanted to see – 'we're free Sunday evening so we could go to the cinema to see this before you fly back on Monday.'

She caught another flash of something like hurt on Matt's face, like he knew she was closing herself off from him. She moved her phone screen closer to him so that he could read the review better and watched him as he read. She loved his face. She loved *him*. She ought to talk to him and explain how her health issues had defined her childhood and how she never wanted to be the object of sympathy. She was absolutely certain that if he knew the whole story he'd be lovely to her, like her friends had been.

But she couldn't start talking about it if he was already being over-sympathetic. And they needed time together, more time than they ever had. It wasn't the kind of conversation you could get through quickly. Maybe she'd explain it to him in a couple of weeks' time. When she felt a bit more ready and he wasn't travelling so much. Maybe in a month's time.

He looked up and saw her watching him. She smiled at him. He smiled back, and said, 'Great,' a second or two later.

———

Two weeks later, Lily was eating the last mouthful of the pasta salad from her packed lunch when she realised that she was ready. She was going to bite the bullet. She was going to scatter the ashes tomorrow on her day off. Initially she'd been tempted to ask Doreen and a few of her granny's other close friends to go with her, but then she'd thought that that might be really offensive to her parents, who she didn't want to ask, so she'd decided to go alone. She could have asked her own best friends to go with her, but she couldn't ask them and not Matt, and he hadn't been around enough for much serious conversation. So she hadn't told anyone that she was going and she'd waited until Matt was away for work again – not difficult because he was away a *lot* at the moment.

She put the salad Tupperware back in her bag and stood up to go and wash her hands before getting back to her patients. It was a busy day on the maternity ward today and there was definitely no time for a full lunch break but she'd hopefully have time to book her train ticket to Eastbourne later.

From Eastbourne she was going to get a bus to a place called East Dean and walk up to Beachy Head. And probably bawl her eyes out in the wind. It felt really soon to be doing it but leaving it didn't feel like a good idea, because once you'd left it for a while, when was the right time to do it? Like, what day did you finally decide that the person had been gone long enough?

· · ·

God, she thought a couple of hours later. This shift had been going on since forever. She wanted to go home and prepare for tomorrow. 'Are you alright?' Manuel, one of the other midwives, asked her. 'You've been staring into the distance for ages.'

'Sorry, yes, totally fine, just a bit tired,' Lily said. 'I need to go back and check on my patient in Room Six, actually. Honestly, don't know what's wrong with me. Away with the fairies.'

She was alone in the flat that evening, after the end of what really had felt like an extra-long shift, when her phone rang and she saw Aaliyah's number on the screen.

She always picked up when her friends phoned.

She really didn't want to this evening.

She actually wasn't going to. It felt like an evening for being alone, wearing pyjamas and eating comfort food.

She stood up to go into the kitchen, pushing away a slight feeling of guilt for not having answered the call.

Her phone was ringing again. She went back to the sofa to see who it was. Aaliyah again.

Lily *really* wanted to be alone this evening.

But what if something bad had happened?

'Hi, Aaliyah,' she said.

'Hi. Can you meet for drinks this evening?'

'I'm so sorry but I kind of need a night in.' The absolute last thing she wanted to do this evening was go out. Actually, why did Aaliyah want to go out on a Monday evening?

'Okay, I wanted to tell you this in person but I'm just going to say it now. I have news,' Aaliyah said. 'Patrick and I got *engaged* yesterday. Can you come for a drink to celebrate? Just us and Tess and Meg. Patrick has to work late this evening. Pleeeease.'

'Oh wow.' Lily *so much* wasn't up for a celebratory evening but you couldn't say no to someone when they had news like that. 'That's huge. So many congratulations. Give me an hour and I'll be there.'

A couple of hours later, she and Aaliyah and Tess were onto their second bottle of the house Prosecco at the wine bar round the corner from Aaliyah's flat.

'Wonder where Meg is,' Tess said, looking at her watch. 'I have a bad feeling about her being so late.'

Tess was right. Within five minutes, Meg had arrived, clutching a congratulations card but visibly tear-stained.

'Congratulations. I'm *so* pleased for you,' Meg said in a wobbly voice. She hugged Aaliyah and gave her the card. 'So pleased. Really, really pleased.' She sank down next to Lily on the banquette she was sitting on and pulled her jacket off.

'Here you go.' Tess pushed a very full glass of Prosecco over to her.

Meg downed it in one.

'Wow,' said Aaliyah. 'That opening the throat thing impresses me every time.'

Meg wasn't talking; she was just pouring. And downing.

'Wow,' all three of the rest of them said this time.

Meg slammed her glass down on the table when she'd finished it and said, 'So Rupert dumped me. Because he has someone else. Who he's been sleeping with for months.'

'Ouch,' Tess said.

Lily looked at Aaliyah, who was looking at her engagement ring and *clearly* weighing up whether it was okay to show it to Meg. What a bloody nightmare.

'I'm so sorry,' she said to Meg. 'I think we should look at Aaliyah's *gorgeous* engagement ring and talk about her wedding plans and then you can tell us about the bastard.'

Meg reached out for the Prosecco bottle again and Tess scrambled to pass it to her.

'You're right,' Meg said. 'We're going to focus totally on Aaliyah this evening. *Congratulations*.' She picked up her third glassful and started more speed-drinking. 'Congratulations,' she said again when she'd finished that glass. 'Show me the ring. Talk to me about wedding planning and honeymoons and sex with the same gorgeous man for the rest of your life, and the gorgeous children you're going to have, and the lovely house you'll live in with your lovely, rich husband-to-be. *Show me the ring.*'

'Er, Meg,' Tess said.

'I'm fine. I'm sorry. I really am so pleased for you,' Meg said. 'I love Patrick and the two of you are so good together and it's wonderful.'

Within under an hour, Meg was slumped silently comatose in the rounded corner of the banquette and, actually, Aaliyah, Tess and Lily were having a lovely conversation.

At about eleven, Aaliyah looked at her watch and said, 'I need to go home now. To my *fiancé*. I *love* being engaged. What are we going to do with Meg?'

'I can take her home,' Tess said. 'Although I do have a bit of a problem which is that I'm on an early shift tomorrow morning so I don't think I'll be able to stay with her. Are you working early tomorrow, Lily? If you aren't, could you maybe take her home and stay? If you don't mind?'

Lily thought about her planned Beachy Head trip. She could totally tell the others about it. And they'd understand. They'd more than understand. They'd be lovely to her about it. But she'd probably cry and this evening she didn't want to be Poor Lily again, so she didn't want to tell them. And Aaliyah *obviously* had to go home to Patrick. And Tess *obviously* had to go to work in the morning. And Lily *could* postpone her trip.

Meg suddenly sat up and wailed, 'Oh my God, what's

wrong with me? I'm *never* going to get married. I thought he was *The One*.'

Yep, it wasn't looking like Meg would get over this quickly. Lily was going to have to postpone.

Her phone vibrated. *Please* let it not be Matt checking in again to see if she was okay.

God. Awful. She was actively not wanting to get messages from her boyfriend, who she really did love. There had to be something wrong there.

She pulled her phone out. The message was actually from a work friend asking if she fancied a cinema trip later in the week. Phew.

Oh. And there *was* one from Matt. Asking how she was.

Great, thank you, she replied. *Busy day at work. Out for a drink with Aaliyah this evening because... SHE AND PATRICK GOT ENGAGED!!!*

She could see that he was typing for *ages* before his response actually came through: *Wow – congratulations to them. Can't wait to see you.*

And she just *knew* that he'd typed something about hoping she was doing okay and had then deleted it. She could *feel* his concern emanating from her phone. He was *so* solicitous at the moment. And always away. And the more caring-from-afar he was, the more she couldn't talk to him. And the more she didn't talk, the more she could see he was getting hurt. It was like a vicious circle they just couldn't get out of.

She *should* talk to him.

They probably just needed to spend more time together, to have the opportunity to talk properly. That would improve matters. Maybe.

Or maybe they actually just weren't right for each other. Love probably wasn't enough on its own if you couldn't communicate the way your partner wanted you to.

No. She was overreacting, probably because she was upset

this evening after thinking so much about scattering the ashes. Matt would be working in London for two or three weeks solid next month. They'd get the opportunity then to spend lots of time together and she'd talk properly to him then, and everything would be okay.

EIGHT

MATT

Then – eight years before

The flat was dark and empty when Matt opened the front door. He felt his face fall. He'd been hoping all the way home that Lily might have come over this evening to stay the night, knowing that he'd be back. They'd exchanged keys a couple of months ago and had been spending increasing amounts of time staying over with each other, although less time since Lily had lost her grandmother. Which kind of didn't feel right; he'd been lucky enough not to lose anyone yet but he was pretty sure that he'd want to be around Lily more, rather than less, if he were bereaved. Although everyone reacted differently to things of course.

She'd been a little monosyllabic over the phone recently in addition to not being around so much. Like her bereavement had caused her to put barriers up between them. Maybe they needed to spend more quality time together.

Seriously. He was thinking like some kind of self-help manual.

He unzipped his suitcase and took his dirty laundry and stuck it and a liquid tab in the washing machine, pressed On, and then stood up and looked around the kitchen.

It was immaculate. Lily must have cleaned it again after he left last weekend. Since she'd lost her grandmother a month ago, she'd been on an extreme cleaning drive. She was always quite big on housework, definitely better than he was, but nothing on this scale normally. Like, she couldn't sit down and relax. If she came over for a quiet night in, she didn't actually sit and talk or watch TV, she cleaned. Anything. Like silver that he hadn't even known *was* silver. In fact, it probably wasn't. It was probably stainless steel. She'd scrubbed and polished her own flat to within an inch of its life too.

The over-cleaning was a little bit weird. It felt like she really wasn't dealing that well with her loss. And that she should perhaps talk about it. But it also felt like every time he tried to talk to her, she retreated from him and he was driving a wedge between them. But how could they have a relationship if they didn't talk?

He checked his watch. Quarter to midnight. He really wanted to hear her voice just for a couple of minutes but he shouldn't call her because it was way too late. Hopefully he'd see her tomorrow evening.

'That was so good.' Matt put his knife and fork together sideways on his plate the next evening. 'I want to take a third helping but I might actually explode.'

'Yeah, don't do that. You'd make a mess all over my lovely clean kitchen. Also, I have a lemon polenta cake for pudding that you have to try.' Lily moved over to the worktop and took the cover off a serving plate with a flourish.

'Wow. That looks amazing.'

'If I say it myself, it *will* be amazing. My granny's recipe,' she said, her back to him as she took plates from a drawer.

Matt opened his mouth to ask her how she was doing now and then saw how her shoulders had tensed.

'Sounds like I'm going to end up being tempted into two slices,' he said lightly.

Lily took forks out of her cutlery drawer, very slowly, like she was waiting to see if he was going to say anything else, and then turned round, smiling.

'Prepare to be *very* impressed by my baking,' she said.

The rest of the evening was great. They told each other all about what had been going on with their friends – Lily had a lot to say about Aaliyah's engagement and Meg's latest break-up – and work, and it was great. Obviously they just needed to spend more time together. It wasn't ideal how often he had to work away at the moment and how Lily had to work nights sometimes when he was home. Building your career was important, though.

————

They didn't see each other again for ten days after Matt left on Wednesday morning after a *great* night together and not much sleep.

He'd been to New York and flew in on the red eye on the Saturday morning, which was perfect – apart from the lack of sleep on the flight – because he'd arrive just in time for breakfast with Lily to start their weekend off nicely. He was going straight to her flat, because he couldn't wait to see her, basically. New York was his last work trip for a while, so finally they were going to get to spend more time together.

Lily was in her pyjamas when he knocked and let himself in, sitting on her sofa with her feet curled under her, reading a magazine. His heart clenched and his stomach dipped when he saw her, the way it always hit him the first time he hadn't seen her for a while – or even just a day – how much he loved her and how lucky he was to have her.

'Hey.' He plonked a kiss on her forehead, and then sat down next to her, winding his fingers into her thick hair and pulling her in gently for a proper kiss. God, that was good.

'Missed you,' he said eventually. 'I need to take a post-flight shower if that's okay. Want to join me?'

'Yes, I think I do.' Her naughty smile was *gorgeous*.

After their shower, they wound up in bed together and it wasn't until nearly lunchtime that they were ready to get up.

'I love you,' Matt told Lily. This felt like the best time they'd had together for weeks. Like whatever distance had developed between them had gone. 'I'm really looking forward to being in London with you for the next few weeks.'

'I love you too.' She smiled at him and he caught his breath. He could happily spend the rest of his life seeing her smile like that. 'And me too.'

He really wanted to spend the rest of his life with her. Definitely.

Wow. When he thought about it he'd maybe known that from the first time they met, but he hadn't articulated it internally until now.

But he *totally* wanted to spend the rest of his life with her. And he'd like – *love* – to make that formal. Maybe he should start planning a proposal.

He leaned in and kissed her and said, 'I love you,' again.

She laughed and said, 'And I love you too.'

This was one of those magical moments in life that you'd probably remember forever.

. . .

Forty-five minutes later, Matt was still lying lazily back on the pillows as Lily pulled on jeans and a top. He glanced over to her bedside table as she took her earrings from there. There was an unstamped envelope addressed in her grandmother's handwriting on there.

'How are you feeling about your granny now?' he asked.

She had her back to him as he spoke and he had an excellent view of her shoulders, which visibly stiffened again. She got tense every time he mentioned her grandmother. She stopped moving for a couple of seconds and then turned round, slowly, looking like she was paying way more attention to fixing her earring in than you normally would unless you were very drunk or something.

And then she took a deep breath, looked him in the eye and smiled, like she was making a big effort, and said, 'Up and down. I'll tell you more later today. I probably have too much to say for right now. We'll miss the skating if we don't get going, and those slots are hard to come by.'

'Of course.' Matt smiled at her. Wow. This felt a big step, like she'd just made some kind of decision to open up to him. 'Great.' He smiled at her again. 'Yep. I'd better get dressed too now so that we can go and strut our Torvill-and-Dean stuff.'

As he moved to push back the duvet, his phone rang. He picked it up to check the screen. His boss, Julian. On a Saturday. Bloody hell.

'So sorry,' he said. 'I'm going to have to take this quickly.'

Ten minutes later, when Julian had finished barking out unreasonable demands, Matt said, 'Could I call you back in an hour or so when I've firmed up my plans?'

'Make it twenty minutes.'

Right.

'Everything okay?' Lily had been busying herself tidying the already tidy room while he talked.

'Yeah. Kind of. I mean, yes, great, we've just been awarded this high-profile contract in the Middle East.'

'Great. Exciting.'

'Yep. But it's going to mean someone going out there tomorrow and being there the majority of the time for the next couple of months. Dubai.'

'And?'

'Yes. Julian wants me to go. And realistically I'm going to have to say yes. Otherwise I might even lose my job, and architect jobs aren't exactly growing on trees right now. Plus I'm building a career for the future.' *Their* future, he very much hoped. 'I won't have to do this forever. In due course I'll be able to choose my projects.'

'Of course. Yep, I totally understand.'

'Would you mind if we postponed skating? I need to do a couple of hours' work today. We could meet at around six p.m. before we go out this evening?'

'Yes, of course.' Her smile looked a little forced. God, they'd been planning to talk about how she was feeling about her grandmother after skating.

'I have maybe half an hour now. If you'd like to tell me about how you're feeling about your granny?'

Lily looked at him and shook her head. 'There isn't much to say. I'm fine. I mean, I'm sad, obviously, but, you know, dealing with it. It is what it is.' And it was like the invisible barrier had come down again.

'You sure?' he asked, to try to encourage her to speak.

'Yes. Everyone gets bereaved sometimes, don't they? It's the natural order of things. People do lose older relatives. And everyone deals with it. I'm no different from anyone else. It sounds like you should get going. Why don't you text me when you've finished your work?'

If they were going to be spending the rest of their lives together, they had to be able to talk about stuff. Whether they had three weeks or only half an hour. Surely? He was pretty sure he could talk about anything with her; but surely she had to feel the same way about him.

'You can still be hurting a lot, though. Grieving,' he said. 'And it's okay to talk about that. Good, even. And about anything else that you have an issue with. Like, your parents?' Why hadn't he ever met them properly?

She didn't look at him, instead focusing with apparent great concentration on doing up her watch.

'Need some help?' he asked.

'Thank you but I think I've done it.' She fixed the clasp and shook her wrist slightly and then smiled at him, but it wasn't a proper smile.

It felt like they needed to get over whatever this was, and they needed to do it fast, given that he was leaving again tomorrow.

'I worry that you're internalising things,' he said.

'Nope.' Lily shook her head. 'All good.'

'Really? Are you sure? I feel like stuff's going on with you, in your head, and you just aren't talking to me about it.'

'Honestly, no, I'm fine. Everyone's different. Not everyone needs to talk the whole time.'

'Okay, then. If you're sure.' God, why did it sound like they were having an argument? They weren't arguing; they were just talking. Surely? Why had he sounded so arsy? 'I'm sorry. That didn't sound the way I meant it to.'

'Nothing to apologise for.' She moved to the other side of the room and perched on the chair there, facing him. 'If anyone should apologise, it sounds like it should be me. Like I can't be the person you want me to be. Like I should be talking a lot more about things. But, you know, we don't actually get to spend that much time together at the moment. And it doesn't feel natural to talk about deep stuff the whole time.' She stared down at her hands, twisting her fingers together, and then raised her head and looked at him. 'I feel like I'm maybe the wrong person for you. Or you're the wrong person for me. Or our timing's all wrong.'

'No. *No*. You're perfect. I love you the way you are. Obviously. And I hope I'm right for you.' Was he? Maybe he wasn't. Oh God. 'And our timing will improve when we're both less busy.'

'But when are we going to be less busy? What if we never are? Or not for a long time? And in the meantime you want me to talk about my feelings and right now I just don't want to, because we don't have enough *time* to talk; we only really have time to have fun.'

He pushed the covers fully back and swung his legs off the bed. 'We can talk for a bit now and have fun this evening.'

'It doesn't feel like that's enough, though, does it?'

'It can be enough,' Matt said. *Why* had he started this?

This time it wasn't just her shoulders that went rigid but her entire body. 'I don't think it can. I really don't think I'm right for you, for where you are in your life, with your career right now.'

'What? No. No! You *are* right for me. You're *perfect* for me.' Although, it didn't feel like things could be totally right between them if she didn't want to talk to him. She was probably talking to her girlfriends instead. She was blatantly very close to them.

'You aren't sure, though, are you?' She didn't say it aggressively, or challengingly, just completely matter-of-factly.

'Yes, I am,' he said. She was kind of right, though, insofar as he wasn't actually sure what they were even talking about now.

'So I think that's it,' she said.

'What? What's it?'

'I think I'm not right for you' she said, like she was explaining something to a child. 'I think we're in this horrible vicious circle where we're going to make each other more and more miserable and we can't get out of it.'

'*What*? No. Really, no. I *love* you.' Matt was suddenly

extremely aware, and not in a good way, that he was completely naked. He began to pull his clothes on, fast.

'I love you too and I want the best for you and I hope you'll be very happy and I'm so sorry,' she said as he zipped his jeans.

'*No.* This is ridiculous. We should talk about this.'

'I don't think there's anything else to say,' Lily said. And then she walked out of the room.

Matt followed her into the hall.

'I'm so sorry—' her voice caught '—but I think you should leave.'

'But *I love you.*'

'I love you too,' she said. 'I'm so sorry.' And then she walked back into her bedroom and closed the door.

Matt knocked on the door but there was no answer. He lifted his hand to knock a second time and then put it down. He couldn't keep hassling her, could he? If she wanted to split up, there wasn't a lot he could do about it. It felt like he'd pushed her into it, somehow, in a way he didn't understand. He shouldn't keep banging on her door like an intruder if she wanted him to go.

'Goodbye,' he said, and picked up his bags from where he'd dumped them just next to the front door and left the flat.

And seconds later, he was walking down her road, alone, carrying his luggage.

How, *how*, had that happened?

One minute he'd been lying in bed, watching his gorgeous girlfriend, who he really adored, get dressed, after a morning of amazing sex, and thinking about *proposing* to her, and the next, things had morphed into a *break-up.*

Really, how had that happened?

NINE

LILY

Now

Lily couldn't help watching Matt stride across the garden. She'd always loved the way he held himself when he walked. He had the whole broad-shouldered, slim-waist-and-hips, manly thing going on, and when he walked it was like he didn't want to waste any time. It wasn't like he hurried; he was just an efficient mover. She'd *always* enjoyed watching him move. Except right now, she wanted to *yell* at him. Which was something she never did.

But how *dare* he? *She* hadn't told him stuff? Okay, that was true. And that was in fact why they'd split up. Because she just *couldn't* confide in him when they'd had such limited time together. He'd tried to help her through the loss of her granny but the only way she'd known how to deal with it had been to pretend on the surface that it wasn't happening while going silently bonkers inside, because she found it hard to accept sympathy from too many people.

She'd only told Tess, Aaliyah and Meg about her childhood after getting to know them very well. She'd never told anyone else. She *would* have told Matt, if they'd been in the same city on a regular basis, but the time had never seemed right.

And of course he might not have understood because his whole life, he himself, were so straightforward that he could *always* talk about his feelings.

Such as they were.

Because they couldn't have been that deep, could they, since he'd married Gemma less than a year after he and Lily had split up.

Which was entirely his prerogative but had *really* hurt when Tess told her about it and ridiculously still hurt even now if she thought about it.

'Lily? Hun? Are you alright?' Aaliyah had sat down in Matt's vacated seat without Lily even noticing. 'You look... angry?'

'Angry? No.' Lily shook her head. 'Nothing to be angry about. Certainly not angry.' She felt her forehead furrowing into a frown and straightened it with an effort. She actually almost *never* did overt anger other than the surface kind at things like strangers driving badly. In fact, she *didn't* really usually get that angry. Ever.

Bloody Matt, though. Right now, she was *seething*. Anyway. No one, except Tess possibly, should be having a strop at Tess's wedding-eve dinner. 'Come on. Why don't we go and find Tess? See if she wants to walk back down to the hotel yet.'

'Good plan. She definitely wants an early night and I wouldn't mind one myself. Tomorrow will obviously be a big one and then I'm on my early flight on Saturday and back to the kids, which I can't wait for, but I'd *love* one more earlyish night now lying star-shaped in the middle of my lovely big bed, all on my own, just me and the TV remote and maybe a little glass of something.'

Lily laughed and stood up.

Tess was talking to her parents when Lily and Aaliyah spotted her. When she saw them she began some quite extreme eye signals.

'Hello, hello,' she said when they reached her. 'Have you come to nag me to leave and get a good night's sleep? Thought so. Okay then. You've twisted my arm. Night, Mum. Night, Dad.' She gave both her parents a quick hug and then practically shoved them away from her and linked arms with Lily and Aaliyah and began to walk towards the garden gate.

'Thank you, thank you, thank you for saving me,' she said to them. 'Obviously I adore Mum and Dad, but *honestly*, my mother's turned into some kind of crazy mother-of-the-bride-zilla over this wedding. You should *hear* her. You honestly wouldn't believe the change in her. I can hardly believe it myself. She's so chilled normally. But honestly. Have I checked whether my flowers will clash with my dad's tie? Have I asked the hotel for slices of cucumber to put over my eyes this evening? Have I worn my shoes around the hotel a little bit so that they don't pinch my toes tomorrow? So. Much. Nagging.'

'I mean that is *unimaginable*,' Aaliyah said, dripping sarcasm.

'I know.' Tess shook her head, seemingly oblivious.

Meg was walking towards them holding Pythagoras's hand. 'I think we're going to say good night,' she said. 'I'll see you in the morning.'

'You'll do *what*?' Tess screeched. 'Are you *joking*? You can't spend the night with Pythagoras if that's what you were planning. I need all my bridesmaids around me.'

'Are *you* joking?' Meg asked.

'Are you being *rude* to me? The night before my wedding?'

Aaliyah did an across-the-throat, stop-talking-right-now action behind Tess while Lily mouthed, 'She's definitely not joking,' at Meg.

'So we're all going to be going back to the hotel together,' said Tess.

'But I have to leave on Saturday,' said Meg, her voice wobbling.

Pythagoras winked at Lily and Aaliyah, and gently tugged Meg towards him and spoke into her ear.

Meg nodded. 'Great,' she said. 'Let's go back to the hotel now then.'

'Are you going to sneak out when I'm not looking?' asked Tess.

'Of course not,' Meg said, eyebrows raised the way they always were when she was lying. 'What am I, a naughty child?'

'Darling.' Tess's mum was running towards them, sprinting actually, looking like she'd be in serious contention for some kind of over-sixties world record. 'Don't do that facepack I was telling you about. Penelope says it can cause spots in the short-term. *Do not do it.*'

'Oh my God,' said Meg to Lily, Aaliyah and Pythagoras, while Tess and her mum hyperventilated together, loudly, about spots on a wedding day. 'Complete. Effing. Bridezillas. The pair of them. I am *so pissed off.*'

'OMG.' Aaliyah had been on her phone, checking for messages from her husband about their kids. 'You think you've seen bridezilla... have you seen the weather forecast for tomorrow?'

'No, what?' Lily said. Was there going to be a massive heat-wave? Did that happen on small islands? Didn't sea breezes keep temperatures to manageable levels?

Aaliyah whispered something – weird; Aaliyah was not a whisperer – and the others all moved closer because she'd whispered too quietly.

'Couldn't hear that,' Meg said.

'Rain,' Aaliyah whisper-hissed.

'Rain?' Lily said. The whole wedding apart from the ceremony itself was planned for outside.

'Nooooo,' Meg said.

'Sshhh,' Aaliyah whispered.

Pythagoras took his own phone out and swiped. 'It's true.' He pointed at his screen and they all leaned in to look. 'We're going to be on the edge of a summer storm out at sea. Rain is expected in the morning.'

'Rain?' Lily repeated. Tess would go *mad* if it was still raining by 3 p.m. when the actual ceremony was due to begin.

'Again, sshhh,' Aaliyah said. 'Don't *tell* her. It might not happen, and if it does we'd be better off not living through a tantrum beforehand.'

'But I thought it *never* rains in the summer here,' Lily whispered. 'That's why no one ever checks the forecast. Not even obsessive brides.'

'Well, apparently, never say never,' Meg said.

'It does occasionally,' Pythagoras said. 'I'm sure it will clear up by the afternoon, though.'

'Wow,' Lily said. 'Let's hope it does.' It didn't bear thinking about if it didn't.

'It might not happen,' Pythagoras said, 'and if it does it will probably just be a light shower.'

They all looked at each other.

'Yeah, let's not mention it,' Aaliyah said.

'But what if there's something we could do in advance?' Lily said. 'Shouldn't we make a contingency plan?'

'The venue's bound to have one,' said Meg. 'They must know their own weather.'

'Are you *joking*?' screeched Tess. They all turned to look at her. Had she overheard them? 'My mum says my hair flowers might wilt in the heat if I'm not careful. What are we going to *do*?'

Lily, Aaliyah and Meg looked at each other and all nodded.

Yep. The rain might not happen and, if it did, they could deal with it tomorrow.

———

There was the most tremendous crashing and banging going on somewhere very close to Lily. What was happening? There was screaming too. Heart thudding, her hands suddenly all thumbs, she fought with her duvet and managed to get an arm out to find her phone to call for help.

Oh, okay, no, the screaming sounded like Tess. And the banging was coming from outside. Clearly, Lily wasn't about to be murdered in her bed; clearly, Tess wanted to speak to her about something.

'*Lilyyyyyy.*' Tess was still banging away on the door. It sounded like someone was banging on the window too. Weird.

'Coming,' Lily called. She stumbled out of bed and across the room while Tess carried on with the banging, and opened the door. 'Morning.'

Tess nearly fell inside the room, hand in the air mid-bang, hair like a crow's nest, eyes staring.

'What's *happened*?' Lily asked.

'It's *raining*.' Oh, okay.

'Only lightly, though,' Lily said, thinking of Pythagoras's words last night.

'Lightly?' screeched Tess. 'It's a fucking deluge.' She marched across to Lily's shutters and opened them. And *that's* what the banging on the window had been. Gigantic hailstones.

'Woah,' said Lily. 'I've never seen hailstones as big as that.'

'Focusing on the *essentials*,' Tess said, 'everywhere is *soaked* and it's my *wedding day*. And my wedding is *outside*.'

'Yes,' said Lily. God.

They stood and stared at each other for a couple of moments and then big tears began to fall from Tess's eyes.

'It's going to be okay,' Lily said. 'We'll find somewhere inside. It'll be fine. Really. Definitely. Like Penelope's house or somewhere. Or a restaurant. Somewhere. We'll definitely find somewhere. Or it might dry up quickly. What time is it?'

'Seven thirty.'

'Well, there you go. It's very early still. It never rains here in the summer. It'll clear up.'

'But what if it doesn't?'

'It will.' Lily looked at her phone. She'd really like to check the forecast right now, but maybe not with Tess watching. It didn't sound like she'd checked it herself yet. 'Shall we maybe go and wake Aaliyah and Meg up?' For moral support and some extra brainpower. Because what if it *didn't* stop raining?

'Morning.' Aaliyah was holding her door open and squinting at them through a green face mask.

'Oh my God, Aaliyah,' Tess said. 'What if that gives you *spots*?'

'She literally never gets spots,' Lily said. 'And also...'

'Yeah, true. A spot isn't going to be the biggest disaster of the day,' Tess said. 'It's raining.'

'Just a bit, though?' Aaliyah's face mask creased slightly.

Lily shook her head while Tess said, 'No, it's a massive storm.'

'Is it actually?' The face mask creased a bit more and then Aaliyah turned round and headed towards her window. Tess and Lily followed her.

'Shit,' breathed Aaliyah when she had her shutters open.

'Shit is right,' Tess said. 'What the *fuck* are we going to do?'

'We're going to get Meg to ask Pythagoras for help,' Aaliyah said. 'He seems to know everyone and he has a whole restaurant and he seems very helpful by nature.'

'It's too small,' Tess said. 'I have a hundred and forty people here.'

'You got a hundred and forty people to fly out to Greece?' Aaliyah said. 'Wow. How did I not know that before?'

'And again focusing on the essentials,' Tess said, 'I'm going to have nowhere to host them.'

'Yep, sorry. I'm sure we'll be able to sort something out.'

'She isn't there, is she?' Tess said after they'd all knocked a *lot* on Meg's door. 'She bloody snuck off with Pythagoras last night, didn't she? How *dare* she?'

'Tess.' Lily took both Tess's hands. 'I know that the rain's a huge shock but this isn't Meg's fault and she hasn't done anything wrong. She's an adult. We're all adults. Yes, she's your bridesmaid today, but you can't really get upset with someone for spending the night with somebody before your wedding.'

'Why not? The England football team aren't allowed to have sex the night before a big match, are they? I definitely read that during the last World Cup.'

'Do we think an England footballer's job is slightly different from a bridesmaid's, though?' Aaliyah's face mask was cracking quite a lot now. 'One has to be on top physical form and run miles over the course of ninety minutes competing against some of the fittest and best athletes in the world and the other has to stand still and hold flowers and smile a lot and look beautiful? Do we think a sex embargo is necessary to enable someone to wear a dress and smile for a few hours?'

'She's supposed to be *supporting* me,' Tess said.

'Diva,' Aaliyah mouthed behind her back.

'Let's phone her,' Lily said. 'And she can ask Pythagoras if he has any ideas.'

'No answer,' she said a couple of minutes later.

'And the forecast is for rain all day,' Aaliyah said.

'*What?*' Tess snatched Aaliyah's phone. 'I'm going to call the wedding off.'

'No you aren't,' Lily said. 'You have a hundred and forty guests here, remember.'

'Well, what are we going to *do*?' wailed Tess.

'You're going to have some breakfast and watch something nice on TV and then have a shower and then get your hair and make-up done. And we are going to sort something out. Honestly,' Lily said, 'it's going to be fine. We *will* sort it. Could I just get Carole's number? She might know some people.'

When they'd got Tess into her room and had her sitting in bed watching some *Grey's Anatomy*, they closed her door and set off down the corridor.

'I've got to get this face mask off before I do anything else,' said Aaliyah, outside her own door, 'and maybe have a shower. Meet in the foyer in half an hour?'

'Make it fifteen minutes? We might have a *lot* to do.'

Lily made it to the hotel lobby twenty-five minutes later and Aaliyah five minutes after her.

'Took me bloody ages to get all that green stuff off,' she said. 'Shouldn't have left it on for so long.'

'The hotel receptionist has *no* ideas and says that the owner is away on Paros today and won't be contactable barring death or a fire, and Meg's still not answering her phone,' Lily told her, 'so I'm thinking let's call Carole.'

No answer.

'What's *wrong* with everyone?' Lily said. 'It's eight thirty and they have a wedding to go to this afternoon. Why aren't they answering their bloody phones?'

'We really need some help,' Aaliyah said. 'I'm really sorry but I'm wondering whether we – I say *we*, I mean *you* – should call Matt. He might have Carole's husband's number or someone else's, and he might have some ideas.'

'There must be someone else,' Lily said. After the awfulness of last night, her plan with Matt had been to never, ever speak to him again.

'Well, who? Tom and Tess's parents will be getting ready for the wedding and Tess's mum will also be busy having a nervous breakdown. We need to get going on making plans right now because we'll need to let everyone know where it's going to be and try to decorate it to make it look weddingy.'

'We do need to start sorting things out fast,' Lily said. 'Maybe people are just in the shower at the moment.'

Five minutes later no one had answered Lily's repeated calls and voice messages.

'Soooooo...' Aaliyah's right foot was definitely twitching, like she wanted to stamp it. '... in addition to being someone whose number we have, Matt is an *architect*. So he could really help us.'

'Architect,' Lily said. 'Not wedding planner.'

'He designs stuff, though, doesn't he? Which we don't. Just bloody phone him. Surely?' And Aaliyah actually did stamp her foot.

'So I'll call Matt now,' Lily said.

TEN

MATT

Matt's phone was ringing as he opened his en-suite door after his shower.

Lily.

Really? Why?

He stared at the phone buzzing away on his bedside table.

He'd been pretty sure when he'd left the dinner last night that he absolutely didn't want to talk to her again. He'd continued to feel like that while obsessing about their – highly unsatisfying – conversation during a relatively sleepless night.

Now that there *was* the option to speak to her again, though, he felt like, on balance, he wanted to seize the phone, shout a lot and then beg her to meet up with him.

He was going to answer it. He stretched his hand out and... it stopped ringing.

He could take that as a sign that it would be better for them not to speak. Or he could phone her back.

He picked the phone up.

Actually, no. Probably better not to. Or should he?

God, he was never usually indecisive like this.

It suddenly started ringing again and he nearly jumped out of his skin. He was never usually jumpy either.

Okay, he was going to answer it.

'Lily,' he said.

'Matt. Hi. So it's raining *really* heavily.' It took him a couple of seconds to process her words because they were so different from what he'd been expecting to hear.

'Rain?'

'Yes, rain. Really heavy rain. And it's the wedding.'

'Right.' He moved over to the window to check. Yep, it was absolutely chucking it down. 'Yep, that's very heavy rain.'

'Yes, and the entire reception is planned for outside with no gazebo or anything so we need to sort something out and Aaliyah and I can't do it by ourselves and she thought that you, especially with all your architect knowledge, might be able to help, so she suggested that I call you.' Lily sounded pretty keen to let him know that it hadn't been her idea to call. What a nightmare. He didn't really have any option other than to agree to help.

'Right. Okay. Where are you now? Shall I meet you both at your hotel? I'll try calling Carole on my way. She'll be our best bet for ideas.'

When he'd ended the call with Lily he discovered that while his phone had been busy Tom had left him three – increasingly panicky – messages, saying that he didn't really know much at all about the wedding because Tess had wanted to organise it all without his input but he was pretty sure she wouldn't have bargained for this weather and he was also pretty sure she wouldn't want to speak to him before the ceremony so would Matt mind again checking if everything was alright. Yup.

Twenty minutes later, wearing a raincoat borrowed from the owner of his hotel but still soaked to the bone, he was greeting Lily and Aaliyah in their hotel lobby.

'Tess is watching TV at the moment and we've told her that everything's under control and that we have Architect Matt sorting everything out,' Lily said, not smiling a lot and looking somewhere slightly to the right of his face.

'Yeah, we actually do an entire module on wedding reception planning in the very first term of an architecture degree,' he said, rolling his eyes, aiming for mild humour rather than arsiness. For everyone else's sake they were clearly going to have to park any animosity and behave normally around each other today.

'I'd be annoyed by the sarcasm if I hadn't said something similar myself,' said Lily, shifting her eyes so that she was looking at his actual face for a moment, and raising a hint of a smile. 'Unfortunately, it seems like we're out of good options, so architect-helper it is.'

'Honoured to be helping you on those terms,' Matt said. 'So where's the reception due to be held?'

'It's in the field attached to a local restaurant. The interior of the restaurant's quite small and there are a hundred and forty people coming, so we can't just do the reception inside. Even if there were space to eat there, which there isn't, there wouldn't be any room for the musicians and dancing.'

'I think we should go and check it out in person,' Aaliyah said.

'I'm going to give Carole another call,' Matt said. 'She knows a lot of people. Plus her car would come in handy.'

Carole still wasn't answering.

'Seriously,' he said. 'Is everyone taking the longest showers ever today?'

'Lily said something very similar to that too, before. It's actually scary how much you two echo each other sometimes.'

Aaliyah beamed at them both, very butter-wouldn't-melt. 'Just saying.'

Lily shook her head, gave her friend a clear *Shut up* smile and went over to the hotel reception. 'Do you have any umbrellas we could borrow?' she asked.

'I'm sorry.' The woman behind the reception raised her shoulders and spread her hands. 'We buy them when we need them and throw them away.'

'That's so bad for the environment,' Lily said. 'I wonder whether you should re-think that.'

'Lily,' hissed Aaliyah. 'The wedding.'

'Yeah, sorry. Where can we buy the umbrellas from?' Lily asked.

'The shop isn't open now.'

'Okay, well thank you,' Lily said.

'So bloody unhelpful,' Aaliyah said, quite loudly. Lily nudged her, Aaliyah gave her a comedy sneer and Lily rolled her eyes upwards and then laughed. Matt almost had to look away from them to deal with a sudden stab of pure misery; *he'd* had closeness like that with Lily once – *such* closeness – and now... nothing.

'It's *pissing* it down.' Lily poked her head out of the hotel's entrance. 'We're going to get *so* wet.'

'You could wear this jacket?' he offered.

'That's a very kind offer,' Lily said, 'but it's already soaked and also, by the looks of you, I don't think it's even waterproof.'

'Do you not have an umbrella *with* you?' He'd suddenly remembered that she *always* had an umbrella in the very large bags she always carried. He was sure she'd had one of those bags with her when he'd seen her this week.

'I took it out because I thought it definitely wouldn't rain and my bag was already really heavy.' Yep, knowing Lily her bag would have been full of a lot of 'just in case' items like a travel first aid kit, socks, spare toothbrush, you name it. They'd once been to the beach for the day with Matt's best friend and his then girlfriend, and the girlfriend's flip-flop had broken, and Lily had saved the day by producing an 'emergency pair' of brand-new flip-flops from her bag.

'I think we're just going to have to accept that we're going to get very, very wet, and get going,' Aaliyah said.

'Oh my God,' she said within literally under a minute. 'We might as well be swimming fully clothed. This is actual torture.'

'Once you're as wet as this, you just have to embrace it.' Lily shook her head like a dog, so that drops of water from her hair splattered around her, held her arms out and pirouetted in the road. She looked ridiculous and perfect and gorgeous, and both Matt and Aaliyah began to laugh. Matt really wanted to join her. He shoved his hands in his wet pockets and stayed still where he was.

Aaliyah put her hands on her hips, shook her head, still laughing, and said, 'Honestly.'

On Lily's third spin, she slipped and began to fall in a kind of arc through the air with the impetus of her spin propelling her. Matt and Aaliyah both leapt forward and the three of them collided, while Aaliyah yelled, 'You muppet,' and Lily yelped.

'Everyone okay?' Matt asked when they were all steady again. The other two nodded.

'Sorry about that.' Lily grinned at them both. 'Maybe I should take the embracing-it down a couple of notches.'

Matt couldn't help grinning back. Her hair was plastered to her head and her clothes to her body, she had rain dripping off her eyelashes, her nose, her ears, she'd obviously had a bit of eye make-up on and what remained of it was in streaks down her face; but all you really saw was her huge smile.

God.

'Come on,' Aaliyah said, shattering the moment very effectively – for a few seconds, he'd barely even remembered that she was there – and starting to walk again. 'We have a wedding reception to save.'

'Woah. It's a mud bath.' Lily was the first one to break their awed silence. She wasn't wrong. The hand-wringing restaurant owner, Johanna, had walked them through the clean white interior of the restaurant to windows next to the large back doors – firmly closed against the elements right now – through which the guests would have accessed the reception in the field, and now they were all standing – in increasingly large puddles of water from the drips rolling down their bodies – goggling at the exterior.

'Tess's wedding shoes are lovely,' Aaliyah said. 'They'll be ruined.'

'And her dress. And everyone else's. Everything'll be ruined,' Lily said. 'We need to either find an indoor venue or erect some kind of outdoor shelter. With some kind of boarding over the ground.'

'Simple,' Matt said.

'Not simple,' said Aaliyah, 'and that's why we brought you and your architect brain on board. What have you got?'

'Same as what Lily said.'

'Really?' Aaliyah genuinely looked like she'd been expecting more.

'Sorry, I should have mentioned the prefab wedding reception venue kit that I have stashed in my architect's suitcase. That you can build in only three hours. Yes, really.'

Lily rolled her eyes. 'Clearly we need to ask around the whole island as fast as we can and if that doesn't work we need to do the exterior thing.' She turned to Johanna. 'Do you know of anywhere we could hold the reception inside?'

Johanna was still hand wringing. 'I am very sorry but no,'

she said. 'There will be nowhere. It is very busy with tourists. Everywhere will be reserved.'

Lily nodded. 'Sounds like if we change venue it would need to be to a private one, which feels pretty much impossible at five minutes' notice. So we're probably going to need to board this up. Johanna, do you know any builders?'

'I will try to find someone.'

'I'm going to call Meg again. Maybe Pythagoras knows some different people.' Lily tugged on the phone in the back pocket of her jeans, which now looked welded onto her body. Very nicely, actually. And, really? Was his mind going to keep going in this direction? Pathetic. 'I hope my phone's survived the rain.'

'I'm going to try Carole again.' Matt extracted his own phone from his sodden but less welded-on jeans with a fair amount of difficulty. There was no answer.

'Yes. My phone still works.' Lily paused and then rattled off a quick voice message for Meg. 'This is *so* annoying. We need Meg. Well, we need Pythagoras.'

'You know I think he might actually be her One?' Aaliyah said. 'Like, he's the first boyfriend she's ever properly introduced us to. We've met him more times in three days than we've met any of her other boyfriends ever, almost, and it isn't just because we're all on the same island. She could absolutely have avoided us. And he's lovely to talk to. When we were cooking together, he spent ages asking about Patrick and the kids.'

'I'm *really* happy for Meg,' Matt said, annoyed that all this *The One* chat was making him think about the first time he and Lily had met, 'but clearly we're in a rush, so we should get going? I think we should phone every restaurant we can find on Google and then, if that fails, walk up to Penelope's and wake Carole up if she hasn't got back to us by then. She likes her lie-ins. She could easily not surface until late morning.'

'Good plan.' Lily turned one of her most winning smiles on Johanna and said, 'Would you mind if we stayed in here while we made a few calls? Will you be able to cater it still if we do it elsewhere? Like, how far can the food travel?'

'We will sort something out,' Johanna said. 'And, yes, yes, please, stay here to make your calls.'

'This is just one reason,' Aaliyah said fifteen minutes later, when they'd discovered that everywhere was indeed completely booked up because it was peak holiday season, 'that Tess should have had the wedding at a different time of year.'

'She wanted to do it now so that the weather would be perfect,' Lily said.

'Unfortunate,' Matt said. 'Come on. Let's go and find Carole.'

'We're in a really big rush now.' Lily turned to Johanna. 'I know that this is a *huge* ask and I'm so sorry, but is there any chance you could give us a quick lift, just ten minutes up the road? Or know someone else who could help us, like a taxi, but right now if possible? We could all sit on plastic bags so that we don't ruin the car.'

'I have an old car I will be very happy to take you in. No plastic bags are necessary.'

The three of them followed Johanna out of the restaurant and round a corner into a little side road until she stopped next to a gobsmackingly rusty car. It was hard to tell through the rain and the rust what colour it was.

'I am very sorry but you will all have to sit in the back,' she told them, pointing through the front passenger window. Yup. It looked like there was no seat there, just some broken bits of metal and broken chair and wire. 'You should sit in the middle because you're the shortest.' She pointed at Lily. Then she opened the left rear door and nodded at Matt. 'You climb across, please. You cannot open the door on the other side.'

'We're in a *rush*,' Aaliyah said as Matt clambered with difficulty across the back seat and then began to fold his legs in front of him in the footwell. The car was not spacious.

'I think he's doing his best.' Lily sounded as though she was trying not to laugh.

When Matt was settled, she climbed in herself. He tensed as she bumped against him a couple of times. Ridiculous. You'd think that he'd manage not to be hugely physically conscious of her when they were both fully clothed and unpleasantly damp to the skin and stuck in a small car with Lily's friend and his cousin's wedding venue host, but apparently not. She shifted around next to him, like she was wiggling her bottom into place, and he tensed further. His heart was definitely beating a little faster too. Really, *how* was it possible that he could be feeling like this with Johanna and Aaliyah right here with them. In an effort to distract himself, he turned his head to the right and looked out of the window. There wasn't a lot to see. Rain and greyness.

Lily finished the wiggling and sat still. She seemed to be taking a lot of care not to touch him at all now, holding herself about an inch away from him absolutely everywhere. And, God, despite how sodden they were, he could pretty much feel her across that inch, feel the tension in her body too, know where firmness yielded to softness, know also – he thought, anyway – that she was aware of him in the same way.

And then Aaliyah got in and said, 'Budge up,' and shoved Lily over so that she lurched into Matt, which made it even more difficult not to be very conscious of her. He turned to look out of the window again but it was already steaming up on the inside.

Aaliyah got the door solidly closed on her third slamming attempt, and then groped behind her shoulder.

'I think the car pre-dates the introduction of seatbelts,' Lily said.

'Off we go,' Johanna said, releasing the handbrake, revving

and doing something violent with the throttle. 'We will take a shorter way to get there as fast as possible.'

'Let's hope Carole has some bright ideas,' said Aaliyah, seemingly oblivious to the awkwardness on Matt and Lily's side of the car. 'Yes, Tess has been a complete bloody nightmare over this wedding but this *is* an actual bride's-worst-nightmare situation and despite the fact that she's been hell on legs for weeks I'm actually feeling sorry for her.'

Matt felt Lily nod.

'Carole's great.' He moved his left elbow in so that it wouldn't brush too much against Lily's side. 'I'm sure we'll sort something between us.'

Johanna took a sharp left onto what felt like an unmade-up road. It was impossible to see much out of Matt's window now – he really hoped that Johanna could see better than he could – but this couldn't be more than a track.

'Are you at all scared?' whispered Lily to him and Aaliyah as they juddered along, picking up speed. 'Do you think we're going too fast? Like we might hit a stone and the car could just disintegrate?'

'No, speed is good in this situation,' said Aaliyah. 'Time being of the essence.'

'We're travelling inland without any steep drops on either side, so as long as we don't have a head-on collision I think we should be okay,' Matt said. 'We'd be unlucky for today to be the day its final disintegration happens. Visibility has to be very poor, though.'

'Honestly,' Aaliyah said, 'you're a proper pair of overcautious backseat drivers.'

Maybe ten seconds later, the front right of the car plunged down, they all screamed and shouted a lot of *Woah* and *Shiiiiit* and advice for Johanna, who definitely did the wrong thing with the steering and the pedals because the car started lurching and revving madly before tipping slowly and thudding over onto its right side.

Matt could hear all three of the women's voices doing a lot of shocked screaming and no one sounded too physically distressed, so hopefully none of them were too seriously injured, and he knew that he had nothing more than maybe the odd bruise, but it didn't feel like they were in a *great* situation. He couldn't see a lot, because both Lily and Aaliyah had fallen on top of him, but he was pretty sure from what he'd heard and what he could feel that a lot of the car had crumpled.

'Is everyone okay?' he shouted. 'If you can move and you don't think you have broken bones I think we need to get out fast in case the petrol tank explodes.'

'Do we think that's a little overdramatic?' Aaliyah said from somewhere above him.

'Are you *joking*?' Lily sounded very muffled. Maybe Aaliyah was on top of her face. 'You said we were overcautious and we immediately had a fairly big crash and now you're thinking it's overdramatic worrying about a possible explosion?'

Okay, good, so they were both alright.

'Johanna?' Matt called. 'Are you okay?'

'Yes I am but I'm not sure if I can get out by myself,' Johanna said. 'I am very sorry.'

'Not your fault,' Matt said.

'Really?' Aaliyah said.

'It clearly wasn't on purpose,' Lily said.

'Right, so let's get out as fast as we can.' Matt moved a bit and Lily said '*Ow.*'

'Sorry. Can one of you open the door on the top side?'

There was some thrashing around and then Aaliyah said, 'Done it. It's open. I'm going to get out.' There was a lot more thrashing, which wasn't that comfortable, and then a lot of the weight on top of Matt disappeared very suddenly, and then almost immediately Aaliyah yelled, 'Owwwww. Fuck, fuck, fuck.'

'Aaliyah,' screamed Lily, right in Matt's ear. 'Are you okay?'

'Hurt my ankle. *Really* hurt it.' Aaliyah sounded like she was panting.

'That does not sound good,' Lily whispered. Then she shouted, 'You're going to be totally fine. We're coming to help you right now.' Then she went back to whispering. 'I don't think I can get myself out because I'm kind of upside down.'

'Okay.' Matt could see a lot better now that there were only two of them in the back. 'I think the easiest thing is if I pull myself out and then help you and Johanna out.' He was a lot taller and a lot heavier than Lily.

'Okay. Be *really* careful. Total disaster if you hurt yourself too. You have to help Johanna out before me.' Lily was right; out of courtesy he did have to get Johanna out first.

Matt hauled himself up to the top and then got out a lot more carefully than Aaliyah had. He lifted a moaning Aaliyah out of the hole she'd fallen into and carried her, fast, down the track out of harm's way, before helping Johanna extricate herself, also as fast as he could, feeling increasingly panic-stricken about Lily still stuck in there. He turned round to get her, his heart beating uncomfortably quickly with worry, just in time to see her jump nimbly down from the car onto the track, away from the hole. He grabbed her hand and they ran down the road to the other two.

'You two are *such* worriers,' Aaliyah said. 'Look at you sprint there. The car is not going to blow up.'

Aaliyah had been wrong about a fair few things so far this journey. They all turned as one and looked at the car. And waited, expectantly.

And it did not blow up.

'I'm genuinely surprised about that,' Matt said.

'Your head's bleeding,' Lily told Johanna.

'It doesn't hurt,' Johanna said. 'Please ignore it.'

'Hmm.' Lily narrowed her eyes. 'I hope you aren't just being brave.'

'I'm *not* being brave,' Aaliyah said. 'My ankle *really* hurts. I can't walk. You two are going to have to go and get help while Johanna and I stay here.'

'You and me?' Johanna didn't look delighted.

'Yes,' said Aaliyah. 'I think they'll be quicker than you.'

Lily looked between Aaliyah, Johanna and Matt like she wasn't too keen on Aaliyah's suggestion either, and then after a couple of seconds nodded. Matt agreed. He wasn't keen to go for a walk with Lily, but Aaliyah was right.

'I'm so sorry that we're asking so much of you, Johanna,' Lily said, 'but since there are four of us it kind of makes sense to split into two twos. How's your head feeling? I just need to ask you a few questions.' She ran through some *How many fingers am I holding up* and *Who's the prime minister of Greece* type questions that people always asked you when they thought you might be concussed. 'Yep, I think we're okay to leave the two of you.'

'Yes, *go*.' Aaliyah did shooing motions with her hands.

'Which way is it?' Lily asked.

Johanna – the woman whose shortcut had got them into this position – started a complicated route description, and Lily actually started listening, like her route might be in any way worth taking.

'That's great,' Matt said the first time Johanna drew breath. 'We'll check the rest on Google Maps. Let's go.'

'It's hard to see properly with this rain,' he said a minute or two later, 'but I think it's about two kilometres along these tracks.'

'Two kilometres?' Lily said. 'Oh my *God*. That's like five minutes in a car but it's going to take us a good half hour and we're going to be so ridiculously wet. I can't actually believe this is happening.'

'Come on.' Matt started walking. 'You not embracing it any more?'

'I don't want to bloody embrace it,' Lily muttered. 'You embrace water. This is mainly mud. *Woah.*' Suddenly, she was slipping down the slope of the track, away from him.

Matt lunged for her and caught her arm.

'I think we should hold hands,' he said.

'Um, okay?' Lily said after a couple of beats just standing staring at him.

God, he hoped she didn't think he was wanting to hold hands in a romantic way.

'*Because* I think my shoes have better grips than yours. But we could hold arms. Arms would be good. Let's hold arms. If you like. Because my shoes are quite grippy. And yours apparently aren't so much. But only if you want to. And *oh my God* I sound ridiculous, like I'm implying that if we *do* walk arm-in-arm it's going to be akin to sex. What I meant was, why don't we hold onto each other because my shoes are grippier than yours?'

Lily sniggered. 'All I can say is, it's a good job this isn't the first time I've met you. I'd be running for the hills now.' She took another couple of steps and slipped again, grabbed hold of his arm and said, 'Yes please, I'd like to take you up on your awkwardly worded offer.'

He stretched his right hand out and she put her left one into it, and they started walking again, the rain slightly lighter now, but the mud underfoot gobsmackingly squelchy.

And it was odd. He really hadn't expected ever to hold Lily's hand again. When they were together, they'd always felt so *right* together. They still felt right, but also, clearly, wrong, even more so because now, after last night, he'd finally learned that he really hadn't known her as well as he'd thought he had. At least the tension between them had broken.

He cleared his throat and then realised that he didn't have much to say right now.

Lily turned to look at him through the rain, raised her eyebrows slightly, and then looked back in front of her when he didn't speak. It was hard to see her properly due to the rain and the fact that her head was below his, but he was pretty sure she was smiling.

Which was a big step up from anger. If they were even supposed to be feeling angry with each other. It felt like their conversation last night had definitely been a huge argument but he wasn't sure now where they'd got to at the end of it.

They trudged on through the mud like that for a while as the heavens continued to chuck gallons upon gallons of water over them, holding hands the whole time. Which was fortunate, because Lily's shoes *really* weren't made for slippery mud-walks, and she nearly fell another three times.

'Thank you,' she said each time.

And, 'No problem,' Matt replied each time.

And other than that, they didn't really speak. The walk was actually quite hard work plus the driving rain in their faces made it difficult to talk, but from his side, the main reason for not speaking was that it all just felt a little – very – awkward.

After what had to be a good twenty minutes' more walking and another couple of near-spectacular slips, Lily said, '*Surely* we must be nearly there now. That *has* to have been nearly two kilometres.'

'I know.' Matt got his phone out and they peered at it together while huge raindrops splattered the screen. 'Bloody hell,' he said. 'I think we missed the turning. Look.' He let go of Lily's hand and pointed the track out to her.

Lily took the phone and squinted at it. 'Noooo. You're right. I actually want to cry.' She squinted some more. 'Is that really the time? Ten to ten?'

'Yup.'

'How can that be true, though? I feel like literally days have passed since Tess woke me up this morning. Maybe that's UK time? In which case we have a *big* problem.'

'Nope. Greek time.'

'Wow. Well, that's good. Very good. We still have time to work whatever miracle we're going to be working. What's the quickest way to Penelope's?'

'I'm thinking straight across that field,' Matt said. 'If you're up for a bit of hedge climbing and even more mud.'

'Yep, totally ready now to move on to embracing mud.'

Matt put his phone back in his pocket and they set off hand-in-hand again.

'There's no gate. There's no stile. Just this enormous great bloody hedge,' Lily panted a few minutes later. 'This is *such* a cock-up. We should have gone round by the road.'

'I think that was about five miles.' Matt looked at the hedge. 'Come on. We can get over that together. I'll give you a leg up.'

He hoisted her up and then followed her and, shit, he'd over-estimated the strength of the hedge, and it wasn't going to hold them for long.

The hedge buckled, quite slowly, but fast enough for them both to tumble off and land together in a jumble of limbs on the other side.

'Oh my *God*.' Lily was lying on her back with rain splattering onto her mud-streaked face. 'I can't actually believe this is happening. There's no point even *trying* to stay remotely clean.' She turned to look at Matt lying next to her. 'We're *covered*. I mean, it's in our *hair*. It's everywhere. It's probably *inside* us. We've probably *eaten* mud.'

She was right. She had mud everywhere. Hair. Face. Body. She looked ridiculous.

She looked gorgeous.

ELEVEN

LILY

Lily could see in his eyes that something had just shifted inside Matt as they were lying there on their – actually very comfortable – bed of mud looking at each other. His eyes had softened. They'd gone from laughing to... to the way he used to look at her when they were just about to kiss.

They were very close to each other. Lily could see the rise and fall of his chest, the movement of his throat as he swallowed. And she could feel his eyes on her body too. She looked into his eyes again and he smiled, very slowly.

She knew that smile like she knew the look in his eyes. She could feel its effect right to her stomach.

Matt sucked in a deep breath, his eyes on her lips.

There was complete silence other than the sounds of the rain and their breathing. It was like they were the only two people in the world. No one at all knew that they were here.

Matt leaned closer towards her. Their chests were touching now. She could *feel* his breathing pattern, the gorgeous weight of him pressed against her. She reached her arms round his neck and he moved towards her.

Nothing in the world could stop them now. Lily was almost

throbbing from head to toe with lust. As Matt reached to kiss her, she licked her lips to moisten them. And, oh *God*, that was *disgusting*.

'*Mud.*' She turned her head to the side and spat. 'Eurgh.' She spat again. 'I'm sorry. But *yuck.*'

She looked back at Matt. She still had her arms round his neck and he somehow had his arms round her too.

'Saved by the mud,' he said, half smiling, still with that incredibly tender expression in his eyes.

'Well, I hope it was mud.' Lily barely knew what she was saying and she was pretty sure that her voice was ridiculously hoarse.

Matt moved a little closer and kissed her forehead, very gently.

'You're going to have mud in your mouth too now.' Yeah, her voice was *really* hoarse now, but *wow* that had been a gorgeously intimate little kiss. His lips on her skin for the first time in eight years.

'Mmm,' he said.

Lily couldn't think of a better place in the world to be right now than here. She wriggled a little and wound her fingers into his hair, and Matt pulled her closer.

'I missed you,' he said into her hair.

'Me too.'

They lay there, just holding each other, moving against each other a little, but not kissing, not looking at each other, just being there, still fully clothed, but almost as one. They'd had a *lot* of intimate experiences when they were together, but Lily could barely think of one as, just, *perfect* as this felt right now. Yes, they'd hurt each other in different ways in the past. Yes, they'd had a big argument last night – was that only last night? – and, yes, they were in the middle of someone else's wedding-day crisis but right now...

'Oh God,' she said, pulling her head back from where it was nestled in Matt's shoulder. 'We have a *wedding* to save.'

'Oh my God, so we do.' His voice had gone all gravelly in a way she recognised. Lily was fairly sure that if she'd been standing her legs would have gone all weak at the sound of it.

'We have to go,' she said.

'Mmm.' Matt let go of her back and very gently pushed her hair away from her face. 'You look beautiful. Mud suits you.'

Lily smiled at him. And then remembered the wedding again. 'Matt, we *have* to go. There's a wedding to save and we seem to be the only superheroes available.'

'You're right.' Matt struggled to his feet and then held a hand out to Lily. 'Come on, Wonder Woman.'

'Coming, Mud Man. If no one else will save the wedding, then we must. New Wonder Woman quote.' She put her hand into Matt's and heaved herself onto her feet, and then they set off across the field, as fast as they could, slipping and sliding, but staying upright, and having way more fun than she'd ever have imagined.

'What the chuffing hell have you been doing?' Carole was on the front doorstep of Penelope's house, wearing an insanely frilly pink nightdress and fluffy slippers. 'What were you *thinking*? You've got to be ready for the *wedding* in only five hours' time. It's going to take longer than that to wash the mud off you.' She stopped talking and looked over their shoulders. 'Well, will you look at that? That's some rainbow.'

Lily and Matt both turned round to look and simultaneously both put their hands up to shield their eyes.

From the sun.

'It's bloody *sunny*,' Lily said. 'And, actually, only bloody *drizzling* now.' The heavy rain had literally just stopped almost the second they'd knocked on Penelope's door. 'We need to check the forecast.' She began the process of pulling her phone out of her jeans again. It was really difficult to get it out because the jeans were stuck so tightly to her. She glanced up as she grappled with it and caught Matt's eyes on her bottom and had to try hard not to smirk.

Finally she had the phone out. She swiped through to her weather app. And the forecast had changed.

'I don't know whether to be pleased or not,' she said. 'There's like a twenty per cent chance of rain for the rest of the day and even if it does rain it will probably be sunny at the same time. So it might not rain at all, and all of this—' she gestured with her hands at her own and Matt's mud-splattered bodies '— might have been for no good reason.'

'If there's a twenty per cent chance I think we have to assume it really could rain again,' said Matt. 'And there's no way the mud bath in the restaurant field is going to have dried out by mid-afternoon. So yes it was worth it.'

'I mean, no it *wasn't*,' Lily said. 'We could just have waited until now and come up here in mild drizzle. Or Carole could have driven down to us given that she's now awake. I mean, *totally* pointless.'

'Worse than pointless, I'd say.' Carole pointed both forefingers at them. 'It's going to take forever to get you cleaned up. How did you get so muddy?'

'Tess got upset about the rain so we went to check the restaurant and discovered that the field where the reception was going to be is a mud bath and we couldn't contact you by phone so the restaurant owner gave us a lift to find you to ask for advice and we had a crash and walked,' Lily explained. It sounded quite simple when you summed it up but it actually felt like they'd had a *huge* morning. Made way huger, if she was honest, by all the attraction that had been going on between her and Matt.

'Obviously as it turns out, yes, it was completely pointless,'

Matt said, 'but had we just driven straight here and found you it wouldn't have been, would it?'

'We need to send help to Aaliyah and Johanna,' Lily said.

'We'll send Norm.' Carole turned round and screeched, '*Norm*,' at foghorn volume. Then she turned back to them. 'Sounds like we all need coffee.'

When Carole had put on a feather-trimmed chiffon dressing gown over her nightdress and thumped Penelope's coffee machine into submission, Lily and Matt – both standing barefoot on a plastic sheet in the middle of the kitchen – filled her in on the current state of the reception venue and the current state of Tess's mind.

'So in summary we either need to de-mud and protect the restaurant outside space or we need to find an alternative venue,' Carole said, looking round Penelope's enormous kitchen with an appraising eye. 'Yes, I think we could do it here. Penelope permitting.' Then she wrinkled her face. 'And you two need to shower. And we don't have a lot of time for all of this because we have to get ready for the wedding. Especially Lily.' She opened her mouth and shouted, 'Penelope.'

'Yes, dear?' Penelope must have been right outside the kitchen, because she was in there with them within about three seconds of Carole's yell. She must also have been up since the crack of dawn because she was immaculate in another floral ensemble with her hair amazingly coiffed.

And within what couldn't have been more than two minutes later, she'd volunteered up her whole house and garden – it turned out that she had several gazebos because she liked to throw parties all-year round – and had told Matt and Lily to follow her so that she could show them where to shower.

'Matt, Lily,' Carole said as they got to the kitchen door.

They both turned round and she said, 'Say cheese,' and took several photos of them. 'Couldn't resist,' she told them. 'Hilarious. We can show everyone later.'

Soon, Penelope was showing Matt and Lily together into an unoccupied ground floor spare bedroom and its en suite so that they could shower.

'I'm going to find some clothes for you both,' she said. 'For underwear you can both borrow some of the new swimwear that we have for guests who unexpectedly want to take a dip, and for outer clothes you can wear some of mine, Lily, and *you* —' she turned to Matt, moved closer to him and stroked, literally *stroked*, his – nicely visible through his damp t-shirt – pecs '— will have to wear some of the gardener's clothes, because my husband isn't as *big* as you.' And then she stroked both his biceps at once. Her laugh could only be described as tinkly and coquettish and the look on Matt's face could only be described as terrified. 'I'll just pop and find them while you're in the shower. It's a big one so you might as well go in together, but no naughty business—' she lifted one of her hands from Matt's arm so that she could wag a finger '—because there's no time for it.'

Matt shook his head and said, 'Not together,' while Lily said, 'No, no, we aren't a couple.'

'What?' Penelope said. 'I thought someone told me you were. You *look* great together. And you seem great together. As though you have a connection. Alright, well, it's up to you whether you shower together or not. Might be nice though?' She winked, gave Matt's biceps one more long stroke, walked over to the bedroom door and left, turning to blow kisses at them as she went.

'Wow,' Matt said. 'I'm no longer surprised by the waterfall phallus.'

'I know. I was wondering the whole time if I should *say* something about the fact that she was basically sexually harassing you. I mean, if a man stroked a woman like that there'd be an uproar and rightly so.'

'That's actually a very good point and thank you for nearly saying something. Although I'm big and ugly enough to look after myself and I was also thinking of saying something, or at least moving away from her, except I didn't want to offend her because of the wedding venue issue and the shower.'

'And *that* is exactly how people, mainly women but obviously men too, have been taken advantage of since time immemorial,' said Lily. 'Being scared to offend people. Next thing she'll be asking you to sleep with her if we want to use her house for the venue.'

'Yeah, that would be a step too far, even to save my cousin's wedding.'

'Yeah, I think so.' Lily smiled at him and his gaze shifted to her lips and he visibly swallowed, and Lily found herself swallowing too. 'So we should have our showers now,' she said, after a pause. Shower. The last time they'd been properly alone together, the day they'd split up, they'd spent the morning having the most amazing sex and they'd showered together, and it had been fantastic. Imagine if they were to get into the shower together now, strip each other's mud-caked clothing off, wash the mud off each other...

'Lily?'

'Sorry, yes?'

'I said why don't you go first? If Penelope comes back in while I'm waiting, I'll be brave and hold her off.'

'Ha, yes, great, okay, then. Thanks.' Lily's voice was sounding far too high-pitched. She hurried into the bathroom, blinked at the peach-ness of it – the sanitaryware was peach, the tiles were peach, the mirror surround was peach – and closed and locked the door behind herself and went over to the basin. Woah. She looked *atrocious*.

She pulled all her clothes off and left them in the peach-coloured, shell-shaped bidet next to the shower, took her inhaler out of her hoodie pocket and did a couple of puffs – humidity always made her chest a bit tight – and stepped into the shower.

And now, as the water ran over her body, she was thinking about that last shower with Matt again. And about their split, which had been one of the saddest things that had ever happened to her. It had felt right, though. Matt had clearly just wanted, *needed*, an open, heart-wearing-on-sleeve girlfriend, and Lily couldn't be the person he needed. As evidenced by the fact that he'd leapt straight into marriage with someone else. Better to have split up then than to have made each other thoroughly miserable and split further down the line.

And all of a sudden she wasn't thinking about sharing a shower with Matt any more, she was just feeling miserable and deflated. She picked up the shower gel. Best to stop thinking and get on with washing all the mud off.

Her skin was still tingling from the very hot water and the extreme scrubbing she'd had to do, when there was a knock on the bathroom door. Now she was tingling for another reason. She was very naked and Matt was just on the other side of the door.

She wrapped a large, fluffy white towel securely around herself and called, 'Yes?'

'Penelope brought clothes for both of us while you were in the shower,' Matt said from the other side of the door. 'I'll just put them on the floor here for you and you can reach round for them. I'll turn my back.'

'Great.' Her voice was too high-pitched again.

'Oh my *goodness*,' she said when she'd retrieved the clothes. They were very... Penelope.

'Yeah,' Matt said from the other side of the door.

Lily got herself dressed as fast as she could, because time was clearly of the essence, but couldn't resist taking a couple of seconds to check herself out in the bathroom mirror.

Well. When you'd been fantasising about the last time you'd had sex with your gorgeous ex-boyfriend, maybe it was good to be reminded that right now, from the feet up, you had: a big bruise on one shin from somewhere on your mud-walk; some scratches on the other shin; battered knees; a very frilly and very floral, slightly too small, mini twinset; slightly greyish arms and face but non-grey chest because you'd been wearing a crew neck t-shirt when you rolled in mud; and wet hair and no make-up apart from some very smudged mascara. The exact opposite of God's gift to anyone who had an eye for an attractive woman.

This was arguably up there with the Rod Stewart haircut. None of this was how she would have chosen to look in front of Matt.

She was just going to have to style it out.

She opened the bathroom door, spread her arms wide and said, 'Ta-dah.'

Matt looked at her, clamped his lips hard together and said something that sounded like *Ermumph*.

'You think this is funny,' Lily said, 'you should see the bikini I'm wearing underneath. It's *exactly* the kind of bikini the owner of a phallic water feature would have. Quite obscene. Also quite uncomfortable.'

Matt stopped with the lip clamping and laughed out loud.

'I'm just looking forward to seeing you in the gardener's clothes,' Lily said. 'Since you're too *big* for Howard's.'

'You're going to be disappointed,' Matt said. 'They're just regular clothes. T-shirt and shorts.'

'Dammit. What swimwear do you have?'

'Not so great. Some very snug-looking speedos. But fortunately no one will be able to see those. Right. I'm looking forward to this shower.'

And off Lily's mind went again, conjuring up images of Matt in the shower.

And it was Tess's wedding day, and they had a lot to do.

'I'm going to go and see what's happening with Carole and the wedding plans,' Lily said. 'I'll see you in the kitchen.'

Lily found Johanna and Aaliyah in there. Norm had picked them up while she was showering.

Aaliyah, sitting on a chair in the corner of the room, snorted with laughter when Lily walked into the room, and whipped her phone up and started snapping. 'Love your outfit. And your slightly mud-coloured cheeks. Carole's already shown us the photos of you and Matt in full muddy glory. We'll have a whole Lily's Day Out collection of photos for you to curate soon.'

Lily glared at her. 'You're supposed to be a very close *friend*,' she said. 'Oh my word. Your *ankle*.' It was wrapped in a bandage that was nearly as OTT as Tom's finger one. 'Can't anyone do a normal-sized bandage round here? Tess is going to *freak*. And, also, are you okay?'

'Penelope's husband Howard's a retired GP and he very kindly took a look at it. He thinks it's a sprain and that I need to have it bandaged up. And it does really hurt without it and Howard doesn't want me to do permanent damage to myself and I'm keen not to either. I'm thinking Tess might be okay about it because our dresses are long and I can stand behind people and not get the foot in the photos.'

'What shoe are you going to wear though?'

They had pale-blue suede kitten-heeled shoes that matched their bridesmaid dresses. Aaliyah's bandaged foot had to be about five sizes bigger than normal.

'Penelope's lent me some size nine Crocs that belong to her swimming pool cleaner.'

'What colour?'

'Neon orange.'

'No way. This is beyond ridiculous,' Lily said. 'Everything that can go wrong is going wrong. I feel like having a tantrum myself and I'm not even the bride.'

'Stop panicking. Everything's going to be *fine*,' Carole said.

'Johanna has all the food in her restaurant kitchen and she doesn't think we can feasibly transport it up here, so I've called a builder friend and we're going to put some boards down to cover all the mud, and we're going to put Penelope's gazebos up and decorate them, and as I said it'll be *fine*. So, really, there was no need for you and Matt to go for your cross-country hike. You could just have stayed in the hotel until it stopped raining and called me when I woke up and we'd be in the same position as now except Aaliyah wouldn't have a sprained ankle and you two wouldn't have got so muddy. Just saying.'

'But we didn't *know* it was going to stop raining or that you'd wake up soon or that the car would break down,' Lily said. 'And at least Tess was happy that we were doing something.'

'Not so happy now,' Aaliyah said, holding her phone up. 'Just took a very stressed call. *Grey's Anatomy* isn't doing it for her any more. She needs wedding prep action. Howard's offered us a lift and Carole can come with Matt when he's ready. We need to get back down to the hotel and start our hair and make-up.'

'And maybe scrub a bit more, Lily,' Carole said. 'You're still quite muddy.'

'I've *had* my shower,' Lily said, 'and the mud will not come off.'

'You look lovely,' Aaliyah said, 'and no one will notice a tiny residue of mud.'

'Oh, God, I look *really* muddy, don't I? Tess is going to *kill* us,' Lily said.

'I'll stand on one leg and you can wear a lot of foundation. It'll be fine.' Aaliyah stood up on her good foot and began to hop across the kitchen. 'And also nothing compared to the whole rain thing.'

. . .

'It's going to be a disaster.' Tess was sitting in front of the mirror in her room with most of her hair in rollers while the hairdresser did clever things with tongs and the wispy bits at the front. 'We haven't planned for an interior wedding. We don't have the right décor.'

'It's going to be amazing.' Meg was sitting cross-legged on Tess's bed, looking far too happy. 'When you're marrying the person you love, your surroundings don't matter at all; it's just about declaring that love in front of the people who matter to you the most.'

'Okay, so that's true in a fairy-tale romance,' Tess said, her voice beginning to crescendo, 'but in real life I've spent three and a half years and way more money than we could really afford planning this bloody wedding and I've postponed it seven times because of Covid and I want it to be perfect. And I had not factored in having to decorate a gazebo and now we're going to have to do that at very short notice and we don't have time because we have to get *ready*.'

'Decorating a gazebo isn't that different from decorating the courtyard,' Aaliyah said.

'Yes, it is. The gazebo will obscure the beautiful plants growing round the edge of the courtyard.'

'I think we need to look on the bright side—' Aaliyah didn't sound as though *she* was looking on the bright side; she sounded as though she was about to flip '—everything's going to be *fine* because a lot of very kind people are helping, and you're getting married to the man you love in a gorgeous location in front of a lot of family and friends.'

'And also,' Lily said, fast, because Tess's eyes were now looking suspiciously damp and they did *not* need a bride with a tear-blotched face to deal with, 'gazebos are open down the sides, aren't they, it isn't a tent, so we'll still be able to see the sides of the courtyard, *and* Carole and Penelope have volunteered to decorate the ceiling.'

'Are you *joking*?' Tess screeched. 'Have you seen Penelope's house? And garden? And the way she dresses? No *way* is she decorating *my wedding reception venue*. It's going to have to be you three. No. I need some help here. Meg, you stay, you're the best with make-up. Aaliyah and Lily, you go. For one hour max because then you need to get ready.'

'Oh-kay.' Aaliyah turned round and opened the door.

'Everything's going to be alright.' Lily bent down to hug Tess and Tess screeched again.

'Your nails. What's *happened* to them?'

'Bit of a cross country hike.' Lily put her hands behind her back.

'We'll sort those too,' Aaliyah said. 'I have nail things with me.'

'But they need to be exactly the same colour as ours,' Tess wailed.

'They'll be near enough.' Aaliyah was clearly speaking through very gritted teeth. 'Let's go.'

Within a couple of hundred yards down the road towards the restaurant, Lily was really uncomfortable. Aaliyah didn't look too happy either. Her hobble was getting more and more pronounced.

'How's your ankle?' Lily asked. 'I have a bikini of Penelope's on under this and it's a thong and it's too small and walking's causing what I can only describe as extreme chafing. And this top's really nylonny and it's bloody baking now and any minute I'm going to start sweating. Look at that sky. Not a cloud in sight. I can't *believe* what we did this morning.'

'I know. We're idiots. Although, in our defence, Tess did tell us to go and we didn't know that Johanna would crash and it did look like it was going to carry on raining.' Aaliyah hobbled another couple of steps. 'My ankle's quite sore.' She looked at Lily and gave a snort of laughter. 'Lily, the way you're walking.'

'Having to clench my bum cheeks. It helps.'

· · ·

Eventually they were at the restaurant and being ushered through to the back by Johanna.

And there were Matt, Howard and Norm and a couple of waiters from the restaurant, lugging large boards around to cover the ground.

Lily stopped walking and just *stared* for a moment. Where she looked like a floral clown post Penelope-makeover, Matt looked absolutely gorgeous in the gardener's clothes, especially bent over the way he was, with his back to her, the muscles across his back and shoulders flexing, and his thighs looking equally good.

'You thinking *phwoar*?' stage-whispered Aaliyah. 'Because I am and I'm very happily married.'

'Yeah, no, just catching my breath after the walk.'

'Yes, I can imagine it must have been very hard keeping up with me sprinting along on my sprained ankle.' Aaliyah pulled a chair out and plonked herself down in it. 'I'll just rest my ankle here for a minute. You go and talk to Matt – sorry, I mean go and get on with the decorating.'

'You know what?' Lily said. 'I'm thinking we just get some green tendrilly stuff and twist that round the poles at the corners of the gazebo and then maybe hang some terracotta plant pots from the ceiling and we're away. We don't need to do anything fancy. We *do* need to make the floor completely flat, though, to make sure no one trips over,' she said, moving towards Matt and Norm.

'Got that covered,' said Matt. 'This is just a base layer to make things flat, and then we're going to put much bigger sheets over that and weight everything down at the corners.'

'Not just a pretty backside,' Aaliyah shouted.

Matt turned round and shook his booty at her, while Howard did a surprisingly loud wolf whistle and Lily smiled and tried to push away the thought that, basically, she *loved* it when Matt made her laugh. And she'd always loved it when *she* made *him* laugh. He had a great rumble of a laugh, and it always felt like a privilege if you were the person who'd caused the rumble.

It really hadn't been very good for her spending so much time with him this morning. At this rate she was almost going to miss him when the wedding was done.

'I think I can decorate it how you'd like.' Johanna took out her phone. 'Why don't you give me your numbers and I can send photos for you to comment.'

'Good plan.' Lily nodded. It wouldn't hurt to have some extra getting-ready time and she'd be a lot better off state-of-mind-wise not having too much opportunity to ogle Matt.

Three hours later, after a lot of showering and hairstyling and make-upping, a lot of stress from Tess, a lot of messages from Johanna and not a lot of opportunity for Lily to think about Matt but, despite that, quite a lot of obsessing done, they were ready. Ready for Tess's big – *huge* – day to start properly.

'There.' The hairdresser gave a final tweak to Tess's veil and moved backwards, and Tess stood in front of them.

'Oh wow,' breathed Lily. '*Stunning.*'

'You look fabulous,' Aaliyah said.

'Beautiful. *I* want to get married.' Meg's voice was tremulous. '*Ow.*' Lily looked down. Meg was rubbing her ankle. It seemed like Aaliyah had just kicked her with her good leg.

'Tess's actual wedding day,' hissed Aaliyah. 'All about her.'

'Of course,' Meg said, looking huffy. Well, at least Aaliyah was finally on board with the all-about-Tess thing. 'Tess, you look insanely gorgeous.'

'I actually do, don't I?' Tess sniffed.

'Don't cry,' Aaliyah yelled. 'Let's not test out the waterproof mascara.'

'We need photos.' Lily started snapping away with her phone while Tess posed. 'And now some selfies of the four of us. And then we should let the photographer in.'

'You all look amazing too,' Tess said. 'Thank you *so* much for being bridesmaids. And I'm sorry if I've been a *tiny* bit demanding. I've found the whole wedding planning thing a little bit stressful.'

'You haven't been demanding at *all*,' they all – even Aaliyah – chorused while they pretend-hugged at arm's length to avoid creasing all their dresses.

'Lily, your tan looks *amazing*,' Tess said.

'Thank you,' Lily said, surprised. What tan? They'd only been there for four days and she'd been loading on the Factor 50 like nobody's business because she always burned too easily at first exposure to the sun each summer.

She took another quick look at herself in the full-length mirror on Tess's bedroom wall. One of the few good things about Tess's everything-must-be-perfect approach was that she'd insisted on them all trying dress after dress after dress until they found a style (strapless, floor length and classic simplicity), fabric (silk) and colour (pale blue) that suited all of them.

Aaliyah had worked her magic again with Lily's hair, and Tess had lent her some foundation, which – now Tess had pointed it out – Lily could see was working really well with the mud underneath to give her a good-tan look, and, bearing Matt in mind, Lily had put a *lot* of effort into creating smoky eyes for herself, and, if she said it herself, she hadn't looked this good in a long time. And there was, in fact, no way she would be looking this good at all if she didn't have her mud-undercoating on her face.

The mud tan was perfect timing for leaving Matt with a

good impression. They wouldn't be seeing each other after today and she had her pride and he'd bloody married someone else within a year of their split and if she was honest she *really* wanted him to remember her with a bit of lust and longing. Much like the way she was unfortunately going to be remembering him, it seemed.

———

Walking down the aisle of the gorgeous chapel that Tess and Tom had chosen to get married in was a heart-stopping experience. Tess had finally relaxed just outside the church, when her dad put his arm out for her to take and said, 'I'm so proud of you, darling,' and they'd all nearly cried, and she was now exuding seriously misleading zen as she processed forwards. Tom – with, seriously, the most *enormous* bandage on his hand – was standing at the front beaming at Tess as though she was the most wonderful – the only – person in the entire universe, exuding extreme happiness. And all the guests sitting there in their wedding outfits were also beaming away, exuding huge goodwill. The chapel was beautifully cool inside. *And*, most heart-stopping of all, even though it shouldn't be, Matt was sitting on the end of a pew towards the front, and as Lily approached him, and he looked up at her, she saw that look again in his eyes and a seemingly involuntary smile that went way beyond mere appreciation of how she looked; when they were together, that was how he'd always look right before he told her how much he loved her.

And the look in her eyes was probably mirroring the look in his. Because right now, despite all the hurt of knowing that he'd moved on so quickly, and the fact that she *knew* they hadn't been right for each other, borne out by their conversation last night, all she could think was how much they'd always talked and laughed together, how good it had been, how much she'd loved his company, how attractive she'd always found him, how much she'd *loved* him.

Meg nudged her and she tore her gaze away from Matt's. Oops, she'd almost walked straight into Tess. She needed to forget all about Matt and focus on the important things. And not just during the ceremony.

TWELVE

MATT

Matt ran his finger round the inside of his shirt collar. Had his shirt shrunk in the wash? Or had his neck grown?

Lily looked amazing. Like, out-of-this-world beautiful. The kind of beautiful that was making him fantasise about whisking her away from this wedding and spending days, weeks, months, years making love to her somewhere private, just the two of them.

Lily had just smiled at him like no one else existed and like she felt the same way about him that he felt about her.

He and Lily had history and this wasn't good.

And now he had to sit through a whole wedding, only a few feet away from her.

Matt hadn't entirely enjoyed a wedding ceremony since his own one, when to his incredible shame – it was fortunate that no one could read his mind – he'd thought, really out of the blue, about Lily right in the middle of the service, as the vicar was talking about the responsibilities of marriage and the meaning of the vows they were about to take, and briefly wondered how he'd have been feeling if she'd been standing there next to him instead of Gemma. He'd even very briefly wondered how she'd look in a wedding dress and veil. And then he'd suddenly come to his senses and realised where he was and how truly awful his thoughts had been, and he'd completely lost concentration and lost his place in the wedding service. It had been very obvious, and Gemma, the vicar and the congregation had all laughed with great good humour; he'd heard one of his aunts say in a loud whisper that he was obviously overcome by the joy of the occasion and that it was *too adorable*; and he'd felt like the biggest fraud who had ever walked the earth.

He'd forced his mind away from Lily – who he had been sure he'd completely moved on from; the weird thoughts during the service must just have been wedding day nerves – and had thoroughly enjoyed the rest of the day and their honeymoon.

And he'd been a good, devoted, loyal husband for four years – other than very occasionally in his head, at other people's weddings, when he'd thought about thinking about Lily during his own wedding and been furious with himself. But then he'd found Gemma in bed with Victor, the man replacing their kitchen roof, and Gemma had told him that she'd 'wanted a bit of rough' – her words – and that he, Matt, was too *nice*.

He'd felt a lot less nice ever since.

He really did want to know exactly why Lily had ended things. At the time, she'd talked about not wanting to talk, and vicious circles, and he'd known that after she'd lost her grand-mother it had felt like there was a barrier between them, but he'd never really known how to breach that barrier or what exactly had happened between them. And he'd been so hurt when she'd refused to see him again, saying that she thought it was better for both of them to have a clean break, that he'd forced himself to stop thinking about her and had ended up throwing himself – too soon in retrospect – into a relationship with someone very different.

He watched Lily, Aaliyah and Meg step back from Tess as she took her place next to Tom.

He couldn't reconcile the Lily he'd known and loved – and yes, still had feelings for, if he was honest – with the woman who'd apparently not wanted to tell him really important stuff about herself. Obviously it was entirely her prerogative not to tell him anything at all, but if you were close to someone you'd surely mention if you had severe asthma. But, again, her prerogative not to. Hurtful, though. God, so confusing.

Lily in the mud had been like the Lily he knew, and they'd had a great morning together.

Lily was sitting herself down now, a couple of rows in front of him. As she sat, smoothing the skirt of her dress under her as she lowered herself, she turned slightly and glanced at him and gave him a tiny half-smile.

Matt shivered, smiled back and then turned his eyes very deliberately towards the bride and groom.

He applied extreme willpower and focused very hard on his cousin and friend's wedding ceremony for the next half an hour and didn't look properly at Lily again until the wedding party began to proceed back down the aisle. And, *God*, she really did look beautiful today. Glowing. Great hair, amazing eye make-up, a gorgeous dress. But the most beautiful thing of all was her smile, which didn't need any make-up or stylist.

'Matty?'

'Sorry, Carole, I missed what you said?'

'Just a platitude about how beautiful all the bridesmaids look,' Carole said. 'Which I believe you've already noticed for yourself.'

'Ha, yes, I have. Yes, they look lovely. All of them.'

He actually just really wanted to drink in as much as he could of Lily, like a guilty pleasure. He wasn't going to see her again after today, so it really couldn't hurt if he watched her while he still could.

Without being weirdly stalker-like. But there was nothing wrong with watching all the photos being taken.

'Matt?' His cousin Rory was waving a hand in front of his face. Quite annoying, actually. 'You were a million miles away. I was asking about the building plans at Carole's.' Oh, okay. Yes, he had been miles away, thinking about Lily. Yeah, maybe too much staring.

'They're still in their early stages,' he said, sharing a hearty handshake and shoulder clasp with Rory. 'But the finished product will be amazing. You know Carole. A great eye for detail and a liking for luxury. How are you, anyway? It's good to see you.'

And he got carried away on a wave of greeting relatives who hadn't been at the dinner the night before and friends of Tess and Tom's who he'd met briefly at various events in the past.

Fortunately, there was no sign of rain right now, so the vehicles that Carole had had lined up to ferry everyone from the chapel to the restaurant weren't needed. Tess and Tom were driven the short distance in a beautiful vintage Rolls, which apparently Tess had insisted on having shipped over at a lot of expense from Naxos, beyond Paros – which looked slightly incongruous in the middle of all the simple whitewashed, blue-shuttered buildings surrounded by the still parched grass and deep-pink flowers – and the bridesmaids and Tess and Matt's grandparents were driven in another two, less ostentatious, cars.

Matt realised that he was slightly disappointed that he wasn't going to be arriving at the same time as Lily because he wanted to see how she reacted to the work they'd done in decorating the gazebos. And Tess, and Aaliyah, obviously. He wanted to see their reactions too. Not just Lily's.

Mainly Lily.

It felt like the whole thing had been a bit of a joint project because of the mud walk.

And he still really cared what Lily thought about him. Would things have worked out differently if they could have spent more time together?

'Woah, mate.' God, he'd just walked straight into Donny in front of him, in a world of his own again. Crazy.

When he got to the restaurant, where all the guests were waiting to file through to the back and out into the gazebo area, it turned out that the bridesmaids hadn't gone inside yet, because it had taken Tom a long time to help Tess out of their car and try to sort out her dress to her satisfaction, and then Lily, Aaliyah and Meg had had to intervene to arrange the dress properly.

'His broken finger's really pissing me off,' Tess told Matt. 'He can't do anything properly with it.' She turned to look at Tom and said, 'Honestly, you're such an idiot.'

'Love you too, my darling.' Tom put his arm, bandage and all, round her waist and planted a big smacker on her lips.

Tess grimaced at him for a moment and then her features softened into a big smile, and she put her arms round his neck. 'I'm very happy to be your wife and I love you and I'm sorry if I've been a bit grumpy. I've just found planning this wedding a bit stressful. I wanted everything to be perfect.' She returned her new husband's kiss and then turned back round and said to everyone in the vicinity, 'Come on, let's get this party *started*.' And she lifted her skirts and marched inside.

'Yesssss,' Matt overheard Lily say to Aaliyah as they all moved through the restaurant together. 'We have the old Tess back.'

'Thank God,' said Aaliyah.

'I really hope everyone likes what we did with the gazebos,' Matt said.

'Oh my God, you're geniuses,' Tess said from a few steps in front. 'It looks amazing. Thank you again for helping so much.'

'So nice now. Jekyll and bloody Hyde,' Aaliyah said.

'Pleasure,' said Lily.

'You're very welcome,' said Matt.

'Oh, wow.' Lily stopped walking and looked around her.

'You actually are a genius, Matt. This is the perfect combination of maximum effect from minimum effort. It looks amazing. It wouldn't have looked any better if we'd spent weeks planning it.'

'I am actually very pleased with the result.' Matt nodded. 'And you know you suggested the green tendrils hanging from the ceiling? You know what all of that is? It's bindweed. Which is a weed that was running riot in the garden of the neighbour three doors along. So we actually did him a favour picking it all. Pulled it out by the roots and everything. That's a lot of birds with one stone.'

'I'm so impressed,' Lily said.

Matt felt a warm glow spread through him and smiled at her. And then frowned. He really shouldn't care so much what she thought of his efforts.

'Lily.' A woman who Matt vaguely recognised was walking towards them with her arms outstretched in Lily's direction. 'How *are* you? Gorgeous dress.' She did a circular pointing thing round her own face and said, 'And gorgeous tan. You look *fab*. Come and say hi to Johnny and Laura if you can take some time out of bridesmaiding?'

'I'll see you later,' Lily told Matt.

And off she went. And off his mood went. Deflated, just like that, because she'd gone. Truly pathetic.

Yup. He really needed to find an opportunity to talk to her properly, get some closure once and for all on their relationship.

He spotted her talking to other people several times but didn't find himself standing close to her again until a couple of hours later, when they were about to be seated for dinner.

'I can't believe how dry and hot it's been since lunchtime,' she said, fanning herself. She lowered her voice. 'I think the gazebos are holding the heat in and making it too hot.'

'I know. Worth it, though, in case it had rained again. And I think it'll get cooler later on. I think there's a breeze starting.'

'Can I just say?' A middle-aged woman leaned over to Lily. 'You look so *well* at the moment. That tan really suits you.'

Lily smiled. 'Thank you.' She waited until the woman had moved away and then said to Matt, 'Literally about the twentieth person who's said that to me today. And you know what the tan is? It's the mud combined with foundation. Literally everyone thinks I look healthier and better because I have a layer of mud stuck into my face under my friend's foundation.'

'If it's any consolation, I think you looked lovely before you bathed in the mud,' Matt said, trying not to laugh. She'd definitely got a lot more mud on her face than he had.

'Hmm,' Lily said. 'It's like that time I had the allergic reaction to antibiotics.' Not long after they'd started going out, she'd had a big reaction to some medication and had been covered in hives for a couple of days and after they'd gone down she'd stayed red for weeks and everyone had congratulated her on how lovely she looked having caught the sun. In the middle of December in London.

God, it felt like they had *so* much history together. Like, when they'd been together, they'd shared so much. Until the end when Lily had withdrawn from him.

Of course, as it turned out, they hadn't shared as much as he'd imagined. Now he thought about it, didn't allergies often go hand in hand with asthma and eczema? When she'd had that allergic reaction would have been an obvious time, actually, to have mentioned her asthma, so she'd clearly made a decision not to. Which was of course entirely up to her, but it hurt that she hadn't wanted to open up to him about important things.

Matt really *needed* to have just one proper conversation with her, or he was going to wonder about all of this forever. He was going to ask her right now. He opened his mouth to speak and had got about two words out before Meg popped up and said, 'Hi, Matt, sorry, I need Lily,' and pulled her away by the hand.

A really good thing, actually. If they were going to have a serious conversation, now wasn't the time for it. Although he wasn't going to see her again, was he? Maybe he should ask her if they could meet up in London just for one drink.

Matt's table for dinner was great and included some of the men he'd met at the stag. He sat down and immediately started talking to Tom's cousin Felix's fiancé, Alfredo, who was fantastic company *and* had devised a way of getting the latest test match score without anyone even suspecting he was looking at his phone: the perfect dinner companion. Matt was going to enjoy this dinner and not spend the whole – or any – of it thinking about an ex from way in the past. Which was all that Lily was.

Alfredo was midway through a story about a half-marathon running disaster when Matt thought he heard Lily laugh and had to force himself not to turn round. Which made him realise that he'd been doing really well at not thinking about her. Although, actually, not *that* well because their starters hadn't even arrived yet. She *was* laughing. He loved it when she laughed. Her whole face lit up and her eyes danced. And then she'd often pull a very dry comment out of the bag which made you choke with laughter yourself at the shock of it.

'Matt?' Alfredo said. Oh God. He'd done it again. Been thinking too much about Lily and not enough about his companion. Ridiculous and not okay. He *had* to stop thinking about her and engage with the people on his table.

'Sorry,' he said. 'Little bit tired. Have you heard about the insane morning a few of us had?' Obviously that story involved Lily a lot. *God.*

He told them the rain story as quickly as possible, and then moved the conversation on to holidays – who knew that between eight people over six months there'd be plans to visit eleven countries over five continents – and actually managed to keep his mind genuinely pretty much off Lily.

When his uncle, Tess's dad, smashed a plate on the floor and roared with laughter at all the gasps and screams and told everyone that he was doing his speech *à la* Greek plate smashing, Matt was delighted to realise that this had to be the first time he'd looked round at or thought about Lily for at least... well, probably nearly ten minutes. Not bad, really.

Pretty pathetic, actually.

Anyway, now he kind of *had* to look at her since she was next to his uncle. He loved everything about the way she looked. The way she always began to smile – with her eyes dancing – slightly before the punchline when she sensed that a good one was coming up. The *way* she smiled, the way the smile started small and finished big and made you want to smile and smile and smile yourself. The way she'd just caught the eye of someone on the table next to him and raised her eyebrows slightly and then smiled broadly.

It was a long time since they'd been together and there were a lot of other attractive women in the world.

It felt like yesterday and there was only one Lily.

'When Tess and Tom first met,' his uncle said, 'they were a lot younger than they are now.' Yeah. Same with Matt and Lily. Ten years ago, he'd been young and naïve. Growing up, he'd seen his parents' straightforward, happy marriage and he'd thought that all you had to do was love someone and be loved and that was kind of that. Nope. Apparently not.

Lily looked away from his uncle and straight at Matt. She didn't smile. Nor did he.

He really shouldn't speak to her later. He really actually didn't need to go there.

And his uncle had finished his father-of-the-bride speech and Matt had missed most of it. Annoying; he'd have liked to have heard it. Hopefully someone would have videoed it.

Tom and Tess both did speeches and they were both great, not too long, not too short, and funny. Tess was funnier than Tom, actually. She even alluded to her own bridezilla tendencies, at which Lily, Aaliyah and Meg all clapped, which made a lot of other people laugh.

The dancing started straight after the speeches. Tess and Tom's first dance was one of the best Matt had ever seen. They'd clearly been for lessons and Tess had clearly been more of a natural than Tom. He counted, visibly, throughout and breathed an extremely audible sigh of relief when it was over.

Tess went over to the stage and said, 'Come on, everyone, onto the dance floor. Come and show my gorgeous, wonderful, two-left-footed husband how it's actually done.'

Tom stuck his head next to hers at the mic and said, 'Just to make it very clear: at no point during that dance did I step on either of my wife's feet,' and everybody cheered.

Half an hour later, jacket off, tie loosened and sleeves rolled up, Matt found himself next but one behind Lily doing the conga. The person between them, whose waist Matt was holding and who was holding Lily's waist, was Carlton. Newly divorced and looking for a fling Carlton. Good-looking, very funny Carlton. Right now making Lily laugh Carlton.

And right *now*, the end of the dance, taking the hand of a still-giggling Lily and whisking her into a slow dance Carlton.

Matt was standing right next to Aaliyah, who was clapping as Meg and Pythagoras, who'd just arrived at the reception straight from his own restaurant, started a very smoochy dance. He held out his hand to her.

'Sure,' Aaliyah said.

It was incredible how much willpower it took not to grill her about Lily.

And this was absolutely ridiculous.

Lily had – frankly – broken his heart eight years ago. And this morning he'd enjoyed their walk way too much, and he'd been thinking about her all day. He didn't want to go there again. He shouldn't be planning to ask her in detail again what had happened at the end of their relationship; he should be planning to avoid her. End of.

Tess had planned for them all to be on the beach next to the restaurant after the more formal dances, for some moonlit barefoot dancing on the sand, which was a lot of fun, even when you were trying to avoid someone. A lot more fun, actually, once you'd made the decision that you weren't going to speak to that person again beyond civilities. Apart from the feeling of bereftness.

They were all in the middle of dancing in the moonlight to 'Dancing in the Moonlight' when the moon and stars suddenly pretty much disappeared from sight and next thing the clouds that had covered them developed into some serious rain.

Everyone, as one, sprinted for the gazebos. By pure chance, Matt ended up next to Lily as they all piled under.

'If I'm honest,' she said, 'and I wouldn't say this to anyone else, but you *were* there this morning: I'm kind of glad that it's raining now.'

'Yeah, me too.' He nodded. 'Otherwise we'd be feeling pretty stupid.'

'Exactly.' She smiled at him. *God*, he was going to miss her smile. All over again. Which was why he shouldn't chat to her any more now.

'Anyway,' he said, 'I should go and speak to—' he saw his aunt over her shoulder '—Tess's mum. Check she's okay. If I don't see you tomorrow, have a great journey back. Great to have seen you again.'

'Yes, great,' Lily said. 'You have a good journey too. Great to have seen you.'

Yes. *Great*.

THIRTEEN

LILY

The band finished reassembling inside the end gazebo and struck up 'Rockabye', and Mick, a tall man dressed in a very natty green suit, diamond-patterned shirt and pointy shoes, who Lily had vaguely noticed during the week as part of Tom's stag group when she'd been sneaking glances at Matt under cover of her sunglasses, took Lily and Aaliyah's hands and began to spin them both round, Aaliyah balancing weirdly because of her dodgy foot.

By the time the song finished, he had them both twirling like they were ballerinas in a jewellery box and Lily's head was spinning so much that she was wondering whether she was going to ruin the reception by projectile vomiting. In the final bar, he sent them both into a final pirouette before letting go of them and, as the next song started, began some energetic popping. Lily and Aaliyah both stood there swaying slightly, blinking and clapping him.

'Come on,' he shouted.

'I honestly can't do that,' Lily shouted back, laughing.

'Me either.' Aaliyah shook her head, pointing at her

bandaged leg and Croc, and started a bit of gentle, non-stom-ach-upsetting-style side-to-side rocking, and Lily joined her.

She slid her eyes right when she was sure that no one was looking at her. Matt was doing his own dancing thing – which Lily knew like the back of her hand – and it was a struggle to keep her eyes off him. He was a much more average dancer than Mick – a lot less flamboyant – but just solid and gorgeous and lovely and very, very sexy. He did a – slightly failed – shimmy thing with a couple of the other men and then laughed with them and, honestly, Lily felt a bolt of attraction right to her core. From a good fifteen feet away.

Looking at him was actually too much. She turned her head slightly, gave Aaliyah a 'Yay, I'm having *so* much fun and I'm not thinking about Matt at *all*' smile, and then focused again on Mick, who was pulling some truly bonkers moves now.

And then she looked back at Matt. It was like there was an invisible string drawing her eyes in his direction.

And he glanced over towards her, like he'd felt her watching him. He locked eyes with her, and carried on dancing, watching her, not smiling, just... dancing.

Lily blinked. Her throat was drying. She could barely remember how to work her own limbs. She just couldn't think about anything except Matt and the way his body was moving. And the fact that this morning they'd been lying face to face on the ground together with their arms round each other, and then taken showers with only a door separating them. And that in the past they'd shared so much love.

She took a couple of steps towards him, and he just carried on watching her, dancing, like he was dancing *at* her, or *for* her, and then someone shouted, 'Lily,' in her ear. About three times.

Lily tore her eyes from Matt and looked round.

'Shall we go and get a drink?' Mick said, waggling his eyebrows suggestively.

'I...' Lily took a quick glance back at Matt. He'd turned

away from her and was laughing with one of Tess's new work friends, a very attractive woman of about their age.

'Just the two of us?' Mick said.

Lily suddenly felt really tired. She snuck another look at Matt. What could be that funny? He looked as though he was having so much fun.

She didn't want to have a drink with Mick. She just wanted to go to bed. Except she should really wait until Tess and Tom left. Why hadn't they left, actually? Surely they didn't want to start their honeymoon with a really late night?

'I'm actually fine at the moment,' she told Mick. 'Thank you. Very much. I need to go and talk to Tess.' She grabbed Aaliyah's hand and pulled her across the dance floor towards where a little group were watching Tess and her dad dance together while Tom danced with Tess's mum.

'Lily, Aaliyah, darlings,' Tess's mum said at the end of the song. 'Best bridesmaids. I'm proud of you all. Hasn't everything gone *marvellously*? Where's Meg?'

Where was Meg, actually?

'She left with Pythagoras a good hour ago,' Aaliyah said, 'under cover of all the rain hysteria. Their last night together.'

'Fair enough,' Lily said. 'She's going to be devastated to leave him.'

'I think she might genuinely decide to try to stay here with him,' Aaliyah said. 'Seriously. And I wouldn't even be that worried about her. I really like Pythagoras.'

'Me too. The nicest man she's met in the entire fifteen odd years we've known each other.'

'Pity she lives in Edinburgh and he lives here.'

'Tess, Tom, it's late,' Tess's mum said, clapping her hands loudly. 'I wonder whether you should think about leaving.' The false eyelashes on her right eye slipped as she did an exaggerated wink. 'I'm looking forward to hearing about your honeymoon pregnancy.'

'Oh my God,' said Tess to Aaliyah and Lily. 'Morphing seamlessly from mother-of-the-bride-zilla to desperate-to-be-a-grandmother-zilla.'

'I heard that,' Tess's mum said. 'I love you, darling. I just want you to be happy.'

'I love you too, Mum.' Tess reached out to her mum and pulled her into a hug.

Lily looked over her shoulder while everyone else smiled at Tess and her mum. Matt was dancing now with the woman he'd been talking to. *Clearly* no reason he shouldn't, but Lily didn't want to watch.

'I actually think we *should* leave now,' Tess said to Tom. 'What do you think?'

'I agree.' Tom smiled at Tess adoringly and put his enormously bandaged hand round her waist.

Lily waited until everyone had finished throwing rice and petals over Tess and Tom and they were out of sight and the goodbye-and-congratulations cheers were dying down, and began to walk towards the exit herself.

Tom's cousin Felix grabbed her hand as she tried to squeeze past him and pulled her back towards the dance floor with him. 'Dance with me, Lily,' he pleaded. 'Alfredo's been propping up the bar all evening and not dancing at *all*. I *need* you.'

Lily laughed, trying really hard not to look over her shoulder to see where Matt was.

'Do you have your *eye* on someone here?' Felix frowned and followed the line of her vision with a pointed finger.

'No.' Lily shook her head vigorously and started dancing with her eyes fixed on Felix's. 'I was just looking for Aaliyah.'

'She's literally right next to us. You *totally* have your eye on someone. Who?'

'No, *honestly*.'

'Hmm.'

Lily *really* wanted to go to bed. Maybe she could get away with dancing to just one or two songs now. And, yes, perfect, the next song that came on was a slow one.

'I'm *really* tired,' she shouted to Aaliyah, who was hobble-swaying with some of Tess's work friends. 'I'm going to go to bed now.' Then she turned to Felix. 'I think it's time for you to drag Alfredo away from the bar. I'm going to bed. Soooo tired.'

'You're right. It is. We'll both see you tomorrow for our photo session.' They'd agreed that they were going to meet at twelve tomorrow for Lily to help them with some photo cura-tion. 'Sleep well.'

She blew kisses at Felix and Aaliyah and then turned to leave, colliding in the throng of tall people swirling around them with someone large as she was leaving the courtyard. Matt. Ironically, this had been about the first time all evening that she hadn't known almost exactly where he was at any given moment. Talk about behaving like a lovesick teenager, honestly. Such a good thing that within the next few seconds she'd be saying goodbye to him for the foreseeable future. Maybe forever.

'Oops, sorry,' he said. 'You alright? You're obviously a light-weight like me, making a dash for it as soon as decently possible after the bride and groom have left.'

'Yep, *soooo* tired,' Lily said. Her heart was beating so loudly at the hugeness of this moment – the last time she was going to see Matt for a while, maybe ever – that maybe *he* could hear it. 'Probably because of all that hiking in the mud this morning.'

He smiled at her and she found herself smiling back. His face was so familiar. But also changed with age. *He'd* changed, it seemed. He'd always been so open when they were young. Now there was a slight wariness about him. Not all the time, but she'd caught it every so often over the past couple of days. Like the way he was looking at her now; his eyebrows were a little raised and his smile was a tiny bit lopsided. When they were younger, from the very first moment they'd met, he'd just directed wide, happy smiles at her. Until the end of their relationship. Right now, he looked – she didn't know how she'd describe it – maybe slightly cynical, less trusting. Maybe because of his divorce. Maybe a little because of her, Lily, how their relationship had ended. God, she hoped not.

She really wanted to reach up and touch his face, trace the line of his cheekbone. It felt utterly heartbreaking that she had no right to do so any more.

There'd been silence between them for too long.

'It's been a wonderful evening, hasn't it?' she said.

Matt drew a deep breath, like she'd brought him back from somewhere else. 'Yep, fantastic. Fitting, because they're a fantastic couple.'

'They really are.' Lily nodded, far too over-enthusiastically. His last memory of her – if he ever thought of her again – would be of her head bobbing up and down crazily. She stopped the nodding. And now she had her head completely still. Was that normal? To be so still? Now she was acting like she was playing musical statues. What was *wrong* with her? 'So, it's been great to see you,' she said. 'Goodbye.'

'Are you walking back to the hotel by yourself?'

'Yep. Meg's with Pythagoras, and Aaliyah says she's going to be the last woman standing – or hobbling – if it kills her because tomorrow at the crack of dawn she's flying home to her family and tonight she wants to make the most of dancing on an island like she's footloose and fancy-free. I think she might just stay up all night.' And Lily would have carried on dancing with her if she hadn't been so full of not-very-happy thoughts about Matt.

Matt laughed. 'Sounds slightly scary.'

'She said she's going to bear her husband and kids in mind and not actually follow through with any footloose and fancy-free stuff.'

'Good news. Right. Walk with me? I'm going past your hotel.'

'Great.' The sad thing was, it did seem great, because it turned out that she just really wanted to grab a few more final crumbs of time with Matt.

'Look at that gorgeous clear night now the rain's gone again.' Matt pointed up at the star-filled sky. 'Always mind-blowing seeing skies like this when you're normally in London. Also mind-blowing that the sky's like this now when you think about the storm this morning and the rain earlier.'

'I know. I still can't believe that happened. It's so amazingly still now. And silent. It's like we're the only two people in the world.' What? Why had she said that? It sounded like the biggest come-on of all time.

'Yeah.' Matt paused, and then suddenly said, 'Lily, I...' like he was blurting the words out. And then nothing.

It seemed obvious that he wanted to pursue the conversation they'd been in the middle of yesterday evening. She knew that they weren't right for each other, because he wanted, needed, someone different from her. And she didn't want to talk about that, but, actually, it wouldn't really hurt given that they weren't going to see each other again. He was a nice person, a good person, and if he was still hung up after eight years on why they'd split up, then maybe the least she could do was tell him in more detail. She'd be *tempted*, while they were at it, to ask why he'd thought he'd loved her if he could move on so quickly and marry someone else so soon afterwards. But actually she didn't need to go there. And it wasn't like there was only one soulmate for each person, was it? So clearly he'd just met someone else he really loved straight after he and Lily split and that was that. Clearly. *Totally* understandable, and entirely his right.

Okay, so if he still wanted to talk, she'd talk. And then they'd say goodbye and whatever she'd said wouldn't matter.

'Yes?' she asked.

'Just. I...' He stopped again, and then said, 'Shall we walk along the beach? If you can do it footwear-wise? Slightly quicker and great view at night?'

Yep. Why not?

'Good plan.' The beach was only a few metres away and seconds later they were both taking their shoes off. 'Oof.' Lily wiggled her toes in the fine sand. 'Can't believe I danced so much in these shoes.'

'I can't imagine walking even a few feet in shoes like that,' Matt said as he pulled off his socks. 'I think I'm going to have to do some trouser leg rolling.'

Lily laughed as he finished the rolling and struck a pose for her. 'Loving your *Miami Vice* look.'

They wandered along the edge of the water, gentle waves occasionally lapping at their feet, Lily holding her shoes in her left hand and Matt his in his right hand, their other arms brushing from time to time, and, oh *God*, Lily wished they could have been right for each other and that this night could end the way their last beachside walk had ended.

She really didn't want Matt to start the serious chat he clearly wanted to have, and destroy this moment.

'Remember those turtles we saw in Zakynthos,' he said, turning to look at Lily so that their arms brushed even more. Maybe he didn't want to destroy the moment either.

'I was just thinking about that beach too,' she said. After the success of their ten days staying with Carole and Norm, they'd taken a holiday the next year to a different part of Greece and turtle-watched, dolphin-watched, sunbathed, had amazing food and drink and then, obviously, had fantastic sex too. Al fresco the first time and slightly marred by the sand – sex on the beach definitely wasn't all it was cracked up to be – so they'd taken a little swim in the sea and then gone back to their room and had *the* most amazing night.

Matt drew a deep breath.

Lily didn't do anything at all. She just stood and stared at him. It was like she'd lost control of herself. They were standing next to each other in the shallow water, under the clear, moonlit sky, with not another person in sight. If she inched just a tiny bit closer to his gorgeous, solid chest, they'd be touching. And if she inched closer again, they'd *really* be touching, in all sorts of places. Like they had this morning, except without the mud and the need to sort the wedding reception.

Matt reached out and brushed a strand of hair away from Lily's cheek.

She sighed and opened her lips slightly and tilted her head back a little.

Matt smiled a little and didn't move, and they just stood there gazing at each other.

Was this a bad idea? Would she feel like total crap afterwards because she'd be so bereft to say goodbye to him? Would he feel crap too? Nothing serious was going to happen between them because nothing could have changed in the past eight years, so it was definitely going to be goodbye.

Realistically, though, whether or not anything happened tonight, she was going to feel like total crap saying goodbye to him anyway. So, really, they might as well create one more good memory first.

In fact, maybe it would be like getting closure.

Just one kiss would be perfect.

Lily was almost holding her breath now. All she could think about was Matt and what might happen next.

His smile grew, and then he started to lean his head down towards hers.

She reached towards him and he further towards her and their lips met. And, oh wow. It was even better than she remembered. Her memories, her knowledge of him, the love they'd shared; all of that combined with the physical sensation to make the most amazing, wonderful kiss she could ever remember.

The kiss went on for a long time until Lily felt something bang against her leg and pulled away slightly to look down.

'Oh my goodness,' she said. 'The tide. Your trousers. My dress. Our shoes.'

Matt looked down. 'Woah. Where *are* our shoes?'

'Floating. One just bumped against my leg. I think it's over there now.' She pointed a few feet away.

Matt pulled his phone out, put the torch on and scanned around them. 'Look at that.' He pointed too. All four shoes were floating out to sea, quite close together.

'Sweet. Like a little shoe family on a day out at the beach.' Lily hitched her dress up and started to wade. 'Might as well see if we can rescue them.'

'Given how wet we already are,' Matt said, when they'd retrieved the shoes and were standing out of reach of the water, 'I'm thinking what about a moonlit dip?'

Lily felt a slow smile spread across her face. 'You're on.'

'Cool. I'm going in in my trunks. Too conservative to either ruin my entire suit for no good reason or skinny dip.' Matt shrugged out of his jacket and began to undo his shirt buttons and Lily felt her mouth go dry as he moved in front of her in the dim moonlight. There was something incredibly erotic about it, like he was stripping just for her in the near-darkness. She could make out the planes of his chest and abdomen, hear the gentle lapping of the water, smell the salt. Just the two of them, and the sea.

His face was in shadow, but she was pretty sure that he was watching her watching him.

And then he broke the spell.

'I'm going in. You coming?' He took a few steps into the water and then turned to face her.

'Totally coming.' Although, eek, now she was going to have

to strip to her underwear in front of him. Or completely ruin her dress.

Underwear. It was dark and it was only like wearing a bikini and she could run straight into the sea.

'Eurmph,' she said a good minute later, her arms *really* aching from the effort of trying to wind them further round her body than they could feasibly go. 'Can't reach my zip.'

'Let me.' Matt walked back towards her, shaking water from his hands. He moved behind her and, moving her hair gently out of the way, pulled the zipper down, his fingers brushing the skin on her back as he did it. Lily really hoped he couldn't feel or see her sudden goosebumps. 'I think that's done,' he said, his voice hoarse now.

'Great!' Lily's voice was the opposite of hoarse, very squeaky. She took a couple of steps away from him, stepped out of the dress and laid it carefully on a rock. And then stood up. He was looking at her, wearing just those very snug, soaking wet trunks, and a little smile. Oh. God. He stretched out a hand to her and Lily panicked.

She ignored his hand and said, 'I'm going straight in,' and ran towards the water. 'Woah,' she shrieked as it reached her thighs. 'It's a lot colder at night.'

'We'll warm up soon,' said Matt from just behind her.

Lily turned round and looked at him, and he grinned at her and splashed water on her shoulders.

'Cooooold,' she screamed and whacked her hands down really hard just in front of him for a mega splash.

And then he splashed her again and she splashed him back, and then he nudged her and she nudged him and then suddenly they were kissing and their torsos and limbs were moulded together and their hands were everywhere and it was the most gorgeous, erotic, urgent near-love-making experience Lily could remember in a long time. Maybe ever.

And... They weren't alone. There was definitely some noise. Some people talking.

'Who's that?' A couple of men were yelling from the beach. 'Matt?'

'Eek.' Lily let go of him and ducked down into the water. 'I'm in my underwear.'

'Busy right now,' Matt called, moving her round so that he had his back to the shore, shielding her from view.

'Got you. Have a good one, mate.'

Lily and Matt both stayed frozen where they were while the sounds of the men's footsteps and voices disappeared into the distance.

'Honestly—' Lily began to giggle '—I can't actually believe what we've done in one day. Mud and now this.'

'I know,' Matt said. He wasn't laughing, though, and he was letting go of her and taking a step back. And his voice had changed. The warmth, desire, loveliness that had been there minutes before had dissipated.

Lily stared through the moonlit night into his face as she swallowed the remainder of her laughter, trying to work out what had suddenly changed.

'Lily, I'm so sorry. I... I actually can't do this. That was amazing but I need to stop now. I'm going to be honest with you. You broke my heart eight years ago. I've never fully known why we split up. I've always felt that I wanted to understand properly, for closure, but I don't know any more whether I even want to have that conversation, because after spending today with you I think I'm going to struggle to move on again. I'm hurt that when we were together you didn't tell me about your severe childhood asthma and any ongoing issues, although obviously I would never want you to talk to me about anything if you didn't feel comfortable. I suppose I'm hurt that you didn't feel comfortable with me. I'm hurt that you didn't explain properly to me why you wanted to split. And I'm angry that I'm still hurt about any of that because it should all be so spectacularly in the past. So I'm really sorry for suggesting that we swim and then going back on it but if it's alright with you I'd really like to leave now.'

'Of course.'

It felt like she'd just been punched in the stomach. Like all the air had just gone out of her and she couldn't think. It was awful that she'd hurt him so much. And awful that she'd been so hurt herself, when she'd heard about his marriage. Everything he'd just said made total sense. Of course they should stop. Except... That kiss had been breathtaking. And they'd always been so good together.

For a mad moment she was tempted to launch herself at him, wind her arms round his neck, start kissing him again, press her body to his. And... no. He'd made it very clear that he didn't want to do anything.

They waded out of the water in their soaking underwear, both staring straight ahead, only a couple of feet away from each other physically, but miles apart in every other way.

When they got back to where they'd left their clothes, they both, without saying a word, turned their back on the other to get themselves dressed.

Lily found herself wrestling with her thoughts as well as her dress. Of course Matt was right to have stopped them. But knowing that didn't stop her *really* wishing that they *had* carried on. It had been *so good.*

And she just couldn't get her dress back on by herself. She was too wet and shivery and it had been quite hard to get into in the first place.

In the end, she hung it round her neck, to cover her front, and said, 'Ready,' in her best I-really-don't-mind-about-what-just-happened voice. Hopefully she wouldn't bump into anybody on the walk back to her hotel.

'Take my jacket.' Matt handed it to her without meeting her

eye. 'You really can't walk around like that. That underwear's very see-through.' Good to know. 'Plus, you're shivering.' He had his shirt on over his trunks and was holding his trousers and shoes in his hand. If he hadn't had such gorgeously solid thighs, the shirt would have been just about long enough to make him look decent, but as it was, he just looked *sinfully* sexy and not at all properly covered up. Lily wanted to cry. 'I'm going to walk you to your hotel room and you can hand the jacket round the door to me once you're inside.'

Because obviously they weren't going to be seeing each other again for her to hand the jacket back another time.

God. Now she could feel actual tears forming.

They trudged up the beach and along the pavement, staying several feet apart, not speaking. So different from their soaking wet walk this morning when it had felt like they were together. So sad.

Lily glanced at Matt a couple of times. He wasn't looking in her direction at all. His profile looked very stern.

A tear dribbled down her cheek and she felt a wave of misery wash up her from toes to head, leaving her even colder. She couldn't bear to say goodbye to Matt like this. Not again. They should talk now. She should explain to him why from her side she'd felt they had to end their relationship.

And while they were talking, she could ask about his marriage in case he was willing to tell her. It turned out she really wanted to know. She wanted to be able to remember the wonderful times they'd had together without them being tainted by the thought that he just couldn't have loved her that much.

She cleared her throat. 'I think we should talk so that I can explain exactly why I thought we should split up. If you'd like me to explain?'

Matt said nothing for a moment and then said, sounding

unutterably weary, 'I don't want you to feel that you have to talk about something you don't want to talk about.'

'No, really, it's okay. I'm sorry I didn't tell you before. I just couldn't. I'd like to now, if you'd still like to hear.'

'If you're sure, then, yes, I'd like to hear what you have to say.'

They stopped under a palm tree and turned to face each other.

Lily began to gather her thoughts together, and then saw beyond Matt a group of men weaving their way along the road. 'Would you like to come back to my room and talk there?' she asked, indicating the men with her head. 'For privacy.'

Matt glanced at the men and nodded. 'Probably best, if you're okay with that.'

Lily opened the hotel's front door with the key the receptionist had given her earlier in the day and they tiptoed through the lobby and up to her room. She switched the light on and nearly screamed at the sight of herself in the floor-length mirror on the wall opposite. Matt's jacket didn't cover her as well as she'd thought.

'I might just go into the bathroom and get changed,' she said, grabbing dry underwear and shorts and a top on her way.

Matt had himself back in his trousers by the time Lily came out of the bathroom, his shirt loose over the top. His expression was very serious and he seemed so distant and looked so handsome that she just wanted to cry.

FOURTEEN

MATT

'Shall we sit down?' Lily gestured at the single armchair in the corner of the room and sat down on the bed, in a cross-legged position, like she had when they were folding scarves.

'Great, thanks.' It felt a little rude to take the only chair but he was hardly going to sit on her bed, and he didn't want to stand and loom over her.

'Cup of tea?'

'No thanks, I'm good. Actually, a glass of water would be great.'

'Of course.' Lily stood up and Matt looked at his feet while she poured the water for him. If he looked *at* her, he might almost cry at the sadness of it all.

She handed the glass to him, poured one for herself and said, 'So. Straight to it. I never told you a lot about my childhood and that's because I've hardly ever talked about it to anyone, and that's because I was quite friendless as a child and I reinvented myself when I went to uni and I didn't want to go back to being the person I was. Basically, as you now know, I had very severe asthma as a child and got admitted to hospital a lot with life-threatening breathing episodes. My parents worked very long hours and didn't want to take time off work to look after me, so my granny essentially brought me up. I lived with my parents but my granny lived just round the corner and in practice she was the one who was always there so really it was like I lived with her. My parents obviously do love me, I don't want to imply that they don't; just being a stay-at-home parent wasn't for either of them, and I did need a lot of care because I had to miss a lot of school.'

She paused and took a sip of her water. 'My dad coped better than my mum. She spent a *lot* of time talking about my health, and there were a lot of things that I wasn't allowed to do, because they made me ill, and it ended up that the health thing kind of defined both of us. Like, she has this amazing, very high-powered job as a consultant gynaecologist in a hospital, and I'm obviously me, a person with other characteristics, but we just became the ill child and the mother of the ill child, and that was all anyone talked about in relation to either of us. And I didn't really have any friends and the only fun I had was with my granny.'

'I'm sorry.'

'No, no.' She waved her arm, like she was pushing his *sorry* away. 'I don't want sympathy. I didn't have a bad childhood. I mean, no one enjoys having severe asthma, but I was very well looked after. And I had a *great* time with my granny. And some good times with my parents when they weren't being anxious about my health. I just *hated* being the subject of all the sympathy and compassion and pity. I just wanted to be like everyone else. And while I was at school, living with my parents, I couldn't be. So when I went to uni, I decided not to tell anyone about any of that, and I've barely ever confided in anyone about any proper weaknesses really, just surface stuff, and my new identity became like I'm the one who supports others. I rarely confide deep stuff in people. I just say I'm okay. I mean, really, you could say that hardly anyone knows the real me.'

'When you say "hardly anyone"...?' The question sounded pathetic but having started down this route, he should finish, for closure.

Lily looked down and then back up at him. 'I told Tess, Aaliyah and Meg about my childhood during my first-year uni exams when my dad had a heart attack and I got really stressed. And they've been fab and they're there when I need them but without being too in my face. Like they know that I'll say when I'm upset but then I don't really want to talk too much about things.'

'Oh.' Yeah. When he thought about it, of course she'd always been closer to her girlfriends than she had to him. And that really did hurt. It was also food for thought. Maybe they'd been more sensitive to her needs than he had. Yeah, they probably had. He put his hands over his face for a second, suddenly incredibly tired, and then focused again on Lily. 'I'm glad they were there for you.'

Lily blinked hard, like she was trying to get rid of tears. 'I didn't mean to say that you weren't there for me. I know you were. Would have been if I'd let you in. Sorry.'

'No. Please don't apologise. If anyone should, it's me.'

'No. You shouldn't have to apologise either. I suppose it was just a function of us not having the time to get to know each other well enough. No one's fault. I wanted to explain about my childhood to you. I really wanted to. I was planning to. But we never spent enough time together. It isn't the kind of conversation you can just have out of nowhere. The day that we split up, I was planning to. We were going to have a lot of time together then. But then you got called away again for work.'

Matt nodded slowly. That actually made sense. He'd been away for work a lot at that time – still was – and she'd been working shifts at the hospital. And, yes, if you had something big to say and you weren't someone who liked to talk about your feelings, of course you wouldn't just blurt it out in five snatched minutes alone.

Thinking about what he'd seen of her this week, he said, 'If you don't mind me saying, you actually still hold back a fair amount with your friends too, don't you? Like you'll "confide" in people that you hate your new hairstyle, but you won't really tell anyone if you're hurt that Tess apparently cared more about her wedding photos than your feelings. I should have seen that before. But you're *good*; you talk a lot, but not too much, and a lot of people think they know you really well. And we don't.'

She actually flinched at his words, which really didn't make him feel good.

'Yeah, doesn't sound so nice when you summarise it like that.' She looked him straight in the eye. 'That's me, though. And that's it. That's why we couldn't be together. Because you're very open, you genuinely do talk through your feelings, I think, and I realised when my granny died and I couldn't talk to you about how I was feeling that ultimately it wouldn't work between us. We just didn't have enough time together to build a strong enough foundation for our relationship. I can't see anything that could have changed that.'

'But we're talking now.' Even more pathetic. Almost slightly pleading.

'Well, we talked before. We just didn't *talk* talk. I wouldn't say we're *talk* talking now either. We're just talking about why we – I – never *did* manage to *talk* talk.'

'Isn't this the first step towards two people becoming really close, though? Explaining things in their pasts that really affected them? And how they don't want to talk too much about things that have upset them? And the other person understanding that.'

'Right now, I'm just giving you some details about my childhood. If I was really hurting about something, I might tell you but I wouldn't want to spend the whole night talking about it because then I'd feel like I'd flipped straight back into the ill child or the unpopular unable-to-join-in-with-stuff child and that I wouldn't be the person you fell in love with any more.'

'You'll always be the person I fell in love with.' He didn't feel at all pathetic now. He felt like he was fighting for Lily. He put his glass down, moved forward and held his hands out to her. 'I fell in love with your kindness, your humour, your lovely smile. All you.'

She didn't move to take his hands. 'If something bad happened to both of us, which does happen to couples in a life-time together, I don't think we could deal with it similarly enough. I think it would drive a wedge between us. I think the way my grandmother and mother dealt so differently with my health drove a wedge between them, and they were mother and daughter.'

He looked at his outstretched hands and let them fall. Was she right? He wasn't sure. He did know that it seemed like he wasn't going to get through to her right now, like the fight he'd felt he was starting was already lost.

And that was probably for the best. What had he been thinking, actually? It wasn't like they were going to reignite their relationship eight years on. It would be madness. He didn't want to get hurt like that again. If he ever met another serious partner, he'd obviously like it to be someone who wouldn't sleep with the roofer, but probably also someone who'd want to share the important stuff with him rather than dealing with it alone and not split up with him for unspecified reasons, which turned out to be, in many ways, just due to them not having been in the same place at the same time enough.

He nodded. 'Maybe you're right.' It felt like this conversation was over. God. So deeply sad.

They sat in silence for a few moments and then – so

suddenly that he almost jumped – Lily said, 'I have a question for you.'

'Go ahead.'

'I really believed that you loved me.' Not really a question.

'I did.' He *still* did, if he was honest, although it was irrelevant. If there was one thing Lily and Gemma between them had taught him, it was that love was not enough on its own.

'I never understood how you could meet someone else that you loved enough to marry so soon after splitting up with someone you loved. Or said you did. And I really thought you did. Kind of still think you did. I mean, I know you could totally meet two people you could fall in love with in very quick succession. So we should probably forget I asked. It just seemed odd, that's all.'

It felt like Lily was almost wanting to talk about her feelings after all.

'I'm sorry if it hurt you that I met Gemma so soon,' he said, trying to tread cautiously.

Not cautious enough; her face immediately closed.

'Oh, okay, yep,' she said. 'Right here we have a situation where you're kind of thinking that I'll admit to having been hurt and I don't want to admit it. I mean, yes, of course I was hurt. *Really* hurt. Like, not being able to take pleasure in *any*thing for a while level of hurt. But I didn't want to dwell on it, beyond saying to my friends that of course I was really upset but that it was momentary and I'd be fine, and I got through it, and I still don't want to talk about it. I don't want to be on the receiving end of sympathy. I wouldn't be *me* any more.'

God. He just wanted to scoop her up in his arms and hug her and hug her.

'Just so you know,' he said. 'I realised when my relationship with Gemma ended that I didn't love her like I love you. I probably leapt into the relationship because I was hurt and confused and bereft, and I was trying to shove you out of my mind.

Unconsciously, but I think that's what I was doing. And after we'd been married for four years I found her in bed with the builder who'd been replacing our kitchen roof. And quite quickly I discovered that the most heartbreaking thing about our divorce was having to share custody of Elmer, our dog. Whereas the most heartbreaking thing about splitting with you was, and remains... losing you.'

It was only when he'd finished speaking that he realised that he'd used the wrong tense. He'd said he still loved Lily. And also, that was the first time he'd articulated any of that out loud about his marriage. Because until now, it had been too hard to talk about it. Oh, okay. Maybe he and Lily weren't that different. Maybe with more life experience he'd have realised that she needed to cope with her bereavement any way she could, and if that involved not talking to him, he should have accepted that without question. He'd really let her down, actually.

'I...' he said, but Lily shook her head and said, 'Shhh. Please?'

After a long pause, he nodded. It was too late for them.

She looked at him for a long time, and then whispered, 'Thank you.'

She turned her face away and looked at the wall. When she looked back at him, he saw that she had tears rolling down both cheeks. Yeah, that was about how he felt too.

'I'm really glad we got to talk about all of this,' she whispered.

'Me too.'

She wiped her cheeks and stood up with another one of those fluid yoga movements.

Matt stood up too. It felt like a big effort. 'I should go.'

'Yep.' Lily moved over to the door and opened it.

When he got to the door, she stood on tiptoes and put her arms round his neck and pulled him into a fierce hug.

He held her tightly and buried his face in her hair for a long moment. God, he loved her scent.

This was almost certainly the last time he'd ever hold her.

'Goodbye,' she mumbled into his shoulder a few seconds later.

'Bye.' He could barely get the word out.

They let go of each other.

And she closed the door behind him.

He stood and stared at it. It was wooden and panelled, but modern.

He was pretty sure that image of the closed door would be imprinted in his memory forever.

God.

He'd always thought that if he'd known *why* they split up it maybe wouldn't have hurt so much. Not true as it turned out.

Part of him wanted to bang hard on the door and tell her that he loved her and he thought she might still love him and what else did you need in a relationship.

And the rest of him knew that that would be stupid and the best thing for him was to walk away and not get hurt again.

So he walked off along the corridor.

FIFTEEN

LILY

That *noise*. Bloody phone. Lily flung her arm out of bed and smacked the phone and the alarm stopped. Thank the Lord for that. She put her head under a pillow and went back to sleep. And then off the alarm went again. She smacked the phone again and then turned onto her back and peeled open her eyes. Eurgh. So gunky. She should really have taken her make-up off last night.

And, oh. Matt. She should really not have had that conversation with him. She didn't think he'd felt better afterwards and she definitely hadn't. She'd ended up crying for hours and not going to sleep until about 6 a.m.

What time was it now? She reached down to pick up her phone. Eleven thirty. Shit. She should really have set the alarm for a bit earlier.

She was going to have to be quick if she was going to be on time for her lunch meeting with Felix and Alfredo.

She took a quick look at her messages. Yesssss: Felix and Alfredo had overslept and would she mind meeting half an hour later. She would *adore* meeting half an hour later.

She had two messages from Aaliyah and now the meeting

was later she had time to read them before she finished packing her bags and checked out.

Goodbye, hun. Didn't bother going to bed – only stopped dancing for long enough for a quick shower and change in time to get myself on the first ferry. See you back in London. Can't wait to see my babies later!!!!!!!!!!!!!!!

OMG. Have you heard from Meg????? Call her!!!!!!!!!!!!!!!!!!!

And a missed call from Meg.

Lily pressed the button to call her back. Meg answered on the first ring.

'Lily, guess where I am?'

'Um? I don't know?'

'No, you have to guess.' Oh, for God's sake. Why did people do these stupid guessing games? It was rare that you could make any kind of a sensible guess. They were just a boring waste of time.

'On a ferry, at an airport or... I don't know, feeding goats in the hills.'

'I mean, what? Why would I tell you about my journey, and why would I be feeding goats?'

'I don't know,' Lily said. She did not need this right now.

'Take a sensible guess,' Meg instructed her. Really? They were still doing this?

Lily sighed. 'Okay. Um. You're in Pythagoras's restaurant because you've decided to do a Shirley Valentine.'

'Oh my God, you're *psychic*.'

'I'm what?' No *way*.

'We're at Pythagoras's mother's house and I'm meeting all the family for lunch and then I'm staying on for a few days and I'm going to do my classes over Zoom and then he's flying to Edinburgh with me and moving in with me. His cousin's going to look after the restaurant here. We're going to spend a year in Edinburgh together and then a year here and then we're going to work out where we want to live. I'm going to put you on video.'

'No, Meg, I'm...' In bed. Looking like shit.

And, oh, okay, there were literally dozens of people in the picture and Lily was going to upset Meg if she didn't switch to video.

She jumped out of bed and into the armchair – that Matt had been sitting in only a few hours ago – and tried to hold the phone at an angle so that she wasn't *too* visible.

'That's so exciting, Meg. And Pythagoras. I'm so pleased for you both.'

While Meg chatted and explained to the backdrop of Pythagoras's *large* family, and Lily exclaimed and congratulated, she couldn't help remembering that a few days ago she'd been thinking that of the four of them she was definitely negotiating their thirties the best.

But now, Tess was no longer a bridezilla but just a – very happy – bride, married to a lovely man who was very right for her. And Aaliyah was going to be much happier now that she had her new plans for her cleaner and working more. And Meg was going to be all loved up with Pythagoras.

While right now, Lily just felt really miserable.

She should really not have had the conversation with Matt. She'd been very happy with her life before this week.

It was a good thing that she wouldn't be seeing him again.

———

Three hours later, she sat back in her chair in the restaurant where she'd had lunch with Felix and Alfredo and said, 'So I'm really pleased with the progress we've made.'

'We definitely had way too many photos,' Alfredo said.

'I still think we should keep all the ones of the feather boa karaoke night,' Felix said. A little grumpily, actually.

'I think Lily's right, though. Hoarding isn't great.' Alfredo picked up the phone. 'Maybe we should delete some of these now.'

'I'm not ready for that.' Felix looked alarmingly tearful now. 'That was a *good* night.'

Lily took the phone out of Alfredo's hand. 'I'm sure we can come to a compromise. And we don't have to delete them all now. Why don't we just start with a few? The blurry ones to start off with. There were definitely a few blurry ones.'

'Yep, I'm up for binning the blur,' Alfredo said.

'I like the blur. It was a blurry evening. We were very drunk. It's like the photos are telling the story how it actually happened.' Felix had his mouth set in a very firm line.

For God's *sake*. Lily normally *loved* her photo curating work. But today, very over-tired and very over-sad, she wasn't totally in the mood for it. She could do with just crawling into a dark hole somewhere and spending another few hours sobbing her heart out over Matt.

'You know what—' she opened the phone's photo album again '—why don't we park those photos for a while and start with something easy. Yesterday's wedding. It's always easier to curate a collection of photos from something very recent because you haven't yet become ridiculously nostalgic.'

'Oh yes. I totally get that.' Felix was cheering up fast. 'Let's do it.'

And, oh no, Matt was in quite a lot of the photos, because he and Alfredo and a few other men had been hanging out together at the bar quite a lot of the evening. Lily didn't want to delete photos of Matt, she wanted to send them to her own phone and keep them. Clearly, she really shouldn't be preaching to other people about an excess of nostalgia.

Utterly, utterly ridiculous. She was a professional and she needed to remember that.

Half an hour later, after she'd watched and winced as Felix deleted several photos that included a *gorgeous*-looking Matt and had to restrain herself from *peering* at the photos to check out everything he'd been doing last night – God, it was like she was a *stalker* – she looked at her watch and said, 'I'm so sorry, I need to leave for my ferry over to Paros. I'm on a flight to Athens this evening and then straight to London tonight.'

'Same. Let's go together,' Felix said. 'I think we're the only ones travelling this evening. Most people either booked a holiday for the coming week or went back early this morning.'

———

There were a surprisingly large number of people at the little ferry terminal when the three of them pitched up with all their cases in tow. And no ferry. That would be why there were so many people. The ferry was obviously late.

'I hope the ferry arrives soon.' Lily really didn't want to miss her flight. She looked around. 'It's amazing how many people can fit in one smallish ferry. Like, you'd never think all these people could squeeze inside one of those boats we came on, would you?'

'I actually don't think they *could*.' Alfredo was looking around too, and frowning. 'I'm getting a bad feeling. About the ferry. Look at everyone's body language. There's way too much gesturing and surprise going on.'

'I think you're right.' Lily pointed to where a sunburned man in a tight t-shirt and Hawaiian shorts had his face right up close to an official-looking man and was yelling. 'The ferry must have been cancelled. I wonder what time the next one is and whether we'll be able to get on it.'

'Why don't you wait here with the bags while I go and ask

someone.' Alfredo set off towards the crowd and Lily and Felix pulled all the bags into the shade.

'We should check whether our flights are flexible and whether we're insured for things like this.' Felix pulled out his phone as Lily sank onto her suitcase, blinking back tears.

She shouldn't cry; people's travel plans got disrupted all the time. This would be *fine*. It was the lack of sleep and the all-pervasive sadness about Matt that were making her react like this.

She shook her head, sniffed and said, 'Right, so I'm going to check the time of the next ferry and then I'm thinking we should maybe see if we can check back into our hotels, fast, in case we can't get off the island tonight and there's a rush on rooms.'

'Good point.' Felix was swiping. 'I think we should be okay ticket-wise. Have you found yours?'

'Just trawling through my emails now.' Lily found the right one and began to read. Wow. Did they make the small print this complicated on purpose? Even with a full night's sleep and no misery she'd be struggling to interpret all these clauses.

'Okay. You read about your ticket and I'll start calling round hotels.'

Lily had just begun to re-read everything from the start – reading the terms and conditions was one of those situations where you knew all the individual words, or most of them, anyway, but put them together and they could have been Greek – when a pair of tanned leather-thonged feet came to a stop in front of her. Alfredo's.

'It's worse than we thought unfortunately,' he said. 'There's a strike. As in, no ferries at all until the strike stops.'

'Ferry *strike*?' Lily parroted. Nightmare.

'Total disaster,' Felix said. 'We're going to be sleeping on the beach like teenage interrailers. I've been phoning around and all the rooms on the island seem to have been taken by the tourists who arrived this morning, obviously before the strike struck. Saturday's the big swapover day for accommodation.'

'Fortunately,' Alfredo said, 'I bumped into Matt down on the quay.'

Lily looked up and behind Alfredo. And, yes, there was Matt. She couldn't believe she hadn't noticed him there before. She'd obviously been too blindsided by the strike news. *Fortunate* wasn't the word she would have used to describe bumping into him.

He was standing looking down at her, his face completely blank. Why hadn't he left when everyone else did? Carole had said something about him staying with her and Norm on Paros tonight. Why hadn't he already gone?

'Didn't realise you were staying on.' Felix stood up so Lily hauled herself up too.

'I'm not.' Matt turned his eyes from Lily to Felix and smiled briefly. 'I spent the day here doing some work looking at a couple of properties on the island, and now I'm going over to Paros to stay with my aunt Carole. I've just spoken to her, and her husband's going to pick me up in their boat. There's space for the three of you and you might be better off coming with me in case the strike goes on for a while because the only way off Antiparos is by boat.'

'I've already told Matt that I'm pretty sure you'll be with me in agreeing that we'd definitely like a lift,' Alfredo told Felix.

Lily really didn't want to get a lift anywhere with Matt. Spending any more time with him would be too heartbreaking. She didn't want to see him again for a very long time, so that she could lick her wounds, forget all about him and get back to her normal happy state.

'That would be *great*.' Felix took Matt's hand and pumped it up and down.

The men all turned to look at Lily. She'd be mad not to accept the offer. She needed to get home and there'd be flights off Paros, plus it would be easier to find somewhere to stay tonight on a bigger island. And what excuse could she give for not joining them? Okay. Fine. It was just a short boat trip, and there'd be Felix, Alfredo and Norm as well as Matt.

'Great,' she said. 'Thank you so much.'

Matt looked at his watch. 'Norm'll be here in about an hour.' Okay, so there was no way they'd make a flight off Paros this evening in time to get their flights out of Athens. Lucky it looked like her flights could be changed with only a small extra payment. She'd have to find a hotel on Paros.

'I'm thinking an afternoon cocktail and a game of cards,' Felix said. 'Quick, before the bars get over-run by angry stranded tourists.'

'Unbelievable.' Alfredo rolled his eyes, smiling. 'He's *obsessed* with contract whist at the moment.'

Matt looked at Lily and Lily looked at Matt.

'I might actually take the opportunity to do a bit more work,' Matt said. 'Got a lot on.'

Felix narrowed his eyes. 'Are you saying you don't like playing whist?'

Matt laughed. 'I love whist, just genuinely quite busy with work. Doing some stuff for Carole and after visiting a couple of properties here on the island this afternoon I've had a few ideas that I'd like to act on.'

'What about you join us at the same café, we treat you to a huge drink as a very small thank you for saving our bacon with the boat, and you sit in a corner and do your work while we play God's own card game at a different table. And then you can join us when you get bored with your boring work,' Felix said. 'And in the meantime I promise we won't speak to you.'

Matt glanced quickly at Lily, hesitated and then said, 'Sounds like a plan. Although no thanks due.'

. . .

'I'm not surprised you love this game,' Lily told Felix after their third round of whist. 'You're amazing. It's like you're a mind reader.'

'I actually am,' he said. 'I *know* what you're going to play. I *know* how the cards are going to go.'

Lily laughed and took another sip of her mojito. Felix and Alfredo were such good company and the game was genuinely so addictive that she was almost managing not to be conscious the entire time of Matt in the corner with his long legs stretched to the side of his table, the pen he was holding looking tiny in his large, square-fingered hand, his capable fore-arms, dusted with just the right amount of dark hair, resting on the table...

And, woah.

'Lily?' Felix had worked his face in front of hers. 'You're not concentrating, my darling. You need to focus. Still recovering from last night?'

'Yes, exactly, still recovering. I'm very tired. Struggling to stay awake. Exactly.' Not because of Matt at all.

Halfway through their next round, which Lily was sure she was actually going to win, Matt stood up and said, 'Norm just called. He's setting off in a minute, so if we begin to make our way down to the harbour we should get there at about the right time. The crossing's pretty quick, isn't it? Ten minutes?'

'Do we have time to finish this round very quickly?' Lily asked.

'I reckon we do.' Alfredo placed the ace of hearts very deliberately in the middle of the table and Lily and Felix both gasped.

'No way. I was *convinced* I was going to win that one.' Lily put her king of hearts down on top of the ace and stuck her tongue out at Alfredo when he laughed.

'See?' Felix sucked the last drops out of his cocktail glass with his straw. 'It's addictive, isn't it? If we get stranded on Paros at least we'll have cards to keep us happy.'

The walk down to the harbour was similar torture-wise to sitting a few feet away from Matt in the café. Lily walked with Felix, and Matt and Alfredo walked behind them, and Lily *really* wondered, the whole way, whether Matt was watching her.

They were at the harbour in time to see Norm arrive in a medium-sized, very swanky-looking, sparkling white yacht. As he pulled in, he adjusted the cap he was wearing to a very jaunty angle and shouted, 'Ahoy there, me hearties.'

'He been on the booze, do you think?' Felix said.

'Think he might just be enjoying his afternoon out,' Matt said.

'Let's put all the luggage down here,' Norm said, when they were all on board, and led them down the steps in the middle of the deck into what could only be described as a very James Bond-esque black and chocolate-brown suede, leather and marble interior.

'Wow.' Lily looked round, almost expecting to see some scantily clad female spies emerging from behind the banquettes.

'It's my man cave,' said Norm, beaming. He pressed a button and a box full of cigars on the table sprang open. 'It's my equivalent of a garden shed. Everyone needs a little escape from their wife. No offence, Lily, not that you *are* a wife. Yet.'

'Wow again.' Lily didn't have any other words.

'Smoke?' Norm asked them all, pointing at the cigars. 'What, none of you? What's wrong with your generation? All namby-pamby, worrying about your lungs.' He broke into a massive coughing fit and bent double for a few moments, and then said, 'Right, let's get going. You're not going to be able to get on a flight this evening so I'll take you a scenic route. Gives us a break from Carole as well.'

They all looked at each other. It didn't actually sound like he was joking.

'Great,' said Matt eventually.

Norm turned to a glossy wooden drinks cabinet. 'If you won't have a cigar, can I at least give you a whisky or glass of champagne for the trip?'

'This is the life,' said Alfredo. The four of them, all clutching drinks and all wearing shades and their hair pleasantly wind-blown, were sitting around the edge of the deck, while Norm was at the helm.

Matt nodded. 'It's amazing.'

Lily wanted to scream. She didn't want to be here with him, finding him this attractive. She wanted to be on her way home, licking what now felt like very deep wounds, about to never see him again. Once she'd thrown herself into work for a few days, she'd get over seeing him again very quickly. Like, Felix and Alfredo had been a great distraction this afternoon. She just needed other distractions.

'Can I just say?' Felix did a circling motion round his face in Lily's direction. 'You're looking particularly gorgeous. It really suits you having a tan.'

'Thank you.' Lily smiled at Felix and looked up, sure that Matt's eyes were on her. Yep, they were, and his lips were twitching. She *loved* that he always saw the ridiculous in things, and that he had zero ability to remain aloof. And she *hated* that she loved so much about his personality.

Matt mouthed, 'Mud?' and she nodded, and he snorted with laughter. And she got goosebumps literally just at the sound. She really did just need this trip, beautifully scenic as it was, to be over, so that she could walk away from the heartbreak of Matt.

'I forgot to say,' Norm shouted over. 'You're obviously all stuck on Paros for tonight at least and Carole's expecting you to stay with us.'

What? No.

'Are you absolutely sure?' Felix asked.

'Yes, yes.' Norm nudged the helm and the boat turned slightly. 'Loads of spare room and Carole adores hosting. As do I, of course. You're more than welcome. Which is another way of saying if you don't agree Carole will nag you half to death, so you might as well give in now. We'll make a night of it.'

'That's great. Very kind. Thank you so much,' said Alfredo.

Lily looked at Matt, who was staring over the side of the boat somewhere into the distance, and said, 'Thank you so much but I couldn't possibly. I'll find somewhere else to stay.'

'Not sure you will,' said Norm. 'The island's chocker with tourists; never seen it so busy. We got a lot of arrivals this morning and not everyone whose holiday had finished managed to leave. So I doubt you'll find anywhere unless you have about five thousand euros to drop on a very high-end hotel and even those might be at full capacity this weekend. One of the busiest weeks of the year already.'

'So kind,' Lily repeated, 'but I'm sure I can squeeze in somewhere else and I'll probably have an early start tomorrow.' Spending an evening and night under the same roof as Matt really wouldn't help her frame of mind.

She felt her phone vibrate inside her bag and took a quick look in case it was something important. It was Aaliyah texting.

Just landed at Heathrow. Going to see the kids in a minute!!! Oh yeah, and Patrick :) I saw on the news there's a ferry strike I just missed – did you get caught???

Yes I did. Going to have to stay until tomorrow. On Norm's boat right now with Felix and Alfredo and Matt. Norm says Carole wants us all to stay with them!!!

Love Felix and Alfredo – danced with them last night. But OMG. You okay being with Matt??

Totally fine. Not going to stay there tonight. Can't face spending so much time with Matt. Had a really bad conversation with him last night.

Lily was too miserable not to moan to Aaliyah.

Oh my love. So sorry. Will call later. At the carousel now – witch next to me trying to elbow me out of way – will call as soon as I can. Good luck!!!!! Love youuuuuu

Thank you!

Lily added some heart emojis, pressed Send, put her phone down and looked over at Matt, who was still staring into the distance.

Norm steered the boat parallel to Paros, and Lily sighed and looked out of the opposite side of the boat from Matt. At least the scenery *was* amazing so it would look completely normal for both of them to be staring at it for the rest of the journey.

'Helloooooo,' called Carole when they eventually moored on Paros. 'That took a long time, Norm. What were you playing at? Sorry to hear you've all missed your flights tonight but your loss is our gain. We're so pleased to be having you to stay.'

'Oh, I don't think...' Lily began.

'Don't think what?' Carole drew her into a big hug. 'I hope you aren't going to blow me out. You won't find anywhere nice to stay and I need another woman with all these gorgeous men around.' She pinched Felix's bottom and he play-smacked her back. There was no way Lily could politely turn the invitation down.

'Okay, yes, of course. I'd love to. So kind of you.' Lily hugged Carole back. 'Thank you so much.'

She could see Matt over Carole's shoulder, looking his usual tall, dark, handsome self, but a lot more uncomfortable than he usually did.

SIXTEEN

MATT

'Penny for them?' Carole gave Matt an almighty nudge and – totally unprepared for it – he almost staggered. She'd be excellent in a boxing ring. 'You're glowering into the distance like some kind of nineteenth-century brooding hero. What's up?'

'Nothing's up.' Matt tried really hard to drop any glower and smile instead.

'Now you look like you're in pain.'

'Just still a bit hungover from last night,' he said. How was Lily reacting to Carole pointing out that he looked seriously miserable? Was she feeling equally low? And why *was* he so down actually? It was one more evening in Lily's company, and they weren't going to be alone, so there'd be no more one-on-one chat to remind him how sad it was that they wouldn't ever be together. And then tomorrow morning they should all be able to get themselves on either ferries or flights to Athens. So it was just a delay of one night, and then that would be that. He could go back to his Lily-less life, which he *liked*, and forget about her, with closure this time. She was absolutely right: they weren't right for each other. He felt his brows draw into a frown again.

'You *do* look like a brooding hero.' Felix waggled his

eyebrows and pursed his lips in Matt's direction, which did genuinely make Matt smile. A bit. Hard to smile a *lot* with Lily standing there staring out to sea like the completely featureless horizon was *the* most interesting sight ever.

'Cheer up.' Carole nudged Matt again.

'Leave him alone,' Norm said. 'He's probably just irritated that you're nagging him. I know how he feels.'

'Do you *mind?*' Carole turned a glower of her own on Norm.

Lily still had her face – the part visible beneath her sunglasses expressionless – firmly turned in the direction of the horizon.

'Come on.' Norm picked up two of the cases that were scattered at their feet and set off towards Carole's jeep.

When they had all the cases in the back of the jeep, Norm and Lily squished in together on the long front seat next to Carole, and Matt, Felix and Alfredo got in the back.

'This likely to be a nightmare for you, Matt?' Alfredo asked. 'Workwise?'

'No, all good,' Matt said. 'I have a flight out of Athens tomorrow evening anyway, with a flexible ticket, and I'm lucky enough to be my own boss, so the only demanding people I have to deal with are my clients, plus there's a fair amount I can do remotely, so even if I have to stay a day or two longer, it'll be fine.'

'Oh, okay.' Alfredo's voice was inflected like he was surprised. Oh, right. That would be the whole glowering thing Carole had accused Matt of. That he probably had been doing, if he was honest.

'If I was looking a little unenthusiastic back there,' Matt said, 'it was just the hangover thing. Still a bit dehydrated from last night.'

'You really are a lightweight.' Felix shook his head. 'We were there for hours longer than you, and we're fine. I'm going to boast here. We're hardcore. A group of us were dancing until the sun came up. Your friend Aaliyah was there the whole time, Lily. With a sprained ankle, as well, like *nothing* was stopping her.'

'Oh yes,' Lily said. 'She was making the most of her last child-free night. She has three kids. I texted her earlier. She loved you guys.'

'Well, who wouldn't?' Felix said. 'We loved her too. You should have stayed too, Lily.'

'I know I should have done.' Lily half-turned, so that she was facing towards Felix and Alfredo, with her back to Matt. 'Sounded like so much fun.' Matt was pleased she hadn't stayed dancing with the others. It had been depressing but good for him – he was pretty sure – having their conversation. To draw a line under things.

'So, Lily, how are you fixed workwise over the next couple of days? Were you supposed to be doing any shifts at the hospital or were you going to be doing photo curation?' Alfredo asked.

'I'm not working at the hospital until Wednesday. I was going to be doing some curating work but I can work anywhere with good Wi-Fi if I'm not meeting with clients in person, so I'm okay to stay until Monday if necessary.'

'So I had an ulterior motive in asking that,' Alfredo said. 'Can we sneak in some extra curating while we're here?'

'Still not getting rid of the feather boa photos,' Felix said.

Lily and Alfredo both laughed and then Lily said, 'You know, I totally know what you mean. I do think you should prune your photo collection so that you enjoy what you do have and just, you know, the whole clutter thing; it isn't good for you. But I do agree that it's soooo hard parting with certain things. And not just blurry photos of great nights. Like I have this skirt that I used to wear a lot in my big clubbing days and, honestly, there's no way I could get into it now and even if I could I'd just be *way* too self-conscious to wear it because it's *so* short, but I still can't get rid of it because of the memories.'

'I'd like to say that that's why Alfredo still wears clothes he bought fifteen years ago,' said Felix, 'but actually I think he just hates shopping.'

Alfredo shook his head. 'No, I'm just wise. You find a look that suits you, you should stick with it. And I'm doing the environment a favour too.'

'You're basically a clothing angel.' Lily smiled at him.

Before long, Felix was telling Lily all about the end of his last relationship before Alfredo and how Alfredo had pulled him back from the edge, emotionally, and Matt *knew* that soon – almost in return – she'd tell him lots of amusing personal – but not actually emotional – anecdotes. As in, this was morphing into another one of Lily's close friendships where, if you *knew*, and you thought about it, which he clearly never had done in the past, you could see that, yes, she wasn't giving much at all away about herself while Felix was. And that relationship could and would work very well for both of them, unless Lily ever *needed* to talk and then felt she couldn't. Although, of course, she had her three best friends.

It was like she painted a picture of the person she wanted everyone to think she was, with her childhood and miseries erased or hidden.

Which didn't make him love her any less. The picture she painted was a lovely picture and she made everyone around her happy. And she was a great friend. He hoped *she'd* be happy too.

She and Felix were sniggering about some very risqué jokes and Alfredo was beginning to laugh too, Carole was honking with laughter now, and even Norm was chuckling a little. *God*, Matt wished he and Lily could have worked things out. Except, they couldn't. And so this was torture.

'Do you know what I'm thinking?' Carole went very late

into a corner and they all lurched to the left. 'I'm thinking *party* tonight,' she continued when the car had righted itself and they'd all stopped squawking in terror. 'I already had a little gathering planned, but we'll get a few more of the neighbours over, do a barbie, get the pool lit up and do some midnight dipping.'

'Ow,' Alfredo said.

'Sorry.' Matt had involuntarily jerked at the mention of midnight dipping – the memory of last night with Lily – and had jabbed Alfredo in the ribs with his elbow. 'I might have to give the party a miss, Carole. Bit tired.'

'You can sleep on your journey tomorrow.' Carole threw the car round another corner and they all lurched again. 'No-one's party-pooping at my house.'

Two hours later, after hiding – frankly – in his room under the guise of working, Matt was in the garden with the others, plus the 'few' – actually a good fifty – neighbours who Carole had invited over for what was already a raucous party.

They were all in the garden next to the very fancy infinity pool. The whole area was lit up with fairy lights wrapped around trees and bushes, and, seemingly from nowhere, Carole had magicked up several men – clearly assiduous gym-goers – in very tight t-shirts and jeans, who were weaving their way amongst the guests, plying them with very large bright-coloured cocktails and very small snacks.

Lily was with Felix and Alfredo in the middle of a group of other men and women their age, seemingly having a great time, laughing and chatting away.

And Matt basically had the option of joining them, or chatting to Carole and her friends, or Norm and his friends.

Lily's group looked a lot of fun.

Several of Carole's friends seemed to be in the Penelope camp when it came to men, and were all-out ogling the waiters.

And Norm's friends were in a huddle smoking cigars and, from what Matt could hear, moaning about everything from the weather (too hot, like if you chose to live on a Greek island you'd expect snow in July?) to the state of the local golf course (they'd changed things around and made the holes too hard plus there were too many women there now) to Brexit (some were for, some were against, but they all agreed it made it much harder to come by imports of British food you couldn't live without like Marmite and cream crackers and blue cheese).

Matt glanced over again and caught Lily's eye and simultaneously felt his breath catch and his stomach contract at the sight of her beautiful, laughing face. From which the laugh fell when she saw him looking at her.

He looked over at Carole, and one of her friends gave him an exaggerated wink and did a little shimmy with her nearly bare shoulders.

Norm's group it was.

Eventually, around midnight, the perfect escape excuse presented itself. Matt was now in a bigger group because Carole had brought her friends over to join Norm's. For the past half hour he'd been squeezed on a sunlounger between two of Carole's neighbours, both women in their sixties and both women who liked a younger man, it seemed.

'Time to swim.' One of Matt's sunlounger buddies stood up and wriggled her sundress down to display a remarkably tiny bikini before jumping straight into the pool.

She was followed by several of the others, at which point Matt said, 'Great idea. I'm just going to go and change into my trunks.'

He left, doing his best imitation of someone who really was going to get changed into swimming kit and come straight back, the cackles of various women telling him he was welcome to swim nude ringing in his ears.

And within ten minutes, he was in bed, trying to forget the sound of Lily's laugh that had carried to him on the still night air over everyone else's as he'd left, and trying to resist the temptation to sneak a look through the slats of his shutters at what she was doing. When he said *she*, he obviously meant *they*; it wasn't like he was *only* wondering about Lily. Oh, who was he kidding? It was a huge struggle not to obsess about her.

He was very much looking forward to leaving tomorrow.

————

The next morning, they were all up bright and early – or not so bright in the case of Felix in particular, who, in his words, had gone too large last night – to get themselves going on finding a way back to Athens airport for their London flights.

'I'll give you a lift,' Carole told them, still in her dressing gown. 'No rush. No one gets up at the crack of dawn on Paros, especially on Sundays.'

'Ferries are off for at least another couple of days. Maybe all week. Maybe a fortnight.' Norm was chomping away on toast and liberally applied Marmite, clearly not suffering as much from Brexit import issues as some of his friends. 'Better try the airport.'

'It won't be a problem.' Carole wasn't eating this morning; she and Felix were both just mainlining espressos. 'Don't let possible ferry strikes ever put you off visiting. Or any of your I'm sure very lovely friends when we have our holiday let business up and running. There are lots of flights to Athens. We'll have you sorted in a jiffy. Everyone ready to go in twenty minutes?'

'We're going to have the place to ourselves,' Carole told

them as they hurtled down the road to the airport just after eight.

And at quarter past eight this beautiful Sunday morning, the airport was... rammed.

About an hour after their arrival, they'd established that there was no way that they'd be getting on a flight today. Instead of partying last night – or skulking in a bedroom pretending to be getting changed into swim kit in Matt's case – they should have been here, queuing overnight for a flight. The commercial flights had already been fully booked – Matt knew that because he'd been unable to book one for today when he'd booked his Athens to London flight for this evening a couple of months ago, so he'd had to book himself on a ferry to Athens – and the private ones were also booked up.

'If we come back this evening we should be able to book one for tomorrow,' Alfredo said, after a final recce.

'Can we not book it now?' Lily asked.

'No. Apparently not. Something to do with schedules and aeroplanes being in the right place at the right time and the expected temperature of the tarmac, blah, blah, blah. Bottom line is there's no possibility of a flight today unless we have a friend with a private jet and even then there might not be space for them to take off, and we need to be back here at eight p.m.'

'D'you know what?' Carole said after they'd all finished grumbling. 'We should all look on this as a bonus holiday day together. We can have a lovely time. I'm going to organise some tourist things.'

It took a lot less than a second for Matt to work out that he'd be a lot happier if he avoided Lily as much as possible today. No point being reminded of everything he loved about her.

'Normally I'd love to join you,' he told Carole, 'but I have a ton of work to catch up on. So I'll probably just stay at the house and get on with that, if that's alright.'

'I'm pretty sure that I'm speaking for Alfredo too when I say that we'd adore to sightsee but I'm also wondering whether we should make hay while the sun shines and do some more photo curation with lovely Lily.' Felix slipped an arm round Alfredo's waist and Alfredo hooked an arm round Felix's shoulder and they leaned into each other; and Matt looked sideways at Lily and thought about all the times that they'd been just so *together*, like a solid unit, like Felix and Alfredo were. Although it had just been an illusion, hadn't it? He clenched his hands into fists to try to rein in his emotion. Once he and Lily had gone their separate ways, this would all feel a lot better.

He bloody hoped so, anyway.

'Okay, here's the plan.' Carole started herding them out of the airport building towards her car. 'You get on with your work, Matt, and you can all do your photo thing now for an hour or two, and then we'll gather at about noon for an outing, and then you can work again and then we'll come down here, organise the flights for tomorrow, and then we'll have a big end-of-holiday dinner tonight. And Lily, you need to talk me through this photo curating thing because I think I could find you a lot more clients.'

'Oh, wow, thank you so much. And that sounds like a lovely Sunday you have planned for us. So thoughtful. We're very spoilt.' Lily smiled at Carole, without making any eye contact with Matt, who was standing right next to his aunt.

'It does sound perfect.' Felix plonked a big kiss on Carole's cheek and Alfredo smiled at her.

And Matt said, 'Thank you so much, Auntie Carole, that sounds great,' because what else could he say? *No thanks, I just want to hide in my room and never see Lily again because right now it's like I can't actually cope with seeing her because I really love her but it's too late for us?* Nope.

'You're the biggest so you sit in the front with me, Matt,' Carole instructed, 'and the other three can squish up in the back.'

Lily and Felix talked and laughed incessantly all the way back to the villa, with Alfredo chucking in the occasional great one-liner. They were already planning to meet up in London, not just to finish the photo curation but for Felix and Lily to go to a singalong film screening and also fruit picking together (apparently Alfredo was a musical film philistine and also had no interest in jam making). At this rate, Lily would be a bridesmaid at *their* wedding, which apparently they were planning for a couple of years' time, because they wanted it to be perfect. Well, Felix did.

'An adorable groomzilla in the making,' Lily had said when Felix told her that, twinkling at him.

'Matt, what are you doing Saturday lunchtime?' Alfredo asked.

'Erm.' He'd hesitated too long. Always have a good excuse prepared.

'Perfect, sounds like you're around. You have to join us. You can help me stop Felix and Lily bursting into song every five minutes and trying to involve me in berry picking.'

'Great,' Matt said. For God's sake. He wasn't having lunch with Lily in London. He was going to be busy getting over her again. He'd have to remember to manufacture a good excuse for Saturday.

And they were back at the house. Matt was out of the car and striding towards the interior while the others were all still laughing about something.

An hour and a half and a little bit of progress on the guesthouse plans later, Carole hollered for them all to come and join her in her big reception hall.

'I have a big treat for you all,' she said. 'I'll tell you when we get there, but you need to be wearing trousers. Jeans are fine.

Off you go.' She clapped her hands. 'Quick as you can. You too, Norm.'

Norm scowled at her but trotted off with everyone else to get changed.

They reassembled fast, although not fast enough for Carole, who'd been doing a slow – and very loud – clap for the past couple of minutes, and she ushered them at a bit of a run into the car.

'We might be out for slightly longer than you were planning,' she shouted over their yelps as she threw the car round a hairpin bend, 'but it'll be worth it. You're going to have an amazing afternoon. I've brought lunch for us to eat en route.'

'En route where?' Matt was in the back with Felix and Alfredo again while Norm and Lily sat up front.

'Aha, *that's* the secret.' God. The last secret outing Carole had taken Matt on had involved a visit to a burlesque club that he hadn't totally enjoyed. Carole beamed at him over her shoulder and the car swung to the right and Lily grabbed the wheel and pushed it back in the opposite direction.

'Cheeky,' Carole said to Lily.

'Sorry,' Lily said. 'Just a reflex.'

Carole took her hand off the steering wheel to give Lily a hug and the car swung again, Lily shot a hand out and pushed the wheel back again, and Carole tutted again.

'So here we are,' Carole said a few minutes later.

'Riding!' they all exclaimed.

'That's right.' She pulled the handbrake on before the car had actually stopped and they were all flung forwards and then backwards. 'Sorry. Right. Here we go.'

They all got out of the car with varying degrees of enthusiasm and made their way into the stables.

'I'm not sure about this,' Norm said for about the seventeenth time as they got fitted with riding hats. His lower lip was actually trembling slightly.

'I'm sure it will be fine,' Matt told him. 'Really. They aren't going to put us on particularly feisty horses, I'm sure, and we'll have a guide.'

'I'm not so sure.' Norm really did look positively tearful now.

'You know what.' Lily moved closer from where she'd been standing a few feet away. 'I feel exactly the same way.'

'You do?' Norm gave the strap of his hat another tug. 'What if we fall off? Do these hats actually fit properly? People are very susceptible to broken bones at my age.'

'Honestly.' Lily lowered her voice. 'I hate horses. They're terrifying. They're so *big*.'

Matt stared at her. Did she think this was going to *help*?

'But I do get dragged out on rides from time to time,' she said, 'and, honestly, after I've pretty much wet myself each time, I end up going with it because, however much you want to say, "No, bugger off," to your friends, or your partner, or whoever, you kind of can't, so you *have* to go with it, and then, not joking, it's often okay. Like one minute you're thinking, "Oh my God, I'm going to *die*," and the next you're feeling kind of at one with nature and it's lovely. And also, on this particular ride, you're very, very lucky that I'm here, because I am truly, truly not a natural, and horses definitely sense that. I mean, it takes me a lot of attempts to get on. And then I'm stuck there rigid with fear, and yet wobbly, in a rigid way. And I've fallen off before now, which didn't hurt as much as I thought it would. And so on. You name an incompetent riding thing and I'll have done it. So, on the off chance that you aren't a *completely* competent rider, I'm here to keep you company.'

'That's very good to hear.' Norm nodded and looked like he was almost on the brink of smiling.

'So I'm thinking—' Lily lowered her voice further '—you

and me, at the back together. Worst comes to the worst, we can sneak off the horses and walk along leading them and if all the others are miles ahead of us it won't matter because we'll be together.'

'Lily, you're a wonderful young lady.'

'Thank you, Norm.' She smiled at him. 'You're pretty cool too. I love your yacht.' She widened her smile and Norm visibly puffed his chest out. 'So do we have a deal? You aren't going to ride off and leave me? You'll stay at the back with me?'

'Are you both alright?' Matt asked. 'Why don't I ride with you?' He hadn't been on a horse since he was a child, and that didn't count because someone had been leading it with a rope – riding had never really appealed – but how hard could it be? Much as he wanted to avoid Lily, it didn't feel right leaving her and Norm to panic at the back alone.

'That's really kind,' Lily said. 'I think we'll be okay.'

'It would be great if you kept an eye on us,' Norm said, 'but we don't want to ruin your experience. You go ahead.'

Matt fought an urge to laugh at Norm's brave-little-soldier demeanour.

Lily giggled and nudged Norm. 'You totally want to beg Matt to stay with us, don't you?' she said. 'We don't even know if he's any good on a horse. He might be worse than us. He might just be over-cocky.'

Norm laughed. Actually laughed. Lily was a miracle worker.

'Are you joking?' Matt said. 'I'm going to be amazing.'

'Have you ridden before?' Lily tipped her head to one side and raised her eyebrows.

'Not as such,' Matt said, 'but how hard can it be?'

'I'm thinking pride might come before a fall,' Lily said to Norm, and they both sniggered.

Pride didn't come before an actual fall but it did come before a less enjoyable experience than Matt had anticipated.

Carole was like some kind of genius horse whisperer. Felix and Alfredo went on regular riding holidays in Wales and Argentina, they said, and were pretty good. Lily wasn't as proficient as them but she was *way* better than she'd – as it turned out – been pretending to be to cheer up Norm, and Norm and Matt were both pretty shaky on horseback. In slightly different ways.

'It's going too fast,' Norm mumbled for about the twentieth time, while Matt said absolutely nothing at all, like he hadn't the whole time.

Since they'd set off, some time ago – it felt like a long time but in reality was probably well under half an hour, because the sun had barely moved round since then – he'd been fully focused on just trying to stay *on* the horse. He'd kind of thought he'd be *fine* at riding. Normally he had good balance. And he was fit. And he liked playing football. And tennis. And he was alright at them. So why was it so hard to sit on a horse? Well, it wasn't that hard. None of them had actually fallen off yet. But it just felt like he was going to fall off any minute. And that was not a good feeling.

'Stop,' Norm begged, as his horse broke into a little trot.

'Maybe pull on the reins,' Matt suggested. Good to know that his voice still worked.

Norm gave a little tug, nearly fell off and then shouted, 'It worked,' as his horse slowed down, and then the horse reared a little in shock, and Norm wobbled, a lot. Matt would definitely have laughed if he hadn't been sitting on a horse himself and therefore not finding anything at all funny.

'So, um, this is nice, isn't it?' said Lily, slowing down – literally, slowing her horse down, as in, she was actually in control of it – to wait for them.

'Not really,' Norm muttered.

'It's great.' Matt was getting better at multi-tasking talking and riding. 'Loving it.'

'You know.' Lily manoeuvred her horse so that she was riding next to Norm. 'It does get better. It really does. The first time I went riding, I fell off seven times in an hour. It's taken me ten years to get to this point but honestly it's okay. I *hated* it the first time I went but my friend Meg loves it and kept making me go and here I am. On a horse, not hating it, not falling off – yet, anyway – and chatting while riding. But the key thing is, I haven't actually got better, I've just relaxed into it. And, also, I cling on with my knees. Like, really cling. I always have thigh ache afterwards but it does make you feel a lot more secure.'

Matt clenched his thighs and knees around the horse. That did feel good.

'That wasn't what the instructor told us to do, though,' Norm said.

Why hadn't the instructor stayed with them, actually? Wouldn't that have been the responsible thing to do? Why had Carole said they didn't need anyone with them? Why had the riding stable *let* them go without anyone responsible?

'Bugger instructors, Norm,' Lily said. 'We don't want to be *good* riders, do we? We just want to be moderately *happy* riders.'

'You're bloody right,' Norm said, sounding the happiest he'd been since they'd arrived at the stables.

She *was* bloody right. Matt was pretty sure he wasn't at any point going to enjoy this outing, but with the leg-clenching thing there was a chance he was going to stop feeling like death was imminent.

They rode along like that for a while, and Norm actually started chatting to Lily, like he was okay with life on horseback.

Every so often, Lily took one hand off her reins to take some photos, of the scenery and of Norm or the others on their horses. Never Matt. He could see her flicking through the photos immediately, and deleting a few. *While on horseback.* Unbelievable.

He'd love to ask her about the photo curation. And realistically he never would.

Lily moved her horse over to him and leaned over – actually leaned, and did not fall off; how was she *doing* that? – and asked, 'You okay?'

'Yeah.' He managed to nod without feeling like he was about to land on his head. 'As you said, starting to enjoy it.' He had his pride. No way was he going to admit that he was hating this.

'That's good.' She smiled at him like she knew exactly how much he was lying.

She was really annoying him.

And he was really annoying himself because right now he couldn't help noticing how even in a stupid riding hat she just looked beautiful, because all he could see was her lovely smile and her gorgeous eyes.

SEVENTEEN

LILY

Lily couldn't help smiling at Matt. He was *so* far out of his comfort zone.

His horse stepped up his pace a tiny bit and Matt wobbled massively. 'Bloody *hell*,' he said. 'This is a terrible way to spend an afternoon. Bloody Carole.'

Lily caught herself smiling even more. Matt couldn't really pull stroppiness off; it just wasn't him.

'Are you taking my wife's name in vain?' Norm said.

'She's my aunt and yes I am and right now I'm really regretting letting her talk me into this.' Matt lifted a hand to adjust his hat and wobbled alarmingly. 'Oh my *God*. I can't even scratch my head without risking my life.'

'You're so brave.' Lily was struggling not to laugh. Matt was good at *every*thing. But not this.

'Bugger off,' Matt said.

Lily laughed more and relaxed her grip on her reins too much, and nearly lost her balance as her horse did a bit of a feisty side-step.

'Need any help there, Lily?' Matt asked, very sweetly.

'Bugger off yourself.' She gathered her reins and kicked her horse into a little trot.

'Lily, wait,' Norm wailed.

She laughed and slowed her horse.

The three of them ambled along on their horses in near-peace, with only minimal grousing from Matt and Norm, for the next ten or fifteen minutes, and then caught up with the others, who'd been waiting for them.

'This is the treat part,' Carole called, as they drew closer.

'None of this is a treat,' grumbled Matt from just behind Lily. 'I thought we were going to be spending the day on the beach. *That* would have been a treat.'

'Honestly.' Lily turned to look at him. 'You've *totally* been almost enjoying it for the last few minutes.'

'*Maybe.*' Matt grimace-smiled at her. 'In a warped kind of way.'

'Valley of the butterflies,' Carole announced.

'Oh, wow.' Matt sat up straight and looked properly in front of him, and then wobbled a lot. 'I hadn't realised that that's where we were now. Too busy fearing for my life. But I remember coming here as a child – on car and foot, not horse-back – and feeling like it was some magical other-worldly place. Beautiful, and amazing when you spot the butterflies.'

'All sorts of butterflies or one particular kind?' Lily asked.

'Mainly one, I think?' Matt raised his eyebrows in Carole's direction, without wobbling now that he was stationary.

'Yes. Jersey tiger moths,' Carole told them. 'They congregate in huge groups in shady areas but they're quite hard to see because they're well camouflaged against the leaves. Your challenge is to get some great photos of them. Or actually *any* photos of them at all.'

'Not a problem.' Felix pulled his phone out of his pocket.

'At the ready. Lily knows how good at photography I am. No blurry pictures here, honest. Photo genius. In fact, I think we should have a competition to get the best photo. Lily can judge.'

'Fabulous idea,' Carole said. 'Prize for the winner.'

'How are we going to take photos, though?' Matt said. 'Given that we can't use our hands because we're busy riding.'

'You're going to have to be super brave and take a hand off a rein for a second.' Lily lifted her right hand. 'Like this. *Daring.*'

'Your horse isn't moving at the moment,' Matt said. 'It's very different.'

'I'm with Matt,' Norm said. 'I'm not risking my life for a photo.'

'Oh my *God*,' Carole said. 'See what I have to put up with?'

'Are you joking?' Norm was not laughing. 'See what *I* have to put up with.'

'Eek,' Lily said. 'I think you're both wonderful.'

'So do I,' Felix, Alfredo and Matt said as one.

'Humph.' Carole turned round and she and her horse flounced off.

Norm muttered something that sounded suspiciously like *Good riddance.*

They hadn't been in the valley of the butterflies for long before everyone was seeming a lot happier. It was properly gorgeous, almost like a park.

'You're going to lose the photo competition if you won't leave the paths and get searching in some of those shady areas,' Carole told Matt.

'You know what?' Matt tugged hard on his horse's reins. 'Wow. Did you see that? I can stop a horse. When I want to. Anyway: I'm getting off for a break. For a legit reason, which is butterfly hunting.' He took his legs out of the stirrups and swung one leg over and, just as he dismounted, the horse started walking, and he landed in a heap on the ground. 'My *God*, I hate riding,' he said as Lily looked down at him and tried really hard again not to laugh. 'It's really bloody unnatural.' He climbed to his feet, ran after the horse, grabbed the reins and tied them round a tree. 'Yessss. So. Much. Better. I really don't want to get back on.'

'I've never seen you moan so much about *anything*,' Lily said. It was true. He really wasn't a moaner. Angry occasionally. Pissed off sometimes. Upset sometimes. Not a moaner.

'You've never seen me on a horse before.'

She nodded. 'Very true.'

'And I'm thinking you won't see me on one again. I think I'm going to walk back. I'll lead the horse.'

'Me too,' Norm said, 'except I can't get off.'

'Okay.' Matt moved to the front of Norm's horse and stroked her face a few times. 'Maybe if I hold her steady you can get down.'

'I don't know.' Norm had his shoulders all hunched and his face all screwed up, like a nervous small child.

Lily slid down from her own horse, tied him up and then walked over to Norm. 'Why don't I hold Calypso and Matt can help you down?' She got a *great* view of Matt's shoulder and arm muscles flexing as he basically lifted Norm down and held him until he was steady on his feet.

'Norm, you must have some inside information on where these butterflies are. I want that prize. Come and show me?' Matt smiled at Norm and Norm smiled back and, honestly, Lily knew exactly where the butterflies were. In her stomach.

When they'd all finished wandering around, exclaiming over the many butterflies literally clinging to each other, Carole said, 'I thought we could have a little beverage at the café in the village just here before we ride back.'

'Not riding, Carole,' said Norm, 'but I'm happy to partake of a beverage.'

'I'm wondering whether I should start walking now,' Matt said. 'I'm genuinely not getting back on and the walk's going to take a while and we really need to be at the airport in good time to book those slots.'

'You're right. I'll willingly sacrifice a drink in order not to get back on that animal,' Norm said.

Lily looked at Matt and Norm. Did she want to walk back with them? Well, Matt?

She looked at Carole, Felix and Alfredo. They were *much* better riders than she was. There was every chance they'd break into a canter or gallop given the opportunity. She was okay on the basics, like staying on, and she could deal with a bit of trotting from time to time, but that was all.

She looked back at Matt and Norm. Matt was watching her.

'Why don't you come with us, Lily, but you could ride while we walk?' he said. She was pretty sure that he knew that she was hesitating because she felt awkward talking to him but she really didn't want to ride with the others.

'That's actually a very good idea,' she said. No scary too-fast riding but not much opportunity to chat.

It was actually genuinely quite idyllic, meandering back under the late afternoon sun at Norm's walking pace, exchanging the odd word with Matt and Norm but most of the time just listening to the hum of their voices ahead of her and the chattering sound of the cicadas. Idyllic apart from the fact that with literally every second that she spent in Matt's presence it felt like her heart was breaking just a little bit more.

When they made it back to the stables, slightly after the others, who'd apparently managed two ouzos and an espresso each and still overtaken them – good call on wandering back with Matt and Norm rather than getting scared witless riding hell for leather – they all headed towards the car to drive back to the house.

'Everyone in their usual places?' Matt asked.

'At the risk of sounding like a moaner, could I possibly not sit in the middle of the back this time?' Alfredo asked. 'There was something odd about the saddle and my backside's suffering.'

'At the risk of sounding like a six-year-old,' Matt said, 'my backside's sore too and I'm taller than you so I need more space for my legs.'

'I might vomit if I sit in the middle,' Felix said. 'Not joking.'

Lily sniggered. 'All so childish. And so selfish.'

'You bloody sit in the middle of the back then,' Felix said. 'I'd very happily take the teacher's pet place up front.'

'That will not be a problem for me,' said Lily, 'because I am not childish or selfish.'

'Spoken so very unchildishly.' Matt grinned at her.

Lily climbed into the middle of the back, and Alfredo got in on her left, and Matt on her right. And, torture, she was so aware of every *inch* of him. Even *more* now than she had been when they hadn't been getting on. Yeah, it did feel like something had shifted between them today. Like now they were friends again.

Not normal friends, though. You didn't fancy the pants off your friends normally.

'So when are you going to judge the photos, Lily?' Felix looked over his shoulder. 'Because I'm going to win.'

'As soon as we get back?' Lily's leg, shoulders and neck were really starting to hurt from the tension of holding her thigh away from Matt's and her right arm tight to her body, one, so that she wouldn't bump too much against Matt's chest, because it felt kind of personal, and two, so that *he* couldn't bump against *her* chest, because that felt even more personal.

Carole drove them back to the house, and Lily took herself

off to her room for a quick post-riding-expedition shower, ideal for a little break from being so *constantly* aware of Matt.

She had two missed calls from Aaliyah and three from Meg. She and Aaliyah hadn't managed to speak yesterday evening after all because by the time Aaliyah was home and had happily reunited with her kids and put them all to bed and then eaten the – apparently not very nice but very much appreciated because of the effort – beef Wellington her husband had made her, it had been late in Greece, and Lily had been in the middle of Carole's party. And she hadn't spoken at all to Meg today.

God, what if Meg and Pythagoras had split up?

Lily couldn't actually deal with talking to Meg about that right now. After the wedding, it had felt like she and Matt had split all over again, which they clearly totally hadn't because they hadn't got back together, but whenever she thought about that conversation and the fact that after tomorrow morning she wasn't going to see him again, she felt like she was falling into a trough of sadness, and dealing with Meg being devastated on top of that would be maybe a bit too much.

It felt like she was being a bad friend, though. If Meg needed her, she should be there for her. Maybe she could deal with talking to Meg if she had a chat with Aaliyah first.

'Hello,' she said to Aaliyah, who'd answered on the first ring. 'How's your weekend been?'

'Fab. I agreed with the surgery yesterday that I'm going to work an extra day every week and I've agreed that my neighbour's cleaner's going to do a day a week cleaning our house and first thing tomorrow I'm signing the kids up for an extra day and a half a week of nursery and they've been total hell on legs since I got back because I *abandoned* them last week and I really don't mind because tomorrow I have my neighbour's daughter who's back from uni babysitting and I'm going to work. And that's *way* too much chat about me. What about *you*? How was last night? How's today been? How are you feeling about Matt now? What was the bad conversation you had with him? Have you had to see him much today? When are you going to manage to get home?'

'Erm.'

'Okay, yes, too many questions in a row. Tell me about the big one.'

And all of a sudden, words were just falling out of Lily. She told Aaliyah pretty much all the details of her conversation with Matt after the wedding. And then she told her that she knew that she still loved him and always would, although obviously that wouldn't really matter soon because she wouldn't be seeing him again but it really hurt right now.

She told Aaliyah about horse riding today and then thought about when they'd all piled out of the car when they got back just now and she and Matt had been laughing together at something Felix had said, and then they'd brushed arms and there'd been that zing that they'd always had but also, instead of the tension there'd been over the past few days, it had felt like there'd been companionship.

'And now I feel like over the course of today things have shifted back to friendship between us,' she said. 'And that *really* hurts.' Woah. She was really going for it with the spilling her emotions thing. 'Anyway, I've been talking about myself for too long. I'm so pleased for you that you've made all your life changes.'

'Can I just say,' Aaliyah said, 'I totally get everything you've said about Matt and that you've always held stuff back because of a fear that you'll lose the person you want to be, who isn't the sick child that everyone felt sorry for. But you know we don't all just love you because you're always so supportive and amazing but because we love your company and none of us think you're a victim or a different person if you ever act like you need a bit of sympathy or help. And I'm sure Matt feels the same way, or would do given the opportunity. And it sounds like you still really love each other so maybe you should try to find a way to get past this. Anyway, maybe you aren't ready to hear that so maybe I'm just going to leave that thought there.'

'Right,' Lily said. Time to change the subject. 'Thank you. We're going to the airport soon to book a private flight for tomorrow to Athens and then we can all fly home.'

'Okay, fab, so shall we meet at the weekend? Do you want to come over for a barbecue on Sunday?'

'Perfect, thank you. Has Meg been calling you?'

'No?'

'That's odd.' Lily frowned. 'She's been trying to call me. I was worried she and Pythagoras have split up. I thought she'd have tried you too.'

'Hmm. Let's hope not. Good luck with that conversation if she has.'

'I know. It'll be torture. She'll be beyond distraught.'

'I really thought he was her One,' Aaliyah said. 'This time, I kind of feel like she'd be *right* to be distraught if they've split up.'

Lily's phone was beeping. 'Someone's trying to call me,' she said. 'Probably Meg. I'd better go.'

'Good luck.'

Yep, it was Meg.

'Lily, do you have any leads on a flight off Paros? Pythagoras and I need to fly to Edinburgh tomorrow if possible because he has an interview for a head chef job on Tuesday and it would be a *lot* better to do it in person than on Zoom. We can come over this evening if necessary, or in the morning. Pythagoras's cousin can bring us over on his boat.'

'Oh, wow, that's amazing.' Relief. 'We're going to the airport soon to get booked on a flight for tomorrow. I'll book you on the same one and let you know when it is.'

'Thank you so much. I'll text my credit card details to you.' And she'd gone.

Well, wow.

'So you can take six of us?' Lily was clarifying forty-five minutes later.

The pilot, a tall German man with an incredible handlebar moustache and bright-yellow leather shoes, said, 'Yes, absolutely, if you don't mind lying in the luggage hold.' His face was completely straight. Lily gave him a lips-together smile. There was something about him that she didn't like. 'I'm joking, of *course*,' he said. 'I would never put you with the luggage. You can sit on my lap.'

'Ha, hilarious,' she said. 'So you can take the six of us. In seats. Great.'

He leaned into Lily, so close that the moustache brushed her cheek, *grim*, and, as she nearly fell over moving away from the bristles and, eurgh, waxed end bit, said, 'If you come for a drink with me this evening I will only charge you half.' His breath had a very strong smell. Mainly mint but with a bit of onion and garlic coming through.

'Again...' she took another step away from him '...hilarious.'

'And if you do not come for a drink with me, the price will go up, or I will not take you. I have a very nice hotel room.' Oh, for God's sake.

Lily took the lid off her water bottle.

Matt strode forward and said, 'What the *hell* is wrong with you? Are you sexually harassing my friend?' just as Lily accidentally, honest, poured the entire contents of her water bottle down the front of the pilot's trousers.

'Nice.' Matt nodded approvingly as they walked away.

'Now you've lost your seats on my plane,' the pilot shouted after them.

'And you've lost your *dignity*,' Lily yelled back. 'And stop sexually harassing women.' Satisfyingly, a lot of people turned to stare.

'What a shit,' Matt said.

'I'm really annoyed that I didn't have a better comeback. "You've lost your dignity." Not very snappy.'

'I mean, it was *okay*. I can't think of a better one-liner right now. Nothing that isn't very sweary, anyway. And the water spillage was genius.' Matt smiled at her and Lily felt a little glow inside that she should really not be feeling. 'Come on. Let's re-join the queue and see if we can get a flight with someone who isn't a complete sexist arse.'

'What are we doing?' Felix had been sitting on a little wall, the absolute picture of boredom, head and shoulder rolling, shoe scuffing, the works. 'Why are we queuing again?'

'I lost us our seats on that flight,' Lily said.

'Whyyyyy?' howled Felix.

'Totally not Lily's fault. The pilot was a dick.' Matt looked around them. 'The queue isn't moving anywhere fast. Do you still have your playing cards in your bag?'

'Yes I do.' Felix opened his man-satchel and nudged Alfredo. '*See.* There *is* a point to this bag.'

'There really isn't,' Alfredo said. 'How often do you need a pack of cards?'

'Well, surprisingly often as it turns out,' Felix said.

'Men should totally carry bags,' Lily said. 'I adore my bag.' This holiday she'd brought a gold woven leather tote with her and she *loved* it. 'Look at this. Firstly, it's genuinely gorgeous. In my opinion. And secondly, I have *so much* useful stuff in here.'

Matt nodded. 'She does. The number of times something unforeseen happens and Lily's bag comes up trumps. Small things like pens and plasters and scissors. And big things like a toy gun once—' he grinned at her '—and umbrellas, except for the other day.' He was still grinning, and there was that glow again. Although who wouldn't feel a glow that someone remembered stuff about you from eight years ago. It was flattering, obviously.

'You know what I can produce right now?' she said. 'A pen and paper to score our game.'

'I can also produce a pen and paper.' Felix took out a very smart fountain pen and leather-bound notebook.

'I like those a *lot*,' Lily said. '*However*, look at my spangles.' She pulled out the glittery pen and sparkly green notebook she'd bought at Heathrow on the way out.

'Yeah.' Felix nodded. 'Those are good. I'm jealous.'

Lily felt Matt's eyes on her and glanced round at him. He was looking at her with a lopsided smile that gave her goose-bumps, and an unreadable expression in his eyes that made her want to say *What???* Matt had never been unreadable in the past. The unreadable thing was very sexy actually. Kind of more grown up. Enigmatic.

'Lily?' hollered Felix really close to her ear.

'Oh my God, what?' Lily looked round to see what shocking event had occurred.

'Just asked you about five times if you wanted to start the game but you were in a world of your own. Thought I should shout. Also, whose notebook are we using?'

They sat down on the tarmac in a little circle and got going with their game.

And now they were playing, Lily *knew* that she was going to beat Matt, because she just knew him too well.

In fact, as the game progressed, it was *really* hard not to crow.

'Lily, you've got your lips pressed together like you really want to say something to me, like the words are pushing up inside your mouth just bursting to get out.' Matt had his eyebrows raised and his eyes narrowed. 'And I don't think it's complimentary.'

Lily put her hands over her face and tried really hard to

look like her mind was blank.

Matt put the queen of hearts down.

'Yesss.' She couldn't help it. 'I *knew* you were going to play either the jack or the queen.'

'*How* did you know that?'

'Psychic.'

'It's because she knows you so well,' Felix told Matt.

'I didn't know you two knew each other before this?' Alfredo looked from Matt to Lily and back again.

'Really?' Felix said. 'You can't feel the *history* between them?'

Alfredo looked between the two of them some more while Lily made a face at Felix and then checked the cards in her hand very carefully. No way was she looking at Matt right now.

'Oh-kay.' Matt tapped the pile of cards in the centre of their little circle. 'You to play, Lily.' She played the ace of clubs, trying not to smirk. 'Oh my God. Again.'

Eventually they got to the front of the queue and, with a lot of negotiating, managed to book spaces for the four of them and Meg and Pythagoras on a flight on an eight-person plane leaving mid-morning tomorrow. Carole had said that Meg and Pythagoras would be more than welcome to stay over tonight, so they'd be on their way with Pythagoras's cousin any minute.

'I love small planes,' Alfredo said once they were settled in a taxi to go back to Carole's, Matt in the front and the other three in the back. 'Such a different feeling from a large one.'

I know. Like you might fall out of the sky, Lily thought. Best not to mention her flying phobia out loud. No point tipping other people from being okay about flying into joining her in her paranoia.

'You okay about it, Lily?' Matt asked over his shoulder.

'Yep, totally,' she said.

'Really?' Yeah, he was clearly thinking about the first flight they'd taken together. They'd been on their way to a wedding in

Scotland soon after they'd got together, and there'd been turbulence on their plane and it had dropped several feet inside some kind of air pocket and Lily's stomach had dropped a lot further and Lily had grabbed Matt's arm and screamed *Make it stop*. And then she'd been really embarrassed about looking so pathetic but he'd been *lovely* to her. That flight had cemented her feeling that she was falling in love with him.

And right now he was looking at her with a similarly gorgeously concerned expression in his dark eyes and she couldn't have pulled her eyes away from his if you'd paid her.

'It'll be okay,' he said.

'Yes,' she breathed. Right now it felt like anything would be okay if Matt was there.

EIGHTEEN

MATT

Matt really wished he could time travel. Like, go back ten years to the moment he realised that he'd fallen head over heels in love with Lily – of all places on a plane to Scotland when she'd alternated between obvious terror and being lovely to an elderly lady across the aisle – and from there just not mess up. How, though? Take things more slowly? Travel for work less? Hard to know.

Felix coughed and said, 'So you don't like flying, Lily?'

Lily carried on gazing into Matt's eyes for a couple more seconds – her eyes looked heavy, like she couldn't pull them away from him – and then turned slowly to Felix. 'I don't *love* it, but it's fine. Really. I mean, it isn't like we have any other options.'

'Yep, and the conditions will be clear,' Matt pointed out. 'And if they aren't, we won't go. We can just stay a day longer. The majority of aeroplane crashes are weather-related, I'm sure.'

'Well, you've also got terrorism, engine failure, crashes.' Felix was ticking flight disaster reasons off on his fingers like he was enjoying himself. 'I could go on.' The man was an idiot. Lily was looking more miserable by the second.

'It's really hot in here.' Lily started fanning herself with her hand. 'I feel a bit sick.'

Felix gave her a little shove. 'I don't want to be unsympathetic, but if you *do* throw up, please do it on Alfredo. He cares a lot less about his clothes than I do.'

'Why don't we wind the windows down?' Alfredo said, already winding.

Lily leaned her head back against her seat and closed her eyes.

'So what do we think Carole has planned for this evening?' Matt asked, anything to try to distract Lily. She looked very pale. 'She mentioned something about some traditional plate smashing earlier.'

'I don't think she's going down that route.' Lily kept her head back but opened her eyes. 'Norm said it was wasteful and annoying and that he was putting his foot down. So then she suggested clubbing together in Parikia and Norm said not to be so bloody stupid and now we're just going to have another poolside barbecue, which sounds lovely.'

Chat about the evening ahead got them all the way back to Carole and Norm's and they all got out of the taxi just as Carole and her jeep arrived in a swirl of dust.

'Hello.' Meg jumped out and hugged Lily and then waved at the others. 'Thank you so much for reserving the flight for us.'

'Congratulations.' Lily, who looked like she'd recovered completely from her flight stress, pulled Pythagoras into their hug. 'I'm so happy for you both. So exciting.'

'What are we celebrating?' Felix asked.

'Pythagoras is moving to Edinburgh with me tomorrow.' Meg had an enormous smile on her face. During the time that Matt and Lily were together, Meg had had at least three traumatic relationship break-ups that he could recall, and Lily had been there for her every time.

He suddenly wondered whether Meg had been there for Lily when *they'd* split up because that had to have been traumatic for Lily, surely. Maybe Meg had been busy having her own break-up – there'd been something just before he and Lily split. Or maybe Lily wouldn't have let on how upset he was pretty sure she'd been.

'How long have you *known* each other?' Felix was looking between Meg and Pythagoras, eyes like saucers. Alfredo gave him the mother of all nudges to the ribs, and he jumped. '*What*? Just asking.'

'We met last Monday,' Meg said. 'Which probably seems quite quick, I suppose, but sometimes you just know when you meet The One.'

'Yes.' Pythagoras kissed the top of her head. 'You do.'

Well, it sounded utterly ridiculous, frankly, to be moving country for someone you barely knew.

Although... Matt looked over at Lily, because he couldn't help it. Yeah, if he'd been braver and less obsessed with his career in the early years, and followed his heart a lot more, he'd probably have moved country for her almost from the moment he first met her when he nearly tripped over her five miles into the charity walkathon Tess had roped them both into.

Lily had plonked herself down on a rock and said, 'Time for a little rest,' and had pulled a tub of chocolate brownies, a little pack of one-shot-tequila mini bottles and some tissues out of her backpack. Matt could still remember looking at her shimmery orange nail varnish-tipped fingers holding the brownie tub out to him, and then into her eyes when she'd smiled at him and said, 'Always be prepared.' She'd been wearing a pale-blue top with a wide neck that slipped off her shoulder quite a lot, and she'd had her long curly hair up on top of her head and held in place by a bright-green band. She hadn't really looked that prepared for a twenty-six-mile walk, other than the refreshments she'd brought. And she'd smiled her gorgeous smile and her eyes had been laughing and he'd grinned back at her and taken a brownie and a tequila bottle and he'd known that he really wanted to get to know her a lot better. And within a couple of weeks, on that plane, he'd been certain that she was his One.

It still felt like she was his One. It felt like maybe he just needed to convince her of that.

She was returning his gaze now. Was she also thinking about the past?

He couldn't stop looking at her. His lips were forming into a half smile, just for her, and something inside him had changed, settled into certainty. Yes. He should have been a lot braver before, fought harder. Tonight he was going to fight for the chance to restart their relationship.

She was still gazing back at him, but she wasn't smiling, she was just... looking.

They needed to talk more. Right now. It felt like there was no time to waste. They had maybe thirteen hours before the flight tomorrow morning.

He really wished they were alone. He took a step towards Lily and bumped into Alfredo.

'Sorry, mate.' He stepped round Alfredo and carried on walking towards Lily. It sounded like the others were all still talking about how Meg and Pythagoras had met. Felix was exclaiming *very* loudly about how *gorge* their story was.

Not as gorge as it would be if Matt and Lily got back together after all this time. In his opinion, anyway.

'So,' he said, when he was standing in front of her.

'So.' Her eyes were laughing a little and she was doing a small, intimate smile which gave him shivers.

'I thought we should talk.' He should maybe have thought this through a bit better before he got going.

'I think we already talked.' She put her head to one side. The smile hadn't gone yet.

'I think we could stand to talk some more. Well, I could.' Oh, for God's sake. What an idiot. He should have just gone straight in with what he wanted to say. And he shouldn't have done it when they were standing within earshot of Meg, Pythagoras, Felix, Alfredo and Carole.

'Come on.' Carole began to march towards the house. 'Let me show you to your room, Meg and Pythagoras, and then we can reconvene next to the pool, with some drinks.'

Lily went off to her room saying that she'd be down soon, so Matt decided that he'd take the opportunity to change into a shirt, clean his teeth and maybe slap a little bit more aftershave on. Couldn't hurt. Because tonight he was definitely going to go for it, hopefully have a very big conversation. With the woman he loved.

Oh, God. High stakes.

He and Norm were out at the pool first. Norm had taken up station by the enormous stone barbecue next to the pool house, so Matt joined him there.

'Carole's decided I'm barbecuing, so here I am. To be honest, it's a good place to be because she'll be too busy talking to – or I should say *at* – all our – or I should say *her* – guests, to bother coming over here, so I'll get some peace for once.' Norm gave the coals a vicious poke with the barbecue fork.

'Ha,' said Matt. He was pretty sure that Norm wasn't joking, but he wasn't keen to get involved in his aunt and uncle's marital spats. Lily popped into his head – well, not exactly; it was more like she'd taken up permanent residence there since he'd arrived in Greece – and he felt guilty. If someone wanted to talk, she'd always listen. 'You okay, Norm?'

'I'm not actually.' Norm forked the coals around a bit more. 'Fed up.'

'I'm very sorry.'

'I think I need a break.'

'Um, what kind of a break?' Out of the corner of his eye, Matt saw Lily arrive. She'd changed into a long, loose, yellow sundress and she looked gorgeous.

'Just a break.' Norm put his fork down and picked up some tongs and started moving coals around with those instead. 'On my own. With no nagging.' He looked like he *meant* it. Like, maybe things really weren't good between him and Carole.

'What about a holiday? On your own? Things often feel better after a few days away. You'd be very welcome to stay with me in London?' God. Matt was already imagining having Norm stay in his spare room and his mind was boggling.

'I might take you up on that.'

'Great.'

Carole shouted, 'Norm!' and made an exaggerated barbecue tonging gesture with her arms.

Norm looked over at her, physically turned his back to her and said, 'Have you seen the latest cricket score? England all out yet?'

'They were doing a bit better when I came down. Let me check.' Matt took his phone out and showed Norm the screen where he had the cricket up, half-watching Lily as he did so. He really wanted to go and speak to her but she was deep in conversation with Meg now, plus it didn't feel right to abandon Norm to barbecue chef loneliness.

An hour, yes, an entire hour, later, Matt was still with Norm next to the barbecue. Pythagoras and Alfredo had joined them, and they were both great company, but Matt was really running out of time now and he was feeling pretty desperate to go and talk to Lily.

'Norm, over here,' called Carole. 'Time to go and get the puddings from the house. Everyone's done on the meat.'

Norm pinched his mouth, turned round and went into the pool house kitchen and emerged with more steaks, which he put onto the barbecue.

'What are you doing?' Carole yelled.

'Barbecuing as many steaks as I want.'

Wow. This was the first time Matt had witnessed a steak mutiny.

'Talk us through any chef's barbecuing tips,' Alfredo said to Pythagoras.

Under cover of all the barbecue chat, Matt went over and sat down next to Lily, Meg and Felix.

'What's happening with the steaks?' whispered Lily.

Before Matt could speak, Carole said, 'Meg and Lily. Come and help me in the kitchen with the puddings.'

And off they went, leaving Matt and Felix next to the pool. Matt looked at his watch. It was already quarter to eleven and they had to be at the airport by nine tomorrow morning for a ten thirty take-off. He really did not have a lot of time left with Lily, and it wasn't looking like he was going to get to speak to her alone any time soon.

When Meg, Lily and Carole got back with the puddings, the rest of them just goggled. Carole had made a large raspberry pavlova, a large, good old-fashioned trifle, with a lot of jelly, and a large chocolate tart. For eight people.

'I'm going to be offended if there's much food left,' she said, brandishing a cake slice. 'Everyone needs to try every pudding.'

'You shouldn't bully people into overeating,' roared Norm from next to the barbecue. 'That's abuse.'

'Be quiet,' sniffed Carole.

One big portion of pudding for everyone later, Carole said, 'Right, everyone, time for seconds.'

'I can't.' Felix rubbed his stomach very dramatically. 'I'm sorry. I *love* your cooking, Carole, and we're incredibly grateful for your wonderful hospitality, but it takes a lot of effort to maintain this body...' he did an up and down gesture with his hand '... and I'm afraid I can't eat more than one pudding, even for you.'

Carole's whole face crumpled. Oh God.

'I'd love some of the pavlova, please,' Matt said quickly. 'If it's anywhere near as delicious as the tart, it'll be amazing.' He was going to be *so* overfull. Not ideal for when you needed to convince the love of your life to give your relationship another go but needs must.

Carole's face un-crumpled.

Lily smiled at her. 'I'm *really* full, Carole, but I agree the pavlova looks amazing, so could I just try a tiny bit? I mean, really quite tiny. Could I maybe help myself?' She put a minis-cule amount on her plate and spread it out a bit with the back of the cake slice.

'And I'd love to try the trifle.' Alfredo held his plate out.

'I must try the trifle too,' Pythagoras said, 'now that I'm going to be living in England.'

'Edinburgh's in Scotland,' Felix said.

Finally, they'd all finished eating. Norm had been seduced over by the pavlova from his barbecue sulking station, although he'd seated himself a good ten feet away from Carole. Alfredo was leaning back against Felix on a sunlounger, Felix idly playing with his hair. Meg was sitting on Pythagoras's lap. And Lily and Matt were sitting separately.

'I'd love to go for a beach walk in the moonlight,' Felix said. 'Our last night here. Just the two of us. Look at some stars together.'

'Good idea. Sorry, everyone.' Alfredo stood up and held his

hand out to Felix. 'Excuse us. We'll say good night to you now.' They disappeared into the dark night in the direction of the beach, their arms round each other.

Meg looked at Pythagoras and giggled. 'I'd rather just go straight to bed than waste time looking at stars,' she said.

'Excuse *us*,' Pythagoras said, and off they went too, starting in on the smooching before they'd even left the pool area.

'I'd like to go for a moonlit beach walk too,' Carole announced. 'Norm, you can help me clear all this up and then we're going for a walk.'

'*Or*,' said Norm, 'I could go to bed right now in a spare room. Good night.' He nodded at Lily and Matt, not looking at Carole, and walked off.

'Um.' Lily swivelled her eyes backwards and forwards between Norm, Matt and Carole, who was staring after Norm. 'We can help you clear up, Carole.' She started loading plates and bowls onto a tray.

'Absolutely.' Matt started loading another tray.

When they'd got everything inside and Lily had insisted on clearing all the crumbs up to avoid wasps next to the pool, Carole – clearly having decided to leave Norm to his strop – said, 'Like to have a nightcap with me?'

'I thought Lily and I could also take a walk on the beach,' Matt said.

'Oh.' Lily looked at him, and then at Carole.

'Good idea.' Carole practically shoved the two of them outside. 'Good night, my loves. Off you go.'

And finally they were alone.

'So.' Matt turned to face Lily. He could just make out her features in the moonlight. 'Walk?'

'It's very late,' she said, not moving in the direction of the beach. She also wasn't moving in the direction of the house, which was something.

'You can sleep on the plane tomorrow? It's a lovely night. And I'd love to walk if you'd like to?' He held his arm out.

Lily looked at it for a long moment and then took it.

They strolled through trees in silence for a minute or two, the only sounds the lapping of the water and the occasional rustle of leaves and branches from a nocturnal animal.

'Weird to think that in under twelve hours' time we'll be in the middle of Athens airport,' Lily said. 'A world away.' Yeah, and most of that time would be taken up with sleeping and packing and having breakfast and being at the airport with the others. So, no time to waste.

He was going to go straight in with the conversation. With his thoughts. Really, nothing to lose at this point, and so much to gain. And it felt a bit easier saying stuff while you were walking and it was dark and you couldn't see each other's faces.

'I had a question that I wanted to ask.' He could feel her stiffen immediately. Fair enough, but he was going to plough on. The worst that could happen would be that she'd refuse to engage. 'Although I'm not sure how to word it. I suppose I wondered whether the idea of talking about your feelings, hurt, pain, fear, makes you scared that other people will think differently about you, or whether admitting to those feelings will make you feel differently about yourself.'

'Oh.' She paused, for ages. 'Okay,' she said eventually. 'So, yep, basically, yes, I'm scared that people will think differently about me if I start talking in too much detail about my weaknesses, I suppose. And, yes, that wouldn't make me feel good about myself.'

'Weakness is a strong word. At the risk of interfering, I'm not sure you should think of those emotions as weaknesses. Being sad or upset or whatever isn't a weakness or failing, it's just part of normal human life, isn't it? And you're the same person as the ill child you used to be, surely? The same gorgeous sense of humour? The same caring nature? The same tendency to laugh when you really shouldn't? Surely the only difference is that when you were ill you didn't have the opportunity to get to know people well, or they didn't have the opportunity to get to know *you*, plus you weren't able to do what everyone else did, so they assumed that you didn't want to join in when it was just that you couldn't?'

'Um.'

God, maybe he'd been too bulldozing. And, also, he was pretty sure that conversations like this shouldn't be one way.

'Sorry. I'm clearly talking way more about you than you'd like right now,' he said. 'I think when I was young, when we were together, I was very naïve. I'd never really experienced anything difficult. It was easy for me to talk about everything in my life, because I didn't have a lot of deep and meaningful stuff going on really. I've learned quite a lot since then. Getting hurt, and betrayed, makes you grow up. I didn't understand then how people might be a lot deeper, basically, than I was. And how sometimes people just don't want to talk. Last week, Carole tried to talk to me about my marriage and my relationship with you, and I just shut her down. Not as open as I thought I was.'

'So.' Lily cleared her throat. He wished he could see her face properly. Maybe it actually would have been better having this conversation inside with some lights on. 'What are you trying to say?'

'Erm.' Oh God, oh God, oh God. It felt *so important* to get these words right. 'I've spent eight years wanting to know why we split up. And I think that I've finally worked out what it was. Essentially, I didn't understand why someone – you, I mean – wouldn't just be an open book. But I didn't even know that I didn't understand that. And then you pointed that out to me, last week, and I thought how ridiculous. Until I thought about it and realised that *no one's* really an open book. And you'd just had a lot more to deal with when you were younger than I had. And we weren't able to spend enough time together for me to get that. I think what I'm trying to say is that I really, really love you and that I think, hope, I've had enough life experience now to be more understanding.'

Lily didn't speak for a while. For far too long, actually; Matt's stress levels were going to be stratospheric soon. And then she said, 'Wow,' and sniffed.

Matt looked down. Her cheeks were definitely damp. He stopped walking and reached for her hand and gave it a gentle tug so that she was facing him. Very carefully, with his thumbs, he wiped the tears from under her eyes. Then he slid his hands round so that they were cupping her face.

Lily gave a huge sigh and smiled through the tears that were still falling.

And, suddenly, everything seemed as though it could be alright, and, still taking huge care and moving very slowly, he lowered his head to hers and kissed her.

NINETEEN

LILY

Lily sank into Matt's kiss like it was the only place in the world she was meant to be. He'd made everything sound so simple. Like, they were meant to be together and maybe it had just taken a bit of time to work things out. Were things really that simple? It was hard to process thoughts when you were kissing like this. She gave up on the thinking and just went with the kissing.

And everything else that followed.

'Remember,' breathed Matt, as he traced along Lily's collarbone and into the hollows of her neck, and down, 'that time in the woods?'

'Mmm.' Lily remembered – it had been mind-blowing – but she was really struggling to form words. She was basically panting. She started to undo his belt.

'Too sandy.' Matt was panting too.

'Mmm. Find some grass.'

And it was the best sex of Lily's life. Three times.

. . .

They were still there, under palm trees, on what turned out in daylight to be a grassy dune, when the sun began to come up.

'Oh my God.' Lily looked round for her dress. 'People might *see* us.'

'*I* can see you.' Matt's slow smile was just *wicked*. He pulled her towards him and began working some serious magic on her body again.

'No, *really*. Look over there.' Lily wriggled away and pointed.

'Woah.' Matt reached for her dress, fast, and handed it to her, and leapt into his shorts so quickly that he nearly fell over. 'How are we so close to the villa? I felt like we walked quite a long way.'

'Maybe we were distracted.' Lily finally had her dress back on. That felt a *lot* better. 'I can see Norm's head in the garden.'

'That kind of implies he might be able to see us.'

'Yup.'

'Let's go. Let's just style it out. Out for an early-morning walk.' Matt jumped up and then pulled Lily to her feet.

'Wait. Underwear.' Lily picked it all up and Matt stuffed it in his pockets and then they both sniggered like kids.

'Morning, Norm,' they both said on their way past him, not stopping to chat.

'What time is it?' Matt whispered as they went inside.

Lily pointed at the kitchen clock.

'So we have another hour before either of us needs to shower and pack,' he said.

'That's not a lot of time to sleep,' Lily said.

'So little time that there's really no point bothering with sleep at all.'

'I think you're right.' Lily put her fingers to her lips and led him in silence to her room.

. . .

A couple of hours later, they were all standing next to Carole's jeep, in the full glare of the morning sun, surrounded by their bags.

Lily felt herself stagger a little and took a sideways step to stop herself falling over. She was going to die of tiredness. Actually going to die. She was struggling to interpret basic speech and her eyes were dry and prickly, and if she closed them she started swaying on her feet. She was too old to cope with staying up all night, especially when it was followed by having to pack in a rush in boiling heat. She wasn't too old to have *amazing* sex, though.

'Lily, you're smirking at your own thoughts.' Meg was peering at her far too closely. '*Lily.*'

'Mmm?'

'When you've been getting a lot yourself you *totally* know when someone else has got some.' Meg looked over her shoulder at the men and then back at Lily with her eyes wide open. 'Did you sleep with Matt?'

'Shhhh.'

'Oh my goodness. Are you two back together?'

'*Shhhhhhhh.*' That was a very good question. Were they? They hadn't actually said anything about that. They'd been too busy doing stuff. It felt like they needed to talk some more.

'Lily. We need to *talk.*' Meg's jaw was going to hit the floor if she wasn't careful.

Lily looked around for something to point out to distract Meg, and saw Norm walking towards them lugging suitcases.

'Did one of us forget our bags?' she asked.

'No. They're mine.' Norm stopped walking and then chucked his bags into the boot of his car.

'Are you going somewhere?' Lily asked.

'Yep,' he said.

Lily opened her mouth to ask where but before she could get the words out, Alfredo yelled, 'You're joking,' into his phone.

After a lot more yelling, he ended the call and turned to the others and said, 'So we only have four seats on the flight now. We've effectively been gazumped on two of them. We get a refund for those two, like that's any consolation.'

Lily looked at Meg and Pythagoras, who were standing gripping each other's hands tightly.

'Meg and Pythagoras should take two of the seats,' she said. 'Pythagoras has his interview tomorrow.'

'That would be amazing.' Meg looked quite tearful. 'Except I feel terrible if we take them and two of you can't go home yet.'

'No, you two should definitely take them. The rest of us just have normal work days, don't we, not big interviews.' Felix looked round Lily, Matt and Alfredo and they all nodded.

'Thank you so much. You'll all invited to Edinburgh to stay with us and I'm cooking a *big* Greek meal to thank you all.' Pythagoras shook everyone's hands vigorously in turn.

Lily, Matt, Felix and Alfredo looked at each other.

Lily kind of didn't mind the idea of another day and night here with Matt. 'I don't have in-person work until later in the week,' she said.

'Me neither,' Matt said immediately, which made Lily smile. 'You two should take the seats.' He nodded at Alfredo and Felix.

'Thank you so much for offering. Alfredo and I have both managed to switch today's meetings to Zoom but we could both really do with being in the office tomorrow so it wouldn't be great for either of us to stay.' Felix and Alfredo were both high-flying lawyers in London. 'But are you sure?'

'Totally.' Lily and Matt both nodded.

'Then yessss.' Felix hugged them both and Alfredo shook Matt's hand and kissed Lily's cheek. 'Thank you. Drinks on us in London very soon.'

'We'll enjoy having your company for longer.' Carole didn't seem to have noticed Norm's bags. 'Now you four hop in and let's get going as fast as possible so that no one else can gazump you.' She climbed into the driver's seat and started revving.

'Erm, where were you off to, Norm?' Matt asked as Carole's jeep disappeared in a screech of tyres.

'Going to find a friend to stay with and then I might go to England when I can get a flight. I'll play it by ear.'

'What?' Lily and Matt gasped as one.

'It's time to leave.' Norm folded his arms across his chest. 'I can't take it any more.'

'Norm.' Matt put his arm round Norm's shoulders. 'Are you okay? Can I help? What's happened, if I can ask?'

'I've just had enough.'

'Have you told Carole?'

'Not as such. I packed during the night and left her a note this morning. Don't know whether she's read it but, as you saw, she either didn't notice or didn't care that I'd brought my bags out this morning.' Norm looked as though he was on the brink of tears. Lily moved forward and hugged him too.

'I'm sure she can't have read your note,' she said. 'And she was probably just focused on getting people to the airport. That will be why she didn't notice your bags. You and Carole have been together for such a long time and you're great together. I'm sure she wouldn't want you to leave.'

'I think she would. Forty years,' Norm said, 'and all she does is yell at me and try to stop me doing what I want, and we haven't had sex since my birthday in twenty-twelve.'

Lily was actually genuinely surprised by that. Carole seemed like one of those mature women you read about in magazines who was in charge of her own sexuality and had a *lot* of sex.

'You're surprised, aren't you?' Norm said. 'Menopause, loss of libido, *she* says. But I think it's because she doesn't respect me. I think if she was married to Donald Trump she'd be having sex all the time.'

'Donald *Trump?*'

'Yes. She loves him. Not really his politics, but his looks. And his charisma.'

'Wow...' Matt and Lily both said.

'Yes. It's all "*Donald Trump* wears his jumpers so well", "*Donald Trump* has such a great tan", "*Donald Trump*'s probably better at barbecuing than you".'

'Wow,' Lily repeated. 'Norm, I'm so sorry. I wonder whether Carole might have been joking about the Donald Trump thing.'

'I don't know.' Norm shook his head. 'He's a good-looking man. She's been very demanding recently. I think she's frustrated because I'm not Donald.'

'Perhaps just a short break will do you the world of good,' Matt said. 'You're welcome to come and stay with me as I mentioned before if you'd like a holiday.'

'I agree,' Lily said. 'Short breaks do help a lot in these situations.'

'Firstly, thank you but if I go to England I'll probably stay with my brother and his wife. And secondly, no offence but is either of you really qualified to give me relationship advice? I mean, look at you both. Look like you're completely right for each other. Lovely together when you stayed with us all those years ago. Lovely together now. Rampant outdoor sex all night last night. And yet do you have any kind of relationship?' Woah. Norm in this new incarnation was far too forthright.

'Erm,' Matt said.

'That's a conversation for another time,' Lily said. 'Focusing on you and Carole, Norm, she's probably going to be really upset when she finds out.'

'I doubt it.' Norm's chin wobbled and Lily hugged him again.

'Why don't you wait and talk to her?' she said.

'No. I'm going. I think it's over. I don't think she'll care at all that I've gone. She'll probably just be delighted.'

'I really do think you just need to talk. It's never going to be completely over, is it, until both of you want it to be for good. Maybe you do need a bit of time apart but then – and yes I know I'm not one to give relationship advice – but I think after that talking would really help and things will probably be okay then.' She looked up at Matt across Norm's head. He was watching her, smiling crookedly. It felt like there were some parallels between what she'd been saying to Norm and her relationship with Matt.

Norm sniffed. 'Maybe. I don't know. I need to go now, though, before she gets back.' He opened his car door and got inside. 'Goodbye.' And off he drove, with Lily and Matt waving at the car.

'Waving did not feel right there,' said Matt.

'I know. Like he was off on some lovely jaunt instead of walking out on forty years of marriage. I really hope they can resolve this.'

'Me too. Hopefully Carole will go after him when she's read his note.' Matt put his arm round Lily and pulled her against him.

'Lucky we decided to stay so that Carole will have company.' Lily slid her arm round his waist and turned her face up to his and he kissed her.

'You secretly pleased that you don't have to get on a tiny plane today?' he asked.

'Well, duh. Totally.' Also secretly pleased that she was going to get to spend more time with Matt. It would be *so* nice to curl up somewhere cool and have a snooze together now.

'Maybe we could go and grab half an hour's sleep while we wait for Carole to get back,' Matt said.

'Good plan. My room?'

. . .

Some time later, Lily heard a strange sound outside her bedroom window and dragged her eyes open. She smiled at the sight of Matt sprawled in the bed next to her and then reached for her phone to check the time. Woah. They must have been asleep for a good two or three hours.

There was that strange sound again.

She nudged Matt awake and he mumbled something and wrapped his arms round her.

'What's that noise outside the window?' she said. 'Is it crying? Is it Carole?' Crying wasn't really the right word; it was more like wailing.

'What?' Matt let go of her, jumped out of bed and opened the shutters a little to peer through them. He turned round, his eyes wide. 'I think Carole's singing next to the swimming pool. I think that's some classic Aretha Franklin.'

Lily joined him at the window. 'Yeah, I think you're right. It's "Respect". Not that mournful. God. This is awful. I hope she isn't *happy* that Norm's gone. Or ambivalent. Because *he* clearly isn't happy. I'm totally expecting him to want to come back within about two weeks.'

'Two weeks? I think more like two days. Or even two hours. I mean, I think he started wavering before he'd even got in the car. I was thinking a short sharp shock like this might be great for them. But not if Carole's happy that he's gone.'

'I think we should go and find out.'

When they got out to the pool area, Carole, still warbling, was reclining on a sunlounger in a sundress and shades, with a magazine on the little table next to her, holding a cocktail with a straw in it like a mic and looking like she was giving Aretha everything she had.

'She looks really happy,' Lily whispered.

'Maybe it's bravado. Maybe the shades are hiding tears.' Matt took a few steps forward. 'Carole. Hi. Are you okay?'

Carole jumped and squawked and half her cocktail went flying.

'Sorry, we didn't mean to surprise you.' Lily moved closer to her. 'Carole, are you alright?'

'Well, I'm very sticky but this dress goes in the wash, so not to worry.'

'Sticky?'

'From the cocktail?' Carole pulled her shades down and looked at Lily over the top of them before putting them back in place. 'You look very pale, Lily. Are you poorly?'

'I'm fine, thank you,' Lily said, 'just a bit tired. Maybe a bit hungover.' And the mud was finally wearing off. 'You know. But how are you feeling?'

'I'm fine. I'm used to a late night or two. What would you like to do today?' Oh, God. Carole clearly didn't know.

Matt sat down on the lounger next to Carole's. 'Carole, we saw Norm after you left.'

'Did he say where he was going? Is he playing golf?'

'He said something about having left a note for you.' Wow. Matt was brave.

'What? Why?' Carole sat motionless for a second and then said, 'Has something happened? *What's* happened? Where's the note?'

'In the kitchen, I think,' Matt said.

Carole didn't move for another few seconds and then said, 'It's bad, isn't it?' She very suddenly swung her legs off the lounger. The whole thing snapped together around her and the rest of the cocktail went flying, showering Matt.

When they had Carole out of the lounger and on her feet, she marched inside.

'I think we should wait here,' Lily said.

Matt nodded, still brushing cocktail off his lap. 'She wasn't wrong when she said this was sticky. Maybe I'll—'

'The *bastard*,' yelled Carole. She appeared at the kitchen

door and marched back towards them, waving a letter. 'He's bloody left me. He's bloody *left me*. Because *I'm* unreasonable, he says. Complete bloody nonsense. *He's* the unreasonable one.' She walked over to the barbecue and tore and tore the paper until it was in tiny pieces and scattered them in the underneath bit where the coals went. 'Lol. He *hates* it when I put paper in there. Well now he's gone. So I'll put as much paper in as I bloody well like.' And then she did an enormous snort and tears began to stream down her cheeks beneath her sunglasses.

'Oh God,' Matt said.

'I'm so, so sorry.' Lily ran over to where Carole had slumped down onto a chair and put her arms round her. 'Carole, listen. Norm seemed very upset. I think it's just a tiff from his side. I think he'll want to come back soon.'

Carole did another massive snort, took the sunglasses off and wiped her eyes with her arm. 'D'you know what, Lily? I don't *want* him back. Good bloody riddance I say. You leave someone, hurt them, you can't expect them to take you back.'

'I'm not sure that's true.' Matt had walked the length of the swimming pool and was standing in front of them in his sticky shorts.

'It's completely true.' Carole sniffed, hard.

'No, it isn't. And I know for certain that it isn't.' Matt wasn't looking at Carole, he was looking at Lily. 'I would totally get back together with someone who'd split up with me in the past if they had good reason for doing so. Sometimes you might be right for each other, but it's maybe the wrong time, maybe you just need some time apart to grow, learn about life. And then be together forever.'

Lily's breath caught. He wasn't talking about Carole and Norm any more. It felt like he'd just made a huge declaration of intent.

TWENTY

MATT

'What are you talking about?' Carole said. 'You're being ridiculous. Norm and I have been married for forty years. And I'm sixty-five and he's pushing seventy. We don't need to bloody learn about life.'

Lily was half gigantic-smiling and half gigantic-frowning at Matt, indicating Carole with her head and an eye swivel. Yeah, maybe he'd been a little insensitive there. But *God*, it felt like things had fallen into place in his mind and he wanted to speak to Lily about their feelings for each other right now.

'I think what Matt *means*—' Lily hugged Carole again '—is that maybe you and Norm just need a little bit of space from each other like everyone does sometimes but that obviously you're great together and maybe you should call him when you're up to it?'

'Oh, Lily,' Carole wailed. 'What am I going to do without him?' And then she broke into heaving sobs again. Lily pulled her right into her arms and held her and did a zip-it motion at Matt when he opened his mouth to say something to cheer his aunt up.

'Why don't you go and change your shorts?' Lily indicated

over to the house with her head. 'And then maybe fix us all some coffee?'

By mid-afternoon, they – well, Lily, because Matt kept saying the wrong thing and every time he came back from his latest chore and opened his mouth, Lily suggested that he do the dishwasher, clean the pink jeep, make lunch, vacuum the whole of the downstairs of the villa, put the rubbish out, make coffee – had Carole in a better state of mind.

'You're right, Lily,' she said, as Matt put another cup of coffee down in front of her. 'Norm will be back. And if he isn't, I need to accept it. Or maybe I need to go and find him and tell him I'm sorry if I upset him and I love him. In the meantime, I do need to make the most of this time alone. I'd like to have a girls' night here at the house tonight. Let's call Penelope and she can arrange it. She has a boat so she can get over here. Matt, you can be an honorary girl for the evening.'

Right. Not exactly what he'd had in mind for tonight at the airport when he'd leapt at the opportunity to spend another day on the island with Lily. With Lily and no one else.

'Great,' he said, pretty sure that if he objected out loud it would upset Carole and annoy Lily. 'Um?' he began, and Lily gave him the evil eye. 'Great,' he said again.

'Do you know,' Carole said after another cup of coffee, 'I might go and have a lie-down now.' Hurrah.

Matt and Lily both waited – weirdly, both of them quite statue-like, like any movement would look suspicious – until Carole had been safely inside the house for a few seconds, and then turned to each other.

'Fancy a walk?' Matt asked.

'Yup.' Lily smiled at him and it nearly took his breath away.

'So you have a great imagination for chores,' Matt said as they began to stroll towards the gate at the end of the garden.

'Only because you apparently have a great imagination for saying the worst possible thing to cheer Carole up.'

'I know. I didn't realise I had such a knack for it.' He reached out and took her hand. And that was nice. Better than nice. 'You know it's weird: on paper you might say that I'm keener than you, or historically I was keener, on an open-with-your-emotions conversation, but in practice you're good at those conversations, and I'm *bad*.'

'You aren't bad. Except very specifically at cheering Carole up the day that she's found out Norm's left her. Not gifted there. But last night when we were talking it felt like you were making a lot of sense.'

'It did? I mean, *I* thought I was making sense. I think *we* make sense. I'd love the opportunity to restart our relationship. Maybe differently from how we did things last time. Maybe put a lot more effort into spending quality time together.'

'I'd like that.' Lily's smile was so beautiful that he had to kiss her, and then that was basically that for an extended period of time.

'What about if we creep into the house?' Matt wasn't totally up for al fresco sex in broad daylight.

'What if Carole hears us go in, though, and wants to chat?' Lily leaned back into the crook of his arm and adjusted her top back to decency. 'What about going to the pool house?'

'Carole has a pool man, who comes a lot. I'd rather take my chances in the house.'

Lily started giggling as they crept through the house, and then she started coughing she was laughing so much. 'We're like teenagers,' she hiccupped when they'd made it safely into her bedroom.

'I know.' Matt smiled at her and pulled her towards him and kissed her.

. . .

Some time later, Matt opened his incredibly heavy eyes to a thunderous banging. What was that? Where was he?

Oh, okay. He was wrapped around a sound-asleep Lily and he'd been asleep too. Her hair was in his face, their limbs were entwined, they were all tangled up in the bedsheets and they were gloriously naked. Two sleeps in one day. Clearly they were too old for staying up all night.

The banging was getting louder.

'Are you in there, Lily?' shouted Carole. And the door handle began to turn.

Lily – who'd always been a very dead-to-the-world sleeper – was still completely comatose, breathing deeply and regularly, smiling in her sleep. And the door was opening.

'Stop,' yelled Matt. 'I'm here too. Don't come in.'

'Good Lord,' said Carole through the crack in the open door. 'Okay. Well, the girls will be here quite soon. I'll see you downstairs.'

Lily heaved a big sigh, rolled over towards Matt and opened her eyes slowly. And then she smiled and Matt's heart jumped.

When they got downstairs, 'the girls' had already arrived. There were about twenty of them standing on the terrace outside the kitchen, with Carole in the middle of the group, pink champagne in hand, all glammed up, looking a *lot* happier.

'OMG,' she shouted as Matt and Lily made their way over. 'What have you two been *doing*? No, don't give me the details, but OMG.' She turned to all her friends and said, 'Matt and Lily were an item for quite a while when they were younger, then Matt got married to someone else – clearly a mistake, they had a nasty divorce – and *now* it seems like Matt and Lily might be back together again. Or at least sleeping together again.'

'I *knew* there was something between you.' Penelope stepped forward and began stroking Matt's biceps again like she'd never left off from the morning of the wedding. 'You make a *gorgeous* couple.' And then she let go of his arms and began to clap. And then everyone was clapping.

So essentially they were being clapped for having slept together. Which was a new experience for Matt, and, he was guessing, Lily.

'Wow,' said Lily to everyone.

Matt looked at all the women looking at him and Lily and then at Lily and made a snap decision that he was pretty sure Lily would be on board with. 'Carole, this has been great. Lily and I are going out for dinner now. We'll catch you when we get back.' He grabbed Lily's hand and started walking, to a lot of – *seriously* – catcalls and whistles.

'That was a very good call,' Lily said as they speed-walked down the drive. 'Why are we walking so fast?'

'I think we're running away.'

And then they broke into an actual run, until Lily pulled Matt's arm, and panted, 'Stop, I have a stitch.'

They found a great little restaurant tucked away in a quiet residential street in the local village, with the owner delighted to show them to a table and increase his Monday night business.

They talked about nothing serious at all through platters of delicious local cuisine and a bottle of island-produced wine, clapped a violinist sitting in the corner of the room playing a mixture of haunting and jazzy melodies, and basically had a wonderful evening, made even better by the anticipation of the night to come.

'Oh my goodness,' Lily said as they left the restaurant, 'we completely forgot to go back to the airport to try to get on a flight tomorrow.'

'Oh God, yes. I actually do need to get back. Mainly because I need to pick up the dog from Gemma on Wednesday.' Matt looked at Lily – well, the top of her head, because she seemed to be suddenly staring hard straight ahead of her, like she didn't want to hear about his ex-wife or the marital dog. He wasn't sure what to say so he looked at his watch. 'It's far too late to go now.'

After a short pause, Lily looked up and said, 'Looks like we might just have to deal with being forced to spend another day hanging out in a luxury villa on a beautiful Greek island.' She twinkled at him and he felt as though his heart might perhaps burst.

When they rolled back into the house, after a stroll round some of the village's winding streets, Carole and her friends – a lot of men as well as women now – were dancing on the terrace, music blaring, garden lights flashing, waiters still providing copious drinks.

'Pretty sure no one will notice if we just go straight to bed,' Matt said.

'Definitely. They're busy.' Lily indicated towards Penelope and another woman. It took Matt a moment to take in what he was seeing and then he put his hand over his eyes.

'Was that...?'

'Yup. Belly dancing wearing nipple tassels. With some serious appreciation from the male guests.'

'Oh my God. I hope Carole's paying the waiters danger money. We need to get ourselves upstairs fast.'

'I feel inspired,' Lily said as they held hands up the stairs. 'I think I want to be like that when I'm their age.'

Matt tried hard to imagine Lily doing a nipple tassel shimmy in her sixties and realised that whatever she was doing when she was that age, he wanted her to be doing it with him.

———

Matt woke up first in the morning, his arms around Lily again. The room's solidly built shutters were keeping out most of the sun, but from the brightness of the splinters of light that were filtering around their edges, it felt like it had to be at least ten.

This was the perfect way to wake up, the perfect way to start a day.

Lily had always slept longer than he had in the mornings. He lay for a few moments, just holding her, the way he always used to when they were together. Well, until one of them had to jump out of bed for work. They really hadn't ever had enough time together.

In the half-light he could just make out her lashes lying against her cheeks. She heaved a big contented-sounding sigh and snuggled further against him. Yep, he really did want to stay here forever.

He reached for his phone to settle in to read the news while Lily slept.

He had a message from Norm. He'd taken his yacht and sailed to Naxos and was staying with a friend there. They were going to play golf later today and Norm was having a jolly good time actually. Right. Was that something to share with Carole? Probably not.

They ought to get out of bed and try to get themselves on a flight today. Matt was pretty sure that Carole would cope with Norm's departure with the help of her friends, and he did have work to do back in London, and it sounded like Lily did too. He wasn't going to wake her up, though.

She eventually stirred a good half hour later.

'Morning.' He smiled at her blinking at him.

'I feel like I've been drugged. That was such a good sleep.'

'Same. I've missed waking up with you.'

'Me too.' She smiled sleepily, and, again, he was lost.

They finally made it downstairs in time for a late lunch.

'How are you two lovebirds?' Carole looked a lot better than she had this time yesterday.

Matt tried not to wince. He desperately wanted the love-bird description to be right, but it kind of felt like they needed to feel their way to firmer ground with their relationship, if it could be described as a relationship yet, and it didn't feel like a running commentary from Carole would help. Today, he just wanted to enjoy these moments with Lily.

'Let's eat outside,' Carole said. Yeah, it looked like enjoying these moments was going to include Carole.

When they were sitting at the table on the terrace with way more food than three people could reasonably eat, Carole said, 'Have you heard from Norm?' Dammit. Matt should have discussed with Lily what to say to about that, but he'd obviously got sidetracked.

'Um.' He cleared his throat. 'He's on Naxos. Not too far away.'

'What's he doing?' Carole barked.

'Playing golf.' He glanced at Lily, who was frowning and signalling with her eyes. Yeah, he shouldn't have said that.

'Nice to know he's frigging enjoying himself,' said Carole.

'I wouldn't say enjoying himself,' Matt said, a little desperately.

'He loves golf.' Carole speared a tomato viciously. 'More than me, it seems.'

'Um.' Matt took a slice of olive bread. 'This bread smells delicious.'

Lily said, 'Carole, if Norm had seen you here last night he'd have thought you were having a fabulous time with your friends.'

'I actually did have a fabulous time.' Carole cut a piece of ham even more viciously than the tomato.

'Exactly,' Lily said, 'but some might say you're missing Norm. I don't think him playing golf means that he isn't missing you, I think it probably means that he's trying to pretend that he did the right thing leaving and is trying to keep himself happy. I reckon he's actually really upset. I mean, why would he bother texting Matt otherwise? *Maybe* he was trying to make a point, knowing that Matt would tell you.'

'There might be something in that.' Carole helped herself to some salad, less angrily. She pointed at the feta. 'Try some of that cheese with the bread. Oh, I should have told you immediately: the ferries are back on. Fully operational. You're more than welcome to stay as long as you like – you know I'd always love to have you here – but I know you have work commitments both of you. I'd maybe sort your Athens-to-London flights before you leave here, but I think you'll be able to get on a ferry this afternoon and that might be easier than flying from here to Athens. Maybe check the flights from the ferry terminal. They shouldn't be too booked up on a Tuesday evening. Maybe best to go as soon as possible so that you don't miss out?'

'It's like she *wants* us to leave,' said Lily when Carole had shooed them away from the table and said that she absolutely wouldn't hear of them helping to clear lunch up. 'Hopefully because she's planning to call Norm, not because she wants to wallow. Or have too *much* fun.'

Within only a couple of hours, they were sitting on the deck of a ferry, flights changed to that night, waving off Carole, who'd driven them down to the harbour.

'She definitely wanted us to leave,' Lily said.

Matt nodded. 'She did.' And no bad thing, because right now he just wanted to be with Lily without his aunt observing them the whole time. 'So, can we meet up in London? Very soon?'

'I'd like that.' Lily tipped her head back to smile at him and then reached up to kiss him on the lips.

They spent the ferry trip laughing, talking about nothing serious, gazing and marvelling at the scenery – islands and the sparkling, almost-navy sea – and, really, just enjoying each other's company.

The taxi journey from the port at Piraeus to the airport was on paper a lot less scenic and a lot less comfortable but in practice just perfect because they were together. Matt remembered this feeling from the past, that he'd enjoy, or at least be able to deal with, just about anything as long as he was sharing the experience with Lily.

'Quick.' They'd got to the airport and were running as fast as they could with their cases to make it to the check-in in time to get the flight they'd both switched to. Lily's ludicrously full bag kept falling off her shoulder as they ran but she was insistent that Matt shouldn't carry it.

They stopped in front of the check-in screen and Matt started tapping while Lily rummaged for her passport inside her bag. 'Aisle?' In the past she'd always liked to sit in the aisle so that she could pretend she was on a train and not far too many dangerous thousands of feet up above solid ground.

'Of course.'

They wandered the duty-free shops hand-in-hand and it felt great. It couldn't have been any better if they'd been shopping on Athens' fanciest shopping street, because it was just about being together.

'Which one?' Lily held up the back of her hand with three lipstick stripes on it.

Matt opened his mouth to say the furthest right one, and then remembered lessons learned the hard way. Most recently yesterday with Carole. Sometimes there was no value in sharing your own opinions fully. 'Which one do *you* like?' he asked.

'I think the middle one.'

'Me too.' The one nearer her thumb was *way* nicer.

Lily narrowed her eyes. 'You don't actually think that, do you? I'm not a toddler.'

'Well, I do prefer that one.' He pointed. 'But they're all nice?'

'You have terrible taste in lipstick, it seems. I'm getting the middle one.' As she took her purse out to pay, she turned and grinned at him over her shoulder, a wide smile just for him.

Another breathless moment.

TWENTY-ONE
LILY

Lily did her strap up very carefully. She'd definitely read somewhere that *all* flight crash survivors had been properly strapped in when the crash happened. Then she unstrapped herself and took her denim jacket off and did the strap back up. Fear always made her hot. Apart from when it made her freezing cold. Maybe she should put the jacket back on.

'You okay?' Matt looked like he was preparing to *enjoy* their flight. He'd always done that. He was looking out of the window at the runway. He'd still be happily looking out of the windows even when they were billions of feet up in the air over hard land. Or hard water. Water was very hard apparently when you landed on it from a long way up.

'Fine,' Lily managed.

'Hey.' Matt reached his arm round her and squeezed. 'Statistically this is pretty much the safest way of travelling. I mean, I know I say that every time...' like the last eight years had never happened and they still travelled together regularly '... but it's true.'

'Also statistically: if you fall out of the air from a really long way up, you pretty much always die. Just saying. It's too all or nothing.'

'I mean, so's being hit by a car or getting a very serious illness. I think we just have to live life in the moment and not worry about the things we can't do anything about, and just focus on the things that we *can* do something about. Like, if you leave the house on time and there's an unexpected traffic jam and you're going to be really late for a *huge* client meeting, there's literally no point stressing because there's nothing you can do.'

'But you *always* used to get stressed about being late for work.'

'I know. And then a couple of years ago I had an epiphany in a traffic jam, which was caused by a lorryload of melons tipping over three cars in front of me, and I'm *way* more chilled about lateness now.'

'How long did it take to clear the melons?'

'Literally an hour and half.'

'Melon melons or watermelons?'

'Water.'

Wow. So weird. It was like something Matt said had just chimed inside her. She was genuinely feeling kind of zen right now. She looked at him and smiled.

'What?' He was smiling back.

'You're cool.'

'Why thank you.' His smile grew and he leaned over and kissed her cheek. 'Come on. Let's choose a film to watch.'

They were busy arguing over whether to go for a classic James Bond or a just-released psych thriller or a romcom, when Lily realised that the cabin crew were halfway through their start-of-flight instructions.

Oh God. What if there was a crash and they didn't know what to do? She could feel her heart rate picking up and her palms getting clammy. Would Matt notice if she took some very deep breaths and a couple of puffs just in case?

She risked a half-second glance away from the cabin crew to focus on him. He looked up from the film list and smiled at her.

'You okay?' he asked.

'Yeah, totally fine,' she said, switching her focus back to the evacuation demonstration. Actually, maybe there was no need to always pretend that she was okay in front of Matt. 'Actually, not *totally* fine, if I'm honest. I might just take a couple of puffs. My chest's a bit tight.' She took her blue inhaler out. For the first time ever in front of Matt. In the past she'd have been skulking in the loos to use her inhaler.

Matt waited until she'd finished and then took her hand, pointed at the film list and said, 'What about if you choose now and we go to the cinema next week and I choose?' Okay. So all good. He wasn't going to comment on her inhaler. Well, of course he wasn't. Why had she ever thought he would? And if he had, would it have mattered?

'That's an excellent plan.' She picked up the film list. She didn't need to watch the rest of the demonstration because, realistically, there wasn't going to be anything different about the emergency doors and oxygen masks on this flight from any other. And they needed to get going with the film soon so that they could watch the whole thing during the flight.

It was so nice that Matt wanted to go to the cinema with her next week.

Lily was still smiling about the loveliness of feeling like they were going to be doing stuff together again – and, if she was honest, the fact that they were going with her film choice because Matt's choices both looked rubbish – when she realised that they'd already taken off and she hadn't even started her usual near-nervous-breakdown routine surrounding the fact that apparently, due to maths and physics, take-off and landing were more dangerous than actually being up in the air.

'We're up!' she said.

'Yeah, I know. What kind of meal do you think they're going to be bringing us? Proper dinner or just a snack? I'm really hungry.' Matt looked up from where he'd been trying to navigate the film screen. 'I *should* have asked if you're okay before thinking about my stomach. Are you?'

Lily laughed. 'Yep. I actually am. Thank you.' So nice that he wasn't treating her with kid gloves.

The rest of the journey home was amazing. Lily loved craning her neck to see the screen. She loved eating the crap airline food. She loved drinking the airline cheap white wine that tasted of Marmite. She loved the long wait at the luggage carousel and the extreme queue to get out of the airport. Basically, obviously, she loved Matt and she loved being with him. Would she fancy a bit of poop scooping or public loo cleaning, or even taking a flight in a tiny plane? Yes, she really would if she could do any of it with Matt.

'Share a taxi?' he asked when they were *finally*, just after midnight, done with the airport queuing.

'You don't know where I live.' Funny how when they'd been in Greece they'd talked about big stuff and small stuff but not really the medium stuff, their everyday lives, at *all*. 'And I don't know whether you've moved?'

'Still in the same flat.' Matt lived in leafy Muswell Hill in a flat that he'd bought at a discount because no one else could see past the awful state it had been in. He'd worked some architect's magic on it and had turned it into a stunning haven.

'I live quite close to Heathrow, actually. I'm saving up to finally buy somewhere and my rent's nice and low due to the *extreme* aeroplane noise. You're welcome to come back to the flat?'

'I have an early start in the morning.'

Lily felt her face fall.

'No, no, no. What I meant by that was I'm going to have to

get up really early. I did *not* mean that I didn't want to come. I *really* want to come. If that's okay?'

Lily was smiling again. 'It's very okay.'

They were already kissing as they barrelled through the front door, straight to the sofa in Lily's open-plan living room.

'Let me get us some drinks.' She pulled away from him and stood up. Now that they were back home, things suddenly felt more serious. 'I feel like we still need to talk. Coffee? Tea? Water?'

She felt *really* self-conscious as she got their teas. Like Matt was clearly going to be looking around the room while she had her back to him, and like everything between them felt bizarrely more personal now that they weren't on neutral territory any more.

'Thank you,' he said when she handed him his cup of builder's. 'You've made this room lovely. All your pictures and cushions.'

'Thank you. I'm *really* looking forward now to buying my own place and being able to do it up myself. Nearly there. Anyway.'

'Yep, sorry. I wasn't trying to change the subject.'

Lily sat down at the other end of the sofa and said, 'I really do feel like we still need to talk except I'm not even sure what there is to discuss. It's like there was a big barrier between us, from both sides, and it's gone. And I don't know what else to say.'

'Maybe sometimes there just isn't that much to say?'

'Even when the issue was huge?'

'Maybe.'

Lily yawned. 'I think I'm too tired to think.' She moved along the sofa and leaned into Matt. 'Mmm, that's *nice*.'

. . .

Gaaah. Lily groped with her hand for her phone. It couldn't actually *be* the morning, surely. She must have made a mistake when she set it. She found the phone and banged it a few times. The alarm wasn't bloody going off. Actually, the sound wasn't coming from there.

'Matt.' She gave him a little nudge in the ribs. 'Your alarm's going off.'

'Mmph.' He flailed with an arm and the sound stopped, thank the Lord.

It had been like this at the beginning the last time they started going out. Far too little sleep. *The last time*. Like they'd definitely started going out again. It really did feel like they had. Lily gave an actual physical squirm of pleasure.

Matt put his arm round her and buried his face against her. 'Want to stay here all day,' he mumbled.

'I know. But we have work.'

Matt groaned and then pushed himself slowly up into a sitting position. 'Yeah. I do have to go. I have to get home and change. I have a busy schedule today. Back-to-back meetings until mid-afternoon and then picking up Elmer and working the rest of the day from home. I have to fly to Edinburgh tomorrow for a couple of nights but I'm free this evening. Would you like to come over and meet Elmer?' He swung his legs out of bed with another groan and began to gather up clothes.

'I'd love to.' She loved dogs. They grinned at each other inanely for a couple of beats and then Lily said, 'Who's dog-sitting while you're in Edinburgh?'

'My neighbour, Cynthia. Remember her?' Matt reached down and planted a kiss on Lily's lips, and then leaned in for more. A couple of minutes later, he pulled away and said, 'I really do have to go. I'll call you later.'

Lily checked the time on her phone when she'd seen him out of the door. Five thirty. The actual crack of dawn. Definitely time to crawl back into bed and get another hour and a half of sleep in before she started her day properly.

As she drifted back off, images of their week in Greece and snippets of things they'd said to each other swirled around in her head. It still felt like there was a conversation that they should have started and finished properly. Like, could things really be as simple as Matt had made out?

———

Lily arrived on Matt's doorstep that evening straight from work. She rang the bell and waited, her heart thudding like she had... what, first-date nerves? Silly.

Matt opened his front door, half bending down holding Elmer's collar and wearing a huge beam and Lily felt herself beam too.

'He's liable to get a bit over-excited when he meets new people,' Matt said, still smiling broadly at Lily and still holding onto Elmer as she closed the door behind her. 'I should have asked whether you're okay with dogs – any allergies or anything – but I'm guessing you'd have said?'

'I actually would have done,' Lily said. 'If I'm honest, I might not have done in the past, I might have just tried to avoid the situation without saying, but I would tell you now. But luckily I don't have animal allergies.' She bent down to pet Elmer. 'He's *gorgeous*.'

'Yeah, he is. I'm a very proud dog-dad.'

Lily straightened up and opened her shoulder bag. 'I have a couple of little presents for the two of you in here.' She handed a bottle of wine to Matt and took out a natural rubber ball attached to a rope for Elmer. 'Are you okay for him to have this?'

'Absolutely. He's going to be a very happy dog. And this wine looks great. Both completely unnecessary but both very gratefully received. Thank you.' He smiled at her and then kissed her.

They took Elmer for a walk around Highgate Wood before going back to the flat for the dinner Matt had, 'just whipped up from store-cupboard ingredients, honestly,' he said, pushing three supermarket bags and two cookery books into the corner behind him.

'That was delicious.' Lily spooned out her last little bit of the lemon posset pudding Matt had made to follow his prawn and shiitake mushroom dish. 'I'm not saying you weren't a good cook when we were younger...' he'd been a terrible cook then '... but your cooking skills are *amazing* now. Properly impressive.'

'If I'm honest, I don't cook that much, I've just learnt to follow a recipe a lot better. For special occasions.' Matt smiled at Lily and she smiled back at him. 'I'm so pleased we met each other again,' he said.

'Me too.'

Matt moved his chair towards Lily's and she moved hers towards his and put her hand into the one he was holding out to her. And Elmer pushed between the two of them and placed his front paws on Matt's – nicely solid – thigh.

'Does Elmer ever sleep in bed with you?' Lily asked, not *totally* pleased at the prospect of things being constantly interrupted by him, if she was honest.

'Nope. He used to when he was a puppy but we...' Matt tailed off and Lily tried hard not to mind that he'd clearly been about to mention being in bed with Gemma, and actually pretty much succeeded. He shook his head and frowned. 'Sorry.'

'Hey, no, nothing to say sorry about.' Lily looked down at where they were still holding hands, in a slightly rigid way now. 'I ended our relationship, you met Gemma, I met a couple of other people, although nothing long-term, nothing for either of us to apologise about.' She relaxed her hand and squeezed Matt's fingers. 'And of course I don't *love* talking about her but it really is fine. Genuinely.' She smiled at him and his frown eased.

He pushed Elmer gently off his leg and stood up. 'Maybe we could go and watch some TV? And then maybe an early night?'

'I'd love that.'

The three of them curled up together on the sofa, Lily and Matt with their arms round each other and Elmer snuggled up on Matt's other side.

'This—' Matt kissed Lily '—is perfect.' And then his phone started pinging like mad. 'Oh my God, *what*?' he said. 'Oh, okay. It's Norm. He's arrived in Bristol to stay with his brother because he's upset that Carole didn't follow him to Naxos. And he'd like to come and visit. And he has a lot to say. Maybe he wants me to repeat all of this to Carole. I'm just going to send a very quick reply saying I'm very busy this evening but I'll speak to him tomorrow.' He kissed her again.

'Mmm.'

———

The next day, Lily's phone was going silent-vibratingly ballistic as she finished up the last appointment of the morning's antenatal clinic. She took it out of her bag to check it and discovered that she had literally about fifteen missed calls from her mother.

She went completely cold, all over, really fast.

She actually wanted to speak to Matt, tell him she was scared that something terrible had happened. But that was stupid. What she should actually do was speak to her *mother*, and find out for certain what had happened rather than speculate.

Help, she couldn't get her fingers to work on the phone. Okay, stop panicking. Deep breath, focus, finger into home button, press the right things. Okay. She'd done it.

Her mum answered on the first ring.

'Darling, do you have your inhaler to hand?' God. What?

'Is it Dad?'

'Do you have your inhaler?' Her mum was practically shrieking.

'*Yes*. What's happened?'

'Take some puffs first.'

'Please could you just tell me?'

'He had a big heart attack. He's in hospital and he's having surgery shortly. Bypass.'

Everything suddenly went black and starry in front of Lily's eyes and she staggered. She caught the wall of the front garden she was walking past and held onto it until the light-headedness had passed.

'Lily? Lily, are you alright?'

'Yes, I'm fine. Are *you* alright? Shall I come? I can come immediately.' She'd only been working a half day today at the hospital and was doing photo curation this afternoon; she'd have to postpone her clients.

'Darling, there's no point. He'll be in surgery before you get here. Why not plan to visit when he's out? Maybe tonight but more likely tomorrow, I think?'

'Okay.' Oh God.

'Lily, how's your breathing?'

'It's *totally* fine. Totally normal.' Bit of a lie. As soon as she got off the phone she was going to take some puffs. It was the shock.

'Are you *sure*?'

For God's sake. Her father had had a second big heart attack and was about to have major surgery and Lily was thirty-three and her mother was *still* managing to make it about Lily's health.

'Yes. How are *you*? I could still come to the hospital and keep you company?'

'They told me to go home and keep myself occupied so I might do some work. I'll update you when I hear anything.'

'Okay. Well, let me know. I love you.' She did love her mother, a lot; she just wasn't that keen on spending a lot of time with her. And apparently her mother felt the same way because when the chips were down she'd rather occupy herself with work than with Lily's company. Although maybe that was because she was still perma-worried about Lily and she couldn't deal with any extra stress right now.

Oh, God, she could feel her chest getting tight.

Okay, puffs.

And now some deep breaths through her nose, mouth closed, trying to get air right to the bottom of her lungs.

Okay, things were getting better.

And her dad was in great hands in an amazing hospital. Heart bypasses happened all the time, so the surgeons would clearly know exactly what they were doing. She needed to focus on the positives and not panic.

She should probably take a leaf out of her mum's book and not give in to her first instinct, which had been to take the rest of the day off work.

Maybe she'd give Matt a quick call first. Tell him what had happened. It felt like just the sound of his voice would be comforting.

No answer. To voicemail or not to voicemail? Not, obviously. You couldn't leave a message saying *Hi, just to let you know my dad's seriously ill, ciao*, could you.

A message pinged in from him a minute or two later. *Running between meetings. Missing you. On way to Edinburgh soon. Will call tonight.*

Oh. Well, yes. He had a busy job. She couldn't expect him to be free to chat at any given moment. Same with her. She wouldn't be able to talk to someone in the middle of delivering a baby.

Maybe she'd try one of her best friends. Not Tess, obviously, because she was still on her honeymoon.

Aaliyah didn't pick up and again Lily didn't leave a message and then Aaliyah texted back to say *On nursery run, catch you later xxxx*

And Meg didn't pick up, Lily didn't leave a message, and Meg didn't text either but she obviously had a lot on her plate at the moment with Pythagoras having just moved to Edinburgh.

Well, that was fine. Work.

Lily finally got a message from her mum late afternoon to say that the operation seemed to have been a success and her dad had been moved to recovery and Lily would be able to visit him tomorrow. It seemed that there might be some other complications, but hopefully nothing short-term life-threatening.

Lily immediately tried to call her, and she wasn't answering her phone either.

Did no one ever answer phones nowadays?

Well. Obviously it was a relief that her dad had come through the operation but the rest of it didn't sound that good.

Oh, listen to that – her own phone was ringing.

'Hi, Lily.' Her friend Jessica from work sounded like she was panting. 'Phoning you while I run. Just checking you're still good for the cinema this evening? Could we meet a bit earlier?'

'I...' With the whole delayed-in-Greece thing plus Matt and the lack of sleep, Lily hadn't been totally on top of the date. Now she thought about it, yes, she and Jessica had definitely agreed to go out this evening, with another couple of friends from work. She *really* wasn't up for it. But on the other hand, moping in her flat by herself wasn't going to do a lot of good; working had definitely helped her state of mind this afternoon. Plus she never liked to let people down. 'Yep, great.'

. . .

Matt left a voice message while she was in the cinema. 'Hey. I'm missing you. I'm in Edinburgh, just about to go out for dinner but I'll call you later if you're still up. I have news.'

'I'm so sorry but I'm going to wimp out and go straight home,' she told her friends after the film finished. 'I'll come for a drink next time, I promise. I'm still catching up from Greece. We had a lot of late nights.' She hadn't told them about Matt but anyone could have a lot of late nights on holiday, especially when they'd been to a wedding.

She hadn't told them about her dad, either. It would have felt a bit weird telling them when she hadn't even told Matt.

Wow. She and Matt had only been back together, if that's what they were, for literally a few days, although a *lot* had happened in that time. Was she turning into Meg, putting her partner ahead of her friends? No. She'd very happily introduce Matt to all her friends.

'You look miles away,' Jessica said. 'Thinking about your holiday?'

'Yep. It was a good one.' Lily hugged the others and said, 'Have one for me. I'll see you at work and next time I'll be massively up for drinks, I promise.'

She tried Matt again as she arrived home and *finally* a phone was picked up.

'Hey, Lily, guess what, you will not *believe* who just called me. Well, you will, but I'm still quite surprised.'

'Ooh, who?' Lily said automatically. Weird how however low or worried you felt inside, you went straight into saying-the-right-thing mode when someone else spoke first.

'Carole. Not a surprise, except she called me from Bristol.'

'Bristol?'

'Basically, from what I can piece together, she shoved us out the door, spent the rest of the day packing up the house and then set off first thing yesterday morning, narrowly missed

Norm on Naxos, called all his friends and family to track him down and landed in Bristol early evening.'

'Wow. So have they had a big reunion?' Lily was good at this. This was what she'd always done. Surface chat about one, non-emotive, thing, while thinking about another thing. She could totally be interested and surprised about Carole and Norm while going silently *screamingly mad with worry* about her father at the same time. And pissed off with her mother, actually. But a lot more worried than pissed off.

'Lily?'

'Sorry, didn't hear you. Bad line.'

'Basically, Norm's having none of it. He told her to go and stay in a hotel.'

'No way. Oh my goodness. Poor Carole.'

'She's pretty sure that he's just playing hard to get.'

'Wow. I hope she's right.'

'Yup. So how's your evening been?'

'Um, kind of average.' She was done with pretending. It was much better not to. She was actually just going to tell him all about her dad.

'Really? Would that be because you're missing me by any chance?' Oh. Maybe he hadn't heard her tone of voice properly. Actually, there was quite a lot of noise in the background. She'd thought it was the TV but maybe he was out. Somewhere really noisy by the sounds of it; there'd just been a very loud crash.

'What was that?'

'Glasses smashing. A waiter just dropped a tray. I'm in the hotel bar with a couple of colleagues.'

Now was clearly really not the time to talk to him.

'I'm really sorry but I'm going to have to get going,' she said. 'I'm really tired.'

'Can't wait to see you.' Nice that he'd say that in front of other people.

'Me too.' She really wished his job involved a lot less travel. She'd like him to be *here*. 'Night.'

———

He called her in the morning while she was having her breakfast, reading a very brief text update from her mum to the effect that her dad was doing okay and maybe Lily could visit in the evening. It felt like by the evening she'd suggest that Lily wait until tomorrow to visit. Like Lily was too delicate a flower to be able to visit her own father in hospital. Was she going to have to end up having an argument with her mum over this?

'I'm just walking down the Royal Mile. It's sunny but quite fresh. Glorious actually. How's London looking this morning?'

'Pretty much as usual, I think.'

'Lily, are you okay?'

'Yep. Well, just a bit worried. My dad had a heart attack. But he seems to be doing okay now.'

'Oh my *God*, Lily. When did it happen?'

'Yesterday.'

'Lily. I'm so sorry for wittering on about Carole and Norm last night. You should have interrupted and told me.'

'Well, it was difficult to hear you in the bar.' She blinked away tears. Right now it felt too difficult to tell him *how much* she'd wanted to talk to him.

And how it just felt ridiculous that finally she did just want to talk – and talk and *talk* – but he wasn't here for her to talk *to*. Maybe that had been the real problem last time. Maybe it would always be a problem. Maybe this just wasn't ever going to work. In real life, mutual love just wasn't enough, was it? You needed other stuff, like regularly being in the same place at the same time. Maybe they should just leave things between them as a holiday fling.

TWENTY-TWO

MATT

'So, tell me now what happened? If you'd like to?' Matt said. 'Is he in hospital?'

'Yep. Being very well looked after, I hear. I'm sure he'll be fine.' Her voice wasn't very steady.

'Would you like me to come back? I can cancel my meetings or do them remotely.'

'Honestly, that's really kind but it's fine.'

And he'd lost her. He knew he had. She'd just withdrawn from him again, put the barriers straight back up.

'So what kind of a project are you working on in Edinburgh?' She'd got her voice back under control. She sounded for all the world like she wanted to ask the question and was interested. 'Is that the hotel you were telling me about?'

'Lily...' No. What was he going to say? Was he going to tell her that she *had* to stop talking about his job and tell him all about her dad and how she was feeling? Or not tell him about her dad, just chat about anything she'd like to. But just talk to him. No, of course he wasn't going to say that. It was entirely up to her whether or not she wanted to. 'I'm here for you,' he said.

God. Lame. Also, likely to put her back up. 'If you'd like to talk, I mean. Or not.'

'Thank you. I need to go. I have work. Thank you so much for calling.'

God.

This felt like when her grandmother had died. She'd become so distant and he just hadn't been able to overcome the walls she'd erected around herself. Probably partly because he'd never been around. Like he still wasn't. Realistically, things really weren't ever going to work out between them if they could only manage what was effectively a long-distance relationship.

———

Back in London the next evening, he retrieved Elmer from Cynthia in the next-door ground floor flat and sank onto his sofa. A dog hug would be great right now. He should actually get another dog. One he didn't have to share the custody of. Maybe two so that the new dog wouldn't be bereft when Elmer came and went.

His phone buzzed and he pulled it out of his pocket, his heart rate literally up just at the sound of it. Hopefully it was Lily replying to one of the many (too many?) texts he'd sent asking if she was okay. Nope. It was his friend and work partner Ade wanting to know if he was up for a pub lunch tomorrow. Ade's local did amazing Sunday roasts.

He didn't want to have lunch with Ade tomorrow. He wanted to see Lily, and talk, and comfort her and hold her and be with her. Apparently not what she wanted, though.

God, he hoped something terrible hadn't happened to her father. Maybe that was why she hadn't been replying to him. He was going to call her. Maybe Lily would pick up a call where she wouldn't text. During the rest of his stay in Edinburgh and on the journey home he hadn't had time for an actual call, only messages. Which in itself told a story that maybe he should listen to.

And she did pick up.

'Hi, Matt.' It was ridiculously good to hear her voice again.

'Hey. How are you doing? How's your dad?'

'He's hopefully going to be okay. We're waiting to hear. How was your trip?'

'Yeah, good, thanks. The usual. Would you like me to come over? Or you'd be very welcome to come here?'

'Thank you so much. I might just get an early night. Matt...' She paused.

Matt waited. He was pretty sure from the tone of her voice that she wasn't going to say anything that he wanted to hear. Or maybe he did want to hear it. Get confirmation. Maybe some closure.

'I think this was a holiday romance,' she said. 'I don't think it's going to work out now. You know. Work. Travel. Never in the same place for that long. Not enough time to talk properly, basically.'

'I think we could make time.' Turned out he really hadn't wanted to hear it and it didn't feel like he could ever get closure on his relationship with Lily. 'We just need to recognise the issue and make the time.'

'I'm really not sure.'

'Could we meet tomorrow, just for an hour or two? Maybe for a walk or at a pub?' Somewhere neutral. 'If you like? Just, I just...' He couldn't get the right words out. 'I know the most important thing for you right now must be your dad but I feel that, for both of us, what happened between us in Greece was huge. I'd love the opportunity to see you just one more time. If you feel able to do that. Please?' Pleading. Pathetic. He felt pathetic, though.

'Okay, maybe. But I'm working tomorrow. I'll call you.' It

sounded like a tear had caught in her voice. Yeah, he was crying too. Of course she wasn't going to call him.

'Great. I'll look forward to hearing from you. I hope work goes well.' Pretty impressive that he'd got any words out. He pressed the red button on his phone hard and placed the phone very deliberately down on the table next to him, and Elmer whacked him in the face with his tail.

'Yeah. I'll take you for a walk. Come on.' It felt like a real effort to stand up.

———

'Thanks, mate.' Matt raised the glass of beer that Ade had just put down on the table in front of him. 'Cheers.' Sunday lunchtime after a miserable Saturday night and he was really regretting having made the decision to meet Ade for lunch on the basis that wallowing alone wasn't a good thing to do. He did want to wallow right now. And he wanted to do it alone.

'So how was the wedding? Haven't seen you since then.'

'Yeah, it was great.'

Ade peered at him. 'Mate, you alright?'

'Yeah, all good.'

'Sure? You look... I dunno? Rough?' This was the disadvantage of having known someone since uni. They knew you too well and they sensed when you were miserable and they asked if you were okay but sometimes you didn't want to talk about stuff. Especially when there was so much background to fill them in on. Actually, mainly because of the background filling-in. He wouldn't actually mind telling Ade how shit he felt right now if it wouldn't mean so much in the way of explanations.

Yeah, when he thought about it, that was exactly what was wrong between him and Lily, wasn't it? They just hadn't ever spent enough time together. So they'd always needed explanations when they were going through big stuff.

God, he was an idiot. Seriously, what the hell had *ever* been wrong with him, expecting Lily always to spill her heart and soul to him even when they'd barely had time to see each other.

He'd been so bloody young and immature when they'd met.

'Matt?' Ade said.

'I'm feeling kind of crap actually but it's a long story and I kind of don't want to go into it right now. A woman.'

'Mate, I'm sorry. Here any time you want to talk.'

'Thank you.'

Ade looked at Matt and then said, 'You been watching the cricket?'

Matt nodded. He could do cricket chat while he ate his roast. And then he was going to go home and think hard.

TWENTY-THREE

LILY

'We shouldn't have come for Greek food.' Aaliyah poked at the olives with a cocktail stick. 'It's too soon after we ate *actual* Greek food.' It was Wednesday evening, four days on from when Lily had last spoken to Matt – going by last time it would be several weeks before she stopped measuring everything by that – and they were in a restaurant in Acton. 'So tell me everything about your dad.' This was the first time Lily had seen Aaliyah since the wedding because she'd cancelled all her weekend plans to visit her dad both Saturday and Sunday.

'There isn't that much to tell yet. The doctors still aren't sure what the prognosis is but he's stable and he's obviously in good hands, and we're hoping for the best. I visited him this afternoon and he was in good spirits.'

'Fingers crossed.'

'I know.'

'You've had so much on your plate recently,' Aaliyah said. 'How's... everything else?'

'Shit, actually. Matt and I got together, I thought, in Greece. We talked about why we split up before. We almost got over it, but not quite. And then it all happened again. And *God* I miss him.'

'So why *did* you split up? *What* all seemed to happen again?'

A good half hour later, Lily came to the end of a quite phenomenal monologue and took a long sip of water to soothe her throat after all that talking.

Aaliyah shook her head. 'So basically you love him, it sounds like he loves you, but when you went out you were never together that much because of work and so you never opened up to him the way you did with us, and you worried that if you did you might become like the fragile child you used to be again. And you thought maybe he would have thought less of you or you would have thought less of yourself. And now you know that isn't true but you still think you can't have a relationship because you're rarely in the same place at the same time.'

Lily nodded and tried not to sniff.

Aaliyah handed her a napkin. 'I just want to say that you're quite bloody obviously the same person whether you talk about stuff or not. You aren't one of my best friends because your asthma's now under control. You're one of my best friends because I had the opportunity to meet you and you're fab and funny and loyal and great company. You've just spent a long time telling me about your love-life disaster with some misery about your parents thrown in – not *the* lightest of topics – and you still made me laugh and you kept me interested and you stopped at least twice to ask how I'm doing with work and the kids and basically you're completely bloody wonderful. And when other people have issues you're amazing. And when people don't have issues you're also amazing. And Matt obviously thinks so too and I'm thinking you should spend more time together and take things from there.'

'Thank you. I think *you're* amazing. But it isn't physically possible for me to spend enough time with Matt. Literally, whenever I'm not working, it turns out that he's going to be away. It was always like that in the past and apparently it's the same again.' Lily dabbed underneath her eyes with the napkin.

'Let's leave the rest of this disgusting inauthentic moussaka and go to the pub.' Aaliyah drew her into a hug.

The pub wasn't a lot better.

'I've been ruined by Greece.' Lily pointed at her glass of red. 'This is just horrible. It must be the atmosphere in the restaurants out there and the scenery that makes everything taste so good.' Maybe she'd also been ruined by feeling miserable about Matt.

She wouldn't be ruined forever. She'd got over Matt before and she'd get over him again. Although was it harder when you were older?

Aaliyah took a sip from Lily's glass. 'No, that's just shit wine.'

Lily pushed the wine away. 'Maybe we should get going. I'll see you at the weekend.'

As they left the pub, Lily's phone rang. She pulled it out in case it was her mum.

'It's Matt.' Aaliyah was looking over Lily's shoulder completely unashamedly. 'You should answer it and speak to him.'

'I don't know.' Lily stared at the screen.

'Why?'

'Well, what's the actual point? We're never in the same place at the same time.'

Her phone stopped ringing and Lily felt her spirits sink even lower.

'Bloody call him,' Aaliyah said.

'*Fine.*' Lily rolled her eyes.

'Now?'

'No.'

'Why not?'

'Because you're listening for a start.'

'Yep, fair enough,' Aaliyah said. 'But promise me you'll call him when I'm out of earshot.'

'Okay.'

They hugged and set off in their opposite directions.

There wasn't any point calling Matt. She actually wasn't going to.

When she was about a hundred metres down the road a message flashed up on her screen from Aaliyah. *BLOODY CALL HIM.*

Yep.

No.

And then the phone rang again.

Matt.

Fine. You couldn't just ignore people.

'Hi,' she said.

'Hi. Are you okay?'

'Yes, thank you. Are you?'

'Yep. Could we talk? I could meet you now? For a walk?'

'Now?' Lily checked her watch. 'It's ten to ten.'

'I love a London summer evening walk.'

'I'm in Acton.' Even though it was silly, Lily kind of did want to go for a walk with him. But Acton was a long way from Muswell Hill.

'Well, luckily I'm not that far away. I'll meet you?'

'Okay.' And despite the fact that she *knew* that there was no point because they had no future, she was smiling. Maybe he'd been in West London in the hope that she'd agree to meet him.

By the time they met outside Ealing Common Tube station, Lily wasn't smiling any more. This was pointless. If they kept seeing each other on the occasions they were both in London and not working, they'd both just be even more miserable when they inevitably split up.

Matt kissed her on the cheek, which gave her way more goosebumps than it should, literally from head to toe, even though the evening was warm, and immediately said, 'How's your dad doing?'

When she'd finished telling him, wandering across Ealing Common together, walking close together, but not touching, she said, 'And I'm scared that he won't recover fully and my mum will end up behaving towards him the way she behaved towards me when I was a child and we – but especially they, because I don't see them that much – will be really miserable.'

Matt nodded, slowly. 'I totally see that. I wonder if you could try talking to her. And explain to her how you feel? Have you ever tried that?'

'I... No. I haven't. I couldn't.'

Matt stopped talking and turned to face her. 'I think you could. If you thought it would help. You're a very strong person. And maybe it would help you as well as them.'

Lily thought for a moment. 'Weirdly, I think you could be right.' She'd had a lot of chats recently that she'd never expected to have.

'If you wanted any moral support I could come with you.'

Lily shook her head automatically. 'Honestly, no, that's really kind but if I do speak to them I'll do it alone.'

'You don't always have to do things alone. I mean if you don't want to. Obviously I wouldn't want to intrude.' His eyes were full of such kindness that Lily wanted to cry. And to kiss him. And that wasn't a great thing to be thinking right now.

'I doubt we'd be able to find a date that we could all make anyway,' she said. 'My mum still works long hours, I'm busy with work too, and you're away a lot.' She'd *love* to live in a world where she could rely on Matt and he could come with her to meet her parents properly. But she didn't.

'Well, funny you should say that.' Matt took her hands, really not the reaction she'd expected because, if she was honest, her words had been a little spiky. 'I've been thinking. From my perspective it seems like a lot of our problems stemmed from us not being in the same place at the same time so I'm thinking that I need to start working in London a lot more and doing a lot more remote meetings. There's a lot of amazing technology now courtesy of when we were in lockdown that makes you feel like you're actually on site.'

'Oh no.' Lily shook her head. 'I wouldn't want to ruin your career.'

'You really wouldn't be. I have more work than I can feasibly manage anyway. I can just make sure I only take on new projects that are close to home or where I know I can do a lot of the work remotely. And, *also*, if you were to give me your work schedule for the next few weeks, or however long you know in advance, I should be able to arrange things so that I'm only away when you're working nights.'

'Really?'

'Yes, really.' He leaned down and dropped a far-too-brief kiss on her lips. 'I'm thinking I should see you home now and say good night to you and then if you like you could let me have your schedule and I could make a work plan. Maybe we could go for dinner soon when we've had a chance to look at our schedules and work stuff out? And I'd be very happy to meet your mother with you if you like?'

'I... Okay. Yes. Great.' Maybe that could work.

Lily *really* didn't want him to leave her outside her front door when they finished a lingering goodbye and he said, 'I should go.' But, yep, it was probably for the best, given that neither of them really knew whether they could actually make things work.

It was *hard* going inside without him, though.

She had a text from Matt waiting on her phone in the morning when she woke up, asking for her work schedule, and another one from her mum saying that her dad would be going home on Saturday and it was going to be *very* difficult – Lily could hear the *hushed tones* whispering off her screen – and they'd have to be very cautious with him and his health.

Snap decision. She was going to speak to her mum and she really didn't like the idea of doing it and she was going to ask Matt if he could come and if he couldn't – which, realistically, he wouldn't be able to at short notice – fate would have made the decision that she wouldn't involve him.

But, 'Yes, I'll be there,' he replied when she told him over the phone that her mum could manage a meeting the next afternoon, Friday.

And, yes, at one day's notice, he abandoned his Friday afternoon work meetings, which had to be a first, and arrived in good time for the meeting in a café on the South Bank near St Thomas's Hospital, where her mum worked.

'Hi, Mum.' Lily and Matt both stood up to greet her mum. She kissed Lily's cheek – Lily had to make a conscious effort to stop herself rubbing her face afterwards because she was *sure* there'd be a lipstick mark there now – and turned to Matt with her hand outstretched. 'You remember Matt,' said Lily.

'I don't think we've met before.' Her mum sat down and Lily and Matt joined her.

'Yes, you have, at Granny's funeral.'

'Really?' Her mum frowned. 'I suppose I was too worried about you to register much else.' Lily tried very hard not to glare at her. Her mum pushed her glasses up into her hair and peered at Lily's face. 'Are you alright, Lily? Has the worry about your father been impacting your breathing?'

So. Annoying. Yes, *obviously*, it was lovely that her mother cared. But there was so much more to Lily than her breathing and she wanted her mother to see that.

'I'm totally fine,' Lily said.

'Are you sure?' Her mum looked at her phone. 'I don't have long. I have an important meeting at three.'

Lily heaved an internal sigh. What was actually the point of this? Nothing was ever going to change between her and her mum. Matt took her hand and she looked up at him and he smiled at her and mouthed, 'You can totally do this.'

He was right actually. And if her mum was busy she was just going to launch straight in.

'Mum.' She stopped. Maybe she should have rehearsed this. 'I...' The words really weren't coming. Okay. Start positive. 'I love you. Thank you for caring so much about me.'

Her mum, one eye still on her phone, held up a finger to the waiter and called, 'Could we order? We're in a rush. Darling, I have to look out for you because I'm not sure you take enough care of yourself.'

No. Beyond annoying. Lily opened her mouth to let three decades of frustration rip and the waiter popped up in front of them, pencil poised over open notebook, and said, 'What can I get you?'

Her mum took what felt like *minutes* to decide between a macchiato light and a cappuccino light – wasn't she supposed to be pushed for time? – while Lily struggled not to tap her foot. Or just yell, 'Hurry up.'

When she'd finally decided that she was going macchiato, her mum thanked the waiter, turned back to the table and said, 'So what do you do, Matt?'

'Mum, I have something to say.' The words had just burst out of Lily. 'I *hate* the way you mollycoddle me and make my supposed weaknesses define me. It ruined my childhood and, if I hadn't made a big effort to move away from all that, it would have ruined my adulthood too. I'm not pathetic. I'm no more vulnerable than the next person. I'm an averagely strong woman with asthma, which is under control.'

On the word *hate*, her mother had jerked back like she'd been slapped. She now placed her phone with great care on the table, but didn't speak.

Lily was shaking a bit now she'd stopped talking. Matt took her hand.

'I was just worried about you,' her mum said eventually.

'Disproportionately so, I think,' Lily said.

'Tragedies do occur in relation to adults with currently well-managed asthma but a prior history of severe asthma.'

'I'm very sensible. I take my blue inhaler everywhere.' Lily reached down and produced an inhaler from her bag. 'Like this. And I recognise the early signs of a breathing episode. And life is for living.'

During the lengthy silence that followed, Lily fiddled with the tablecloth and Matt continued to hold her hand tightly. Thank goodness he was here.

After what felt like an extremely long time, her mum said, 'I'm sorry. I had the best of intentions. And I believe that how I cared for you was necessary for your well-being.'

Lily just looked at her, suddenly completely out of energy to carry on trying to get through to her. Honestly. This had all been pointless.

Matt cleared his throat into the silence. 'I hope neither of you mind me saying that as a third party I can see how very hard it must have been for both of you. Maybe everyone was doing their best given the situation and maybe sometimes people's bests aren't perfect.'

Lily's mum pursed her lips together and then her phone rang. 'I have to get this,' she said. She picked it up. And then she declined the call. 'It can wait five minutes.' She took a breath. 'Maybe I've always been too busy at work. You were so ill so often and your grandmother had to look after you. I felt guilty.'

'Maybe you were over-compensating,' Lily said.

'Maybe I was.' Her mum's phone rang again. 'Look, I have to go, but maybe we can have dinner soon? Perhaps the three of us with your father?'

'I'd like that.' Lily smiled at her.

'It was good to meet you, Matt.' Her mother shook Matt's hand again and click-clacked out of the café in the power heels she always wore.

'I kind of think that went as well as it could have done. Thank you so much for talking me into it. I think that from my side my relationship with my mother will hopefully improve now.' Lily looked down at their linked fingers and squeezed Matt's hand. 'And thank you so much for coming as well. It was a *lot* better with you here.'

'No problem. I'm glad you feel better. Sometimes things just need to be said. Want to go for a walk?'

They strolled along the South Bank until they got to Waterloo Bridge, talking about the architecture and the history of the area.

'Thank you again,' Lily said to Matt as they walked up onto the bridge.

'No, thank *you*. I always love a captive audience for my nerdy architect facts.' He pulled her into a hug and kissed her before letting her go and taking her hand to draw her further along the bridge. 'This is my favourite urban view anywhere in the world. St Paul's. The Oxo Tower. Both banks. The meeting of old and new architecture. The London Eye. The only city view better than this is being here at night.'

Lily nodded and looked around. It was a good view. Not as good a view as Matt though, the way he was smiling at her.

'What?' she said. She had goosebumps again. That look in his eye.

'So I have something to show you on my phone,' he said.

'Okay.'

He leaned against the wall of the bridge and did some swiping, and pointed to his screen.

Lily peered at it. 'That's a... spreadsheet?'

'Yup. Dates along here, your schedule here and then my new schedule.' He looked at her.

'Wow. You're so *anal*. You have colours and everything.'

'Yeah, I do like a spreadsheet. But that isn't the *point*. At the risk of mansplaining Excel, the spreadsheet shows that I've switched everything around workwise so that I'm going to be in London most of the time and only away when you're working shifts.'

'*Oh*. Sorry. I was fixating on the colours. Are you *sure*?'

'Yes, I'm sure. I'd do anything to be able to spend more time with you.' He put his phone back in his pocket and took both her hands in his. 'I love you, Lily.'

She pressed her lips together and sniffed.

'Are you crying?' Matt's smile had faltered.

'Happy tears.' They were falling onto her cheeks now. 'I love you too.'

'Thank God for that.' He pulled her closer. 'So could we... try again? Now that we're going to be able to spend time together?'

Lily nodded, unable to speak.

Matt leaned down and kissed her, and then, surrounded by hordes of commuters and early evening theatre-goers and tourists, with a backdrop of the best view in the world, they kissed and kissed like there was no tomorrow.

EPILOGUE

LILY

A year later

'Over here, Norm,' Carole panted. 'Oh my *God*, life was easier when I treated you like a slave.'

Norm put his end of the table they were carrying down and walked round and gave Carole a big smacker on the lips. 'I love you, Carole,' he said. 'Why don't you go and do what you're best at and I'll get some of the boys to help with this? And then we'll all sit and have a beer and a rest while you do your thing? And then we'll get the barbecue fired up before I get changed.'

'Norm, you're on.' Carole put her end of the table down and then stopped. 'If you're sure?'

'Totally sure.' He gave her another kiss.

'Thank you, my darling.' Carole gave him a big squeeze and then marched over to the stage they had set up at one end of the garden and picked up her megaphone. 'Listen, everyone,' she hollered. 'Only two hours to go until the ceremony starts and a lot of work still to do. You need to *focus*.'

Lily smiled at Matt and he put his arm round her and kissed her.

'Better get on,' he told her. 'I need to go and pick the priest up. Those vows won't renew themselves.'

'Too right they won't. I haven't had such a stressful pre-event experience since Tess and Tom's wedding day.'

Matt lowered his voice. 'Imagine how Carole must have been on her *actual* wedding day?'

Lily nodded. 'Thank goodness we have a full day off tomorrow between this and Meg's wedding. I think she's getting a teensy bit uptight now too.'

'I just got a message from Cynthia.' Matt tapped his pocket where his phone was. 'The dogs are doing well.' Lily smiled at him. They were the very proud parents of two poochon puppies – a cross between a toy poodle and a bichon frise – and they could both talk for hours about them. 'You okay?'

'Just a bit worried about my dad. I got another message from my mum. He's back in hospital.'

Matt hugged her into him. 'We can fly home early if we need to.'

'Thank you.' He'd been amazing over the past year through her dad's illness. 'It sounds like he's stable at the moment.'

'Matt,' yelled Carole. 'Where's the priest? Only one hour and fifty-six minutes until the ceremony starts.'

'On my way.' Matt raised the car keys in Carole's direction, kissed Lily again and said, 'Back soon. I love you,' and began a jog towards the corner of the garden while Lily admired his legs and bum.

Three hours later, Carole and Norm were standing under a flower-decorated arch kissing – sweet – while everyone clapped.

'Carole's an amazing force of nature,' Alfredo said while Felix snapped away manically with his phone camera. 'I can't

believe how much she gets organised with so little fuss.' Carole
had suggested to Norm a couple of months ago that they renew
their vows and they'd decided to do it the same week that Meg
was getting married since Lily and Matt, Tess and Tom, Felix
and Alfredo and Aaliyah and her family would already be over
for Meg's wedding and staying in Carole and Norm's newly
finished holiday cottages.

'Meg could learn a lot from her,' Tess grumbled. 'Complete
bloody bridezilla. She literally just asked me – told me in fact –
to stay out of the sun so that I wouldn't be sunburnt for her
wedding.'

'Are you having a *laugh*?' Aaliyah said. 'I mean, if Meg *is*
high maintenance right now, she learnt from the *queen* of all
bridezillas last summer.'

Tess glared at her and Lily said, 'How are you both feeling?'

Aaliyah put her hand into her back and stroked her baby
bump. 'I'm okay except my feet are already swollen to about
twice their normal size and we've only been here two days and
it's going to get hotter tomorrow. Bloody Greece and its bloody
so-called perfect summer weather.' She'd got a lot more chilled
last year after upping her working hours and getting her cleaner
and au pair, but she'd got a bit tetchier again after getting pregnant with a surprise fourth baby.

'At least you're only in your middle trimester.' Tess stroked
her own bump. 'It's a lot harder work when you're seven months
pregnant.'

'I mean, I do have three other children to look after *while*
pregnant.' Aaliyah's eyes were like gimlets and her mouth very
straight. Baby bumps at dawn.

'Clearly it's harder the first time.' Tess was glaring even
more now. '*Your* body knows what to do. Been there done that.'

'Seriously.' Aaliyah turned and said to no one in particular,
'It's like no one's ever been pregnant before.'

'Um...' Lily said.

'Okay. I think I have enough photos for now.' Felix did a little bow. 'I need more champagne.'

'He's taken literally thousands already today.' Alfredo smiled fondly at Felix. 'You're going to have some serious curation to do, Lily.'

'Hey, only a bit. I want to keep most of them.' Felix tucked his phone securely into the inside pocket of his very suave lime-green suit jacket. 'I've got some corkers in there. I got a great one of the priest picking his nose earlier. I'm telling you now, Lily, that no way am I deleting it, even if the snot's blurred. Ooh look.' He pointed and pulled his phone back out. 'Not done with the photos after all. I need some of the gorgeous newly-weds-to-be.'

Meg and Pythagoras were walking towards them, holding hands, in another one of their matching colour combos, pale green this time, a very wide, very short dress for Meg and a suit for Pythagoras. A lot of people would struggle to pull off either of their looks, but they both looked gorgeous, and together they were absolutely stunning. Lily and Matt had been up to visit them a couple of times in Edinburgh and they'd been doing the couple-dressing thing all-year round. And genuinely looking good the whole time.

'I've come to say goodbye.' Pythagoras shook hands and kissed them. 'Time for me to go back over to Antiparos. I'll see you all in the church.'

'Oh my God,' Meg screamed. 'I'm getting married on Saturday to my perfect One.'

A few hours later, as they danced next to the swimming pool amidst the dying embers of the party, a long time after Tess, Aaliyah and Meg had all gone to bed, Matt leaned into Lily's ear and said, 'I think now's the time for us to make a move.'

Lily looked round in the direction of his gaze and gasped.

'We should *definitely* go.' There was a lot of nipple tassel belly dancing going on and some of Norm's friends had stripped to their trousers and greased their chests and were now doing some Chippendale-style dancing and, woah, some of the trousers were starting to come off.

Norm, standing with his arm round Carole, caught sight of Lily and Matt, nudged Carole and waved.

Carole cupped her hands round her mouth and shouted, 'Lilyyyyy, Matty, over here.'

'No way,' Matt said. He did a big wave and shouted, 'Good night,' and grabbed Lily's hand and they began to speed-walk in the direction of the cottage Carole had them staying in to try out for her first paying guests, who'd be arriving next week.

'I adore your aunt and uncle,' Lily said, opening the cottage front door, 'but they can be scary at times.'

'Likewise your friends. This wedding preparation thing's a nightmare.'

'I know. It's the big wedding in Greece thing. Maybe if they'd done a small one somewhere it would have been a lot less stressful.'

'You know what I'm thinking?' Matt pushed the door closed behind him and put his arms around her.

'Mmm?' Lily could never concentrate when he was kissing her like that.

'I'm thinking I'd love to marry you.'

'Mmm?' Now she was concentrating better, despite the kissing.

'What are your thoughts about getting married but having a small wedding?'

'Very, very up for it,' Lily panted between kisses.

Matt lifted her into his arms and made for the bedroom. 'I love you.'

'Me too.'

A LETTER FROM JO

Thank you so much for reading *Just Friends*. I really hope that you enjoyed it!

If you did enjoy it, and would like to keep up to date with all my latest releases, just sign up at the following link. Your email address will never be shared and you can unsubscribe at any time.

www.bookouture.com/jo-lovett

I had so much fun writing Lily and Matt's story. I love the 'What if the One That Got Away reappeared in your life' question and of course I loved being able to travel vicariously to Greece.

I was lucky enough to be able to spend a few weeks island hopping in the Cyclades with one of my sisters when I was younger, and of the several beautiful islands that we visited, Antiparos was the one I loved the most. It's been lovely to have an excuse to revisit those memories!

Lily has a history of severe asthma. Two of my children have a similar history and I wanted to mention here how grateful my family are to the amazing paediatric doctors and nurses at our local hospital. And now that the children are older, hospital admissions are a relatively distant memory and life's a lot easier in that respect.

I hope the story made you smile or laugh and that you loved Lily, Matt and their friends and family as much as I did!

If you enjoyed the story, I would be so pleased if you could leave a short review. I'd love to hear what you think.

Thank you for reading.

Love, Jo xx

 twitter.com/JoLovettWrites